FALSE IMPRESSION

ALSO BY JEFFREY ARCHER

NOVELS

Not a Penny More, Not a Penny Less

Shall We Tell the President?

Kane and Abel

The Prodigal Daughter

First Among Equals

A Matter of Honor

As the Crow Flies

Honor Among Thieves

The Fourth Estate

The Eleventh Commandment

Sons of Fortune

SHORT STORIES

A Quiver Full of Arrows

A Twist in the Tale

Twelve Red Herrings

To Cut a Long Story Short

The Collected Short Stories

PLAYS

Beyond Reasonable Doubt

Exclusive

The Accused

SCREENPLAY

Mallory: Walking Off the Map

PRISON DIARIES

Volume One: Hell

Volume Two: Purgatory

Volume Three: Heaven

FALSE IMPRESSION

JEFFREY ARCHER

ST. MARTIN'S PRESS ⚏ NEW YORK

TO TARA

www.stmartins.com

Library of Congress Cataloging-in-Publication Data

Archer, Jeffrey, 1940–
    False impression / Jeffrey Archer.—1st U.S. ed.
      p. cm.
    ISBN 0-312-35372-3
    EAN 978-0-312-35372-8
    1. Missing persons—Fiction. 2. Art thefts—Fiction. 3. Revenge—Fiction. I. Title.

PR6051.R285F35 2006
823'.914—dc22   2005054291

First published in Australia by Macmillan, an imprint of Pan Macmillan Ltd.

First U.S. Edition: March 2006

10 9 8 7 6 5 4 3 2 1

ACKNOWLEDGMENTS

I would like to thank the following people for their invaluable help with this book: Rosie de Courcy, Mari Roberts, Simon Bainbridge, Victoria Leacock, Kelley Ragland, Mark Poltimore (chairman, nineteenth- and twentieth-century paintings, Sotheby's), Louis van Tilborgh (curator of paintings, Van Gogh Museum), Gregory DeBoer, Rachel Rauchwerger (director, Art Logistics), the National Art Collections Fund, Courtauld Institute of Art, John Power, Jun Nagai, and Terry Lenzer.

9/10

1

Victoria Wentworth sat alone at the table where Wellington had dined with sixteen of his field officers the night before he set out for Waterloo.

General Sir Harry Wentworth sat at the right hand of the Iron Duke that night, and was commanding his left flank when a defeated Napoleon rode off the battlefield and into exile. A grateful monarch bestowed on the general the title Earl of Wentworth, which the family had borne proudly since 1815.

These thoughts were running through Victoria's mind as she read Dr. Petrescu's report for a second time. When she turned the last page, she let out a sigh of relief. A solution to all her problems had been found, quite literally at the eleventh hour.

The dining-room door opened noiselessly and Andrews, who from second footman to butler had served three generations of Wentworths, deftly removed her ladyship's dessert plate.

"Thank you," Victoria said, and waited until he had reached the door before she added, "And has everything been arranged for the removal of the painting?" She couldn't bring herself to mention the artist's name.

"Yes, m'lady," Andrews replied, turning back to face his mistress. "The picture will have been dispatched before you come down for breakfast."

"And has everything been prepared for Dr. Petrescu's visit?"

"Yes, m'lady," repeated Andrews. "Dr. Petrescu is expected around midday on Wednesday, and I have already informed cook that she will be joining you for lunch in the conservatory."

"Thank you, Andrews," said Victoria. The butler gave a slight bow and quietly closed the heavy oak door behind him.

By the time Dr. Petrescu arrived, one of the family's most treasured heirlooms would be on its way to America, and although the masterpiece would never be seen at Wentworth Hall again, no one outside the immediate family need be any the wiser.

Victoria folded her napkin and rose from the table. She picked up Dr. Petrescu's report and walked out of the dining room and into the hall. The sound of her shoes echoed in the marble hallway. She paused at the foot of the staircase to admire Gainsborough's full-length portrait of Catherine, Lady Wentworth, who was dressed in a magnificent long silk and taffeta gown, set off by a diamond necklace and matching earrings. Victoria touched her ear and smiled at the thought that such an extravagant bauble must have been considered quite risqué at the time.

Victoria looked steadfastly ahead as she climbed the wide marble staircase to her bedroom on the first floor. She felt unable to look into the eyes of her ancestors, brought to life by Romney, Lawrence, Reynolds, Lely, and Kneller, conscious of having let them all down. Victoria accepted that before she retired to bed she must finally write to her sister and let her know the decision she had come to.

Arabella was so wise and sensible. If only her beloved twin had been born a few minutes earlier rather than a few minutes later, then *she* would have inherited the estate and undoubtedly handled the problem with considerably more panache. And worse, when Arabella learned the news, she would neither complain nor remonstrate, just continue to display the family's stiff upper lip.

Victoria closed the bedroom door, walked across the room, and placed Dr. Petrescu's report on her desk. She undid her bun, allowing the hair to cascade onto her shoulders. She spent the next few minutes brushing her hair before taking off her clothes and slipping on a silk nightgown, which a maid had laid out on the end of the bed. Finally she stepped into her bedroom slippers. Unable to avoid the responsibility any longer, she sat down at her writing desk and picked up her fountain pen.

FALSE IMPRESSION

WENTWORTH HALL

September 10th, 2001

My dearest Arabella,

I have put off writing this letter for far too long, as you are the last person who deserves to learn such distressing news.

When dear Papa died and I inherited the estate, it was some time before I appreciated the full extent of the debts he had run up. I fear my lack of business experience, coupled with crippling death duties, only exacerbated the problem.

I thought the answer was to borrow even more, but that has simply made matters worse. At one point I feared that because of my naïveté we might even end up having to sell our family's estate. But I am pleased to tell you that a solution has been found.

On Wednesday, I will be seeing—

Victoria thought she heard the bedroom door open. She wondered which of her servants would have considered entering the room without knocking.

By the time Victoria had turned to find out who it was, she was already standing by her side.

Victoria stared up at a woman she had never seen before. She was young, slim, and even shorter than Victoria. She smiled sweetly, which made her appear vulnerable. Victoria returned her smile, and then noticed she was carrying a kitchen knife in her right hand.

"Who—," began Victoria as a hand shot out, grabbed her by the hair, and snapped her head back against the chair. Victoria felt the thin, razor-sharp blade as it touched the skin of her neck. In one swift movement the knife sliced open her throat as if she were a lamb being sent to slaughter.

Moments before Victoria died, the young woman cut off her left ear.

9/11

2

ANNA PETRESCU TOUCHED the button on the top of her bedside clock. It glowed 5:56 A.M. Another four minutes and it would have woken her with the early morning news. But not today. Her mind had been racing all through the night, only allowing her intermittent patches of sleep. By the time she finally woke, Anna had decided exactly what she must do if the chairman was unwilling to go along with her recommendations. She switched off the automatic alarm, avoiding any news that might distract her, jumped out of bed and headed straight for the bathroom. Anna remained under the cold shower a little longer than usual, hoping it would fully wake her. Her last lover—heaven knows how long ago that must have been—thought it amusing that she always showered *before* going out for her morning run.

Once she had dried herself, Anna slipped on a white T-shirt and blue running shorts. Although the sun had not yet risen, she didn't need to open the bedroom curtains of her little room to know that it was going to be another clear, sunny day. She zipped up her tracksuit top, which still displayed a faded P where the bold blue letter had been unstitched. Anna didn't want to advertise the fact that she had once been a member of the University of Pennsylvania track team. After all, that was nine years ago. Anna finally pulled on her Nike training shoes and tied the laces very tight. Nothing annoyed her more than having to stop in the middle of her

9

morning run to retie her laces. The only other thing she wore that morning was her front door key, attached to a thin silver chain that hung around her neck.

Anna double-locked the front door of her four-room apartment, walked across the corridor, and pressed the elevator button. While she waited for the little cubicle to travel grudgingly up to the tenth floor, she began a series of stretching exercises that would be completed before the elevator returned to the ground floor.

Anna stepped out into the lobby and smiled at her favorite doorman, who quickly opened the front door so that she didn't have to stop in her tracks.

"Morning, Sam," Anna said, as she jogged out of Thornton House onto East Fifty-fourth Street and headed toward Central Park.

Every weekday she ran the Southern Loop. On the weekends she would tackle the longer six-mile loop, when it didn't matter if she was a few minutes late. It mattered today.

Bryce Fenston also rose before six o'clock that morning, as he too had an early appointment. While he showered, Fenston listened to the morning news: a suicide bomber who had blown himself up on the West Bank—an event that had become as commonplace as the weather forecast or the latest currency fluctuation didn't cause him to raise the volume.

"Another clear, sunny day, with a gentle breeze heading southeast, highs of seventy-seven, lows of sixty-five," announced a chirpy weather girl, as Fenston stepped out of the shower. A more serious voice replaced hers to inform him that the Nikkei in Tokyo was up fourteen points and Hong Kong's Hang Seng down one. London's FTSE hadn't yet made up its mind in which direction to go. He considered that Fenston Finance shares were unlikely to move dramatically either way, as only two other people were aware of his little coup. Fenston was having breakfast with one of them at seven, and he would fire the other at eight.

By 6:40 A.M., Fenston had showered and dressed. He glanced at his reflection in the mirror; he would like to have been a couple of inches taller and a couple of inches thinner. Nothing that a good tailor and a pair of Cuban shoes with specially designed insoles couldn't rectify. He would also like to have grown his hair again, but not while there were so many exiles from his country who might still recognize him.

Although his father had been a tram conductor in Bucharest, anyone who gave the immaculately dressed man a second glance as he stepped out of his brownstone on East Seventy-ninth Street and into his chauffeur-driven limousine would have assumed that he had been born into the Upper East Side establishment. Only those who looked more closely would have spotted the small diamond in his left ear—an affectation that he believed singled him out from his more conservative colleagues. None of his staff dared to tell him otherwise.

Fenston settled down in the back of his limousine. "The office," he barked before touching a button in the armrest. A smoked gray screen purred up, cutting off any unnecessary conversation between him and the driver. Fenston picked up a copy of *The New York Times* from the seat beside him. He flicked through the pages to see if any particular headline grabbed his attention. Mayor Giuliani seemed to have lost the plot. Having installed his mistress in Gracie Mansion, he'd left the first lady only too happy to voice her opinion on the subject to anyone who cared to listen. This morning it was *The New York Times*. Fenston was poring over the financial pages when his driver swung onto FDR Drive, and he had reached the obituaries by the time the limousine came to a halt outside the North Tower. No one would be printing the only obituary he was interested in until tomorrow, but, to be fair, no one in America realized she was dead.

"I have an appointment on Wall Street at eight thirty," Fenston informed his driver when he opened the back door for him. "So pick me up at eight fifteen." The driver nodded, as Fenston marched off in the direction of the lobby. Although there were ninety-nine elevators in the building, only one went directly to the restaurant on the 107th floor.

As Fenston stepped out of the elevator a minute later—he had once calculated that he would spend a week of his life in elevators—the maître d' spotted his regular customer, bowed his head slightly, and escorted him to a table in the corner overlooking the Statue of Liberty. On the one occasion Fenston had turned up to find his usual table occupied, he'd turned around and stepped straight back into the elevator. Since then, the corner table had remained empty every morning—just in case.

Fenston was not surprised to find Karl Leapman waiting for him. Leapman had never once been late in the ten years he had worked for Fenston Finance. Fenston wondered how long he had been sitting there, just to be certain that the chairman didn't turn up before he did. Fenston looked down at a man who had proved, time and time again, that there was no sewer he wasn't willing to swim in for his master. But then Fenston was the only person who had been willing to offer Leapman a job after he'd been released from jail. Disbarred lawyers with a prison sentence for fraud don't expect to make partner.

Even before he took his seat, Fenston began speaking. "Now we are in possession of the Van Gogh," he said, "we only have one matter to discuss this morning. How do we rid ourselves of Anna Petrescu without her becoming suspicious?"

Leapman opened a file in front of him and smiled.

3

NOTHING HAD GONE as planned that morning.

Andrews had instructed cook that he would be taking up her ladyship's breakfast tray just as soon as the painting had been dispatched. Cook had developed a migraine, so her number two, not a reliable girl, had been put in charge of her ladyship's breakfast. The security van turned up forty minutes late, with a cheeky young driver who refused to leave until he'd been given coffee and biscuits. Cook would never have stood for such nonsense, but her number two caved in. Half an hour later, Andrews found them sitting at the kitchen table, chatting.

Andrews was only relieved that her ladyship hadn't stirred before the driver finally departed. He checked the tray, refolded the napkin, and left the kitchen to take breakfast up to his mistress.

Andrews held the tray on the palm of one hand and knocked quietly on the bedroom door before opening it with the other. When he saw her ladyship lying on the floor in a pool of blood, he let out a gasp, dropped the tray, and rushed over to the body.

Although it was clear Lady Victoria had been dead for several hours, Andrews did not consider contacting the police until the next in line to the Wentworth estate had been informed of the tragedy. He quickly left the bedroom, locked the door, and ran downstairs for the first time in his life.

———

Arabella Wentworth was serving someone when Andrews called.

She put the phone down and apologized to her customer, explaining that she had to leave immediately. She switched the OPEN sign to CLOSED and locked the door of her little antiques shop only moments after Andrews had uttered the word *emergency,* not an opinion she'd heard him express in the past forty-nine years.

Fifteen minutes later, Arabella brought her mini to a halt on the gravel outside Wentworth Hall. Andrews was standing on the top step, waiting for her.

"I'm so very sorry, m'lady," was all he said before he led his new mistress into the house and up the wide marble staircase. When Andrews touched the bannister to steady himself, Arabella knew her sister was dead.

Arabella had often wondered how she would react in a crisis. She was relieved to find that although she was violently sick when she first saw her sister's body, she didn't faint. However, it was a close thing. After a second glance, she grabbed the bedpost to help steady herself before turning away.

Blood had spurted everywhere, congealing on the carpet, the walls, the writing desk, and even the ceiling. With a Herculean effort, Arabella let go of the bedpost and staggered toward the phone on the bedside table. She collapsed onto the bed, picked up the receiver, and dialed 999. When the phone was answered with the words, "Emergency, which service?" she replied, "Police."

Arabella replaced the receiver. She was determined to reach the bedroom door without looking back at her sister's body. She failed. Only a glance, and this time her eyes settled on the letter addressed "My dearest Arabella." She grabbed the unfinished missive, unwilling to share her sister's last thoughts with the local constabulary. Arabella stuffed the epistle into her pocket and walked unsteadily out of the room.

4

ANNA JOGGED WEST along West Fifty-fourth Street, past the Museum of Modern Art, crossing Sixth Avenue before taking a right on Seventh. She barely glanced at the familiar landmarks of the massive $^{LO}_{VE}$ sculpture that dominated the corner of West Fifty-fifth Street or Carnegie Hall as she crossed West Fifty-seventh. Most of her energy and concentration was taken up with trying to avoid the early morning commuters as they hurried toward her or blocked her progress. Anna considered the jog to Central Park nothing more than a warm-up and didn't start the stopwatch on her left wrist until she passed through Artisans' Gate and ran into the park.

Once Anna had settled into her regular rhythm, she tried to focus on the meeting scheduled with the chairman for eight o'clock that morning.

Anna had been both surprised and somewhat relieved when Bryce Fenston had offered her a job at Fenston Finance only days after she'd left her position as the number two in Sotheby's Impressionist department.

Her immediate boss had made it only too clear that any thought of progress would be blocked for some time after she'd admitted to being responsible for losing the sale of a major collection to their main rival, Christie's. Anna had spent months nurturing, flattering, and cajoling this particular customer into selecting Sotheby's for the disposal of their family's estate, and had naïvely assumed when she shared the secret with her lover that he would be discreet. After all, he was a lawyer.

When the name of the client was revealed in the arts section of *The New York Times,* Anna lost both her lover and her job. It didn't help when a few days later the same paper reported that Dr. Anna Petrescu had left Sotheby's "under a cloud"—a euphemism for *fired*—and the columnist helpfully added that she needn't bother to apply for a job at Christie's.

Bryce Fenston was a regular attendee at all the major Impressionist sales, and he couldn't have missed Anna standing by the side of the auctioneer's podium taking notes and acting as a spotter. She resented any suggestion that her striking good looks and athletic figure were the reason Sotheby's regularly placed her in so prominent a position, rather than at the side of the auction room along with the other spotters.

Anna checked her watch as she ran across Playmates Arch: two minutes eighteen seconds. She always aimed to complete the loop in twelve minutes. She knew that wasn't fast, but it still annoyed her whenever she was overtaken, and it made her particularly mad if it was by a woman. Anna had come in ninety-seventh in last year's New York Marathon, so on her morning jog in Central Park she was rarely passed by anything on two legs.

Her thoughts returned to Bryce Fenston. It had been known for some time by those closely involved in the art world—auction houses, leading galleries, and private dealers—that Fenston was amassing one of the great Impressionist collections. He, along with Steve Wynn, Leonard Lauder, Anne Dias, and Takashi Nakamura, were regularly among the final bidders for any major new acquisition. For such collectors, what often begins as an innocent hobby can quickly become an addiction, every bit as demanding as any drug. For Fenston, who owned an example of all the major Impressionists except Van Gogh, even the thought of possessing a work by the Dutch master was an injection of pure heroin, and once purchased he quickly craved another fix, like a shaking addict in search of a dealer. His dealer was Anna Petrescu.

When Fenston read in *The New York Times* that Anna was leaving Sotheby's, he immediately offered her a place on his board with a salary that reflected how serious he was about continuing to build his collection. What tipped the balance for Anna was the discovery that Fenston also originated from Romania. He continually reminded Anna that, like her, he had escaped the oppressive Ceauşescu regime to find refuge in America.

Within days of her joining the bank, Fenston quickly put Anna's expertise to the test. Most of the questions he asked her at their first meeting, over lunch, concerned Anna's knowledge of any large collections still in the hands of second- or third-generation families. After six years at Sotheby's, there was barely a major Impressionist work that came under the hammer that hadn't passed through Anna's hands or at least been viewed by her and then added to her database.

One of the first lessons Anna learned after joining Sotheby's was that old money was more likely to be the seller and new money the buyer, which was how she originally came into contact with Lady Victoria Wentworth, elder daughter of the Seventh Earl of Wentworth—old, old money—on behalf of Bryce Fenston—nouveau, nouveau riche.

Anna was puzzled by Fenston's obsession with other people's collections, until she discovered that it was company policy to advance large loans against works of art. Few banks are willing to consider "art," no matter what form, as collateral. Property, shares, bonds, land, even jewelery, but rarely art. Bankers do not understand the market and are reluctant to reclaim the assets from their customers, not least because storing the works, insuring them, and often ending up having to sell them is not only time-consuming but impractical. Fenston Finance was the rare exception. It didn't take Anna long to discover that Fenston had no real love, or particular knowledge, of art. He fulfilled Oscar Wilde's dictum: *A man who knows the price of everything and the value of nothing.* But it was some time before Anna discovered his real motive.

One of Anna's first assignments was to take a trip to England and value the estate of Lady Victoria Wentworth, a potential customer, who had applied for a large loan from Fenston Finance. The Wentworth collection turned out to be a typically English one, built up by the second earl, an eccentric aristocrat with a great deal of money, considerable taste, and a good enough eye for later generations to describe him as a gifted amateur. From his own countrymen he acquired Romney, West, Constable, Stubbs, and Morland, as well as a magnificent example of a Turner, *Sunset over Plymouth.*

The third earl showed no interest in anything artistic, so the collection gathered dust until his son, the fourth earl, inherited the estate and with it his grandfather's discriminating eye.

Jamie Wentworth spent nearly a year exiled from his native land taking what used to be known as the Grand Tour. He visited Paris, Amsterdam, Rome, Florence, Venice, and St. Petersburg before returning to Wentworth Hall in possession of a Raphael, Tintoretto, Titian, Rubens, Holbein, and Van Dyck, not to mention an Italian wife. However, it was Charles, the fifth earl, who, for all the wrong reasons, trumped his ancestors. Charlie was also a collector, not of paintings, but of mistresses. After an energetic weekend spent in Paris—mainly on the racecourse at Longchamp but partly in a bedroom at the Crillon—his latest filly convinced him to purchase from her doctor a painting by an unknown artist. Charlie Wentworth returned to England having discarded his paramour but stuck with a painting that he relegated to a guest bedroom, although many aficionados now consider *Self-Portrait with Bandaged Ear* to be among Van Gogh's finest works.

Anna had already warned Fenston to be wary when it came to purchasing a Van Gogh, because attributions were often more dubious than Wall Street bankers—a simile Fenston didn't care for. She told him that there were several fakes hanging in private collections and even one or two in major museums, including the national museum of Oslo. However, after Anna had studied the paperwork that accompanied the Van Gogh *Self-Portrait,* which included a reference to Charles Wentworth in one of Dr. Gachet's letters, a receipt for eight hundred francs from the original sale and a certificate of authentication from Louis van Tilborgh, curator of paintings at the Van Gogh Museum in Amsterdam, she felt confident enough to advise the chairman that the magnificent portrait was indeed by the hand of the master.

For Van Gogh addicts, *Self-Portrait with Bandaged Ear* was the ultimate high. Although the maestro painted thirty-five self-portraits during his lifetime, he attempted only two after cutting off his left ear. What made this particular work so desirable for any serious collector was that the other one was on display at the Courtauld Institute in London. Anna was becoming more and more anxious about just how far Fenston would be willing to go in order to possess the only other example.

Anna spent a pleasant ten days at Wentworth Hall cataloguing and valuing the family's collection. When she returned to New York, she advised the board—mainly made up of Fenston's cronies or politicians who were only too happy to accept a handout—that should a sale ever prove necessary, the assets would more than cover the bank's loan of thirty million dollars.

Although Anna had no interest in Victoria Wentworth's reasons for needing such a large sum of money, she often heard Victoria speak of the sadness of "dear Papa's" premature death, the retirement of their trusted estates manager, and the iniquity of 40 percent death duties during her stay at Wentworth Hall. "If only Arabella had been born a few moments earlier . . ." was one of Victoria's favourite mantras.

Once she was back in New York, Anna could recall every painting and sculpture in Victoria's collection without having to refer to any paperwork. The one gift that set her apart from her contemporaries at Penn, and her colleagues at Sotheby's, was a photographic memory. Once Anna had seen a painting, she would never forget the image, its provenance, or its location. Every Sunday she would idly put her skill to the test by visiting a new gallery or a room at the Met, or simply by studying the latest catalogue raisonné. On returning to her apartment, she would write down the name of every painting she had seen before checking it against the different catalogues. Since leaving university, Anna had added the Louvre, the Prado, and the Uffizi, as well as the National Gallery in Washington, the Phillips Collection, and the Getty Museum, to her memory bank. Thirty-seven private collections and countless catalogues were also stored in the database of her brain, an asset Fenston had proved willing to pay over the odds for.

Anna's responsibility did not go beyond valuing the collections of potential clients and then submitting written reports for the board's consideration. She never became involved in the drawing up of any contract. That was exclusively in the hands of the bank's in-house lawyer, Karl Leapman. However, Victoria did let slip on one occasion that the bank was charging her 16 percent compound interest. Anna had quickly become aware that a combination of debt, naïveté, and a lack of any financial, expertise were the ingredients on which Fenston Finance thrived. This was a bank that seemed to relish its customers' inability to repay their debts.

Anna lengthened her stride as she passed by the carousel. She checked her watch—off twelve seconds. She frowned, but at least no one had overtaken her. Her thoughts returned to the Wentworth collection and the recommendation she would be making to Fenston that morning. Anna had decided she would have to resign if the chairman felt unable to accept her advice, despite the fact that she had worked for the company for less than a year and was painfully aware that she still couldn't hope to get a job at Sotheby's or Christie's.

During the past year, she had learnt to live with Fenston's vanity and even tolerate the occasional outburst when he didn't get his own way, but she could not condone misleading a client, especially one as naïve as Victoria Wentworth. Leaving Fenston Finance after such a short time might not look good on her résumé, but an ongoing fraud investigation would look a lot worse.

5

"WHEN WILL WE find out if she's dead?" asked Leapman, as he sipped his coffee.

"I'm expecting confirmation this morning," Fenston replied.

"Good, because I'll need to be in touch with her lawyer to remind him—" he paused "—that in the case of a suspicious death—" he paused a second time "—any settlement reverts to the jurisdiction of the New York State Bar."

"Strange that none of them ever query that clause in the contract," said Fenston, buttering another muffin.

"Why should they?" asked Leapman. "After all, they have no way of knowing that they're about to die."

"And is there any reason for the police to become suspicious about our involvement?"

"No," replied Leapman. "You've never met Victoria Wentworth, you didn't sign the original contract, and you haven't even seen the painting."

"No one has outside the Wentworth family and Petrescu," Fenston reminded him. "But what I still need to know is how much time before I can safely—"

"Hard to say, but it could be years before the police are willing to admit they don't even have a suspect, especially in such a high-profile case."

"A couple of years will be quite enough," said Fenston. "By then, the interest on the loan will be more than enough to ensure that I can hold on to the Van Gogh and sell off the rest of the collection without losing any of my original investment."

"Then it's a good thing that I read Petrescu's report when I did," said Leapman, "because if she'd gone along with Petrescu's recommendation, there would have been nothing we could do about it."

"Agreed," said Fenston, "but now we have to find some way of losing Petrescu."

A thin smile appeared on Leapman's lips. "That's easy enough," he said, "we play on her one weakness."

"And that is?" asked Fenston.

"Her honesty."

Arabella sat alone in the drawing room, unable to take in what was happening all around her. A cup of Earl Grey tea on the table beside her had gone cold, but she hadn't noticed. The loudest noise in the room was the tick of the clock on the mantelpiece. Time had stopped for Arabella.

Several police cars and an ambulance were parked on the gravel outside. People going about their business dressed in uniforms, white coats, dark suits, and even face masks came and went without bothering her.

There was a gentle tap on the door. Arabella looked up to see an old friend standing in the doorway. The chief superintendent removed a peaked cap covered in silver braid as he entered the room. Arabella rose from the sofa, her face ashen, her eyes red from crying. The tall man bent down and kissed her gently on both cheeks and then waited for her to sit back down before he took his place in the leather wing chair opposite her. Stephen Renton offered his condolences, which were genuine; he'd known Victoria for many years.

Arabella thanked him, sat up straight, and asked quietly, "Who could have done such a terrible thing, especially to someone as innocent as Victoria?"

"There doesn't seem to be a simple or logical answer to that question," the chief superintendent replied. "And it doesn't help that it was several hours before her body was discovered, allowing the assailant more than enough time to get clean away." He paused. "Do you feel up to answering some questions, my dear?"

Arabella gave a nod. "I'll do anything I can to help you track down the *assailant.*" She repeated the word with venom.

"Normally, the first question I would ask in any murder inquiry is do you know if your sister had any enemies, but I confess that knowing her as I did that doesn't seem possible. However, I must ask if you were aware of any problems Victoria might have been facing, because—" he hesitated "—there have been rumors in the village for some time that following your father's death, your sister was left with considerable debts."

"I don't know, is the truth," Arabella admitted. "After I married Angus, we only came down from Scotland for a couple of weeks in the summer and every other Christmas. It wasn't until my husband died that I returned to live in Surrey"—the chief superintendent nodded but didn't interrupt—"and heard the same rumors. Local gossips were even letting it be known that some of the furniture in my shop had come from the estate in order that Victoria could still pay the staff."

"And was there any truth in those rumors?" asked Stephen.

"None at all," replied Arabella. "When Angus died and I sold our farm in Perthshire, there was more than enough to allow me to return to Wentworth, open my little shop, and turn a lifelong hobby into a worthwhile enterprise. But I did ask my sister on several occasions if the rumors of Father's financial position were true. Victoria denied there was any problem, always claiming that everything was under control. But then she adored Father, and in her eyes he could do no wrong."

"Can you think of anything that might give some clue as to why . . ."

Arabella rose from the sofa and, without explanation, walked across to a writing desk on the far side of the room. She picked up the blood-spattered letter that she had found on her sister's table, walked back, and handed it across to him.

Stephen read the unfinished missive twice before asking, "Do you have any idea what Victoria could have meant by 'a solution has been found'?"

"No," admitted Arabella, "but it's possible that I'll be able to answer that question once I've had a word with Arnold Simpson."

"That doesn't fill me with confidence," said Stephen.

Arabella noted his comment but didn't respond. She knew that the chief superintendent's natural instinct was to mistrust all solicitors who appeared unable to disguise a belief that they were superior to any police officer.

The chief superintendent rose from his place, walked across and sat next to Arabella. He took her hand. "Call me whenever you want to," he said gently, "and try not to keep too many secrets from me, Arabella, because I'll need to know everything, and I mean everything, if we're to find who murdered your sister."

Arabella didn't reply.

"Damn," muttered Anna to herself when an athletic, dark-haired man jogged casually past her, just as he'd done several times during the last few weeks. He didn't glance back—serious runners never did. Anna knew that it would be pointless to try and keep up with him, as she would be "legless" within a hundred yards. She had once caught a sideways glimpse of the mystery man, but he then strode away and all she had seen was the back of his emerald green T-shirt as he continued toward Strawberry Fields. Anna tried to put him out of her mind and focus once again on her meeting with Fenston.

Anna had already sent a copy of her report to the chairman's office, recommending that the bank sell the self-portrait as quickly as possible. She knew a collector in Tokyo who was obsessed with Van Gogh and still had the yen to prove it. And with this particular painting there was another weakness she would be able to play on, which she had highlighted in her report. Van Gogh had always admired Japanese art, and on the wall behind the self-portrait he had reproduced a print of *Geishas in a Landscape,* which Anna felt would make the painting even more irresistible to Takashi Nakamura.

Nakamura was chairman of the largest steel company in Japan, but lately he'd been spending more and more time building up his art collection, which, he'd let it be known, was to form part of a foundation that would eventually be left to the nation. Anna also considered it an advantage that Nakamura was an intensely secretive individual, who guarded the details of his private collection with typical Japanese inscrutability. Such a sale would allow Victoria Wentworth to save face—something the Japanese fully understood. Anna had once acquired a Degas for Nakamura, *Dancing Class with Mme. Minette,* which the seller had wished to dispose of privately, a service the great auction houses offer to those who want to avoid the prying eyes of journalists who hang around the sale rooms. She was confident that Nakamura would offer at least sixty million dollars for the rare Dutch masterpiece. So if Fenston accepted her proposal—and why shouldn't he?—everyone would be satisfied with the outcome.

When Anna passed the Tavern on the Green, she once again checked her watch. She would need to pick up her pace if she still hoped to be back at Artisans' Gate in under twelve minutes. As she sprinted down the hill, she reflected on the fact that she shouldn't allow her personal feelings for a client to cloud her judgment, but frankly Victoria needed all the help she could get. When Anna passed through Artisans' Gate, she pressed the stop button on her watch: twelve minutes and four seconds. *Damn.*

Anna jogged slowly off in the direction of her apartment, unaware that she was being closely watched by the man in the emerald green T-shirt.

6

JACK DELANEY STILL wasn't sure if Anna Petrescu was a criminal.

The FBI agent watched her as she disappeared into the crowd on her way back to Thornton House. Once she was out of sight, Jack resumed jogging through Sheep Meadow toward the lake. He thought about the woman he'd been investigating for the past six weeks, an inquiry that was hampered by the fact that he didn't need Anna to find out that the Bureau was also investigating her boss, who Jack had no doubt *was* a criminal.

It was nearly a year since Richard W. Macy, Jack's supervising special agent, had called him into his office and allocated him a team of eight agents to cover a new assignment. Jack was to investigate three vicious murders on three different continents that had one thing in common: each of the victims had been killed at a time when they also had large outstanding loans with Fenston Finance. Jack quickly concluded that the murders had been planned and were the work of a professional killer.

Jack cut through Shakespeare Garden as he headed back toward his small apartment on the West Side. He had just about completed his file on Fenston's most recent recruit, although he still couldn't make up his mind if she was a willing accomplice or a naïve innocent.

Jack had begun with Anna's upbringing and discovered that her uncle, George Petrescu, had emigrated from Romania in 1972 to settle in Danville, Illinois. Within weeks of Ceauşescu appointing himself president, George had written to his brother imploring him to join him in America. When Ceauşescu declared Romania a socialist republic and made his wife, Elena, his deputy, George wrote to his brother renewing his invitation, which included his young niece, Anna.

Although Anna's parents refused to leave their homeland, they did allow their seventeen-year-old daughter to be smuggled out of Bucharest in 1987 and shipped off to America to stay with her uncle, promising her that she could return the moment Ceauşescu had been overthrown. Anna never returned. She wrote home regularly, begging her mother to join them in the States, but she rarely received a response. Two years later she learned that her father had been killed in a border skirmish while attempting to oust the dictator. Her mother also repeated that she would never leave her native land, her excuse now being, "Who would tend to your father's grave?"

That much, one of Jack's squad members had been able to discover from an essay Anna had written for her high school magazine. One of her classmates had also written about the gentle girl with long fair plaits and blue eyes who came from somewhere called Bucharest and knew so few words of English that she couldn't even recite the Pledge of Allegiance at morning assembly. By the end of her second year, Anna was editing the magazine, from which Jack had gathered so much of his information.

From high school, Anna won a scholarship to Williams University in Massachusetts to study art history. A local newspaper recorded that she also won the intervarsity mile against Cornell in a time of four minutes forty-eight seconds. Jack followed Anna's progress to the University of Pennsylvania, where she continued her studies for a Ph.D., her chosen thesis subject the Fauve Movement. Jack had to look up the word in *Webster's*. It referred to a group of artists led by Matisse, Derain, and Vlaminck who wished to break away from the influence of Impressionism and move toward the use of bright and dissonant color. He also learned how the young Picasso had left Spain to join the group in Paris, where he shocked the public with paintings that *Paris Match* described as "of no lasting importance"; "sanity will return," they assured their readers. It only made Jack want to read more about Vuillard, Luce, and Camois—artists he'd never heard of. But that would have to wait for an off-duty moment, unless it became evidence that would nail Fenston.

After Penn, Dr. Petrescu joined Sotheby's as a graduate trainee. Here

Jack's information became somewhat sketchy, as he could allow his agents only limited contact with Anna's former colleagues. However, he did learn of her photographic memory, her rigorous scholarship, and the fact that she was liked by everyone from the porters to the chairman. But no one would discuss in detail what "under a cloud" meant, although he did discover that she would not be welcome back at Sotheby's under the present management. And Jack couldn't fathom out why, despite her dismissal, she considered joining Fenston Finance. For that part of his inquiry, he had to rely on speculation, because he couldn't risk approaching anyone she worked with at the bank, although it was clear that Tina Forster, the chairman's secretary, had become a close friend.

In the short time Anna had worked at Fenston Finance, she had visited several new clients who had recently taken out large loans, all of whom were in possession of major art collections. Jack feared that it could only be a matter of time before one of them suffered the same fate as Fenston's three previous victims.

Jack ran onto West Eighty-sixth Street. Three questions still needed answering. One, how long had Fenston known Petrescu before she joined the bank? Two, had they, or their families, known each other in Romania? And three, was she the hired assassin?

Fenston scrawled his signature across the breakfast bill, rose from his place, and, without waiting for Leapman to finish his coffee, marched out of the restaurant. He stepped into an open elevator, but waited for Leapman to press the button for the eighty-third floor. A group of Japanese men in dark blue suits and plain silk ties joined them, having also had breakfast at Windows on the World. Fenston never discussed business matters while in an elevator, well aware that several of his rivals occupied the floors above and below him.

When the elevator opened on the eighty-third floor, Leapman followed his master out, but then turned the other way and headed straight for Petrescu's office. He opened her door without knocking to find Anna's assistant, Rebecca, preparing the files Anna would need for her meeting with the chairman. Leapman barked out a set of instructions that didn't invite questions. Rebecca immediately placed the files on Anna's desk and went in search of a large cardboard box.

Leapman walked back down the corridor and joined the chairman in his office. They began to go over tactics for their showdown with Petrescu. Although they had been through the same procedure three times in the past eight years, Leapman warned the chairman that it could be different this time.

"What do you mean?" demanded Fenston.

"I don't think Petrescu will leave without putting up a fight," he said. "After all, she isn't going to find it easy to get another job."

"She certainly won't if I have anything to do with it," said Fenston, rubbing his hands.

"But perhaps in the circumstances, Chairman, it might be wise if I—"

A knock on the door interrupted their exchange. Fenston looked up to see Barry Steadman, the bank's head of security, standing in the doorway.

"Sorry to bother you, Chairman, but there's a FedEx courier out here, says he has a package for you and no one else can sign for it."

Fenston waved the courier in and, without a word, penned his signature in the little oblong box opposite his name. Leapman looked on, but neither of them spoke until the courier had departed and Barry had closed the door behind him.

"Is that what I think it is?" asked Leapman quietly.

"We're about to find out," said Fenston, as he ripped open the package and emptied its contents onto the desk.

They both stared down at Victoria Wentworth's left ear.

"See that Krantz is paid the other half million," said Fenston. Leapman nodded. "And she's even sent a bonus," Fenston, staring down at the antique diamond earring.

Anna finished packing just after seven. She left her suitcase in the hall, intending to return and pick it up on the way to the airport straight after work. Her flight to London was scheduled for 5:40 P.M. that afternoon, touching down at Heathrow just before sunrise the following day. Anna much preferred taking the overnight flight, when she could sleep and still have enough time to prepare herself before joining Victoria for lunch at Wentworth Hall. She only hoped that Victoria had read her report and would agree that selling the Van Gogh privately was a simple solution to all her problems.

Anna left her apartment building for the second time that morning just after 7:20 A.M. She hailed a taxi—an extravagance, but one she justified by wanting to look her best for her meeting with the chairman. She sat in the back of the cab and checked her appearance in her compact mirror. Her recently acquired Anand Jon suit and white silk blouse would surely make heads turn. Although some might be puzzled by her black sneakers.

The cab took a right on FDR Drive and speeded up a little as Anna checked her cell phone. There were three messages, all of which she would deal with after the meeting: one from her secretary, Rebecca, needing to speak to her urgently, which was surprising given they were going to see each other in a few minutes' time; confirmation of her flight from BA; and an invitation to dinner with Robert Brooks, the new chairman of Bonhams.

Her cab drew up outside the entrance to the North Tower twenty minutes later. She paid the driver and jumped out to join a sea of workers as they filed toward the entrance and through the bank of turnstiles. She took the shuttle express elevator and less than a minute later stepped out onto the dark green carpet of the executive floor. Anna had once overheard in the elevator that each floor was an acre in size, and some fifty thousand people worked in a building that never closed—more than double the population of her adopted hometown of Danville, Illinois.

Anna went straight to her office and was surprised to find that Rebecca wasn't waiting for her, especially as she knew how important her eight o'clock meeting was. But she was relieved to see that all the relevant files had been piled neatly on her desk. She double-checked that they were in the order she had requested. Anna still had a few minutes to spare, so she once again turned to the Wentworth file and began reading her report. "The value of the Wentworth Estate falls into several categories. My department's only interest is in . . ."

Tina Forster didn't rise until just after seven. Her appointment with the dentist wasn't until eight thirty, and Fenston had made it clear that she needn't be on time this morning. That usually meant he had an out-of-town appointment or was going to fire someone. If it was the latter, he wouldn't want her hanging around the office, sympathizing with the person who had just lost their job. Tina knew that it couldn't be Leapman, because Fenston wouldn't be able to survive without the man; and although she would have liked it to be Barry Steadman, she could dream on, because he never missed an opportunity to praise the chairman, who absorbed flattery like a beached sea sponge waiting for the next wave.

Tina lay soaking in the bath—a luxury she usually only allowed herself at weekends—wondering when it would be her turn to be fired. She'd been Fenston's personal assistant for over a year, and although she despised the man and all he stood for, she'd still tried to make herself indispensable. Tina knew that she couldn't consider resigning until . . .

The phone rang in her bedroom, but she made no attempt to answer it. She assumed it would be Fenston demanding to know where a particular file was, a phone number, even his diary. "On the desk in front of you" was usually the answer. She wondered for a moment if it might be Anna, the only real friend she'd made since moving from the West Coast. Unlikely, she concluded, as Anna would be presenting her report to the chairman at eight o'clock, and was probably, even now, going over the finer details for the twentieth time.

Tina smiled as she climbed out of the bath and wrapped a towel around her body. She strolled across the corridor and into her bedroom. Whenever a guest spent the night in her cramped apartment they had to share her bed or sleep on the sofa. They had little choice, as she only had one bedroom. Not many takers lately, and not because of any shortage of offers. But after what she'd been through with Fenston, Tina no longer trusted anyone. Recently she'd wanted to confide in Anna, but this remained the one secret she couldn't risk sharing.

Tina pulled open the curtains and, despite its being September, the clear, sparkling morning convinced her that she should wear a summer dress. It might even make her relax when she stared up at the dentist's drill.

Once she was dressed and had checked her appearance in the mirror, Tina went off to the kitchen and made herself a cup of coffee. She wasn't allowed to have anything else for breakfast, not even toast—instructions from the ferocious dental assistant—so she flicked on the television to catch the early morning news. There wasn't any. A suicide bomber on the

West Bank was followed by a 320-pound woman who was suing McDonald's for ruining her sex life. Tina was just about to turn off *Good Morning America* when the quarterback for the 49ers appeared on the screen.

It made Tina think of her father.

7

JACK DELANEY ARRIVED at his office at 26 Federal Plaza just after seven that morning. He felt depressed as he stared down at the countless files that littered his desk. Every one of them connected with his investigation of Bryce Fenston, and a year later he was no nearer to presenting his boss with enough evidence to ask a judge to issue an arrest warrant.

Jack opened Fenston's personal file in the vain hope that he might stumble across some tiny clue, some personal trait, or just a mistake that would finally link Fenston directly to the three vicious murders that had taken place in Marseille, Los Angeles, and Rio de Janeiro.

In 1984, the thirty-two-year-old Nicu Munteanu had presented himself at the American Embassy in Bucharest, claiming that he could identify two spies working in the heart of Washington, information he was willing to trade in exchange for an American passport. A dozen such claims were handled by the embassy every week and almost all proved groundless, but in Munteanu's case the information stood up. Within a month, two well-placed officials found themselves on a flight back to Moscow, and Munteanu was issued an American passport.

Nicu Munteanu landed in New York on February 17, 1985. Jack had been able to find little intelligence on Munteanu's activities during the following year, but he suddenly reemerged with enough money to take over Fenston Finance, a small, ailing bank in Manhattan. Nicu Munteanu changed his name to Bryce Fenston—not a crime in itself—but no one could identify his backers, despite the fact that during the next few years the bank began to accept large deposits from unlisted companies across Eastern Europe. Then in 1989 the cash flow suddenly dried up, the same year Ceauşescu and his wife, Elena, fled from Bucharest following the uprising. Within days they were captured, tried, and executed.

Jack looked out of his window over lower Manhattan and recalled the FBI maxim: never believe in coincidences, but never dismiss them.

Following Ceauşescu's death, the bank appeared to go through a couple of lean years until Fenston met up with Karl Leapman, a disbarred lawyer who had recently been released from prison for fraud. It was not too long before the bank resumed its profitable ways.

Jack stared down at several photographs of Bryce Fenston, who regularly appeared in the gossip columns with one of New York's most fashionable women on his arm. He was variously described as a brilliant banker, a leading financier, even a generous benefactor, and with almost every mention of his name there was a reference to his magnificent art collection. Jack pushed the photographs to one side. He hadn't yet come to terms with a man who wore an earring, and he was even more puzzled why someone who had a full head of hair when he first came to America would choose to shave himself bald. Who was he hiding from?

Jack closed the Munteanu/Fenston personal file and turned his attention to Pierre de Rochelle, the first of the victims.

Rochelle required seventy million francs to pay for his share in a vineyard. His only previous experience of the wine industry seemed to have come from draining the bottles on a regular basis. Even a cursory inspection would have revealed that his investment plan didn't appear to fulfill the banking maxim of being "sound." However, what caught Fenston's attention when he perused the application was that the young man had recently inherited a château in the Dordogne, in which every wall was graced with fine Impressionist paintings, including a Degas, two Pissarros, and a Monet of *Argenteuil*.

The vineyard failed to show a return for four fruitless years, during which time the château began to render up its assets, leaving only outline shapes where the pictures had once hung. By the time Fenston had shipped the last painting back to New York to join his private collection, Pierre's original loan had, with accumulated interest, more than doubled.

When his château was finally placed on the market, Pierre took up residence in a small flat in Marseille, where each night he would drink himself into a senseless stupor. That was until a bright young lady, just out of law school, suggested to Pierre, in one of his sober moments, that were Fenston Finance to sell his Degas, the Monet, and the two Pissarros, he could not only pay off his debt but take the château off the market and reclaim the rest of his collection. This suggestion did not fit in with Fenston's long-term plans.

A week later, the drunken body of Pierre de Rochelle was found slumped in a Marseille alley, his throat sliced open.

Four years later, the Marseille police closed the file, with the words NON RESOLU stamped on the cover.

When the estate was finally settled, Fenston had sold off all the works, with the exception of the Renoir, the Monet, and the two Pissarros; and after compound interest, bank charges, and lawyers' fees, Pierre's younger brother, Simon de Rochelle, inherited the flat in Marseille.

Jack rose from behind his desk, stretched his cramped limbs, and yawned wearily before he considered tackling Chris Adams, Jr., although he knew Adams's case history almost by heart.

Chris Adams, Sr., had operated a highly successful fine art gallery on Melrose Avenue in Los Angeles. He specialized in the American School so admired by the Hollywood glitterati. His untimely death in a car crash left his son Chris, Jr., with a collection of Rothkos, Pollocks, Jasper Johnses, Rauschenbergs, and several Warhol acrylics, including a *Black Marilyn*.

An old school friend advised Chris that the way to double his money would be to invest in the dot.com revolution. Chris, Jr., pointed out that he didn't have any ready cash, just the gallery, the paintings, and *Christina*, his father's old yacht—and even that was half owned by his younger sister. Fenston Finance stepped in and advanced him a loan of twelve million dollars on their usual terms. As in so many revolutions, several bodies ended up on the battlefield: among them, Chris, Jr.'s.

Fenston Finance had allowed the debt to continue mounting without ever troubling their client. That was until Chris, Jr., read in the *Los Angeles Times* that Warhol's *Shot Red Marilyn* had recently sold for over four million dollars. He immediately contacted Christie's in L.A., who assured him that he could expect an equally good return for his Rothkos, Pollocks, and Jasper Johnses. Three months later, Leapman rushed into the chairman's office bearing the latest copy of a Christie's sale catalogue. He had placed yellow Post-It notes against seven different lots that were due to come under the hammer. Fenston made one phone call, then booked himself on the next flight to Rome.

Three days later, Chris, Jr., was discovered in the lavatory of a gay bar with his throat cut.

Fenston was on holiday in Italy at the time, and Jack had a copy of his hotel bill, plane tickets, and even his credit-card purchases from several shops and restaurants.

The paintings were immediately withdrawn from the Christie's sale while the L.A. police carried out their investigations. After eighteen months of no new evidence and dead-ends, the file joined the other LAPD cold cases stored in the basement. All Chris's sister ended up with was a model of *Christina,* her father's much-loved yacht.

Jack tossed Chris, Jr.'s, file to one side and stared down at the name of Maria Vasconcellos, a Brazilian widow who had inherited a house and a lawn full of statues—and not of the garden-center variety. Moore, Giacometti, Remington, Botero, and Calder were among Señora Vasconcellos's husband's bequest. Unfortunately, she fell in love with a gigolo, and when he suggested— The phone rang on Jack's desk.

"Our London Embassy is on line two," his secretary informed him.

"Thanks, Sally," said Jack, knowing it could only be his friend Tom Crasanti, who had joined the FBI on the same day as he had.

"Hi, Tom, how are you?" he asked even before he heard a voice.

"In good shape," Tom replied. "Still running every day, even if I'm not as fit as you."

"And my godson?"

"He's learning to play cricket."

"The traitor. Got any *good* news?"

"No," said Tom. "That's why I'm calling. You're going to have to open another file."

Jack felt a cold shiver run through his body. "Who is it this time?" he asked quietly.

"The lady's name, and Lady she was, is Victoria Wentworth."

"How did she die?"

"In exactly the same manner as the other three, throat cut, almost certainly with a kitchen knife."

"What makes you think Fenston was involved?"

"She owed the bank over thirty million."

"And what was he after this time?"

"A Van Gogh self-portrait."

"Value?"

"Sixty, possibly seventy million dollars."

"I'll be on the next plane to London."

8

AT 7:56, ANNA closed the Wentworth file and bent down to open the bottom drawer of her desk. She slipped off her sneakers and replaced them with a pair of black high-heeled shoes. She rose from her chair, gathered up the files, and glanced in the mirror—not a hair out of place.

Anna stepped out of her office and walked down the corridor toward the large corner suite. Two or three members of the staff greeted her with "Good morning, Anna," which she acknowledged with a smile. A gentle knock on the chairman's door—she knew Fenston would already be seated at his desk. Had she been even a minute late, he would have pointedly stared at his watch. Anna waited for an invitation to enter and was surprised when the door was immediately pulled open and she came face-to-face with Karl Leapman. He was wearing an almost identical suit to the one Fenston had on, even if it wasn't of the same vintage.

"Good morning, Karl," she said brightly, but didn't receive a response.

The chairman looked up from behind his desk and motioned Anna to take the seat opposite him. He also didn't offer any salutation, but then he rarely did. Leapman took his place on the right of the chairman and slightly behind him, like a cardinal in attendance on the Pope. Status clearly defined. Anna assumed that Tina would appear at any moment with a cup of black coffee, but the secretary's door remained resolutely shut.

Anna glanced up at the Monet of *Argenteuil* that hung on the wall behind the chairman's desk. Although Monet had painted this peaceful riverbank scene on several occasions, this was one of the finest examples. Anna had once asked Fenston where he'd acquired the painting, but he'd been evasive, and she couldn't find any reference to the sale among past transactions.

She looked across at Leapman, whose lean and hungry look reminded her of Cassius. It didn't seem to matter what time of day it was, he always looked as if he needed a shave. She turned her attention to Fenston, who was certainly no Brutus, and shifted uneasily in her chair, trying not to appear fazed by the silence, which was suddenly broken, on Fenston's nod.

"Dr. Petrescu, some distressing information has been brought to the attention of the chairman," Leapman began. "It would appear," he continued, "that you sent one of the bank's private and confidential documents to a client before the chairman had been given the chance to consider its implications."

For a moment Anna was taken by surprise, but she quickly recovered and decided to respond in kind. "If, Mr. Leapman, you are referring to my report concerning the loan to the Wentworth Estate, you are correct. I did send a copy to Lady Victoria Wentworth."

"But the chairman was not given enough time to read that report and make a considered judgment before you forwarded it to the client," said Leapman, looking down at some notes.

"That is not the case, Mr. Leapman. Both you and the chairman were sent copies of my report on September first, with a recommendation that Lady Victoria should be advised of her position before the next quarterly payment was due."

"I never received the report," said Fenston brusquely.

"And indeed," said Anna, still looking at Leapman, "the chairman acknowledged such, when his office returned the form I attached to that report."

"I never saw it," repeated Fenston.

"Which he initialed," said Anna, who opened her file, extracted the relevant form, and placed it on the desk in front of Fenston. He ignored it.

"The least you should have done was wait for my opinion," said Fenston, "before allowing a copy of a report on such a sensitive subject to leave this office."

Anna still couldn't work out why they were spoiling for a fight. They weren't even playing good cop, bad cop.

"I waited for a week, Chairman," she replied, "during which time you made no comment on my recommendations, despite the fact that I will be flying to London this evening to keep an appointment with Lady Victoria tomorrow afternoon. However," Anna continued before the chairman could respond, "I sent you a reminder two days later." She opened her file again and placed a second sheet of paper on the chairman's desk. Once again he ignored it.

"But I hadn't read your report," Fenston said, repeating himself, clearly unable to depart from his script.

Stay calm, girl, stay calm, Anna could hear her father whispering in her ear.

She took a deep breath before continuing. "My report does no more, and certainly no less, than advise the board, of which I am a member, that if we were to sell the Van Gogh, either privately or through one of the recognized auction houses, the amount raised would more than cover the bank's original loan plus interest."

"But it might not have been my intention to sell the Van Gogh," said Fenston, now clearly straying from his script.

"You would have been left with no choice, Chairman, had that been the wish of our client."

"But I may have come up with a better solution for dealing with the Wentworth problem."

"If that was the case, Chairman," said Anna evenly, "I'm only surprised you didn't consult the head of the department concerned so that, at least as colleagues, we could have discussed any difference of opinion before I left for England tonight."

"That is an impertinent suggestion," said Fenston, raising his voice to a new level. "I report to no one."

"I don't consider it is impertinent, Chairman, to abide by the law," said Anna calmly. "It's no more than the bank's legal requirement to report any alternative recommendations to their clients. As I feel sure you realize, under the new banking regulations, as proposed by the IRS and recently passed by Congress—"

"And I feel sure you realize," said Fenston, "that your first responsibility is to me."

"Not if I believe that an officer of the bank is breaking the law," Anna replied, "because that's something I am not willing to be a party to."

"Are you trying to goad me into firing you?" shouted Fenston.

"No, but I have a feeling that you are trying to goad me into resigning," said Anna quietly.

"Either way," said Fenston, swiveling around in his chair and staring out of the window, "it is clear you no longer have a role to play in this bank, as you are simply not a team player—something they warned me about when you were dismissed from Sotheby's."

Don't rise, thought Anna. She pursed her lips and stared at Fenston's profile. She was about to reply when she noticed there was something different about him, and then she spotted the new earring. Vanity will surely be his downfall, she thought, as he swiveled back around and glared at her. She didn't react.

"Chairman, as I suspect this conversation is being recorded, I would like to make one thing absolutely clear. You don't appear to know a great deal about banking law, and you clearly know nothing about employment law, because enticing a colleague to swindle a naïve woman out of her inheritance is a criminal offence, as I feel sure Mr. Leapman, with all his experience of both sides of the law, will be happy to explain to you."

"Get out, before I throw you out," screamed Fenston, jumping up from his chair and towering over Anna. She rose slowly, turned her back on Fenston, and walked toward the door.

"And the first thing you can do is clean out your desk because I want you out of your office in ten minutes. If you are still on the premises after that, I will instruct security to escort you from the building."

Anna didn't hear Fenston's last remark as she had already closed the door quietly behind her.

The first person Anna saw as she stepped into the corridor was Barry, who had clearly been tipped off. The whole episode was beginning to look as if it had been choreographed long before she'd entered the building.

Anna walked back down the corridor with as much dignity as she could muster, despite Barry matching her stride for stride and occasionally touching her elbow. She passed an elevator that was being held open for someone and wondered who. Surely it couldn't be for her. Anna was back in her office less than fifteen minutes after she'd left it. This time Rebecca was waiting for her. She was standing behind her desk clutching a large brown cardboard box. Anna walked across to her desk and was just about to turn on her computer when a voice behind her said, "Don't touch anything. Your personal belongings have already been packed, so let's go." Anna turned around to see Barry still hovering in the doorway.

"I'm so sorry," said Rebecca. "I tried to phone and warn you, but—"

"Don't speak to her," barked Barry, "just hand over the box. She's outta here." Barry rested the palm of his hand on the knuckle of his truncheon. Anna wondered if he realized just how stupid he looked. She turned back to Rebecca and smiled.

"It's not your fault," she said, as her secretary handed over the cardboard box.

Anna placed the box on the desk, sat down, and pulled open the bottom drawer.

"You can't remove anything that belongs to the company," said Barry.

"I feel confident that Mr. Fenston won't be wanting my sneakers," said Anna, as she removed her high-heeled shoes and placed them in the box. Anna pulled on her sneakers, tied the laces, picked up the box, and headed back into the corridor. Any attempt at dignity was no longer possible. Every employee knew that raised voices in the chairman's office followed by Barry escorting you from the premises meant only one thing: you were about to be handed your pink slip. This time passersby quickly retreated into their offices, making no attempt to engage Anna in conversation.

The head of security accompanied his charge to an office at the far end of the corridor that Anna had never entered before. When she walked in, Barry once again positioned himself in the doorway. It was clear that they'd also been fully briefed, because she was met by another employee who didn't even venture "good morning" for fear it would be reported to the chairman. He swiveled a piece of paper around that displayed the figure $9,116 in bold type. Anna's monthly salary. She signed on the dotted line without comment.

"The money will be wired through to your account later today," he said without raising his eyes.

Anna turned to find her watchdog still prowling around outside, trying hard to look menacing. When she left the accounts office, Barry accompanied her on the long walk back down an empty corridor.

When they reached the elevator, Barry pressed the down arrow, while Anna continued to cling onto her cardboard box.

They were both waiting for the elevator doors to open when American Airlines Flight 11 out of Boston crashed into the ninety-fourth floor of the North Tower.

9

RUTH PARISH LOOKED up at the departure monitor on the wall above her desk. She was relieved to see that United's Flight 107 bound for JFK had finally taken off at 1:40 P.M, forty minutes behind schedule.

Ruth and her partner, Sam, had founded Art Locations nearly a decade before, and when he left her for a younger woman Ruth ended up with the company—by far the better part of the bargain. Ruth was married to the job, despite its long hours; demanding customers; and planes, trains, and cargo vessels that never arrived on time. Moving great, and not so great, works of art from one corner of the globe to the other allowed her to combine a natural flair for organization with a love of beautiful objects—if sometimes she saw the objects only for a fleeting moment.

Ruth traveled around the world accepting commissions from governments who were planning national exhibitions, while also dealing with gallery owners, dealers, and several private collectors, who often wanted nothing more than to move a favorite painting from one home to another. Over the years, many of her customers had become personal friends. But not Bryce Fenston. Ruth had long ago concluded that the words *please* and *thank you* were not in this man's vocabulary, and she certainly wasn't on his Christmas card list. Fenston's latest demand had been to collect a Van Gogh from Wentworth Hall and transport it, without delay, to his office in New York.

Obtaining an export license for the masterpiece had not proved difficult, as few institutions or museums could raise the sixty million dollars
necessary to stop the painting leaving the country, especially after the
National Galleries of Scotland had recently failed to raise the required
£7.5 million to ensure that Michelangelo's *Study of a Mourning Woman*
didn't leave these shores to become part of a private collection in the
States.

When a Mr. Andrews, the butler at Wentworth Hall, had rung the previous day to say that the painting would be ready for collection in the
morning, Ruth had scheduled one of her high-security air-ride trucks to
be at the hall by eight o'clock. Ruth was pacing up and down the tarmac
long before the truck turned up at her office, just after ten.

Once the painting was unloaded, Ruth supervised every aspect of its
packing and safe dispatch to New York, a task she would normally have
left to one of her managers. She stood over her senior packer as he
wrapped the painting in acid-free glassine paper and then placed it into
the foam-lined case he'd been working on throughout the night so it
would be ready in time. The captive bolts were tightened on the case,
preventing anyone breaking into it without a sophisticated socket set.
Special indicators were attached to the outside of the case that would
turn red if anyone attempted to open it during its journey. The senior
packer stenciled the word FRAGILE on both sides of the box and the number 47 in all four corners. The customs officer had raised an eyebrow
when he checked the shipping papers, but as an export license had been
granted, the eyebrow returned to its natural position.

Ruth drove across to the waiting 747 and watched as the red box disappeared into the vast hold. She didn't return to her office until the heavy
door was secured in place. She checked her watch and smiled. The plane
had taken off at 1:40 P.M.

Ruth began to think about the painting that would be arriving from the
Rijksmuseum in Amsterdam later that evening to form part of the Rembrandt's Women exhibition at the Royal Academy. But not before she had
put a call through to Fenston Finance to inform them that the Van Gogh
was on its way.

She dialed Anna's number in New York and waited for her to pick up
the phone.

10

THERE WAS A loud explosion, and the building began to sway from side to side.

Anna was hurled across the corridor, ending up flat on the canvas as if she'd been floored by a heavyweight boxer. The elevator doors opened and she watched as a fireball of fuel shot through the shaft, searching for oxygen. The hot blast slapped her in the face as if the door of an oven had been thrown open. Anna lay on the ground, dazed.

Her first thought was that the building must have been struck by lightning, but she quickly dismissed that idea as there wasn't a cloud in the sky. An eerie silence followed and Anna wondered if she had gone deaf, but this was soon replaced by screams of "Oh, my God!" as huge shards of jagged glass, twisted metal, and office furniture flew past the windows in front of her.

It must be another bomb, was Anna's second thought. Everyone who had been in the building in 1993 retold stories of what had happened to them on that bitterly cold February afternoon. Some of them were apocryphal, others pure invention, but the facts were simple. A truck filled with explosives had been driven into the underground garage beneath the building. When it exploded, six people were killed and more than a thousand injured. Five underground floors were wiped out, and it took several hours for the emergency services to evacuate the building. Since then, everyone who worked in the World Trade Center had been required to participate in regular fire drills. Anna tried to remember what she was supposed to do in such an emergency.

She recalled the clear instructions printed in red on the exit door to the stairwell on every floor: "In case of emergency, do not return to your desk, do not use the elevator, exit by the nearest stairwell." But first Anna needed to find out if she could even stand up, aware that part of the ceiling had collapsed on her and the building was still swaying. She tried tentatively to push herself up, and although she was bruised and cut in several places, nothing seemed to be broken. She stretched for a moment, as she always did before starting out on a long run.

Anna abandoned what was left of the contents of the cardboard box and stumbled toward stairwell C in the center of the building. Some of her colleagues were also beginning to recover from the initial shock, and one or two even returned to their desks to pick up personal belongings.

As Anna made her way along the corridor, she was greeted with a series of questions to which she had no answers.

"What are we supposed to do?" asked a secretary.

"Should we go up or down?" said a cleaner.

"Do we wait to be rescued?" asked a bond dealer.

These were all questions for the security officer, but Barry was nowhere to be seen.

Once Anna reached the stairwell, she joined a group of dazed people, some silent, some crying, who weren't quite sure what to do next. No one seemed to have the slightest idea what had caused the explosion or why the building was still swaying. Although several of the lights on the stairwell had been snuffed out like candles, the photoluminescent strip that ran along the edge of each step shone brightly up at her.

Some of those around her were trying to contact the outside world on their cell phones, but few were succeeding. One who did get through was chatting to her boyfriend. She was telling him that her boss had told her she could go home, take the rest of the day off. Another began to relay to those around him the conversation he was having with his wife: "A plane has hit the North Tower," he announced.

"But where, where?" shouted several voices at once. He asked his wife the same question. "Above us, somewhere in the nineties," he said, passing on her reply.

"But what are we meant to do?" asked the chief accountant, who hadn't moved from the top step. The younger man repeated the question to his wife and waited for her reply. "The mayor is advising everyone to get out of the building as quickly as possible."

On hearing this news, all those in the stairwell began their descent to the eighty-second floor. Anna looked back through the glass window and was surprised to see how many people had remained at their desks, as if they were in a theater after the curtain had come down and had decided to wait until the initial rush had dispersed.

Anna took the mayor's advice. She began to count the steps as she walked down each flight—eighteen to each floor, which she calculated meant at least another fifteen hundred before she would reach the lobby. The stairwell became more and more crowded as countless people swarmed out of their offices to join them on each floor, making it feel like a crowded subway during rush hour. Anna was surprised by how calm the descending line was.

The stairwell quickly separated into two lanes, with the slowest on the inside while the latest models were able to pass on the outside. But just like any highway, not everyone kept to the code, so regularly everything came to a complete standstill before moving off unsteadily again. Whenever they reached a new stairwell, some pulled into the hard shoulder, while others motored on.

Anna passed an old man who was wearing a black felt hat. She recalled seeing him several times during the past year, always wearing the same hat. She turned to smile at him and he raised his hat.

On, on, on she trudged, sometimes reaching the next floor in less than a minute but more often being held up by those who had become exhausted after descending only a few floors. The outside lane was becoming more and more crowded, making it impossible for her to break the speed limit.

Anna heard the first clear order when she reached the sixty-eighth floor.

"Get to the right, and keep moving," said an authoritative voice from somewhere below her. Although the instruction became louder with each step she took, it was still several more floors before she spotted the first fireman heading slowly toward her. He was wearing a baggy fireproof suit and sweating profusely under his black helmet emblazoned with the number 28. Anna could only wonder what state he'd be in after he'd climbed another thirty floors. He also appeared to be overloaded with equipment: coiled ropes over one shoulder and two oxygen tanks on his back, like a mountaineer trying to conquer Everest. Another fireman followed closely behind, carrying a vast length of hose, six pole arms, and a large bottle of drinking water. He was dripping so much sweat that from time to time he removed his helmet and poured some of the drinking water over his head.

Those who continued to leave their offices and join Anna in her downward migration were mostly silent, until an old man in front of her tripped and fell on a woman. The woman cut her leg on the sharp edge of the step and began to scream at the old man.

"Get on with it," said a voice behind her. "I made this journey after the 'ninety-three bombing, and I can tell you, lady, you ain't seen nothin' yet."

Anna leant forward to help the old man to his feet, hindering her own progress, while allowing others to scramble past her.

Whenever she reached a new landing, Anna stared through the vast panes of glass at workers who remained at their desks, apparently oblivious of those fleeing in front of their eyes. She even overheard snatches of conversation through the open doors. One of them, a broker on the sixty-second floor, was trying to close a deal before the markets opened at nine o'clock. Another was staring out at her, as if the pane of glass was a television screen and he was reporting on a football game. He was giving a running commentary over the phone to a friend in the South Tower.

More and more firemen were now climbing toward her, turning the highway into two-way traffic, their constant cry: "Get to the right, keep moving." Anna kept moving, her speed often dictated by the slowest participant. Although the building had stopped swaying, tension and fear could still be seen on the faces of all those around her. They didn't know what had happened above them and had no idea what awaited them below. Anna felt guilty as she passed an old woman who was being carried down in a large leather chair by two young men, her legs swollen, her breathing uneven.

On, on, on, Anna went, floor after floor, until even she began to feel tired.

She thought about Rebecca and Tina, and prayed they were both safe.

She even wondered if Fenston and Leapman were still sitting in the chairman's office, believing themselves impervious to any danger.

Anna began to feel confident that she was now safe and would eventually wake up from this nightmare. She even smiled at some of the New York humor that was bouncing around her, until she heard a voice behind her scream.

"A second plane has hit the South Tower."

11

JACK WAS APPALLED by his first reaction when he heard what sounded like a bomb exploding on the other side of the road. Sally had rushed in to tell him that a plane had crashed into the North Tower of the World Trade Center.

"Let's hope it scored a direct hit on Fenston's office," he said.

His second thoughts were a little more professional, as expressed when he joined Dick Macy, the supervising special agent, along with the rest of the senior agents in the command center. While other agents hit the phones in an attempt to make some sense of what was happening less than a mile away, Jack told the SSA that he was in no doubt that it was a well-planned act of terrorism. When a second plane crashed into the South Tower at 9:03 A.M., all Macy said was, "Yes, but *which* terrorist organization?"

Jack's third reaction was delayed, and it took him by surprise. He hoped that Anna Petrescu had managed to escape, but when the South Tower came crashing down fifty-six minutes later, he assumed it would not be long before the North Tower followed suit.

He returned to his desk and switched on his computer. Information was flooding in from their Massachusetts field office, reporting that the two attack flights had originated out of Boston and two more were in the air. Calls from passengers in those planes that had taken off from the same airport suggested they were also under the terrorists' control. One was heading for Washington.

President George W. Bush was visiting a school in Florida when the first plane struck, and he was quickly whisked off to Barksdale Air Force Base in Louisiana. Vice President Dick Cheney was in Washington. He'd already given clear instructions to shoot down the other two planes. The order was not carried out. Cheney also wanted to know which terrorist organization was responsible, as the president planned to address the nation later that evening and he was demanding answers. Jack remained at his desk, taking calls from his agents on the ground, frequently reporting back to Macy. One of those agents, Joe Corrigan, reported that Fenston and Leapman had been seen entering a building on Wall Street just before the first plane crashed into the North Tower. Jack looked down at the many files strewn across his desk and dismissed as wishful thinking, "Case Closed."

"And Petrescu?" he asked.

"No idea," Joe replied. "All I can tell you is that she was seen entering the building at seven forty-six and hasn't been seen since."

Jack looked up at the TV screen. A third plane had crashed into the Pentagon. The White House must be next, was his only thought.

"A second plane's hit the South Tower," a lady on the step above Anna repeated. Anna refused to believe that kind of freak accident could happen twice on the same day.

"It's no accident," said another voice from behind, as if reading her thoughts. "The only plane to crash into a building in New York was in 'forty-five. Flew into the seventy-ninth floor of the Empire State Building. But that was on a foggy day, without any of the sophisticated tracking devices they've got now. And don't forget, the air space above the city is a no-fly zone, so it must have been well planned. My bet is we're not the only folks in trouble."

Within minutes, conspiracy theories, terrorist attacks, and stories of freak accidents were being bandied about by people who had no idea what they were talking about. There would have been a stampede if they could have moved any faster. Anna quickly became aware that several people on the staircase were now masking their worst fears by all talking at once.

"Keep to the right, and keep moving," was the constant cry emanating from whatever uniform trudged passed them. Some of the migrants on the downward journey began to tire, allowing Anna to overtake them. She was thankful for all those hours spent running around Central Park and the shot after shot of adrenaline that kept her going.

It was somewhere in the lower forties that Anna first smelled smoke, and she could hear some of those on the floors below her coughing loudly. When she reached the next landing, the smoke became denser and quickly filled her lungs. She covered her eyes and began coughing uncontrollably. Anna recalled reading somewhere that 90 percent of deaths in a fire are caused by smoke inhalation. Her fears were only exacerbated when those ahead of her slowed to a crawl and finally came to a halt. The coughing had turned into an epidemic. Had they all become trapped, with no escape route up or down?

"Keep moving," came the clear order from a fireman heading toward them. "It gets worse for a couple of floors but then you'll be through it," he assured those who were still hesitating. Anna stared into the face of the man who had given the order with such authority. She obeyed him, confident that the worst must surely be behind her. She kept her eyes covered and continued coughing for another three floors, but the fireman turned out to be right, because the smoke was already beginning to disperse. Anna decided to listen only to the professionals coming up the stairwell and to dismiss the opinions of any amateurs going down.

A sudden feeling of relief swept through those emerging from the smoke, and they immediately tried to speed up their descent. But sheer numbers prevented swift progress in the one-way traffic lane. Anna tried to remain calm as she slipped in behind a blind man, who was being led down the stairs by his guide dog. "Don't be frightened by the smoke, Rosie," said the man. The dog wagged its tail.

Down, down, down, the pace always dictated by the person in front. By the time Anna reached the deserted cafeteria on the thirty-ninth floor, the overloaded firemen had been joined by Port Authority officers and policemen from the Emergency Service Unit—the most popular of all New York's cops because they dealt only in safety and rescue, no parking tickets, no arrests. Anna felt guilty about passing those who were willing to continue going up while she went in the opposite direction.

By the time Anna reached the twenty-fourth floor, several bedraggled stragglers were stopping to take a rest, a few even congregating to exchange anecdotes, while others were still refusing to leave their offices, unable to believe that a problem on the ninety-fourth floor could possibly affect them. Anna looked around, desperately hoping to see a familiar face, perhaps Rebecca or Tina, even Barry, but she could have been in a foreign land.

"We've got a level three up here, possibly level four," a battalion commander was saying over his radio, "so I'm sweeping every floor."

Anna watched the commander as he systematically cleared every office. It took him some time because each floor was the size of a football field.

On the twenty-first floor, one individual remained resolutely at his desk; he'd just settled a currency deal for a billion dollars and he was awaiting confirmation of the transaction.

"*Out,*" shouted the battalion commander, but the smartly dressed man ignored the order and continued tapping away on his keyboard. "I said *out,*" repeated the senior fire officer, as two of his younger officers lifted the man out of his chair and deposited him in the stairwell. The unfulfilled broker reluctantly joined the exodus.

When Anna reached the twentieth floor, she encountered a new problem. She had to wade through water that was now pouring in on them from the sprinklers and leaking pipes on every floor. She stepped tentatively over fragments of broken glass and flaming debris that littered the stairwell and were beginning to slow everyone down. She felt like a football fan trying to get out of a crowded stadium that had only one turnstile. When she finally reached the teens, her progress became dramatically faster. All the floors below her had been cleared, and fewer and fewer office staff were joining them on the stairs.

On the tenth floor, Anna stared through an open door into a deserted office. Computer screens were still flickering and chairs had been pushed aside as if their occupants had gone to the washroom and would be back at any moment. Plastic cups of cold coffee and half-drunk cans of Coke littered almost every surface. Papers were scattered everywhere, even on the floor, while silver-framed family photographs remained in place.

Someone following closely behind Anna bumped into her, so she quickly moved on.

By the time Anna reached the seventh floor, it was no longer her fellow workers, but the water and flotsam that were holding her up. She was picking her way tentatively through the debris when she first heard the voice. To begin with, it was faint, and then it became a little louder. The sound of a megaphone was coming from somewhere below them, urging her on. "Keep moving, don't look back, don't use your cell phones—it slows up those behind you."

Three more floors had to be negotiated before she found herself back in the lobby, paddling through inches of water, and on past the express shuttle elevator that had whisked her up to her office only a couple of hours before. Suddenly even more sprinklers jetted down from the ceiling above, but Anna was already drenched to the skin.

The orders bellowing from the megaphones were becoming louder and louder by the moment, and their demands even more strident. "Keep moving, get out of the building, get as far away as you possibly can." Not that easy, Anna wanted to tell them. When she reached the turnstiles she'd passed through earlier that morning, she found them battered and twisted. They must have been brushed aside by wave after wave of firemen when they transported their heavy equipment into the building.

Anna felt disorientated and unsure what to do next. Should she wait for her colleagues to join her? She stood still, but only for a moment, before she heard another insistent command that she felt was being addressed directly at her. "Keep moving, lady, don't use your cell phone, and don't look back."

"But where do we go?" someone shouted.

"Down the escalator, through the mall, and then get as far away from the building as possible."

Anna joined the horde of tired savages as they stepped onto an overcrowded escalator. She allowed it to carry her down to the concourse before taking another escalator up to the open promenade, where she often joined Tina and Rebecca for an al fresco lunch while they enjoyed an open-air concert. No open air now, and certainly no calming sound of a violin—just another voice bellowing, "Don't look back, don't look back." An order Anna disobeyed, which not only slowed her down, but also caused her to fall on her knees retching. She watched in disbelief as first one person then another, who must have been trapped above the nineti-eth floor, jumped out of their office windows to a certain death rather than face the slow agony of burning. "Get back on your feet, lady, and keep movin'."

Anna picked herself up and stumbled forward, suddenly aware that none of the officers in charge of the evacuation were making eye contact with those fleeing from the building or even attempting to answer any of their individual questions. She assumed this must be because it would only slow things down and impede the progress of those still trying to get out of the building.

When Anna passed Borders bookshop, she glanced in the window dis-playing the number-one bestseller, *Valhalla Rising*.

"Keep movin', lady," a voice repeated, even louder.

"Where to?" she asked desperately.

"Anywhere, hut just keep goin'."

"In which direction?"

"I don't care, as long as it's as far away from the tower as possible."

Anna spat out the last bits of vomit as she continued to move away from the building.

When she reached the entrance to the plaza, she came across fire trucks and ambulances that were tending to the walking wounded and those who just simply couldn't manage another step. Anna didn't waste their time. When she finally reached the road, she looked up to see a sign with an arrow covered in black grime. She could just make out the words CITY HALL. Anna began jogging for the first time. Her jog turned into a run and she started to overtake some of those who had departed earlier from the lower floors. And then she heard another unfamiliar noise be-hind her. It sounded like a clap of thunder that seemed to grow louder and louder by the second. She didn't want to look back, but she did.

Anna stood transfixed as she watched the South Tower collapse in front of her eyes, as if it had been constructed of bamboo. In a matter of sec-onds, the remnants of the building came crashing to the ground, throw-ing up dust and debris that mushroomed into the sky, causing a dense mountain of flames and fumes that hovered for a moment, then began to advance indiscriminately through the crowded streets, engulfing anyone and everyone who stood in its way.

Anna ran as she had never run before, but she knew it was hopeless. It could only be a matter of seconds before the gray, ruthless snake was upon her, suffocating all in its progress. Anna wasn't in any doubt that she was about to die. She only hoped it would be quick.

Fenston stared across at the World Trade Center from the safety of an office on Wall Street.

He watched in disbelief as a second plane flew directly into the South Tower.

While most New Yorkers worried about how they could assist their friends, relations, and colleagues at this tragic time, and others what it meant for America, Fenston had only one thought on his mind.

He and Leapman had arrived on Wall Street for their meeting with a prospective client only moments before the first plane crashed into the North Tower. Fenston abandoned his appointment and spent the next hour on a public telephone in the corridor trying to contact someone, anyone, in his office, but no one responded to his calls. Others would have liked to use the phone, but Fenston didn't budge. Leapman was carrying out the same exercise on his cell phone.

When Fenston heard a second volcanic eruption, he left the phone dangling and rushed to the window. Leapman walked quickly across to join him. They both stood in silence as they watched the South Tower collapse.

"It can't be long before the North Tower goes the same way," said Fenston.

"Then I think we can assume that Petrescu will not survive," said Leapman, matter-of-factly.

"I don't give a damn about Petrescu," said Fenston. "If the North Tower goes, then I've lost my Monet, and it isn't insured."

12

Anna began running flat out, more and more aware with each step she took that everything around her was becoming quieter. One by one the screams were dying, and she knew she had to be next. There no longer seemed to be anyone behind her, and for the first time in her life Anna wanted someone to overtake her, anyone, just so she didn't feel like the last person on earth. She now understood what it must be like to be pursued by an avalanche at a speed ten times faster than any human could achieve. This particular avalanche was black.

Anna took deep breaths as she forced her body to achieve speeds that she had never experienced before. She lifted her white silk blouse—now black, sodden, and crumpled—and placed it over her mouth, just moments before she was overtaken by the relentless, all-enveloping gray cloud.

A whoosh of uncontrolled air hurled her forward and threw her onto the ground, but she still tried desperately to keep moving. She hadn't managed more than a few feet before she began choking uncontrollably. She pushed forward for another yard, and then another, until her head suddenly bumped into something solid. Anna placed a hand on the surface of a wall and tried to feel her way along. *But was she walking away from, or back into, the gray cloud?* Ash, dirt, dust were in her mouth, eyes, ears, nose, and hair, and clinging to her skin. It felt as if she was about to be burned alive. Anna thought about the people she had seen jumping because they felt that must be an easier way to die. She now understood their feelings, but she had no building to jump from and could only wonder how much longer it would be before she suffocated. She took her last step, knelt down on the ground, and began to pray.

Our Father . . . She felt peaceful, and was about to close her eyes and give way to deep sleep when out of nowhere she saw a flashing police light. *Who art in Heaven* . . . She made one last effort to get back on her feet and move toward the blue light. *Hallowed be thy name* . . . but the car drifted past, unaware of her plaintive cry for help. *Thy Kingdom come* . . . Anna fell once again and cut her knee on the edge of the sidewalk, *Thy will be done* . . . , but felt nothing. *On earth, as it is in Heaven.* She clung to the edge of the sidewalk with her right hand and somehow managed a few more inches. She was about to stop breathing when she thought she touched something warm. Was it alive? "Help," she murmured feebly, expecting no response.

"Give me your hand," came back the immediate reply. His grip was firm. "Try and stand."

With his help, Anna somehow pushed herself up. "Can you see that triangle of light coming from over there?" the voice said, but she couldn't even see where he was pointing. Anna turned a complete circle and stared into 360 degrees of black night. Suddenly she let out a muffled yelp of joy when she spotted a ray of sunlight trying to break through the heavy overcoat of gloom. She took the stranger's hand and they began inching toward a light that grew brighter and brighter with every step, until she finally walked out of hell and back into New York.

Anna turned to the gray ash-coated figure who had saved her life. His uniform was so covered in dirt and dust that if he hadn't been wearing the familiar peaked cap and badge she wouldn't have known that he was a cop. He smiled and cracks appeared on his face as if he was daubed in heavy makeup. "Keep heading toward the light," he said, and disappeared back into the murky cloud before she could thank him. *Amen.*

Fenston gave up trying to contact his office only when he saw the North Tower collapse in front of his eyes. He replaced the receiver and rushed back down the unfamiliar corridor to find Leapman scrawling SOLD on a "To Rent" board that was attached to the door of an empty office.

"Tomorrow there will be ten thousand people after this space," he explained, "so at least that's one problem solved."

"You may be able to replace an office, but what you can't replace is my Monet," Fenston said ungraciously. He paused. "And if I don't get my hands on the Van Gogh . . ."

Leapman checked his watch. "It should be halfway across the Atlantic by now."

"Let's hope so, because we no longer have any documentation to prove we even own the painting," said Fenston, as he looked out of the window and stared at a gray cloud that hung above the ground where the Twin Towers had once proudly stood.

Anna joined a group of fellow stragglers as they emerged out of the gloom. Her compatriots looked as if they'd already completed a marathon but hadn't yet reached the finish line. Coming out of such darkness, Anna found she couldn't bear to look up at the glaring sun; even opening her dust-covered eyelids demanded effort. On, on, she stumbled, inch by inch, foot by foot, coughing up dirt and dust with every step, wondering how much more black liquid there could possibly be left in her body. After a few more paces she collapsed onto her knees, convinced the gray cloud could no longer overtake her. She continued coughing, spitting, spitting, coughing. When Anna looked up, she became aware of a group of startled onlookers, who were staring at her as if she'd just landed from another planet.

"Were you in one of the towers?" asked one of them. She didn't have the strength to answer and decided to get as far away from their gaping eyes as possible. Anna had only covered a few more paces before she bumped into a Japanese tourist who was bending down trying to take a photograph of her. She angrily waved him away. He immediately bowed even lower and apologized.

When Anna reached the next intersection, she collapsed on the sidewalk and stared up at the street sign—she was on the corner of Franklin and Church. I'm only a few blocks from Tina's apartment, was her first thought. But as Tina was still somewhere behind her, how could she possibly have survived? Without warning, a bus came to a halt by her side. Although it was as full as a San Francisco tram car during rush hour, people edged back to allow her to clamber on. The bus stopped on the corner of every block, allowing some to jump off while others got on, with no suggestion of anyone paying a fare. It seemed that all New Yorkers were united in wanting to play some part in the unfolding drama.

"Oh, my God," whispered Anna, as she sat on the bus and buried her head in her hands. For the first time she thought about the firemen who had passed her on the stairwell, and of Tina and Rebecca, who must be dead. It's only when you know someone that a tragedy becomes more than a news item.

When the bus came to a halt in the Village near Washington Square Park, Anna almost fell off. She stumbled over to the sidewalk, coughing up several more mouthfuls of gray dust that she'd avoided bringing up while she was on the bus. A woman sat down on the curb beside her and offered her a bottle of water. Anna filled her mouth several times before spitting out dollops of black liquid. She emptied the bottle without swallowing a drop. The woman then pointed in the direction of a small hotel where escapees were trooping in and out in a steady stream. She bent down and took Anna by the arm, guiding her gently toward the ladies' room on the ground floor. The room was full of men and women oblivious of their sex. Anna looked at herself in the mirror and understood why onlookers had stared at her so curiously. It was as if someone had poured several bags of gray ash all over her. She left her hands under a flowing tap until only her nails remained black. She then tried to remove a layer of the caked dust from her face—an almost pointless exercise. She turned to thank the stranger, but she, like the cop, had already disappeared to assist someone else.

Anna limped back onto the road, her throat dry, her knees cut, her feet blistered and aching. As she stumbled slowly up Waverly Place, she tried to remember the number of Tina's apartment. She continued on past an uninhabited Waverly Diner before pausing outside number 273.

Anna grabbed at the familiar wrought-iron balustrade like a lifeline and yanked herself up the steps to the front door. She ran her finger down the list of names by the side of the buzzers: Amato, Kravits, Gambino, O'Rourke, Forster . . . Forster, Forster, she repeated joyfully, before pressing the little bell. But how could Tina answer her call, when she must be dead, was Anna's only thought. She left her finger on the buzzer as if it would bring Tina to life, but it didn't. She finally gave up and turned to leave, tears streaming down her dust-caked face, when out of nowhere an irate voice demanded, "Who is it?"

Anna collapsed onto the top step.

"Oh, thank God," she cried, "you're alive, you're alive."

"But you can't be," said a disbelieving voice.

"Open the door," pleaded Anna, "and you can see for yourself."

The click of the entry button was the best sound Anna had heard that day.

13

"YOU'RE ALIVE," REPEATED Tina, as she flung open the front door and threw her arms around her friend. Anna may have resembled a street urchin who had just climbed out of a Victorian chimney, but it didn't prevent Tina from clinging to her.

"I was thinking about how you could always make me laugh, and wondering if I'd ever laugh again, when the buzzer sounded."

"And I was convinced that even if you'd somehow managed to get out of the building, you still couldn't have survived once the tower collapsed."

"If I had a bottle of champagne, I'd open it so that we could celebrate," said Tina, finally letting go of her friend.

"I'll settle for a coffee, and then another coffee, followed by a bath."

"I do have coffee," said Tina, who took Anna by the hand and led her through to the small kitchen at the end of the corridor. Anna left a set of gray footprints on the carpet behind her.

Anna sat down at a small, round, wooden table and kept her hands in her lap, while a soundless television was showing images of the other side of the story. She tried to stay still, aware that anything she touched was immediately smeared with ash and dirt. Tina didn't seem to notice.

"I know this may sound a little strange," said Anna, "but I haven't a clue what's going on."

Tina turned up the sound on the television.

"Fifteen minutes of that," Tina said as she filled the coffeepot, "and you'll know everything."

Anna watched the endless replays of a plane flying into the South Tower, people throwing themselves from the higher floors to a certain death, and the collapse of first the South and then the North Tower.

"And another plane hit the Pentagon?" she asked. "So how many more are out there?"

"There was a fourth," said Tina, as she placed two mugs on the table, "but no one seems certain where it was heading."

"The White House, possibly," suggested Anna, as she looked up at the screen to see President Bush speaking from Barksdale Air Force Base in Louisiana: "Make no mistake, the United States will hunt down and punish those responsible for these cowardly acts."

The images flashed back to the second plane flying into the South Tower.

"Oh, my God," said Anna. "I hadn't even thought about the innocent passengers onboard those planes. Who's responsible for all this?" she demanded, as Tina filled her mug with black coffee.

"The State Department is being fairly cautious," said Tina, "and all the usual suspects—Russia, North Korea, Iran, and Iraq—have all been quick to scream, 'Not me,' swearing they will do everything they can to track down those responsible."

"But what are the newscasters saying? There's no reason for them to be cautious."

"CNN is pointing a finger at Afghanistan and, in particular, at a terrorist group called Al-Qaeda—I think that's how you pronounce it, but I'm not sure as I've never heard of them," Tina said, as she sat down opposite Anna.

"I think they're a bunch of religious fanatics who I thought were only interested in taking over Saudi Arabia so they could get hold of its oil." Anna glanced back up at the television and listened to the commentator, who was trying to imagine what it must have been like to be in the North Tower when the first plane struck. How could you possibly know? Anna wanted to ask him. A hundred minutes telescoped into a few seconds, and then repeated again and again like a familiar advertisement. When the South Tower collapsed and smoke billowed up into the sky, Anna started coughing loudly, shaking ash onto everything around her.

"Are you OK?" asked Tina, jumping up from her chair.

"Yes, I'll be fine," said Anna, draining her coffee. "Would you mind if I turned the TV off? I don't think I can face continually being reminded what it was like to be there."

"Of course not," said Tina, who picked up the remote and touched the off button. The images melted from the screen.

"I can't stop thinking about all our friends who were in the building," said Anna, as Tina refilled her mug with coffee. "I wonder if Rebecca . . ."

"No word from her," said Tina. "Barry is the only person who's reported in so far."

"Yeah, I can believe Barry was the first down the stairs, trampling over anyone who got in his way. But who did Barry call?" asked Anna.

"Fenston. On his mobile."

"Fenston?" said Anna. "How did he manage to escape when I left his office only a few minutes before the first plane hit the building?"

"He'd arrived on Wall Street by then—he had an appointment with a potential client, whose only asset was a Gauguin. So there was no way he was going to be late for that."

"And Leapman?" asked Anna, as she took another sip of coffee.

"One step behind him as usual," said Tina.

"So that's why the elevator door was being held open."

"The elevator door?" repeated Tina.

"It's not important," said Anna. "But why weren't you at work this morning?"

"I had a dental appointment," said Tina. "It had been on my calendar for weeks." She paused and looked across the table. "The moment I heard the news I never stopped trying to call you on your cell, but all I got was a ringing tone. So where were you?"

"Being escorted off the premises," said Anna.

"By a firefighter?" asked Tina.

"No," replied Anna, "by that ape, Barry."

"But why?" demanded Tina.

"Because Fenston had just fired me," said Anna.

"Fired you?" said Tina in disbelief. "Why would he fire you, of all people?"

"Because in my report to the board, I recommended that Victoria Wentworth should sell the Van Gogh, which would allow her not only to clear her overdraft with the bank but hold on to the rest of the estate."

"But the Van Gogh was the only reason Fenston ever agreed to that deal," said Tina. "I thought you realized that. He's been after one for years. The last thing he would have wanted was to sell the painting and get Victoria off the hook. But that's hardly a reason to fire you. What excuse—"

"I also sent a copy of my recommendations to the client, which I considered to be no more than ethical banking practice."

"I don't think it's ethical banking practice that keeps Fenston awake at night. But that still doesn't explain why he got rid of you so quickly."

"Because I was just about to fly to England and let Victoria Wentworth know that I'd even lined up a prospective buyer, a well-known Japanese collector, Takashi Nakamura, who I felt sure would be happy to close the deal quickly if we were sensible about the asking price."

"You picked the wrong man in Nakamura," said Tina. "Whatever the asking price, he's the last person on earth Fenston would be willing to do business with. They've both been after a Van Gogh for years and are regularly the last two bidders for any major Impressionists."

"Why didn't he tell me that?" said Anna.

"Because it doesn't always suit him to let you know what he's up to," said Tina.

"But we were both on the same team."

"You're so naïve, Anna. Haven't you worked out that there's only one person on Fenston's team?"

"But he can't make Victoria hand over the Van Gogh unless—"

"I wouldn't be so sure about that," said Tina.

"Why not?"

"Fenston put a call through to Ruth Parish yesterday and ordered her to pick up the painting immediately. I heard him repeat the word *immediately*."

"Before Victoria was given the chance to act on my recommendations."

"Which would also explain why he had to fire you before you could get on that plane and upset his plans. Mind you," added Tina, "you're not the first person to have ventured down that well-trodden path."

"What do you mean?" said Anna.

"Once anyone works out what Fenston is really up to, they're quickly shown the door."

"Then why hasn't he fired you?"

"Because I don't make any recommendations he isn't willing to go along with," said Tina. "That way, I'm not considered a threat." She paused. "Well, not for the moment."

Anna thumped the table in anger, sending up a small cloud of dust. "I'm so dumb," she said. "I should have seen it coming, and now there's nothing I can do about it."

"I'm not so sure about that," said Tina. "We don't know for certain that Ruth Parish has picked up the painting from Wentworth Hall. If she hasn't, you'll still have enough time to call Victoria and advise her to hold onto the picture until you've had a chance to get in touch with Mr. Nakamura—that way she could still clear her debt with Fenston and he couldn't do anything about it," added Tina, as her cell phone began ringing, "California Here I Come." She checked its caller ID: BOSS flashed up. She put a finger to her lips. "It's Fenston," she warned. "He probably wants to find out if you've been in touch with me," she added, flipping open the phone.

"Do you realize who got left behind in the rubble?" Fenston asked before Tina could speak.

"Anna?"

"No," said Fenston. "Petrescu is dead."

"Dead?" repeated Tina, as she stared across the table at her friend. "But—"

"Yes. When Barry reported in, he confirmed that the last time he saw her she was lying on the floor, so she can't possibly have survived."

"I think you'll find—"

"Don't worry about Petrescu," said Fenston. "I already had plans to replace her, but what I can't replace is my Monet."

Tina was shocked into a moment's silence and was about to tell him just how wrong he was when she suddenly realized that she just might be able to turn Fenston's crassness to Anna's advantage.

"Does that also mean we've lost the Van Gogh?"

"No," said Fenston. "Ruth Parish has already confirmed that the painting is on its way from London. It should arrive at JFK this evening, when Leapman is going to pick it up."

Tina sank down into the chair, feeling deflated.

"And make sure you're in by six tomorrow morning."

"Six A.M.?"

"Yes," said Fenston. "And don't complain. After all, you've had the whole of today off."

"So where do I report?" asked Tina, not bothering to argue.

"I've taken over offices on the thirty-second floor of the Trump Building at 40 Wall Street, so at least for us it will be business as usual." The line went dead.

"He thinks you're dead," said Tina, "but he's more fussed about losing his Monet," she added, as she snapped her cell phone shut.

"He'll find out soon enough that I'm not," said Anna.

"Only if you want him to," said Tina. "Has anyone else seen you since you got out of the tower?"

"Only looking like this," said Anna.

"Then let's keep it that way, while we try and work out what needs to be done. Fenston says the Van Gogh is already on its way to New York and Leapman will pick it up as soon as it lands."

"Then what can we do?"

"I could try and delay Leapman somehow while you pick up the painting."

"But what would I do with it," asked Anna, "when Fenston would be certain to come looking for me?"

"You could get yourself on the first plane back to London and return the picture to Wentworth Hall."

"I couldn't do that without Victoria's permission," said Anna.

"Good God, Anna, when will you grow up? You've got to stop thinking like a schoolteacher and start imagining what Fenston would do if he were in your position."

"He'd find out what time the plane was landing," said Anna. "So the first thing I need to do—"

"The first thing you need to do is have a shower, while I find out what time the plane lands and also what Leapman's up to," said Tina, as she stood up. "Because one thing's for sure, they won't let you pick up anything from the airport looking like that."

Anna drained her coffee and followed Tina out into the corridor. Tina opened the bathroom door and looked closely at her friend. "See you in about—" she hesitated "—an hour."

Anna laughed for the first time that day.

———

Anna slowly peeled off her clothes and dropped them in a heap on the floor. She glanced in the mirror to see a reflection of someone she had never met before. She removed the silver chain from round her neck and placed it on the side of the bath, next to the model of a yacht. She finally took off her watch. It had stopped at eight forty-six. A few seconds later and she would have been in the elevator.

As Anna stepped into the shower, she began to consider Tina's audacious plan. She turned on both taps and allowed the water to cascade down on her for some time before she even thought about washing. She watched the water turn from black to gray, but however hard she scrubbed, the water still remained gray. Anna continued scrubbing until her skin was red and sore, before turning her attention to a bottle of shampoo. She didn't emerge from the shower until she'd washed her hair three times, but it was going to be days before anyone realized that she was a natural blonde. Anna didn't bother to dry herself; she bent down, put the plug in the bath, and turned on the taps. As she lay soaking, her mind revisited all that had taken place that day.

She thought about how many friends and colleagues she must have lost and realized just how lucky she was to be alive. But mourning would have to wait, if she was to have any chance of rescuing Victoria from a slower death.

Anna's thoughts were interrupted by Tina knocking on the door. She walked in and sat on the end of the bath. "A definite improvement," she said with a smile, as she looked at Anna's newly scrubbed body.

"I've been thinking about your idea," said Anna, "and if I could—"

"Change of plan," said Tina. "It's just been announced by the FAA that all aircraft across America have been grounded until further notice and no incoming flights will be allowed to land, so by now the Van Gogh will be on its way back to Heathrow."

"Then I'll need to call Victoria immediately," said Anna, "and tell her to instruct Ruth Parish to return the painting to Wentworth Hall."

"Agreed," said Tina, "but I've just realized that Fenston has lost something even more important than the Monet."

"What could be more important to him than the Monet?" asked Anna.

"His contract with Victoria, and all the other paperwork that proves he owns the Van Gogh along with the rest of the Wentworth estate should she fail to clear the debt."

"But didn't you keep backups?" asked Anna.

Tina hesitated. "Yes," she said, "in a safe in Fenston's office."

"But don't forget that Victoria will also be in possession of all the relevant documents."

Tina paused again. "Not if she was willing to destroy them."

"Victoria would never agree to that," said Anna.

"Why don't you phone her and find out? If she did feel able to, it would give you more than enough time to sell the Van Gogh and clear the debt with Fenston, before he could do anything about it."

"There's only one problem."

"What's that?" asked Tina.

"I don't have her number. Her file is in my office, and I've lost everything, including my cell phone and Palm Pilot, even my wallet."

"I'm sure international directories can solve that problem," suggested Tina. "Why don't you dry yourself and put on a bathrobe? We can sort out some clothes later."

"Thank you," said Anna, gripping her by the hand.

"You might not thank me when you find out what you're having for lunch. Mind you, I wasn't expecting a guest, so you'll have to make do with leftover Chinese."

"Sounds great," said Anna, as she stepped out of the bath and grabbed a towel, wrapping it tightly around her.

"See you in a couple of minutes," said Tina, "by which time the microwave should have completely finished off my gourmet offering." She turned to leave.

"Tina, can I ask you something?"

"Anything."

"Why do you continue to work for Fenston, when you obviously detest the man as much as I do?"

Tina hesitated. "Anything but that," she eventually replied. She closed the door quietly behind her.

14

RUTH PARISH PICKED up her outside line.

"Hi, Ruth," said a familiar voice, about to deliver an unfamiliar message. "It's Ken Lane over at United, just to let you know that our flight 107, bound for New York, has been ordered to turn back, and we're expecting it to touch down at Heathrow in about an hour."

"But why?" asked Ruth.

"Details are a bit sketchy at the moment," Ken admitted, "but reports coming out of JFK suggest there's been a terrorist attack on the Twin Towers. All U.S. airports have been ordered to ground their planes, and won't be allowing any incoming flights until further notice."

"When did all this happen?"

"Around one thirty our time. You must have been at lunch. You can get an update on any news station. They're all carrying it."

Ruth picked up the remote control from her desk and pointed it toward the TV screen.

"Will you be putting the Van Gogh in storage?" asked Ken, "or do you want us to return it to Wentworth Hall?"

"It certainly won't be going back to Wentworth," said Ruth. "I'll lock the painting up in one of our customs-free zones overnight and then put it on the first available flight to New York once JFK lifts the restrictions."

Ruth paused. "Will you confirm an ETA about thirty minutes before your plane is due to touch down so I can have one of my trucks standing by?"

"Will do," said Ken.

Ruth replaced the receiver and glanced up at the TV. She tapped out the number 501 on her remote control. The first image she saw was a plane flying into the South Tower.

Now she understood why Anna hadn't returned her call.

As Anna dried herself, she began to speculate on what possible reason Tina could have to go on working for Fenston. She found herself shaking her head. After all, Tina was bright enough to pick up a far better job.

She pulled on her friend's bathrobe and slippers, placed the key on its chain back around her neck and put on her one-time watch. She looked at herself in the mirror; the outward façade had considerably improved, but Anna still felt queasy whenever she thought about what she had been through only a few hours before. She wondered for how many days, months, years it would be a recurring nightmare.

She opened the bathroom door and maneuvered her way down the corridor, avoiding the ashy footprints she'd left on the carpet. When she walked into the kitchen, Tina stopped laying the table and handed over her cell phone.

"Time to call Victoria and warn her what you're up to."

"What am I up to?" asked Anna.

"For starters, ask her if she knows where the Van Gogh is."

"Locked up in a customs-free zone at Heathrow would be my bet, but there's only one way to find out." Anna dialed 00.

"International operator."

"I need a number in England," said Anna.

"Business or residential?"

"Residential."

"Name?"

"Wentworth, Victoria."

"Address?"

"Wentworth Hall, Wentworth, Surrey."

There was a long silence before Anna was informed, "I'm sorry, ma'am, that number is ex-directory."

"What does that mean?" asked Anna.

"I can't give out the number."

"But this is an emergency," insisted Anna.

"I'm sorry, ma'am, but I still can't release that number."

"But I'm a close personal friend."

"I don't care if you're the Queen of England, I repeat, I'm unable to give out that number." The line went dead. Anna frowned.

"So what's plan B?" asked Tina.

"No choice but to get myself to England somehow and try to see Victoria so I can warn her what Fenston's up to."

"Good. Then the next thing to decide is which border you're going to cross."

"What chance have I got of crossing any border, when I can't even go back to my apartment and pick up my things—unless I want the whole world to know I'm alive and kicking."

"There's nothing to stop me going to your place," said Tina. "Tell me what you want and I can pack a bag and—"

"No need to pack," said Anna. "Everything I want is ready and waiting in the hallway—don't forget I was expecting to fly to London this evening."

"Then all I need is the key to your apartment," said Tina.

Anna unclasped the chain round her neck and handed over her key.

"How do I get past the doorman?" asked Tina. "He's bound to ask who I've come to see."

"That won't be a problem," said Anna. "His name is Sam. Tell him you're visiting David Sullivan and he'll just smile and call for the elevator."

"Who's David Sullivan?" asked Tina.

"He's got an apartment on the fourth floor and rarely entertains the same girl twice. He pays Sam a few dollars every week to keep them all blissfully unaware that they are not the only woman in his life."

"But that doesn't solve the cash problem," said Tina. "Don't forget you lost your wallet and credit card in the crash, and all I have to my name is about seventy dollars."

"I took three thousand dollars out of my account yesterday," said Anna. "Whenever you're moving a valuable painting, you can't risk any holdups, so you have to be prepared to take care of the odd baggage handler along the way. I've also got another five hundred in the drawer by the side of my bed."

"And you'll need to take my watch," said Tina.

Anna took off her watch and swapped it with Tina's.

Tina studied Anna's watch more closely. "You're never going to be allowed to forget what time it was when that plane flew into the building," she said, as the microwave beeped.

"This may well be inedible," Tina warned her, as she served up a dish of yesterday's chicken chow mein and egg fried rice. Between mouthfuls, the two of them considered the alternatives for getting out of the city and which border would be safest to cross.

By the time they had devoured every last scrap of leftovers along with another pot of coffee, they had gone over all the possible routes out of Manhattan, although Anna still hadn't settled on whether she should head north or south. Tina placed the plates in the sink and said, "Why don't you decide on which direction you think would be quickest, while I try to get myself uptown and in and out of your apartment without Sam becoming suspicious."

Anna hugged her friend again. "Be warned," she said, "it's hell on earth out there."

Tina stood on the top step of her apartment building and waited for a few moments. Something felt wrong. And then she realized what it was. New York had changed over a day.

The streets were no longer full of bustling, haven't-got-time-to-stop-and-chat people, who made up the most energetic mass on earth. It felt more like a Sunday to Tina. But not even Sunday. People stood and stared in the direction of the World Trade Center. The only background music was the noise of perpetual sirens, which continually reminded the indigenous population—if they needed reminding—that what they had been watching on television in their homes, clubs, bars, even shop windows, was taking place just a few blocks away.

Tina walked down the road in search of a taxi, but the familiar yellow cabs had been replaced by the red, white, and blue of fire engines, ambulances, and police cars, all heading in one direction. Little clusters of citizens gathered on street corners to applaud the three different services as they raced by, as if they were young recruits leaving their homeland to fight a foreign foe. You no longer have to travel abroad to do that, thought Tina.

Tina walked on and on, block after block, aware that just like the weekend, commuters had fled to the hills, leaving the locals to man the pumps. But now there was another unfamiliar group roaming around the city in a daze. New York had, over the past century, absorbed citizens from every nation on earth, and now they were adding another race to their number. This most recent group of immigrants looked as if they had arrived from the bowels of the earth, and like any new race could be distinguished by their color—ash gray. They roamed around Manhattan, like marathon runners limping home hours after the more serious competitors had departed from the scene. But there was an even more visual reminder for anyone who looked up that autumn evening. The New York skyline was no longer dominated by its proud, gleaming skyscrapers because they were overshadowed by a dense, gray haze that hung above the city like an unwelcome visitor. Occasionally there were breaks in the ungodly cloud, when Tina noticed for the first time shards of jagged metal sticking out of the ground—all that was left of one of the tallest buildings in the world. The dentist had saved her life.

Tina walked past empty shops and restaurants in a city that never closed. New York would recover but would never be the same again. Terrorists were people who lived in far-off lands: the Middle East, Palestine, Israel, even Spain, Germany, and Northern Ireland. She looked back at the cloud. They had taken up residence in Manhattan and left their calling card.

Tina once again waved unhopefully at the rare sight of a passing taxi. It screeched to a halt.

15

ANNA STROLLED BACK into the kitchen and began washing the dishes. She was keeping herself occupied in the hope that her mind wouldn't continually return to those faces coming up the stairs, faces she feared would remain etched on her memory for the rest of her life. She had discovered a downside to her unusual gift.

She tried to think about Victoria Wentworth instead, and how she might stop Fenston from ruining someone else's life. Would Victoria believe that Anna hadn't known Fenston always planned to steal the Van Gogh and bleed her dry? Why should she, when Anna was a member of the board and had been fooled so easily herself?

Anna left the kitchen in search of a map. She found a couple on a bookshelf in the front room above Tina's desk: a copy of *Streetwise Manhattan* and *The Columbia Gazetteer of North America*, propped up against the recent bestseller on John Adams, second president of the United States. She paused to admire the Rothko poster on the wall opposite the bookshelf—not her period, but she knew he must be one of Tina's favorite artists, because she also had another in her office. No longer, thought Anna, her mind switching back to the present. She returned to the kitchen and laid the map of New York out on the table.

Once she'd decided on a route out of Manhattan, Anna folded up the map and turned her attention to the larger volume. She hoped that it would help her make up her mind which border to cross.

Anna looked up Mexico and Canada in the index, and then began making copious notes as if she was preparing a report for the board to consider; she usually suggested two alternatives, but always ended her reports with a firm recommendation. When she finally closed the cover on the thick, blue book, Anna wasn't in any doubt in which direction she had to go if she hoped to reach England in time.

Tina spent the cab journey to Thornton House considering how she would get into Anna's apartment and leave with her luggage without the doorman becoming suspicious. As the cab drew up outside the building, Tina moved a hand to her jacket pocket. She wasn't wearing a jacket. She turned scarlet. She'd left the apartment without any money. Tina stared at the driver's identity information on the back of the front seat: Abdul Affridi—worry beads dangling from the rearview mirror. He glanced around, but didn't smile. No one was smiling today.

"I've come out without any money," Tina blurted, and then waited for a string of expletives to follow.

"No problem," muttered the driver, who jumped out of his cab to open the door for her. Everything had changed in New York.

Tina thanked him and walked nervously toward the entrance door, her opening line well prepared. The script changed the moment she saw Sam seated behind the counter, head in hands, sobbing.

"What's the matter?" Tina asked. "Did you know someone in the World Trade Center?"

Sam looked up. On the desk in front of him was a photo of Anna running in the marathon. "She hasn't come home," he said. "All my others who worked at the WTC returned hours ago."

Tina put her arms round the old man. Yet another victim. How much she wanted to tell him Anna was alive and well. But not today.

Anna took a break just after eight and began flicking through the TV channels. There was only one story. She found that she couldn't go on watching endless reports without continually being reminded of her own small walk-off part in this two-act drama. She was about to turn off the television when it was announced that President Bush would address the nation. "Good evening. Today, our fellow citizens . . ." Anna listened intently, and nodded when the president said, "The victims were in airplanes, or in their offices; secretaries, businessmen and women . . ." Anna once again thought about Rebecca. "None of us will ever forget this day . . . ," the president concluded, and Anna felt able to agree with him. She switched off the television as the South Tower came crashing down again, like the climax of a disaster movie.

Anna sat back down and stared at the map on the kitchen table. She double-checked—or was it triple-?—her route out of New York. She was writing detailed notes of everything that needed to be done before she left in the morning when the front door burst open and Tina staggered in—a laptop over one shoulder, dragging a bulky case behind her. Anna ran out into the corridor to welcome her back. She looked exhausted.

"Sorry to have taken so long, honey," said Tina, as she dumped the luggage in the hallway and walked down the freshly vacuumed corridor and into the kitchen. "Not many busses going in my direction," she added, "especially when you've left your money behind," she added, as she collapsed into a kitchen chair. "I'm afraid I had to break into your five hundred dollars, otherwise I wouldn't have been back until after midnight."

Anna laughed. "My turn to make you coffee," she suggested.

"I was only stopped once," continued Tina, "by a very friendly policeman who checked through your luggage and accepted that I'd been sent back from the airport after being unable to board a flight. I was even able to produce your ticket."

"Any trouble at the apartment?" asked Anna, as she filled the coffeepot for a third time.

"Only having to comfort Sam, who obviously adores you. He looked as if he'd been crying for hours. I didn't even have to mention David Sullivan, because all Sam wanted to do was talk about you. By the time I got into the elevator, he didn't seem to care where I was going." Tina stared around the kitchen. She hadn't seen it so clean since she'd moved in. "So have you come up with a plan?" she asked, looking down at the map that was spread across the kitchen table.

"Yes," said Anna. "It seems my best bet will be the ferry to New Jersey and then to rent a car, because according to the latest news all the tunnels and bridges are closed. Although it's over four hundred miles to the Canadian border, I can't see why I shouldn't make Toronto airport by tomorrow night, in which case I could be in London the following morning."

"Do you know what time the first ferry sails in the morning?" asked Tina.

"In theory, it's a nonstop service," said Anna, "but in practice, every fifteen minutes after five o'clock. But who knows if they'll be running at all tomorrow, let alone keeping to a schedule."

"Either way," said Tina, "I suggest you have an early night, and try to snatch some sleep. I'll set my alarm for four thirty."

"Four," said Anna. "If the ferry is ready to depart at five, I want to be first in line. I suspect getting out of New York may well prove the most difficult part of the journey."

"Then you'd better have the bedroom," said Tina with a smile, "and I'll sleep on the couch."

"No way," said Anna, as she poured her friend a fresh mug of coffee. "You've done more than enough already."

"Not nearly enough," said Tina.

"If Fenston ever found out what you were up to," said Anna quietly, "he'd fire you on the spot."

"That would be the least of my problems," Tina responded without explanation.

Jack yawned involuntarily. It had been a long day, and he had a feeling that it was going to be an even longer night.

No one on his team had considered going home, and they were all beginning to look, and sound, exhausted. The telephone on his desk rang.

"Just thought I ought to let you know, boss," said Joe, "that Tina Forster, Fenston's secretary, turned up at Thornton House a couple of hours ago. Forty minutes later she came out carrying a suitcase and a laptop, which she took back to her place."

Jack sat bolt upright. "Then Petrescu must be alive," he said.

"Although she obviously doesn't want us to think so," said Joe.

"But why?"

"Perhaps she wants us to believe she's missing, presumed dead?" suggested Joe.

"Not us," said Jack.

"Then who?"

"Fenston, would be my bet."

"Why?"

"I have no idea," said Jack, "but I have every intention of finding out."

"And how do you propose to do that, boss?"

"By putting an OPS team on Tina Forster's apartment until Petrescu leaves the building."

"But we don't even know if she's in there," said Joe.

"She's in there," said Jack, and put the phone down.

9/12

16

DURING THE NIGHT, Anna managed to catch only a few minutes of sleep as she considered her future. She came to the conclusion that she might as well return to Danville and open a gallery for local artists while any potential employers could get in touch with Fenston and be told his side of the story. She was beginning to feel that her only hope of survival was to prove what Fenston was really up to, and she accepted that she couldn't do that without Victoria's full cooperation, which might include destroying all the relevant documentation, even her report.

Anna was surprised how energized she felt when Tina knocked on the door just after four.

Another shower, followed by another shampoo, and she felt almost human.

Over a breakfast of black coffee and bagels, Anna went over her plan with Tina. They decided on some ground rules they should follow while she was away. Anna no longer had a credit card or a cell phone, so she agreed to call Tina only on her home number and always from a public phone booth—never the same one twice. Anna would announce herself as "Vincent," and no other name would be used. The call would never last for more than one minute.

Anna left the apartment at 4:52 A.M., dressed in jeans, a blue T-shirt, a linen jacket, and a baseball cap. She wasn't sure what to expect as she stepped out onto the sidewalk that cool, dark morning. Few people were out on the streets, and those that were had their heads bowed—their downcast faces revealed a city in mourning. No one gave Anna a second glance as she strode purposefully along the sidewalk pulling her suitcase, the laptop bag slung over her shoulder. It didn't matter in which direction she looked; a foggy, gray haze still hung over the city. The dense cloud had dispersed, but like a disease it had spread to other parts of the body. For some reason, Anna had assumed when she woke it would have gone, but, like an unwelcome guest at a party, it would surely be the last to leave.

Anna passed a line of people who were already waiting to give blood in the hope that more survivors would be found. She was a survivor, but she didn't want to be found.

Fenston was seated behind his desk in his new Wall Street office by six o'clock that morning. After all, it was already eleven in London. The first call he made was to Ruth Parish.

"Where's my Van Gogh?" he demanded, without bothering to announce who it was.

"Good morning, Mr. Fenston," said Ruth, but she received no reply in kind. "As I feel sure you know, the aircraft carrying your painting was turned back, following yesterday's tragedy."

"So where's my Van Gogh?" repeated Fenston.

"Safely locked up in one of our secure vaults in the restricted customs area. Of course, we will have to reapply for customs clearance and renew the export license. But there's no need to do that before—"

"Do it today," said Fenston.

"This morning I had planned to move four Vermeers from—"

"Fuck Vermeer. Your first priority is to make sure my painting is packed and ready to be collected."

"But the paperwork might take a few days," said Ruth. "I'm sure you appreciate that there's now a backlog following—"

"And fuck any backlog," said Fenston. "The moment the FAA lift their restrictions, I'm sending Karl Leapman over to pick up the painting."

"But my staff are already working round the clock to clear the extra work caused by—"

"I'll only say this once," said Fenston. "If the painting is ready for loading by the time my plane touches down at Heathrow, I will triple, I repeat triple your fee."

Fenston put the phone down, confident that the only word she'd remember would be *triple.* He was wrong. Ruth was puzzled by the fact that he hadn't mentioned the attacks on the Twin Towers or made any reference to Anna. Had she survived, and if so, why wasn't *she* traveling over to pick up the painting?

Tina had overheard every word of Fenston's conversation with Ruth Parish on the extension in her office—without the chairman being aware. Tina vainly wished that she could contact Anna and quickly pass on the information—an eventuality neither of them had considered. Perhaps Anna would call this evening.

Tina flicked off the phone switch, but left on the screen that was fixed to the corner of her desk. This allowed her to watch everything and, more important, everybody who came in contact with the chairman, something else that Fenston wasn't aware of, but then he hadn't asked. Fenston would never have considered entering her office when the press of a button would summon her, and if Leapman walked into the room—without knocking, as was his habit—she would quickly flick the screen off.

When Leapman took over the short lease on the thirty-second floor, he hadn't shown any interest in the secretary's office. His only concern seemed to be settling the chairman into the largest space available, while he took over an office at the other end of the corridor. Tina had said nothing about her IT extras, aware that in time someone was bound to find out, but perhaps by then she would have gathered all the information she needed to ensure that Fenston would suffer an even worse fate than he had inflicted on her.

When Fenston put the phone down on Ruth Parish, he pressed the button on the side of his desk. Tina grabbed a notepad and pencil and made her way through to the chairman's office.

"The first thing I need you to do," Fenston began, even before Tina had closed the door, "is find out how many staff I still have. Make sure they know where we are relocated, so they can report for work without delay."

"I see that the head of security was among the first to check in this morning," said Tina.

"Yes, he was," Fenston replied, "and he's already confirmed that he gave the order for all staff to evacuate the building within minutes of the first plane crashing into the North Tower."

"And then led by example, I'm told," said Tina tartly.

"Who told you that?" barked Fenston, looking up.

Tina regretted the words immediately, and quickly turned to leave, adding, "I'll have those names on your desk by midday."

She spent the rest of the morning trying to contact the forty-three employees who worked in the North Tower. Tina was able to account for thirty-four of them by twelve o'clock. She placed a provisional list of nine names who were still missing, presumed dead, on Fenston's desk before he went to lunch.

Anna Petrescu was the sixth name on that list.

By the time Tina had placed the list on Fenston's desk, Anna had finally made it to Pier 11, by cab, bus, foot, and then cab again, only to find a long line of people waiting patiently to board the ferry to New Jersey. She took her place at the back of the line, put on a pair of sunglasses, and pulled down the peak of her baseball cap so it nearly covered her eyes. She stood with her arms tightly folded, the collar of her jacket turned up, and her head bowed, so that only the most insensitive individual would have considered embarking on a conversation with her.

The police were checking the IDs of everyone leaving Manhattan. She looked on as a dark-haired, swarthy young man was taken to one side. The poor man looked bemused when three policemen surrounded him. One fired questions, while another searched him.

It was almost an hour before Anna finally reached the front of the line. She took off her baseball cap to reveal her long, fair hair and cream skin.

"Why are you going to New Jersey?" inquired the policeman as he checked her ID.

"A friend of mine was working in the North Tower, and she's still missing." Anna paused. "And I thought I'd spend the day with her parents."

"I'm sorry, ma'am," said the policeman. "I hope they find her."

"Thank you," said Anna, and quickly carried her bags up the gangway and onto the ferry. She felt so guilty about lying that she couldn't look back at the policeman. She leaned on the railing and stared across at the gray cloud that still enveloped the site of the World Trade Center and several blocks either side. She wondered how many days, weeks, or even months it would be before that dense blanket of smoke dispersed. What would they finally do with the desolate site, and how would they honor the dead? She raised her eyes and stared up at the clear blue sky above her. Something was missing. Although they were only a few miles from JFK and La Guardia, there wasn't a plane in the sky, as if they had all, without warning, migrated to another part of the world.

The old engine juddered into action and the ferry began to drift slowly away from the pier on its short journey across the Hudson to New Jersey.

One o'clock struck on the pier tower. Half a day had gone.

"The first flights out of JFK won't be taking off for another couple of days," said Tina.

"Does that include private aircraft?" asked Fenston.

"There are no exceptions," Tina assured him.

"The Saudi royal family are being allowed to fly out tomorrow," interjected Leapman, who was standing by the chairman's side, "but they seem to be the only exception."

"Meanwhile, I'm trying to get you on what the press are describing as the priority list," said Tina, who decided not to mention that the port authorities didn't consider his desire to pick up a Van Gogh from Heathrow quite fell into the category of emergency.

"Do we have any friends at JFK?" asked Fenston.

"Several," said Leapman, "but they've all suddenly acquired a whole lot of rich relations."

"Any other ideas?" asked Fenston, looking up at both of them.

"You might consider driving across the border into Mexico or Canada," suggested Tina, "and taking a commercial flight from there," knowing only too well that he wouldn't consider it.

Fenston shook his head and, turning to Leapman, said, "Try and turn one of our friends into a relation—someone will want something," he added. "They always do."

17

"I'LL TAKE ANY car you've got," said Anna.

"I have nothing available at the moment," said the weary-looking young man behind the Happy Hire Company desk, whose plastic badge displayed the name HANK. "And I don't anticipate anything being returned until tomorrow morning," he added, failing to fulfil the company's motto displayed on the countertop, NO ONE LEAVES HAPPY HIRE WITHOUT A SMILE ON THEIR FACE. Anna couldn't mask her disappointment.

"I don't suppose you'd consider a van?" Hank ventured. "It's not exactly the latest model, but if you're desperate . . ."

"I'll take it," said Anna, well aware of the long line of customers waiting behind her, all no doubt willing her to say no. Hank placed a form in triplicate on the countertop and began filling in the little boxes. Anna pushed across her driver's license, which she had packed along with her passport, enabling him to complete even more boxes. "How long do you require the vehicle?" Hank asked.

"A day, possibly two—I'll be dropping it off at Toronto airport."

Once Hank had completed all the little boxes, he swiveled the form around for her signature.

"That'll be sixty dollars, and I'll need a two-hundred-dollar deposit."

Anna frowned and handed over $260.

"And I'll also need your credit card."

Anna slipped another hundred-dollar bill across the counter. The first time she'd ever attempted to bribe someone.

Hank pocketed the money. "It's the white van in bay thirty-eight," he told her, handing over a key.

When Anna located bay thirty-eight, she could see why the little two-seater white van was the last vehicle on offer. She unlocked the back door and placed her case and laptop inside. She then went to the front and squeezed herself into the plastic-covered driver's seat. She checked the dashboard. The odometer read 98,617, and the speedometer suggested a maximum of 90, which she doubted. It was clearly coming to the end of its rental life, and another four hundred miles might well finish it off. She wondered if the vehicle was even worth $360.

Anna started the engine and tentatively reversed out of the parking lot. She saw a man in her rearview mirror, who quickly stepped out of the way. It was less than a mile before she discovered the vehicle was built for neither speed nor comfort. She glanced down at the route map she'd placed on the passenger seat beside her, then began to look for signs to the Jersey Turnpike and the Del Water Gap. Although she hadn't eaten since breakfast, Anna decided she needed to put a few miles on the clock before she started thinking about food.

"You were right, boss," said Joe, "she's not going to Danville."

"So where *is* she headed?"

"Toronto airport."

"Car or train?" he asked.

"Van," replied Joe.

Jack tried to calculate how long the journey would take and concluded that Petrescu ought to reach Toronto by late the next afternoon.

"I've already fixed a GPS on her rear bumper," Joe added, "so we'll be able to track her night and day."

"And be sure you have an agent waiting for her at the airport."

"He's already been detailed," said Joe, "with instructions to let me know where she intends to fly."

"She'll be flying to London," said Jack.

By three that afternoon, Tina had been able to remove four more names from the missing list. Three of them had been voting in the primary elections for mayor, while the fourth had missed her train.

Fenston studied the list, as Leapman placed a finger on the only name he was interested in. Fenston nodded when his eyes settled on the Ps. He smiled.

"Saved having to do it ourselves," was Leapman's only comment.

"What's the latest from JFK?" Fenston asked.

"They're allowing a few flights out tomorrow," said Leapman, "visiting diplomats, hospital emergencies, and some senior politicians vetted by the State Department. But I've managed to secure us an early slot for Friday morning." He paused. "Someone wanted a new car."

"Which model?" asked Fenston.

"A Ford Mustang," replied Leapman.

"I would have agreed to a Cadillac."

Anna had reached the outskirts of Scranton by three thirty that afternoon but decided to press on for a couple more hours. The weather was clear and crisp and the three-lane highway crowded with cars heading north, almost all of them overtaking her. Anna relaxed a little once tall trees replaced skyscrapers on both sides. Most of the highways had a fifty-five-mile speed limit, which suited her particular mode of transport. But she still had to hold on to the steering wheel firmly to make sure the van didn't drift into another lane. Anna glanced down at the tiny clock on the dashboard. She would try and make Buffalo by seven, and then perhaps take a break.

She checked her rearview mirror, suddenly aware of what it must feel like to be a criminal on the run. You couldn't use a credit card or a cell phone, and the sound of a distant siren doubled your heartbeat. A life spent wary of strangers, as you looked over your shoulder every few minutes. Anna longed to be back in New York, among her friends, doing the job she loved. Her father once said—"Oh, God," said Anna out loud. Did her mother think she was dead? What about Uncle George and the rest of the family in Danville? Could she risk a phone call? Hell, she wasn't very good at thinking like a criminal.

Leapman walked into Tina's office unannounced. She quickly flicked off the screen on the side of her desk.

"Wasn't Anna Petrescu a friend of yours?" Leapman asked without explanation.

"Yes, she is," said Tina, looking up from her desk.

"Is?" said Leapman.

"Was," said Tina, quickly correcting herself.

"So you haven't heard from her?"

"If I had, I wouldn't have left her name on the missing list, would I?"

"Wouldn't you?" said Leapman.

"No, I wouldn't," said Tina, looking directly at him. "So perhaps you'll let me know if she gets in touch with you," she added.

Leapman frowned and left the room.

Anna pulled off the road and swung into the forecourt of an uninviting-looking diner. She was pleased to see there were only two other vehicles in the parking lot, and when she entered the building just three customers were seated at the counter. Anna took a seat in a booth with her back to the counter, pulled down her baseball cap, and studied the one-sided, greasy plastic menu. She ordered a tomato soup and the chef's special, grilled chicken.

Ten dollars and thirty minutes later, she was back on the road. Although she'd drunk nothing but coffee since breakfast, it wasn't long before she began to feel sleepy. She'd covered 310 miles in just over eight hours before stopping to eat, and now she was having to make an effort to keep her eyes open.

FEEL TIRED? TAKE A BREAK, advised a bold sign on the side of the highway, which only caused her to yawn again. Ahead of her, she spotted a twelve-wheeler truck turning off the road into a rest stop. Anna glanced at the clock on the dashboard—just after eleven. She'd been on the road for nearly nine hours. She decided to catch a couple of hours' rest before tackling the rest of the journey. After all, she could always sleep on the plane.

Anna followed the articulated truck into the rest stop and then drove across to the farthest corner. She parked behind a large stationary vehicle. She jumped out of the van and made sure all the doors were locked before climbing into the back, relieved that there was no other vehicle nearby. Anna tried to make herself comfortable, using her laptop bag as a pillow. She couldn't have been more uncomfortable but fell asleep within minutes.

"Petrescu still worries me," said Leapman.

"Why should a dead woman worry you?" asked Fenston.

"Because I'm not convinced she's dead."

"How could she have survived that?" asked Fenston, looking out of the window at the black shroud that refused to lift its veil from the face of the World Trade Center.

"We did."

"But we left the building early," said Fenston.

"Perhaps *she* did. After all, you ordered her off the premises within ten minutes."

"Barry thinks otherwise."

"Barry's alive," Leapman reminded him.

"Even if Petrescu did escape, she still can't do anything," said Fenston.

"She could get to London before I do," said Leapman.

"But the painting is safely under lock and key at Heathrow."

"But all the documentation to prove you own it was in your safe in the North Tower, and if Petrescu is able to convince—"

"Convince who? Victoria Wentworth is dead, and try not to forget that Petrescu is also missing, presumed dead."

"But that might prove to be just as convenient for her as it is for us."

"Then we'll have to make it less convenient."

9/13

18

A LOUD, REPEATED banging jolted Anna out of a deep sleep. She rubbed her eyes and looked through the windshield. A man with a pot belly hanging out of his jeans was thumping on the hood of the van with a clenched fist. In his other hand he was carrying a can of beer that was frothing at the mouth. Anna was about to scream at him when she realized that someone else was at the same time trying to wrench open the back door. An ice-cold shower couldn't have woken her any quicker.

Anna scrambled into the driver's seat and quickly turned the key in the ignition. She looked in her side-view mirror and was horrified to see that another forty-ton truck was now stationed directly behind her, leaving her with almost no room to maneuver. She pressed the palm of her hand on the horn, which only encouraged the man holding the beer can to clamber up onto the hood and advance toward her. Anna saw his face clearly for the first time, as he leered at her through the windshield. She felt cold and sick. He leaned forward, opened his toothless mouth, and began licking the glass, while his friend continued trying to force open the back door. The engine finally spluttered into life.

Anna yanked the steering wheel round to give her the tightest possible turns, but the space between the two trucks only allowed her to advance a few feet before she had to reverse. Power steering was not one of the van's extras. When she shot back, Anna heard a yell from behind as the second man threw himself to one side. Anna crashed into first gear and pressed her foot back down on the accelerator. As the van leaped forward, the pot-bellied man slid off the hood and onto the ground with a thud. Anna thrust the gearstick back into reverse, praying this time there would be enough room to escape. But before she had pulled the steering wheel fully around, she glanced to the side to see that the second man was now staring at her through the passenger window. He clamped both of his massive hands on the roof and began rocking the van slowly backward and forward. She slammed her foot on the pedal and the van dragged him slowly forward, but she still failed to make it through the gap, if only by inches. Anna rammed the gear into reverse for a third time and was horrified to see the first man's hands reappear on the front of the hood, as he pulled himself back up onto his feet. He lurched forward, stuck his nose flat against the windshield, and gave her a thumbs-down sign. He then shouted to his buddy, "I get to go first this week." His buddy stopped rocking the car and burst out laughing.

Anna broke out into a cold sweat when her eyes settled on the pot-bellied man, walking unsteadily toward his truck. A quick glance in her side-view mirror and she could see his mate climbing up into his cab.

It didn't take Anna more than a split second to work out exactly what they had in mind. She was about to become the meat in their next sandwich. Anna hit the accelerator so hard that she careered into the truck behind her just as he turned on his full headlights. She crashed the gears back into first as the engine of the front truck roared into life, belching a cloud of black smoke all over the windshield. Anna yanked the steering wheel over with a jerk and once again thrust her foot hard down on the accelerator. The van jumped forward, just as the truck in front of her began to reverse. She collided with the corner of the front truck's massive mudguard, which tore off her bumper followed by her passenger-side mudguard. She then felt herself being shunted from behind as the rear truck plowed into her, ripping off her rear bumper. The little van came hurtling out of the gap with inches to spare and spun around a full 360 degrees before it came to a halt. Anna looked across to see the two trucks, unable to react in time, crash into each other.

She accelerated across the parking lot, raced past several stationary trucks and out onto the highway. She continued to look in her rearview mirror as the two trucks disentangled themselves. A loud screeching of

brakes and a cacophony of horns followed as she narrowly missed collid-
ing with a stream of vehicles coming down the highway, several of which
had to career across two lanes to avoid her. The first driver left his hand
on the horn for some time, leaving Anna in no doubt of his feelings. Anna
waved an apologetic hand to the overtaking vehicle as it shot past her,
while she continued to glance into her side-view mirror, dreading seeing
either of the trucks pursuing her. She jammed her foot down on the accelerator until it touched the floor, determined to find out the maximum
speed the van could manage: sixty-eight miles per hour was the answer.

Anna checked her side-view mirror once again. A vast eighteen-
wheeler was coming up behind her on the inside lane. She gripped the
steering wheel firmly and jammed her foot back down on the accelerator,
but the van had no more to offer. The truck was now eating up the
ground, yard by yard, and in moments she knew it would convert itself
into a bulldozer. Anna thrust the palm of her left hand down on the horn,
and it let out a bleat that wouldn't have disturbed a flock of starlings from
their nests. A large, green sign appeared on the side of the road, indicating the turnoff for the I-90, one mile.

Anna moved into the middle lane and the massive truck followed her
like a magnet hoping to sweep up any loose filings. The truck driver was
now so close that Anna could see him in her side-view mirror. He gave
her another toothless grin and then honked his horn. It let forth a sound
that would have drowned out the last bars of a Wagner opera.

Half a mile to the exit, the new sign promised. She moved across to the
fast lane, causing a line of advancing cars to throw on their brakes and
slow down. Several pressed their horns this time. She ignored them and
slowed down to fifty when they became an orchestra.

The eighteen-wheeler drew up beside her. She slowed down, he
slowed down; quarter of a mile to the turnoff, the next sign declared. She
saw the exit in the distance, grateful for the first shafts of the morning sun
appearing through the clouds, as none of her lights were now working.

Anna knew that she would have only one chance, and her timing had to
be perfect. She gripped the steering wheel firmly as she reached the exit
for the I-90 and drove on past the green triangle of grass that divided the
two highways. She suddenly jammed her foot back down on the accelerator, and although the van didn't leap forward, it spurted and managed to
gain a few yards. Was it enough? The truck driver responded immediately

and also began to accelerate. He was only a car's length away when Anna suddenly swung the steering wheel to the right and carried on across the middle and inside lanes before mounting the grass verge. The van bounced across the uneven triangle of grass and onto the far exit lane. A car traveling down the inside lane had to swerve onto the hard shoulder to avoid hitting her, while another shot past on the outside. As Anna steadied the van on the inside lane, she looked across to see the eighteen-wheeler heading on down the highway and out of sight.

She slowed down to fifty, although her heart was still beating at three times that speed. She tried to relax. As with all athletes, it is speed of recovery that matters. As she swung onto the I-90, she glanced in her side-view mirror. Her heartbeat immediately returned to 150 when she saw a second eighteen-wheeler bearing down on her.

Pot-belly's buddy hadn't made the same mistake.

19

As the stranger entered the lobby, Sam looked up from behind his desk. When you're a doorman, you have to make instant decisions about people. Do they fall in the category of "Good morning, sir" or "Can I help you?" or simply "Hi"? Sam studied the tall, middle-aged man who had just walked in. He was wearing a smart but well-worn suit, the cloth a little shiny at the elbows, and his shirt cuffs were slightly frayed. He wore a tie that Sam reckoned had been tied a thousand times.

"Good morning," Sam settled on.

"Good morning," replied the man. "I'm from the Department of Immigration."

That only made Sam nervous. Although he'd been born in Harlem, he'd heard stories of people being deported by mistake.

"How can I help you, sir?" he asked.

"I'm checking up on those people who are still missing, presumed dead, following the terrorist attack on Tuesday."

"Anyone in particular?" asked Sam cautiously.

"Yes," said the man. He placed his briefcase on the counter, opened it, and extracted a list of names. He ran a finger down the list and came to a halt at the Ps. "Anna Petrescu," he said. "This is the last known address we have for her."

"I haven't seen Anna since she left for work on Tuesday morning," said

Sam, "though several people have asked about her, and one of her friends came around that night and took away some of her personal things."

"What did she take?"

"I don't know," said Sam. "I just recognized the suitcase."

"Do you know the girl's name?"

"Why do you want to know?"

"It might help if we could get in touch with her. Anna's mother is quite anxious."

"No, I don't know her name," admitted Sam.

"Would you recognize her if I showed you a photograph?"

"Might," said Sam.

Once again, the man opened his briefcase. This time he extracted a photo and passed it across to Sam. He studied it for a moment.

"Yes, that's her. Pretty girl," he paused, "but not as pretty as Anna. She was beautiful."

As she swung onto the I-90, Anna noticed that the speed limit was seventy. She would have been happy to break it, but however hard she pressed down on the accelerator she could still only manage sixty-eight miles per hour.

Although the second truck was still some way behind, it was closing on her rapidly, and this time she didn't have an exit strategy. She prayed for a sign. The truck must have been only fifty yards behind her, and closing by the second, when she heard the siren.

She was delighted at the thought of being pulled over, and didn't care whether she would be believed when she explained why she had careered across two lanes of the highway and onto the exit ramp, not to mention why her van was missing both bumpers and a mudguard and that none of its lights were working. She began to slow down as the patrol car sped past the truck and slipped in behind her. The officer looked back and indicated that the truck driver should pull over. Anna watched in her passenger-side mirror as both vehicles came to a halt on the hard shoulder.

It was over an hour before she was calm enough to stop looking in her side-view mirror every few minutes.

After another hour she even began to feel hungry and decided to pull into a roadside café for breakfast. She parked the van, strolled in, and took a seat at the far end of the counter. She perused the menu before ordering "the big one"—eggs, bacon, sausage, hash browns, pancakes, and coffee. Not her usual fare, but then not much had been usual about the past forty-eight hours.

Between mouthfuls, Anna checked her route map. The two drunken men who'd pursued her had helped her keep to her schedule. Anna calculated that she had already covered around 380 miles, but there were still at least another fifty to go to reach the Canadian border. She studied the map more closely. Next stop, Niagara Falls, which she estimated would take her another hour.

The television behind the counter was reporting the early morning news. The hope of finding any more survivors was fading. New York had begun mourning its dead and setting about the long and arduous task of cleaning up. A memorial service, attended by the president, was to be held in Washington, D.C., as part of a national day of remembrance. The president then intended to fly on to New York and visit Ground Zero. Mayor Giuliani was next to appear on the screen. He was wearing a T-shirt proudly emblazoned with the letters NYPD and a cap with NYFD printed across the peak. He praised the spirit of New Yorkers and pledged his determination to put the city back on its feet as quickly as possible.

The news camera cut to JFK, where an airport spokesman confirmed that the first commercial flights would resume their normal schedule the following morning. That one sentence determined Anna's timetable. She knew she had to touch down in London before Leapman took off from New York if she was to have any chance of convincing Victoria . . . Anna glanced out of the window. Two trucks were pulling into the parking lot. She froze, unable to watch as the drivers climbed out of their cabs. She was checking the fire exit as they entered the café. They both took seats at the counter, smiled at the waitress, and didn't give Anna a second look. She had never previously understood why people suffered from paranoia.

Anna checked her watch: 7:55 A.M. She drained her coffee, left six dollars on the table, and walked across to the phone booth on the far side of the diner. She dialed a 212 number.

"Good morning, sir, my name is Agent Roberts."

"Morning, Agent Roberts," replied Jack, leaning back in his chair, "have anything to report?"

"I'm standing in a vehicle rest stop somewhere between New York and the Canadian border."

"And what are you doing there, Agent Roberts?"

"I'm holding a bumper."

"Let me guess," said Jack. "The bumper was at one time attached to a white van driven by the suspect."

"Yes, sir."

"And where is the van now?" asked Jack, trying not to sound exasperated.

"I have no idea, sir. When the suspect drove into the rest stop to take a break, I must admit, sir, I also fell asleep. When I woke, the suspect's van had left, leaving the bumper with the GPS still attached."

"Then she's either very clever," said Jack, "or she's been involved in an accident."

"I agree." He paused, and then added, "What do you think I should do next, sir?"

"Join the CIA," said Jack.

"Hi, it's Vincent, any news?"

"Yep, just as you thought, Ruth Parish has the painting locked up in the secure customs area at Heathrow."

"Then I'll have to unlock it," said Anna.

"That might not prove quite that easy," said Tina, "because Leapman flies out of JFK first thing tomorrow morning to pick up the painting, so you've only got another twenty-four hours before he joins you." She hesitated. "And you have another problem."

"Another problem?" said Anna.

"Leapman isn't convinced you're dead."

"What makes him think that?"

"He keeps asking about you, so be especially careful. Never forget Fenston's reaction when the North Tower collapsed. He may have lost half a dozen staff, but his only interest was the Monet in his office. Heaven knows what he'd do if he lost the Van Gogh as well. Dead artists are more important to him than living people."

Anna could feel the beads of sweat breaking out on her forehead as the line went dead. She checked her watch: thirty-two seconds.

"Our 'Friend' at JFK has confirmed we've been allocated a slot at seven twenty tomorrow morning," Leapman said. "But I haven't informed Tina."

"Why not?" asked Fenston.

"Because the doorman at Petrescu's building told me that someone looking like Tina was seen leaving there on Tuesday evening."

"Tuesday evening?" repeated Fenston. "But that would mean—"

"And she was carrying a suitcase."

Fenston frowned but said nothing.

"Do you want me to do anything about it?"

"What do you have in mind?" asked Fenston.

"Bug the phone in her apartment for a start. Then if Petrescu is in contact with her, we'll know exactly where she is and what she's up to."

Fenston didn't reply, which Leapman always took to mean yes.

CANADIAN BORDER 4 MILES declared a sign on the side of the road. Anna smiled—a smile that was quickly removed when she swung round the next corner and came to a halt behind a long line of vehicles that stretched as far as the eye could see.

She stepped out onto the road and began to stretch her tired limbs. Anna grimaced as she looked across at what was left of her battered transport. How would she explain that to the Happy Hire Company? She certainly didn't need to part with any more cash—the first $500 of any damage, if she remembered correctly. While continuing to stretch, she couldn't help noticing that the other side of the road was empty; no one seemed to be in a rush to enter the United States.

Anna progressed only another hundred yards during the next twenty minutes, ending up opposite a gas station. She made an instant decision—breaking another habit of a lifetime. She swung the van across the road and onto the forecourt, drove past the pumps, and parked the van next to a tree—just behind a large sign declaring SUPERIOR CAR WASH. Anna retrieved her two bags from the back of the van and started out on the four-mile trek to the border.

20

"I'M SO SORRY, my dear," said Arnold Simpson, as he looked across his desk at Arabella Wentworth. "Dreadful business," he added, dropping another sugar lump into his tea. Arabella didn't comment as Simpson leaned forward and placed his hands on the partners' desk, as if about to offer up a prayer. He smiled benignly at his client and was about to offer an opinion when Arabella opened the file on her lap and said, "As our family's solicitor, perhaps you can explain how my father and Victoria managed to run up such massive debts and in so short a period of time?"

Simpson leaned back and peered over his half-moon spectacles. "Your dear father and I," he began, "had been close friends for over forty years. We were, as I feel sure you are aware, at Eton together." Simpson paused to touch his dark blue tie with the light blue stripe, which looked as if he'd worn it every day since he'd left school.

"My father always described it as 'at the same time,' rather than 'together,'" retorted Arabella. "So perhaps you could now answer my question."

"I was just coming to that," said Simpson, momentarily lost for words as he searched around the scattered files that littered his desk. "Ah, yes," he declared eventually, picking up one marked LLOYD'S OF LONDON. He opened the cover and adjusted his spectacles. "When your father became a name at Lloyd's in nineteen seventy-one, he signed up for several syndicates, putting up the estate as collateral. For many years, the insurance industry showed handsome returns and your father received a large annual income." Simpson ran his finger down a long list of figures.

"But did you point out to him at the time," asked Arabella, "the meaning of unlimited liability?"

"I confess," said Simpson, ignoring the question, "that like so many others, I did not anticipate such an unprecedented run of bad years."

"It was no different from being a gambler hoping to make a profit from a spin at the roulette wheel," said Arabella. "So why didn't you advise him to cut his losses and leave the table?"

"Your father was an obstinate man," said Simpson, "and, having ridden out some bad years, remained convinced that the good times would return."

"But that didn't prove to be the case," said Arabella, turning to another of the numerous papers in her one file.

"Sadly not," confirmed Simpson, who seemed to have sunk lower in his chair so that he nearly disappeared behind the partners' desk.

"And what happened to the large portfolio of stocks and shares that the family had accumulated over the years?"

"They were among the first assets your father had to liquidate to keep his current account in surplus. In fact," continued the solicitor, turning over another page, "at the time of your father's death, I fear he had run up an overdraft of something over ten million pounds."

"But not with Coutts," Arabella said, "as it appears some three years ago he transferred his account to a small bank in New York called Fenston Finance."

"That is correct, dear lady," said Simpson. "Indeed, it has always been a bit of a mystery to me how that particular establishment came across—"

"It's no mystery to me," retorted Arabella, as she extracted a letter from her file. "It's clear that they singled him out as an obvious target."

"But I still can't work out how they knew—"

"They only had to read the financial pages of any broadsheet. They were reporting the problems faced by Lloyd's on a daily basis, and my father's name appeared regularly, along with several others, as being placed with unfortunate, if not crooked, syndicates."

"That is pure speculation on your part," said Simpson, his voice rising.

"Just because you didn't consider it at the time," replied Arabella, "doesn't mean it's speculation. In fact, I'm only surprised that you allowed your *close friend* to leave Coutts, who had served the family for over two hundred years, to join such a bunch of shysters."

Simpson turned scarlet. "Perhaps you are falling into the politician's habit of relying on hindsight, madam."

"No, sir," replied Arabella. "My late husband was also offered the opportunity to join Lloyd's. The broker assured him that the farm would be quite enough to cover the necessary deposit, whereupon Angus showed him the door."

Simpson was speechless.

"And how, may I ask, with you as her principal advisor, did Victoria manage to double that debt in less than a year?"

"I am not to blame for that," snapped Simpson. "You can direct your anger at the tax man, who always demands his pound of flesh," he added as he searched for a file marked DEATH DUTIES. "Ah, yes, here it is. The Exchequer is entitled to 40 percent of any assets on death, unless the assets are directly passed on to a spouse, as I feel sure your late husband would have explained to you. However, I managed, with some considerable skill, even if I do say so myself, to reach a settlement of eleven million pounds with the inspectors, which Lady Victoria seemed well satisfied with at the time."

"My sister was a naïve spinster who never left home without her father and didn't have her own bank account until she was thirty," said Arabella, "but still you allowed her to sign a further contract with Fenston Finance, which was bound to land her in even more debt."

"It was that or putting the estate on the market."

"No, it wasn't," replied Arabella. "It only took me one phone call to Lord Hindlip, the chairman of Christie's, to be told that he would expect the family's Van Gogh to make in excess of thirty million pounds were it to come up for auction."

"But your father would never have agreed to sell the Van Gogh."

"My father wasn't alive when you approved the second loan," countered Arabella. "It was a decision *you* should have advised her on."

"I had no choice, dear lady, under the terms of the original contract."

"Which you witnessed, but obviously didn't read. Because not only did my sister agree to go on paying 16 percent compound interest on the loan, but you even allowed her to hand over the Van Gogh as collateral."

"But you can still demand that they sell the painting, and then the problem will be solved."

"Wrong again, Mr. Simpson," said Arabella. "If you had read beyond page one of the original contract, you would have discovered that should there be a dispute, any decision will revert to a New York court's jurisdiction, and I certainly don't have the wherewithal to take on Bryce Fenston in his own backyard."

"You don't have the authority to do so, either," retorted Simpson, "because I—"

"I am next of kin," said Arabella firmly.

"But there is no will to indicate to whom Victoria intended to leave the estate," shouted Simpson.

"Another duty you managed to execute with your usual prescience and skill."

"Your sister and I were at the time in the process of discussing—"

"It's a bit late for that," said Arabella. "I am facing a battle here and now with an unscrupulous man, who seems to have the law on his side thanks to you."

"I feel confident," said Simpson, once again placing his hands on the desk in a prayerlike position as if ready to give the final blessing, "that I can wrap this whole problem up in—"

"I'll tell you exactly what you can wrap up," said Arabella, rising from her place, "all those files concerning the Wentworth estate, and send them to Wentworth Hall." She stared down at the solicitor. "And at the same time, enclose your final account"—she checked her watch—"for one hour of your invaluable advice."

21

ANNA WALKED DOWN the middle of the road, pulling her suitcase behind her, with the laptop hanging over her left shoulder. With each stride
she took, Anna became more and more aware of passengers sitting in
their stationary cars, staring at the strange lone figure as she passed them.

The first mile took fifteen minutes, and one of the families who had
settled down for a picnic on the grass verge by the side of the road offered her a glass of wine. The second mile took eighteen minutes, but she
still couldn't see the border post. It was another twenty minutes before
she passed a 1 MILE TO THE BORDER sign, when she tried to speed up.

The last mile reminded her which muscles ached after a long, tiring
run, and then she saw the finish line. An injection of adrenaline caused
her to step up a gear.

When Anna was about a hundred yards from the barrier, the staring
looks made her feel like a line jumper. She averted her eyes and walked a
little more slowly. When she came to a halt on the white line, where each
car is asked to turn off its engine and wait, she stood to one side.

There were two customs officials on duty that day, having to deal with
an unusually long line for a Thursday morning. They were sitting in their
little boxes, checking everyone's documents much more assiduously than
usual. Anna tried to make eye contact with the younger of the two officers in the hope that he would take pity on her, but she didn't need a mir-

ror to know that after what she'd been through during the past twenty-four hours, she couldn't have looked a lot better than when she staggered out of the North Tower.

Eventually, the younger of the two guards beckoned her over. He checked her travel documents and stared at her quizzically. Just how far had she trudged with those bags? He checked her passport carefully. Everything seemed to be in order.

"What is your reason for visiting Canada?" he asked.

"I'm attending an art seminar at McGill University. It's part of my Ph.D. thesis on the pre-Raphaelite movement," she said, staring directly at him.

"Which artists in particular?" asked the guard casually.

A smart-ass or a fan? Anna decided to play along. "Rossetti, Holman Hunt, and Morris, among others."

"What about the other Hunt?"

"Alfred? Not a true pre-Raphaelite, but—"

"But just as good an artist."

"I agree," said Anna.

"Who's giving the seminar?"

"Er, Vern Swanson," said Anna, hoping the guard would not have heard of the most eminent expert in the field.

"Good, then I'll get a chance to meet him."

"What do you mean?"

"Well, if he's still the professor of art history at Yale he'll be coming from New Haven, won't he, and as there are no flights in and out of the U.S., this is the only way he can cross the border."

Anna couldn't think of a suitable response and was grateful to be rescued by the woman behind her, who began commenting to her husband in a loud voice about how long she'd been waiting in line.

"I was at McGill," said the young officer with a smile, as he handed Anna back her passport. Anna wondered if the color of her cheeks betrayed her embarrassment. "We're all sorry about what happened in New York," he added.

"Thank you," said Anna, and walked across the border. *Welcome to Canada.*

"Who is it?" demanded an anonymous voice.

"You've got an electrical fault on the tenth floor," said a man standing outside the front door, dressed in green overalls, wearing a Yankee baseball cap, and carrying a toolbox. He closed his eyes and smiled into the security camera. When he heard the buzzer, the man pushed open the door and slipped in without any further questions.

He walked past the elevator and began to climb the stairs. That way there was less chance of anyone remembering him. He stopped when he reached the tenth floor, glancing quickly up and down the corridor. No one in sight; 3:30 P.M. was always a quiet time. Not that he could tell you why, it was simply based on experience. When he reached her door, he pressed the buzzer. No reply. But then he had been assured that she would still be at work for at least another couple of hours. The man placed his bag on the floor and examined the two locks on the door. Hardly Fort Knox. With the precision of a surgeon about to perform an operation, he opened his bag and selected several delicate instruments.

Two minutes and forty seconds later, he was inside the apartment. He quickly located all three telephones. The first was in the front room on a desk, below a Warhol print of Marilyn Monroe. The second was by her bed, next to a photograph. The intruder glanced at the woman in the center of the picture. She was standing between two men who looked so alike they had to be her father and brother.

The third phone was in the kitchen. He looked at the fridge door and grinned; they were both fans of the 49ers.

Six minutes and nine seconds later he was back in the corridor, down the stairs, and out of the front door.

Job completed in less than ten minutes. Fee $1,000. Not unlike a surgeon.

Anna was among the last to step onto the Greyhound bus that was due to leave Niagara Falls at three o'clock.

Two hours later, the bus came to a halt on the western shore of Lake Ontario. Anna was first down the steps, and without stopping to admire the Mies van der Rohe buildings that dominate the Toronto skyline, she hailed the first available cab.

"The airport, please, and as fast as possible."

"Which terminal?" asked the driver.

Anna hesitated. "Europe."

"Terminal three," he said, as he moved off, adding, "Where you from?"

"Boston," Anna replied. She didn't want to talk about New York.

"Terrible, what happened in New York," he said. "One of those moments in history when everyone remembers exactly where they were. I was in the cab, heard it on the radio. How about you?"

"I was in the North Tower," said Anna.

He knew a smart-ass when he saw one.

It took just over twenty-five minutes to drive the seventeen miles from Bay Street to Lester B. Pearson International Airport, and during that time the driver never uttered another word. When he finally pulled up outside the entrance to terminal three, Anna paid the fare and walked quickly into the airport. She stared up at the departure board as the digital clock flicked over to twenty-eight minutes past five.

The last flight to Heathrow had just closed its gates. Anna cursed. Her eyes scanned the list of cities for any remaining flights that evening: Tel Aviv, Bangkok, Hong Kong, Sydney, Amsterdam. *Amsterdam.* How appropriate, she thought. Flight KL692 departs 18:00 hours, gate C31, now boarding.

Anna ran to the KLM desk and asked the man behind the counter, even before he'd looked up, "Can I still get on your flight to Amsterdam?"

He stopped counting the tickets. "Yes, but you'll have to hurry as they're just about to close the gate."

"Do you have a window seat available?"

"Window, aisle, center, anything you like."

"Why's that?"

"Not many people seem to want to fly today, and it's not just because it's the thirteenth."

"JFK has reconfirmed our slot at seven twenty tomorrow morning," said Leapman.

"Good," said Fenston. "Phone me the moment the plane takes off. What time do you touch down at Heathrow?"

"Around seven," replied Leapman. "Art Locations will be waiting on the runway to load the painting on board. Three times the usual fee seems to have concentrated their minds."

"And when do you expect to be back?"

"In time for breakfast the following morning."

"Any news on Petrescu?"

"No," Leapman said. "Tina's only had one call so far, a man."

"Nothing from—"

Tina entered the room.

"She's on her way to Amsterdam," said Joe.

"Amsterdam?" repeated Jack, tapping his fingers on the desk.

"Yes, she missed the last flight to Heathrow."

"Then she'll be on the first flight into London tomorrow morning."

"We already have an agent at Heathrow," said Joe. "Do you want agents anywhere else?"

"Yes, Gatwick and Stansted," said Jack.

"If you're right, she'll be in London only hours before Karl Leapman."

"What do you mean?" asked Jack.

"Fenston's private jet has a slot booked out of JFK at seven twenty tomorrow morning, and the only passenger is Leapman."

"Then they probably plan to meet up," said Jack. "Call Agent Crasanti at our London embassy and ask him to put extra agents at all three airports. I want to know exactly what those two are up to."

"We won't be on our own territory," Joe reminded him. "If the British were to find out, not to mention the CIA—"

"At all three airports," Jack repeated, before putting the phone down.

Moments after Anna stepped onto the plane, the door was locked into place. She was guided to her seat and asked to fasten her seat belt, as they were expecting to take off almost immediately. Anna was pleased to find the other seats in her row were unoccupied, and as soon as the seat-belt sign had been turned off, she pulled up the armrests in her row and lay down, covering herself with two blankets before resting her head on a real pillow. She had dozed off even before the plane had reached its cruising height.

Someone was gently touching her shoulder. Anna cursed under her breath. She'd forgotten to mention that she didn't want a meal. Anna looked up at the stewardess and blinked sleepily. "No thank you," she said firmly, and closed her eyes again.

"I'm sorry, but I have to ask you to sit up and fasten your seat belt," said the stewardess politely. "We're expecting to land in about twenty minutes. If you would like to alter your watch, the local time in Amsterdam is six fifty-five A.M."

9/14

22

LEAPMAN WAS AWAKE long before the limousine was due to pick him up. This was not a day for oversleeping.

He climbed out of bed and headed straight for the bathroom. However closely he shaved, Leapman knew he would still have stubble on his chin long before he went to bed. He could grow a beard over a long weekend. Once he'd showered and shaved, he didn't bother with making himself breakfast. He'd be served coffee and croissants later by the company stewardess on the bank's private jet. Who in this run-down apartment building in such an unfashionable neighbourhood would believe that in a couple of hours Leapman would be the only passenger on a Gulfstream V on its way to London.

He walked across to his half-empty closet and selected his most recently acquired suit, his favorite shirt, and a tie that he would be wearing for the first time. He didn't need the pilot to look smarter than he was.

Leapman stood by the window, waiting for the limousine to appear, aware that his little apartment was not much of an improvement on the prison cell where he'd spent four years. He looked down on Forty-third Street as the incongruous limousine drew up outside the front door.

Leapman climbed into the back of the car, not speaking to the driver as the door was opened for him. Like Fenston, he pushed the button in the armrest and watched as the smoke-gray window slid up, cutting him off from the driver. For the next twenty-four hours, he would live in a different world.

Forty-five minutes later the limousine turned off the Van Wyck Expressway and took the exit to JFK. The driver swept through an entrance that few passengers ever discover and drew up outside a small terminal building that served only those privileged enough to fly in their own aircraft. Leapman stepped out of the car and was escorted to a private lounge, where the captain of the company's Gulfstream V jet was waiting for him.

"Any hope of taking off earlier than planned?" Leapman asked, as he sank into a comfortable leather armchair.

"No, sir," the captain replied, "planes are taking off every forty-five seconds, and our slot is confirmed for seven twenty."

Leapman grunted and turned his attention to the morning papers. *The New York Times* was leading on the news that President Bush was offering a fifty-million-dollar reward for the capture of Osama bin Laden, which Leapman considered to be no more than the usual Texan approach to law and order over the past hundred years. *The Wall Street Journal* listed Fenston Finance off another twelve cents, a fate suffered by several companies whose headquarters had been based in the World Trade Center. Once he got his hands on the Van Gogh, the company could ride out a period of weak share prices while he concentrated on consolidating the bottom line. Leapman's thoughts were interrupted by a member of the cabin crew.

"You can board now, sir. We'll be taking off in around fifteen minutes."

Another car drove Leapman to the steps of the aircraft, and the plane began to taxi even before he'd finished his orange juice, but he didn't relax until the jet reached its cruising altitude of thirty thousand feet and the FASTEN SEAT BELT sign had been turned off. He leaned forward, picked up the phone, and dialed Fenston's private line.

"I'm on my way," he said, "and I can't see any reason why I shouldn't be back by this time tomorrow—" he paused "—with a Dutchman sitting in the seat next to me."

"Call me the moment you land," was the chairman's response.

Tina flicked off the extension to the chairman's phone.

Leapman had been dropping into her office more and more recently—

always without knocking. He made no secret of the fact that he believed Anna was still alive and in touch with her.

The chairman's jet had taken off from JFK on time that morning, and Tina had listened in on his conversation with Leapman. She realized that Anna only had a few hours' start on him, and that was assuming she was even in London.

Tina thought about Leapman returning to New York the following day, that sickly grin plastered on his face as he handed over the Van Gogh to the chairman. Tina continued to download the latest contracts, having earlier e-mailed them to her private address—something she only did when Leapman was out of the office and Fenston was fully occupied.

The first available flight to London Gatwick that morning was due out of Schiphol at ten o'clock. Anna purchased a ticket from British Airways, who warned her that the flight was running twenty minutes late as the incoming plane had not yet landed. She took advantage of the delay to have a shower and change her clothes. Schiphol was accustomed to overnight travelers. Anna selected the most conservative outfit from her small wardrobe for her meeting with Victoria.

As she sat in Caffè Nero sipping coffee, Anna turned the pages of the *Herald Tribune*: 50-MILLION-DOLLAR-REWARD, read a headline on the second page—less of a bounty than the Van Gogh would fetch at any auction house. Anna didn't waste any time reading the article as she needed to concentrate on her priorities once she came face-to-face with Victoria.

First she had to find out where the Van Gogh was. If Ruth Parish had the picture in storage, then she would advise Victoria to call Ruth and insist that it be returned to Wentworth Hall without delay, and add that she'd be quite happy to advise Ruth that Fenston Finance couldn't hold onto the painting against Victoria's wishes, especially if the only contract in existence were to disappear. She had a feeling Victoria would not agree to that, but if she did, Anna would get in touch with Mr. Nakamura in Tokyo and try to find out if—"British Airways flight eight-one-one-two to London Gatwick is now ready for boarding at Gate D-fourteen," announced a voice over the public-address system.

As they crossed the English Channel, Anna went over her plan again and again, trying to find some fault with her logic, but she could think of only two people who would consider it anything other than common sense. The plane touched down at Gatwick thirty-five minutes late.

Anna checked her watch as she stepped onto English soil, aware that it would only be another nine hours before Leapman landed at Heathrow. Once she was through passport control and had retrieved her baggage, Anna went in search of a rental car. She avoided the Happy Hire Company desk and stood in line at the Avis counter.

Anna didn't see the smartly dressed young man who was standing in the duty-free shop whispering into a cell phone, "She's landed. I'm on her tail."

Leapman settled back in the wide leather chair, far more comfortable than anything in his apartment on Forty-third Street. The stewardess served him a black coffee in a gold-rimmed china cup on a silver tray. He leaned back and thought about the task ahead of him. He knew he was nothing more than a bagman, even if the bag today contained one of the most valuable paintings on earth. He despised Fenston, who never treated him as an equal. If Fenston just once acknowledged his contribution to the company's success and responded to his ideas as if he was a respected colleague rather than a paid lackey—not that he was paid that much...If he just occasionally said thank you—it would be enough. True, Fenston had picked him up out of the gutter but only to drop him into another.

He had served Fenston for a decade and watched as the unsophisticated immigrant from Bucharest climbed up the ladder of wealth and status—a ladder he had held in place, while remaining nothing more than a sidekick. But that could change overnight. She only needed to make one mistake, and their roles would be reversed. Fenston would end up in prison, and he would have a fortune at his disposal that no one could ever trace.

"Would you care for some more coffee, Mr. Leapman?" asked the stewardess.

Anna didn't need a map to find her way to Wentworth Hall, although she did have to remember not to go the wrong way around the numerous traffic islands en route.

Forty minutes later, she drove through the gates of Wentworth Hall. Anna had no special knowledge of the Baroque architecture that dominated the late seventeenth- and early eighteenth-century homes of aristocratic England before she stayed at Wentworth Hall. The pile—Victoria's description of her home—had been built in 1697 by Sir John Vanbrugh. It was his first commission before he moved on to create Castle Howard and, later, Blenheim Palace, for another triumphant soldier—after which he became the most sought-after architect in Europe.

The long drive up to the house was shaded by fine oaks of the same vintage as the hall itself, although gaps were now visible where trees had succumbed to the violent storms of 1987. Anna drove by an ornate lake full of Magoi Koi carp—immigrants from Japan—and on past two tennis courts and a croquet lawn, sprinkled with the first leaves of autumn. As she rounded the bend, the great hall, surrounded by a thousand green English acres, loomed up to dominate the skyline.

Victoria had once told Anna that the house had sixty-seven rooms, fourteen of them guest bedrooms. The bedroom she had stayed in on the first floor, the Van Gogh room, was about the same size as her apartment in New York.

As she approached the hall, Anna noticed that the crested family flag on the east tower was fluttering at half-mast. As she brought the car to a halt, she wondered which of Victoria's many elderly relatives had died.

The massive oak door was pulled open even before Anna reached the top step. She prayed that Victoria was at home, and that Fenston still had no idea she was in England.

"Good morning, madam," the butler intoned. "How may I help you?"

It's me, Andrews, Anna wanted to say, surprised by his formal tone. He had been so friendly when she stayed at the hall. She echoed his formal approach. "I need to speak to Lady Victoria, urgently."

"I'm afraid that will not be possible," replied Andrews, "but I will find out if her ladyship is free. Perhaps you would be kind enough to wait here while I inquire."

What did he mean, *that will not be possible, but I will find out if her ladyship* . . .

As Anna waited in the hall, she glanced up at Gainsborough's portrait of Catherine, Lady Wentworth. She recalled every picture in the house, but her eye moved to her favorite at the top of the staircase, a Romney of *Mrs.*

Siddons as Portia. She turned to face the entrance to the morning room, to be greeted with a painting by Stubbs of *Actaeon, Winner of the Derby,* Sir Harry Wentworth's favorite horse—still safely in his paddock. If Victoria took her advice, at least she could still save the rest of the collection.

The butler returned at the same even pace.

"Her ladyship will see you now," he said, "if you would care to join her in the drawing room." He gave a slight bow before leading her across the hall.

Anna tried to concentrate on her six-point plan, but first she would need to explain why she was forty-eight hours late for their appointment, although surely Victoria would have followed the horrors of Tuesday and might even be surprised to find that she had survived.

When Anna entered the drawing room, she saw Victoria, head bowed, dressed in mourning black, seated on the sofa, a chocolate Labrador half asleep at her feet. She couldn't remember Victoria having a dog and was surprised when she didn't jump up and greet her in her usual warm manner. Victoria raised her head, and Anna gasped, as Arabella Wentworth stared coldly up at her. In that split second, she realized why the family's crest had been flying at half mast. Anna remained silent as she tried to take in the fact that she would never see Victoria again and would now need to convince her sister, whom she had never met before. Anna couldn't even remember her name. The mirror image did not rise from her place or offer to shake her hand.

"Would you care for some tea, Dr. Petrescu?" Arabella asked in a distant voice that suggested she hoped to hear her reply, *No, thank you.*

"No, thank you," said Anna, who remained standing. "May I ask how Victoria died?" she said quietly.

"I assumed you already knew," replied Arabella dryly.

"I have no idea what you mean," said Anna.

"Then why are you here," asked Arabella, "if it's not to collect the rest of the family silver?"

"I came to warn Victoria not to let them take away the Van Gogh before I had a chance to—"

"They took the painting away on Tuesday," said Arabella, pausing. "They didn't even have the good manners to wait until after the funeral."

"I tried to call, but they wouldn't give me her number. If only I'd got through," Anna mumbled incoherently, and then added, "And now it's too late."

"Too late for what?" asked Arabella.

"I sent Victoria a copy of my report recommending that—"

"Yes, I've read your report," said Arabella, "but you're right, it's too late for that now. My new lawyer has already warned me that it could be years before the estate can be settled, by which time we'll have lost everything."

"That must have been the reason he didn't want me to travel to England and see Victoria personally," Anna said without explanation.

"I'm not sure I understand," said Arabella, looking more closely at her.

"I was fired by Fenston on Tuesday," said Anna, "for sending a copy of my report to Victoria."

"Victoria read your report," said Arabella quietly. "I have a letter confirming that she was going to take your advice, but that was before her cruel death."

"How did she die?" asked Anna gently.

"She was murdered in a vile and cowardly fashion," said Arabella. She paused and, looking directly at Anna, added, "And I have no doubt that Mr. Fenston will be able to fill in the details for you." Anna bowed her head, unable to think of anything to say, her six-point plan in tatters. Fenston had beaten both of them. "Dear Victoria was so trusting, and, I fear, so naïve," continued Arabella, "but no human being deserved to be treated in that way, let alone someone as good-natured as my sweet sister."

"I am so sorry," said Anna, "I didn't know. You have to believe me. I had no idea."

Arabella looked out of the window across the lawn and didn't speak for some time. She turned back to see Anna, trembling.

"I believe you," Arabella eventually said. "I originally assumed that it was you who was responsible for this evil charade." She paused again. "I see now that I was wrong. But, sadly, it's all too late. There's nothing we can do now."

"I'm not so sure about that," said Anna, looking at Arabella with a fierce determination in her eyes. "But if I'm to do anything, I'll have to ask you to trust me, as much as Victoria did."

"What do you mean, trust you?" said Arabella.

"Give me a chance," said Anna, "to prove that I wasn't responsible for your sister's death."

"But how can you hope to do that?" asked Arabella.

"By retrieving your Van Gogh."

"But as I told you, they've already taken the painting away."

"I know," said Anna, "but it still has to be in England, because Fenston has sent a Mr. Leapman to pick up the picture." Anna checked her watch. "He'll be landing at Heathrow in a few hours' time."

"But even if you managed to get your hands on the painting, how would that solve the problem?"

Anna outlined the details of her plan and was pleased to find Arabella nodding from time to time. Anna ended by saying, "I'll need your backing, otherwise what I have in mind could get me arrested."

Arabella remained silent for some time, before she said, "You're a brave young woman, and I wonder if you even realize just how brave. But if you're willing to take such a risk, so am I, and I'll back you to the hilt," she added.

Anna smiled at the quaint English expression, and said, "Can you confirm who collected the Van Gogh?"

Arabella rose from the sofa and crossed the room to the writing desk, with the dog following in her wake. She picked up a business card. "A Ms. Ruth Parish," she read, "of Art Locations."

"Just as I thought," said Anna. "Then I'll have to leave immediately, as I only have a few hours before Leapman arrives."

Anna stepped forward and thrust out her hand, but Arabella didn't respond. She simply took her in her arms and said, "If I can do anything to help you avenge my sister's death . . ."

"Anything?"

"Anything," repeated Arabella.

"When the North Tower collapsed, all the documentation concerning Victoria's loan was destroyed," said Anna, "including the original contract. The only copy is in your possession. If—"

"You don't have to spell it out," said Arabella.

Anna smiled. She wasn't dealing with Victoria any longer.

She turned to leave and had reached the hall long before the butler had time to open the front door.

Arabella watched from the drawing-room window as Anna's car disappeared down the drive and out of sight. She wondered if she would ever see her again.

"Petrescu," said a voice, "is just leaving Wentworth Hall. She's heading back in the direction of central London. I'm following her and will keep you briefed."

23

ANNA DROVE OUT OF Wentworth Hall and headed back toward the
M25, looking for a sign to Heathrow. She checked the clock on the dashboard. It was almost 2 P.M., so she had missed any chance of calling Tina,
who would now be at her desk on Wall Street. But she did need to make
another call if there was to be the slightest chance of her coup succeeding.

As she drove through the village of Wentworth, Anna tried to recall
the pub where Victoria had taken her to dinner. Then she saw the familiar crest flapping in the wind, also at half-mast.

Anna swung into the forecourt of the Wentworth Arms and parked her
car near the entrance. She walked through the reception and into the bar.

"Can you change five dollars?" she asked the barmaid. "I need to make
a phone call."

"Of course, love," came back the immediate reply. The barmaid
opened the cash register and handed Anna two pound coins. Daylight
robbery, Anna wanted to tell her, but she didn't have time to argue.

"The phone's just beyond the restaurant, to your right."

Anna dialed a number that she could never forget. The phone rang
only twice before a voice announced, "Good afternoon, Sotheby's."

Anna fed a coin into the slot, and said, "Mark Poltimore, please."

"I'll put you through."

"Mark Poltimore."

"Mark, it's Anna, Anna Petrescu."

"Anna, what a pleasant surprise. We've all been anxious about you. Where were you on Tuesday?"

"Amsterdam," she replied.

"Thank God for that," said Mark. "Terrible business. And Fenston?"

"Not in the building at the time," said Anna, "and that's why I'm calling. He wants your opinion on a Van Gogh."

"Authenticity or price?" asked Mark. "Because when it comes to provenance, I bow to your superior judgment."

"There's no discussion on its provenance," said Anna, "but I would like a second opinion on its value."

"Is it one we would know?"

"*Self-Portrait with Bandaged Ear,*" said Anna.

"The Wentworth *Self-Portrait*?" queried Mark. "I've known the family all my life and had no idea they were considering selling the painting."

"I didn't say they were," said Anna without offering further explanation.

"Are you able to bring the painting in for inspection?" asked Mark.

"I'd like to, but I don't have secure enough transport. I was hoping you might be able to help."

"Where is it now?" asked Mark.

"In a bonded warehouse at Heathrow."

"That's easy enough," said Mark. "We have a daily pickup from Heathrow. Would tomorrow afternoon be convenient?"

"Today, if possible," said Anna. "You know what my boss is like."

"Hold on. I'll just need to find out if they've already left." The line went silent, although Anna could hear her heart thumping. She placed the second pound coin in the slot—the last thing she needed was to be cut off. Mark came back on the line. "You're in luck. Our handler is picking up some other items for us around four. How does that suit you?"

"Fine, but could you do me another favor and ask them to call Ruth Parish at Art Locations, just before the van is due to arrive?"

"Sure. And how long do we have to value the piece?"

"Forty-eight hours."

"You'd come to Sotheby's first if you ever considered selling the *Self-Portrait,* wouldn't you, Anna?"

"Of course."

"I can't wait to see it," said Mark.

Anna replaced the receiver, appalled by how easily she could now lie. She was also becoming aware just how simple it must have been for Fenston to deceive her.

She drove out of the Wentworth Arms car park, aware that everything now depended on Ruth Parish being in her office. Once she reached the orbital road, Anna remained in the slow lane as she went over all the things that could go badly wrong. Was Ruth aware that she had been fired? Had Fenston told her she was dead? Would Ruth accept her authority to make such a crucial decision? Anna knew that there was only one way she was going to find out. She even considered calling Ruth, but decided any prior warning would only give her more time to check up. If she was to have any chance at all, she needed to take Ruth by surprise.

Anna was so deep in thought as she considered every possibility that she nearly missed her exit for Heathrow. Once she had turned off the M25, she drove on past the signs for terminals one, two, three and four, and headed for the cargo depots just off the Southern Perimeter Road.

She parked her car in a visitor's space directly outside the offices of Art Locations. She sat in the car for some time, trying to compose herself. Why didn't she just drive off? She didn't need to become involved or even consider taking such a risk. She then thought about Victoria and the role she had unwittingly played in her death. "Get on with it, woman," Anna said out loud. "They either know or they don't, and if they've already been tipped off, you'll be back in the car in less than two minutes." Anna looked in the mirror. Were there any giveaway signs? "Get on with it," she admonished herself even more firmly, and finally opened the car door. She took a deep breath as she strolled across the tarmac toward the entrance of the building.

She pushed through the swing doors and came face-to-face with a receptionist she'd never seen before. Not a good start.

"Is Ruth around?" Anna asked cheerily, as if she popped by the office every day.

"No, she's having lunch at the Royal Academy to discuss the upcoming Rembrandt exhibition."

Anna's heart sank.

"But I'm expecting her back at any moment."

"Then I'll wait," Anna said with a smile.

She took a seat in reception. She picked up an out-of-date copy of *Newsweek*, with Al Gore on the cover, and flicked through the pages. She found herself continually looking up at the clock above the reception desk, watching the slow progress of the minute hand: 3:10, 3:15, 3:20.

Ruth finally walked through the door at 3:22 P.M. "Any messages?" she asked the receptionist.

"No," replied the girl, "but there is a lady waiting to see you."

Anna held her breath as Ruth swung around.

"Anna," she exclaimed. "It's good to see you." First hurdle crossed. "I wondered if you'd still be on this assignment after the tragedy in New York." Second hurdle crossed. "Especially when your boss told me that Mr. Leapman would be coming across to collect the picture personally." Third hurdle crossed. No one had told Ruth she was missing, presumed dead.

"You look a bit pale," continued Ruth. "Are you all right?"

"I'm fine," said Anna, stumbling over the fourth hurdle, but at least she was still on her feet, even if there were another six hurdles to cross before the finish line.

"Where were you on the eleventh?" asked Ruth with concern. "We feared the worst. I would have asked Mr. Fenston, but he never gives you a chance to ask anything."

"Covering a sale in Amsterdam," Anna replied, "but Karl Leapman called me last night and asked me to fly over and double-check that everything was in place, so that when he arrives all we have to do is load the picture onto the plane."

"We're more than ready for him," said Ruth testily, "but I'll drive you across to the warehouse and you can see for yourself. Just hang on for a minute. I need to see if I've had any calls and let my secretary know where I'm going."

Anna paced anxiously up and down, wondering if Ruth would call New York to check her story. But why should she? Ruth had never dealt with anyone else in the past.

Ruth was back within a couple of minutes. "This just arrived on my desk," she said, handing Anna an e-mail. Anna's heart sank. "Confirming that Mr. Leapman is scheduled to land around seven, seven thirty, this evening. He expects us to be waiting on the runway, ready to load the painting, as he's hoping to turn round in less than an hour."

"That sounds like Leapman," said Anna.

"Then we'd better get moving," said Ruth, as she began walking toward the door.

Anna nodded her agreement, followed her out of the building, and jumped into the passenger seat of Ruth's Range Rover.

"Terrible business, Lady Victoria," said Ruth, as she swung the car around and headed for the south end of the cargo terminal. "The press are making a real meal of the murder—mystery killer, throat cut with a kitchen knife—but the police still haven't arrested anyone."

Anna remained silent, the words *throat cut* and *mystery killer* reverberating in her mind. Was that why Arabella told her that she was a brave woman?

Ruth pulled up outside an anonymous-looking concrete building, which Anna had visited several times in the past. She checked her watch: 3:40 P.M.

Ruth flashed a security pass to the guard, who immediately unlocked the three-inch steel door. He accompanied them both down a long, gray concrete corridor that always felt like a bunker to Anna. He stopped at a second security door, this time with a digital pad. Ruth waited for the guard to stand back before she entered a six-digit number. She pulled open the heavy door, allowing them to enter a square concrete room. A thermometer on the wall indicated a temperature of 20 degrees centigrade.

The room was lined with wooden shelves, which were stacked with pictures waiting to be transported to different parts of the world, all packed in Art Locations's distinctive red boxes. Ruth checked her inventory before walking across the room and looking up at a row of shelves. She tapped a crate showing the number 47 stenciled in all four corners.

Anna strolled across to join her, playing for time. She also checked the inventory: number forty-seven, Vincent Van Gogh, *Self-Portrait with Bandaged Ear*, 24 by 18 inches.

"Everything seems to be in order," said Anna, as the guard reappeared at the door.

"Sorry to interrupt you, Ms. Parish, but there are two security men from Sotheby's outside, say they've been instructed to pick up a Van Gogh for valuation."

"Do you know anything about this?" asked Ruth, turning to face Anna.

"Oh, yes," said Anna, not missing a beat, "the chairman instructed me to have the Van Gogh valued for insurance purposes before it's shipped to New York. They'll only need the piece for about an hour, and then they will send it straight back."

"Mr. Leapman didn't mention anything about this," said Ruth. "It wasn't in his e-mail."

"Frankly," said Anna, "Leapman's such a philistine, he wouldn't know the difference between Van Gogh and Van Morrison." Anna paused for a moment. Normally she never took risks, but she couldn't afford to let Ruth call Fenston and check. "If you're in any doubt, why don't you call New York and have a word with Fenston?" she said. "That should clear the matter up."

Anna waited nervously as Ruth considered her suggestion.

"And have my head bitten off again?" said Ruth eventually. "No, thank you. I think I'll take your word for it. That's assuming you will take responsibility for signing the release order?"

"Of course," said Anna, adding, "That's no more than my fiduciary duty as an officer of the bank," hoping her reply sounded suitably pompous.

"And you'll also explain the change of plan to Mr. Leapman?"

"That won't be necessary," said Anna. "The painting will be back long before his plane lands."

Ruth looked relieved and, turning to the guard, said, "It's number forty-seven."

They both accompanied the guard as he removed the red packing case from the shelf and carried it out to the Sotheby's security van.

"Sign here," said the driver.

Anna stepped forward and signed the release document.

"When will you be bringing the picture back?" Ruth asked the driver.

"I don't know anything about—"

"I asked Mark Poltimore to return the painting within a couple of hours," interjected Anna.

"It had better be back before Mr. Leapman lands," said Ruth, "because I don't need to get on the wrong side of that man."

"Would you be happier if I accompanied the painting to Sotheby's?" asked Anna innocently. "Then perhaps I can speed up the whole process."

"Would you be willing to do that?" asked Ruth.

"It might be wise given the circumstances," said Anna, and she climbed up into the front of the van and took the seat between the two men.

Ruth waved as the van disappeared through the perimeter gate and joined the late-afternoon traffic on its journey into London.

24

Bryce Fenston's Gulfstream V executive jet touched down at Heathrow at 7:22 P.M., and Ruth was standing on the tarmac waiting to greet the bank's representative. She had already alerted customs with all the relevant details so that the paperwork could be completed just as soon as Anna returned.

For the past hour, Ruth had spent more and more time looking toward the main gate, willing the security van to reappear. She had already rung Sotheby's and was assured by the girl in their Impressionist department that the painting had arrived. But that was more than two hours ago. Perhaps she should have called the States to double-check—but why question one of your most reliable customers. Ruth turned her attention back to the jet and decided to say nothing. After all, Anna was certain to turn up in the next few minutes.

The fuselage door opened and the steps unfolded onto the ground. The stewardess stood to one side to allow her only passenger to leave the plane. Karl Leapman stepped onto the tarmac and shook hands with Ruth before joining her in the back of an airport limousine for the short journey to the private lounge. He didn't bother to introduce himself, just assumed she would know who he was.

"Any problems?" asked Leapman.

"None that I can think of," replied Ruth confidently, as the driver pulled up outside the executive building. "We've carried out your instructions to the letter, despite the tragic death of Lady Victoria."

"Yeah," said Leapman, as he stepped out of the car. "The company will be sending a wreath to her funeral," and without pausing, added, "Is everything ready for a quick turnaround?"

"Yes," said Ruth. "We'll begin loading the moment the captain has finished refueling—shouldn't be more than an hour. Then you can be on your way."

"I'm glad to hear it," said Leapman, pushing through the swing doors. "We have a slot booked for eight thirty and I don't want to miss it."

"Then perhaps it might be more sensible if I left you to oversee the transfer," said Ruth, "but I'll report back the moment the painting is safely on board."

Leapman nodded and sank back in a leather chair. Ruth turned to leave.

"Can I get you a drink, sir?" asked the barman.

"Scotch on the rocks," said Leapman, scanning the short dinner menu.

As Ruth reached the door, she turned and said, "When Anna comes back, would you tell her I'll be over at customs, waiting to complete the paperwork?"

"Anna?" exclaimed Leapman, jumping out of his chair.

"Yes, she's been around for most of the afternoon."

"Doing what?" Leapman demanded, as he advanced toward Ruth.

"Just checking over the manifest," Ruth said, trying to sound relaxed, "and making sure that Mr. Fenston's orders were carried out."

"What orders?" barked Leapman.

"To send the Van Gogh to Sotheby's for an insurance valuation."

"The chairman gave no such order," said Leapman.

"But Sotheby's sent their van, and Dr. Petrescu confirmed the instruction."

"Petrescu was fired three days ago. Get me Sotheby's on the line, now."

Ruth ran across to the phone and dialed the main number.

"Who does she deal with at Sotheby's?"

"Mark Poltimore," Ruth said, handing the phone across to Leapman.

"Poltimore," he barked, the moment he heard the word Sotheby's, then realized he was addressing an answering machine. Leapman slammed down the phone. "Do you have his home number?"

"No," said Ruth, "but I have a mobile."

"Then call it."

Ruth quickly looked up the number on her palm pilot and began dialing again.

"Mark?" she said.

Leapman snatched the phone from her. "Poltimore?"

"Speaking."

"My name is Leapman. I'm the—"

"I know who you are, Mr. Leapman," said Mark.

"Good, because I understand you are in possession of our Van Gogh."

"*Was,* would be more accurate," replied Mark, "until Dr. Petrescu, your art director, informed us, even before we'd had a chance to examine the painting, that you'd had a change of heart and wanted the canvas taken straight back to Heathrow for immediate transport to New York."

"And you went along with that?" said Leapman, his voice rising with every word.

"We had no choice, Mr. Leapman. After all, it was her name on the manifest."

25

"HI, IT'S VINCENT."

"Hi. Is it true what I've just heard?"

"What have you heard?"

"That you've stolen the Van Gogh."

"Have the police been informed?"

"No, he can't risk that, not least because our shares are still going south and the picture wasn't insured."

"So what's he up to?"

"He's sending someone to London to track you down, but I can't find out who it is."

"Maybe I won't be in London by the time they arrive."

"Where will you be?"

"I'm going home."

"And is the painting safe?"

"Safe as houses."

"Good, but there's something else you ought to know."

"What's that?"

"Fenston will be attending your funeral this afternoon."

The phone went dead. Fifty-two seconds.

Anna replaced the receiver, even more concerned about the danger she was placing Tina in. What would Fenston do if he were to discover the reason she always managed to stay one step ahead of him?

She walked over to the departures desk.

"Do you have any bags to check in?" asked the woman behind the counter. Anna heaved the red box off the luggage cart and onto the scales. She then placed her suitcase next to it.

"You're quite a bit over weight, madam," she said. "I'm afraid there will be an excess charge of thirty-two pounds." Anna took the money out of her wallet while the woman attached a label to her suitcase and fixed a large FRAGILE sticker on the red box. "Gate forty-three," she said, handing her a ticket. "They'll be boarding in about thirty minutes. Have a good flight."

Anna began walking toward the departures gate.

Whoever Fenston was sending to London to track her down would be landing long after she had flown away. But Anna knew that they only had to read her report carefully to work out where the picture would be ending up. She just needed to be certain that she got there before they did. But first she had to make a phone call to someone she hadn't spoken to for over ten years to warn him that she was on her way. Anna took the escalator to the first floor and joined a long line waiting to be checked through security.

"She's heading toward gate forty-three," said a voice, "and will be departing on flight BA two-seven-two to Bucharest at eight forty-four. . . ."

Fenston squeezed himself into a line of dignitaries as President Bush and Mayor Giuliani shook hands with a select group who were attending the latest service at Ground Zero.

He hung around until the president's helicopter had taken off and then walked across to join the other mourners. He took a place at the back of the crowd and listened as the names were read out. Each one was followed by the single peal of a bell.

Greg Abbot.

He glanced around the crowd.

Kelly Gullickson.

He studied the faces of the relations and friends who had gathered in memory of their loved ones.

Anna Petrescu.

Fenston knew that Petrescu's mother lived in Bucharest and wouldn't be traveling to the service. He looked more carefully at the strangers who were huddled together and wondered which one of them was Uncle George from Danville, Illinois.

Rebecca Rangere.

He glanced across at Tina. Tears were filling her eyes, certainly not for Petrescu.

Brulio Real Polanco.

The priest bowed his head. He delivered a prayer, then closed his Bible and made the sign of a cross. "In the name of the Father, the Son, and the Holy Ghost," he declared.

"Amen," came back the unison reply.

Tina looked across at Fenston, not a tear shed, just the familiar movement from one foot to the other—the sign that he was bored. While others gathered in small groups to remember, sympathize, and pay their respects, Fenston left without commiserating with anyone. No one else joined the chairman as he strode off purposefully toward his waiting car.

Tina stood among a little group of mourners, although her eyes remained fixed on Fenston. His driver was holding open the back door for him. Fenston climbed into the car and sat next to a woman Tina had never seen before. Neither spoke until the driver had returned to the front seat and touched a button on the dashboard to cause a smoked-glass screen to rise behind him. Without waiting, the car eased out into the road to join the midday traffic. Tina watched as the chairman disappeared out of sight. She hoped it wouldn't be long before she called again—so much to tell her, and now she had to find out who the waiting woman was. Were they discussing Anna? Had Tina put her friend in unnecessary danger? Where was the Van Gogh?

The woman seated next to Fenston was dressed in a gray trouser suit. Anonymity was her most important asset. She had never once visited Fenston at either his office or his apartment, even though she had known him for almost twenty years. She'd first met Nicu Munteanu when he was bagman for President Nicolae Ceauşescu.

Fenston's primary responsibility during Ceauşescu's reign was to distribute vast sums of money into countless bank accounts across the world—bribes for the dictator's loyal henchmen. When they ceased to be loyal, the woman seated next to Fenston eliminated them, and he then redistributed their frozen assets. Fenston's speciality was money laundering, to places as far afield as the Cook Islands and as close to home as Switzerland. Her speciality was to dispose of the bodies—her chosen instrument a kitchen knife available in any hardware store in any city and, unlike a gun, not requiring a licence.

Both knew, literally, where the bodies were buried.

In 1985, Ceauşescu decided to send his private banker to New York to open an overseas branch for him. For the next four years, Fenston lost touch with the woman seated next to him, until in 1989 Ceauşescu was arrested by his fellow countrymen, tried, and finally executed on Christmas Day. Among those who avoided the same fate was Olga Krantz, who crossed seven borders before she reached Mexico, from where she slipped into America to become one of the countless illegal immigrants who do not claim unemployment benefits and live off cash payments from an unscrupulous employer. She was sitting next to her employer.

Fenston was one of the few people alive who knew Krantz's true identity. He'd first watched her on television when she was fourteen years old and representing Romania in an international gymnastics competition against the Soviet Union.

Krantz came second to her teammate Mara Moldoveanu, and the press were already tipping them for the gold and silver at the next Olympics. Unfortunately, neither of them made the journey to Moscow. Moldoveanu died in tragic, unforeseen circumstances, when she fell from the beam attempting a double somersault and broke her neck. Krantz was the only other person in the gymnasium at the time. She vowed to win the gold medal in her memory.

Krantz's exit was far less dramatic. She pulled a hamstring warming up for a floor exercise, only days before the Olympic team was selected. She knew she wouldn't be given a second chance. Like all athletes who don't quite make the grade, her name quickly disappeared from the headlines.

Fenston assumed he would never hear of her again, until one morning he thought he saw her coming out of Ceauşescu's private office. The short, sinewy woman may have looked a little older, but she had lost none of her agile movement, and no one could forget those steel gray eyes.

A few well-placed questions and Fenston learned that Krantz was now head of Ceauşescu's personal protection squad. Her particular responsibility: breaking selected bones of those who crossed the dictator or his wife.

Like all gymnasts, Krantz wanted to be number one in her discipline. Having perfected all the routines in the compulsory section—broken arms, broken legs, broken necks—she moved on to her voluntary exercise, "cut throats," a routine at which no one could challenge her for the gold medal. Hours of dedicated practice had resulted in perfection. While others attended a football match or went to the movies on a Saturday afternoon, Krantz spent her time at a slaughterhouse on the outskirts of Bucharest. She filled her weekend cutting the throats of lambs and calves. Her Olympic record was forty-two in an hour. None of the slaughtermen reached the final.

Ceauşescu had paid her well. Fenston paid her better. Krantz's terms of employment were simple. She must be available night and day and work for no one else. In a space of twelve years, her fee had risen from $250,000 to $1 million. Not for her the hand-to-mouth existence of most illegal immigrants.

Fenston extracted a folder from his briefcase and handed it across to Krantz without comment. She turned the cover and studied five recent photographs of Anna Petrescu.

"Where is she at the moment?" asked Krantz, still unable to disguise her mid-European accent.

"London," replied Fenston, before he passed her a second file.

Once again she opened it and this time extracted a single color photograph. "Who's he?" she inquired.

"He's more important than the girl," replied Fenston.

"How can that be possible?" Krantz asked, as she studied the photo more carefully.

"Because he's irreplaceable," Fenston explained, "unlike Petrescu. But whatever you do, don't kill the girl until she's led you to the painting."

"And if she doesn't?"

"She will," said Fenston.

"And my payment for kidnapping a man who has already lost an ear?" inquired Krantz.

"One million dollars. Half in advance, the other half on the day you deliver him to me, unharmed."

"And the girl?"

"The same tariff, but only after I have attended her funeral for the second time." Fenston tapped the screen in front of him and the driver pulled up to the curb. "By the way," said Fenston, "I've already instructed Leapman to deposit the cash in the usual place."

Krantz nodded, opened the door, stepped out of the car, and disappeared into the crowd.

9/15

26

"GOOD-BYE, SAM," SAID Jack, as his cell phone began to play the first few bars of "Danny Boy." He let it go on ringing until he was back out on East Fifty-fourth Street because he didn't want Sam to overhear the conversation. He pressed the green button as he continued walking toward Fifth Avenue. "What have you got for me, Joe?"

"Petrescu landed at Gatwick," said Joe. "She rented a car and drove straight to Wentworth Hall."

"How long was she there?"

"Thirty minutes, no more. When she came out, she dropped into a local pub to make a phone call before traveling on to Heathrow, where she met up with Ruth Parish at the offices of Art Locations." Jack didn't interrupt. "Around four, a Sotheby's van turns up, picks up a red box—"

"Size?"

"About three foot by two."

"No prizes for guessing what's inside," said Jack. "So where did the van go?"

"They delivered the painting to their West End office."

"And Petrescu?"

"She goes along for the ride. When the van turned up in Bond Street, two porters unloaded the picture and she followed them in."

"How long before she came back out?"

"Twenty minutes, and this time she was on her own, except she was carrying the red box. She hailed a taxi, put the painting in the back, and disappeared."

"Disappeared?" said Jack, his voice rising. "What do you mean, disappeared?"

"We don't have too many spare agents at the moment," said Joe. "Most of our guys are working round the clock trying to identify terrorist groups that might have been involved in Tuesday's attacks.

"Understood," said Jack, calming down.

"But we picked her up again a few hours later."

"Where?" asked Jack.

"Gatwick airport. Mind you," said Joe, "an attractive blonde carrying a red box does have a tendency to stand out in a crowd."

"Agent Roberts would have missed her," said Jack, as he hailed a cab.

"Agent Roberts?" queried Joe.

"Another time," said Jack, climbing into the back of a cab. "So where was she heading this time?"

"Bucharest."

"Why would she want to take a priceless Van Gogh to Bucharest?" asked Jack.

"On Fenston's instructions, would be my bet," said Joe. "After all, it's his hometown as well as hers, and I can't think of a better place to hide the picture."

"Then why send Leapman to London if it wasn't to pick up the painting?"

"A smokescreen?" said Joe. "That would also explain why Fenston attended her funeral when he knows only too well that she's alive and still working for him."

"There is an alternative we have to consider," said Jack.

"What's that, boss?"

"That she's no longer working for him, and she's stolen the Van Gogh."

"Why would she risk that," asked Joe, "when he wouldn't hesitate to come after her?"

"I don't know, but there's only one way I'm going to find out." Jack touched the red button on his phone, and gave the taxi driver an address on the West Side.

———

Fenston switched off the recorder and frowned. Both of them had listened to the tape for a third time.

"When are you going to fire the bitch?" was all Leapman asked.

"Not while she's the one person who can still lead us to the painting," Fenston replied.

Leapman scowled. "And did you pick up the only word in their conversation that matters?" he asked. Fenston raised an eyebrow. "*Going*," said Leapman. Fenston still didn't speak. "If she'd used the word *coming*. 'I'm coming home'—it would have been New York."

"But she used the word *going*," said Fenston, "so it has to be Bucharest."

Jack sat back in the cab seat and tried to work out what Petrescu's next move might be. He still couldn't make up his mind if she was a professional criminal or a complete amateur. And where did Tina Forster fit into the equation? Was it possible that Fenston, Leapman, Petrescu, and Forster were all working together? If that was the case, why did Leapman only spend a few hours in London before returning to New York? Because he certainly didn't meet up with Petrescu or take the painting back to New York.

But if Petrescu had branched out on her own, surely she realized that it would only be a matter of time before Fenston caught up with her. Although, Jack had to admit, Petrescu was now on her own ground and didn't seem to have any idea how much danger she was in.

But Jack remained puzzled as to why Petrescu would steal a painting worth millions when she couldn't hope to dispose of such a well-known work without one of her former colleagues finding out. The art world was so small and the number of people who could afford that sort of money even smaller. And even if she succeeded, what could she hope to do with the money? The FBI would trace such a large amount within hours, wherever she tried to hide it, especially after Tuesday's events. It just didn't add up.

But if she did take her audacious act to its obvious conclusion, Fenston was in for a nasty surprise, and no doubt would react in character.

As the taxi swung into Central Park, Jack tried to make some sense of all that had happened during the past few days. He had even wondered if he would be taken off the Fenston case after 9/11, but Macy insisted that not all his agents should be following up terrorist leads while other criminals got away with murder.

Jack hadn't found it difficult to obtain a search warrant for Anna's apartment while she remained on the missing list. After all, relatives and friends needed to be contacted to find out if she had been in touch with them. And then there was the outside possibility, Jack had argued in front of a judge, that she might be locked in her apartment, recovering from the ordeal. The judge signed the order without too many questions.

"I hope you find her," he said, a sentiment His Honor had cause to repeat several times that day.

Sam had burst into tears at just the mention of Anna's name. He told Jack that he'd do anything to assist, accompanied him up to her apartment, and even opened the door.

Jack walked around the small, tidy apartment while Sam remained in the hallway. He didn't learn a great deal more than he already knew. An address book confirmed her uncle's number in Danville, Illinois, and an envelope showed her mother's address in Bucharest. Perhaps the only real surprise was a small Picasso drawing hanging in the hallway, signed in pencil by the artist. He studied the matador and the bull more closely, and it certainly wasn't a print. He couldn't believe she'd stolen it and then left the drawing in the hall for everyone to admire. Or was the drawing a bonus from Fenston for helping him to acquire the Van Gogh? If it was, it would at least explain what she was up to now. And then he walked into the bedroom and saw the one clue that confirmed that Tina had been in the apartment on the evening of 9/11. By the side of Anna's bed was a watch. Jack checked the time: 8:46.

Jack returned to the main room and glanced at a photograph on the corner of the writing desk of what must have been Anna with her parents. He opened a box file to discover a bundle of letters that he couldn't read. Most of them were signed "Mama," although one or two were from someone called Anton. Jack wondered if he was a relation or a friend. He looked back up at the photograph and couldn't help thinking that if his mother had seen the picture, she would have invited Anna back to sample her Irish stew.

"Damn," said Jack, loud enough for the cab driver to ask, "What's the problem?"

"I forgot to phone my mother."

"Then you're in big trouble," said the driver. "I should know, I'm Irish too."

Hell, is it that obvious, thought Jack. Mind you, he should have called his mother to let her know that he wouldn't be able to make "Irish stew night," when he usually joined his parents to celebrate the natural superiority of the Gaelic race over all God's other creatures. It didn't help that he was an only child. He must try to remember to call her from London.

His father had wanted Jack to be a lawyer, and both his parents had made sacrifices to make it possible. After twenty-six years with the NYPD, Jack's father had come to the conclusion that the only people who made a profit out of crime were the lawyers and the criminals, so he felt his son ought to make up his mind which he was going to be.

Despite his father's cryptic advice, Jack signed up for the FBI only days after he had graduated from Columbia with a law degree. His father continued to grumble every Saturday about him not being a lawyer, and his mother kept asking if he was ever going to make her a grandmother.

Jack enjoyed every aspect of the job, from the first moment he arrived at Quantico for training, to joining the New York field office, to being promoted to senior investigating officer. He seemed to be the only person who was surprised when he was the first among his contemporaries to be promoted. Even his father begrudgingly congratulated him before he added, "Only proves what a damn good lawyer you would have made."

Macy had also made it clear that he hoped Jack would take over from him once he was transferred back to Washington, D.C. But before that could happen, Jack still had to put in jail a man who was turning any such thoughts of promotion into fantasies. And so far, Jack had to admit, he hadn't so much as landed a glove on Bryce Fenston, and was now having to rely on an amateur to deliver the knockout punch.

He stopped daydreaming and put a call through to his secretary.

"Sally, book me on the first available flight to London with an onward connection to Bucharest. I'm on my way home to pack."

"I ought to warn you, Jack," his secretary replied, "that JFK is stacked solid for the next week."

"Sally, just get me on a plane to London, and I don't care if I'm sitting next to the pilot."

The rules were simple. Krantz stole a new cell phone every day. She'd phone the chairman once, only speak in their native tongue, and when the conversation was finished dispose of the phone. That way, no one could ever trace her.

Fenston was sitting at his desk when the little red light flashed on his private line. Only one person had that number. He picked up the phone.

"Where is she?"

"Bucharest," was all he said, and then replaced the receiver.

Krantz dropped today's cell phone into the Thames and hailed a cab. "Gatwick."

When Jack came down the steps at Heathrow, he wasn't surprised to find Tom Crasanti standing on the runway waiting for him. A car was parked behind his old friend, engine running, the back door held open by another agent.

Neither of them spoke until the door was closed and the car was on the move.

"Where's Petrescu?" was Jack's first question.

"She's landed in Bucharest."

"And the painting?"

"She wheeled it out of customs on a baggage trolley," said Tom.

"That woman's got style."

"Agreed," said Tom, "but then perhaps she has no idea what she's up against."

"I suspect she's about to find out," said Jack, "because one thing's for sure, if she stole the painting, I won't be the only person out there looking for her."

"Then you'll have to keep an eye out for them as well," said Tom.

"You're right about that," said Jack, "and that's assuming I get to Bucharest before she's moved on to her next destination."

"Then there's no time to waste," said Tom, before adding, "We've got a helicopter standing by to take you to Gatwick, and they're holding up the flight to Bucharest for thirty minutes."

"How did you manage that?" asked Jack.

"The helicopter is ours; the holdup is theirs. The ambassador called the Foreign Office. I don't know what he said," admitted Tom, as they came to a halt beside the helicopter, "but you've only got thirty minutes."

"Thanks for everything," said Jack, as he stepped out of the car and began to walk toward the helicopter.

"And try not to forget," Tom shouted above the noise of the whirring blades, "we don't have an official presence in Bucharest, so you'll be on your own."

27

ANNA STEPPED ONTO the concourse of Otopeni, Bucharest's international airport, in the early hours of the morning, pushing a trolley laden with a wooden crate, a large case, and a laptop. She stopped in her tracks when she saw a man rushing toward her.

Anna stared at him suspiciously. He was around five nine, balding, with a ruddy complexion and a thick black moustache. He must have been over sixty. He wore a tight-fitting suit, which suggested he'd once been slimmer. He came to a halt in front of Anna.

"I'm Sergei," he announced in his native tongue. "Anton told me you'd called and asked to be picked up. He has already booked you into a small hotel downtown." Sergei took Anna's trolley and pushed it toward his waiting taxi. He opened the back door of a yellow Mercedes that already had three hundred thousand miles on the clock, and waited until Anna had stepped in before he loaded her luggage into the trunk and took his place behind the wheel.

Anna stared out of the taxi window and thought how the city had changed since her birth—it was now a thrusting, energetic capital, demanding its place at the European table. Modern office buildings and a fashionable shopping center had replaced the drab Communist gray-tiled façade of only a decade before.

Sergei drew up outside a small hotel tucked away down a narrow street. He lifted the red crate out of the trunk while Anna took the rest of the luggage and headed into the hotel.

"I'd like to visit my mother first thing," said Anna, once she'd checked in.

Sergei looked at his watch. "I'll pick you up around nine. That will give you the chance to grab a few hours' sleep."

"Thank you," said Anna.

He watched as she disappeared into the lift carrying the red box.

Jack had first spotted her when he was standing in line to board the plane. It is a basic surveillance technique: hang back, just in case you are being followed. The trick, then, is not to let the pursuer realize that you are on to them. Act normal, never look back. Not easy.

His class supervisor at Quantico would carry out a surveillance detection run every evening after class, when he would follow one of the new recruits home. If you managed to lose him, you were singled out for a commendation. Jack went one better. Having lost him, he then carried out an SDR on his supervisor and followed *him* home without being spotted.

Jack climbed the steps of the plane. He didn't look back.

When Anna strolled out of her hotel a few minutes after nine, she found Sergei standing by his old Mercedes, waiting for her.

"Good morning, Sergei," she said, as he opened the back door for her.

"Good morning, madam. Do you still wish to visit your mother?"

"Yes," replied Anna. "She lives at—"

Sergei waved a hand to make it clear that he knew exactly where to take her.

Anna smiled with pleasure as he drove through the center of town past a magnificent fountain that would have graced a lawn at Versailles. But once Sergei had reached the outskirts of the city, the picture quickly changed from color to black-and-white. By the time her driver had reached the neglected outpost of Berceni, Anna realized that the new regime still had a long way to go if they were to achieve the prosperity-for-all program they had promised the voters following the downfall of Ceauşescu. Anna had, in the space of a few miles, returned to the more familiar scenes of her youth. She found many of her countrymen downcast, looking older than their years. Only the young lads playing soccer in the street seemed unaware of the degradation that surrounded them. It appalled Anna that her mother was still so adamant about remaining in her birthplace after her father had been killed in the uprising. She had tried so many times to convince her to join them in America, but she wouldn't be budged.

In 1987, Anna had been invited to visit Illinois by an uncle she had never met. He'd even sent her two hundred dollars to assist with her passage. Her father told her to leave, and leave quickly, but it was her mother who predicted that she would never come back. She purchased a one-way ticket, and her uncle promised to pay for the return journey whenever she wanted to go home.

Anna was seventeen at the time, and she had fallen in love with America even before the boat had docked. A few weeks later, Ceauşescu began his crackdown on any individual who dared to oppose his draconian regime. Her father wrote to warn Anna that it was not safe for her to come home.

That was his last letter. Three weeks later he joined the rebels and was never seen again.

Anna missed her mother dreadfully and repeatedly begged her to join them in Illinois. But her response was always the same. "This is my homeland, where I was born, and where I shall die. I am too old to begin a new life." Too old, Anna had remonstrated. Her mother was only sixty-one, but they were sixty-one stubborn Romanian years, so Anna reluctantly accepted that nothing would change her mind. A month later, her uncle George enrolled Anna in a local school. While civil unrest in Romania continued unabated, Anna graduated from college and later accepted the opportunity to study for a Ph.D. at Penn, in a discipline that had no language barriers.

Dr. Petrescu still wrote to her mother every month, only too aware that most of her letters were not reaching her because the spasmodic replies often asked questions she had already answered.

The first decision Anna made after she left college and joined Sotheby's was to open a separate bank account for her mother in Bucharest, to which she transferred $400 by standing order on the first day of every month. Although she would rather have—

"I'll wait for you," said Sergei, as the taxi finally came to a halt outside a dilapidated block of flats in Piazza Resitei.

"Thank you," said Anna, as she looked out at the prewar estate where she was born, and where her mother still lived. Anna could only wonder what Mama had spent the money on. She stepped out onto the weed-covered path that she had once thought so wide because she couldn't jump across it.

The children playing soccer in the road watched suspiciously as the stranger in her smart linen jacket, jeans with fashionable tears, and fancy sneakers walked up the worn, potholed path. They also wore jeans with tears. The elevator didn't respond to Anna's button-pressing—nothing changes—which was why, Anna recalled, the most sought-after flats were always those on the lower floors. She couldn't understand why her mother hadn't moved years ago. Anna had sent more than enough money for her to rent a comfortable apartment on the other side of town. Anna's feeling of guilt grew the higher up she climbed. She had forgotten just how dreadful it was, but like the children playing soccer in the street, it had once been all she knew.

When Anna eventually reached the sixteenth floor, she stopped to catch her breath. No wonder her mother so rarely left the flat. On the floors above her resided sixty-year-olds who were housebound. Anna hesitated before she knocked on a door that hadn't seen a splash of paint since she'd last stood there.

She waited for some time before a frail, white-haired lady, dressed from head to toe in black, pulled the door open, but by only a few inches. Mother and daughter stared at each other, until suddenly Elsa Petrescu flung open the door, threw her arms around her daughter, and shouted in a voice as old as she looked, "Anna, Anna, Anna." Both mother and daughter burst into tears.

The old lady continued to cling to Anna's hand as she led her into the flat in which she had been born. It was spotless, and Anna could still remember everything, because nothing had changed. The sofa and chairs her grandmother had left them, the family photographs, all black-and-white and unframed, a coal scuttle with no coal, a rug that was so worn it was hard to make out the original pattern. The only new addition to the room was a magnificent painting that hung on otherwise blank walls. As Anna admired the portrait of her father, she was reminded where her love of art had begun.

"Anna, Anna, so many questions to ask," her mother said. "Where do I begin?" she asked, still clutching her daughter's hand.

The sun was setting before Anna had responded to every one of her mother's questions, and then she begged once again, "Please, Mama, come back with me and live in America."

"No," she replied defiantly, "all my friends and all my memories are here. I am too old to begin a new life."

"Then why not move to another part of the city? I could find you something on a lower—"

"This is where I was married," her mother said quietly, "where you were born, where I lived for over thirty years with your beloved father, and where, when God decrees it is my time, I shall die." She smiled up at her daughter. "Who would tend your father's grave?" she asked, as if she'd never asked the question before. She looked into her daughter's eyes. "You know he was so pleased to see you settled in America with his brother—" she paused "—and now I can see that he was right."

Anna looked around the room. "But why haven't you spent some of the money I've been sending to you each month?"

"I have," said her mother firmly, "but not on myself," she admitted, "because I want for nothing."

"Then what have you spent it on?" Anna queried.

"Anton."

"Anton?" repeated Anna.

"Yes, Anton," said her mother. "You knew that he'd been released from jail?"

"Oh, yes," said Anna, "he wrote to me soon after Ceauşescu was arrested to ask if I had a photo of Papa that he could borrow." Anna smiled as she looked up at the painting of her father.

"It's a good likeness," said her mother.

"It certainly is," said Anna.

"They gave him back his old job at the academy. He's now the Professor of Perspective. If you'd married him, you would be a professor's wife."

"Is he still painting?" she asked, avoiding her mother's next inevitable question.

"Yes," she replied, "but his main responsibility is to teach the graduates at the Universitatea de Arte. You can't make a living as an artist in Romania," she said sadly. "You know, with his talent, Anton should also have gone to America."

Anna looked up again at Anton's magnificent portrait of her father. Her mother was right; with such a gift, he would have flourished in New York. "But what does he do with the money?" she asked.

"He buys canvases, paints, brushes, and all those materials that his pupils can't afford, so you see, your generosity is being put to good use." She paused. "Anton was your first love, Anna, yes?"

Anna wouldn't have believed that her mother could still make her blush. "Yes," she admitted, "and I suspect I was his."

"He's married now, and they have a little boy called Peter." She paused again. "Do you have a young man?"

"No, Mama."

"Is that what brings you back home? Are you running away from something, or someone?"

"What makes you ask that?" Anna asked defensively.

"There is a sadness in your eyes, and fear," she said, looking up at her daughter, "which you could never hide as a child."

"I do have one or two problems," admitted Anna, "but nothing that time won't sort out." She smiled. "In fact, I rather think that Anton might be able to help me with one of them, and I'm hoping to join him at the academy for a drink. Do you have any message you want passed on?" Her mother didn't reply. She had quietly dozed off. Anna rearranged the rug on her mother's lap and kissed her on the forehead. "I'll be back again tomorrow morning, Mama," she whispered.

She slipped silently out of the room. As she walked back down the littered staircase, she was pleased to see the old yellow Mercedes was still parked by the curb.

28

ANNA RETURNED TO her hotel, and after a quick shower and change of clothes, her newly acquired chauffeur took her to the Academy of Art on Piata Universitatii.

The building had lost none of its elegance or charm with the passing of time, and when Anna climbed the steps toward the massive sculptured doors, memories came flooding back of her introduction to the great works of art hanging in galleries she thought she would never see. Anna reported to the front desk and asked where Professor Teodorescu's lecture was taking place.

"In the main theater on the third floor," said the girl behind the counter, "but it has already started."

Anna thanked the young student and, without asking for any directions, climbed the wide marble staircase to the third floor. She stopped to glance at a poster outside the hall:

THE INFLUENCE OF PICASSO ON TWENTIETH-CENTURY ART
Professor Anton Teodorescu
TONIGHT, 7:00 P.M.

She didn't require the arrow to point her in the right direction. Anna gingerly pushed open the door, pleased to find that the lecture theater was in darkness. She walked up the steps at the side of the hall and took a seat toward the back.

A slide of *Guernica* filled the screen. Anton was explaining that the massive canvas was painted in 1937, at the time of the Spanish Civil War, when Picasso was at the height of his powers. He went on to say that the depiction of the bombing and the resulting carnage had taken Picasso three weeks, and the image was unquestionably influenced by the artist's hatred of the Spanish dictator, Franco. The students were listening attentively, several taking notes. Anton's bravura performance reminded Anna why she'd had a crush on him all those years ago, when she not only lost her virginity to an artist, but began a lifelong love affair with art.

When Anton's presentation came to an end, the rapturous applause left Anna in no doubt how much the undergraduates enjoyed his lecture. He'd lost none of his skill in motivating and nurturing the young's enthusiasm for their chosen subject.

Anna watched her first love as he collected together his slides and began to put them in an old briefcase. Tall and angular, his mop of curly, dark hair, ancient brown corduroy jacket, and open-neck shirt gave him the air of a perpetual student. She couldn't help noticing that he had put on a few pounds, but she didn't feel it made him any less attractive. When the last student had filed out, Anna made her way to the front of the hall.

Anton glanced up over his half-moon spectacles, apparently anticipating a question from the student who was approaching him. When he first saw Anna, he didn't speak, just stared.

"Anna," he finally exclaimed. "Thank God I didn't realize you were in the audience, as you probably know more about Picasso than I do."

Anna kissed him on both cheeks and said with a laugh, "You've lost none of your charm or ability to flatter."

Anton held up his hands in mock defeat, grinning widely. "Was Sergei at the airport to pick you up?"

"Yes, thank you," said Anna. "Where did you meet him?"

"In jail," admitted Anton. "He was lucky to survive the Ceauşescu regime. And have you visited your sainted mother?"

"I have," replied Anna, "and she's still living in conditions not much better than a jail."

"I agree, and don't think I haven't tried to do something about it, but at least your dollars, and her generosity, allow some of my best students to—"

"I know," said Anna, "she's already told me."

"You can't begin to know," continued Anton. "So let me show you some of the results of your investment."

Anton took Anna by the hand, as if they were still students, and guided her down the steps to the long corridor on the first floor, where the walls were crammed with paintings in every medium.

"This year's prize-winning students," he told her, holding out his arms like a proud father. "And every entry has been painted on a canvas supplied by you. In fact, one of the awards is in your name—the Petrescu Prize." He paused. "How appropriate if you were to select the winner, which would make not only me, but one of my students, very proud."

"I'm flattered," said Anna with a smile, as she walked toward a long row of paintings. She took her time as she strolled slowly up and down the canvas-filled corridor, pausing occasionally to study an image more closely. Anton had clearly taught them the importance of drawing before he allowed them to move on to other media. *Don't bother with the brush if you can't first handle the pencil,* he liked to repeat. But the range of subjects and bold approach showed that he had also let them express themselves. Some didn't quite come off, while others showed considerable talent. Anna finally stopped in front of an oil entitled *Freedom,* depicting the sun rising over Bucharest.

"I know a certain gentleman who'll appreciate that," she said.

"You haven't lost your touch," said Anton, smiling. "Danuta Sekalska is this year's star pupil, and she's been offered a place at the Slade in London to continue her studies, if only we can raise enough money to cover her expenses." He looked at his watch. "Do you have time for a drink?"

"I certainly do," replied Anna, "because I confess there's a favor I need to ask of you—" she paused "—in fact, two favors."

Anton once again took her by the hand and led her back down the corridor toward the staff refectory. When they entered the senior common room, Anna was greeted by the sound of good-humored chatter as tutors swapped anecdotes while they sat around in groups enjoying nothing stronger than a coffee. They didn't seem to notice that the furniture, the cups, the saucers, and probably even the cookies would have been rejected by any self-respecting hobo visiting a Salvation Army hostel in the Bronx.

Anton poured two cups of coffee. "Black, if I remember. Not quite

Starbucks," he mocked, "but we're getting there slowly." Heads turned as Anton guided his former pupil to a place by the fire. He took a seat opposite her. "Now, what can I do for you, Anna," he asked, "because I am unquestionably in your debt."

"It's my mother," she said quietly. "I need your help. I can't get her to spend a cent on herself. She could do with a new carpet, sofa, a TV, and even a telephone, not to mention a splash of fresh paint on that front door."

"You think I haven't tried?" Anton repeated. "Where do you imagine you get your stubborn streak from? I even suggested she move in with us. It's not palatial, but it's a damn sight better than that dump she's living in now." Anton took a long draft of his coffee. "But I promise I'll try again—" he paused "—even harder."

"Thank you," said Anna, who remained silent while Anton rolled a cigarette. "And I see I failed to convince you to give up smoking."

"I don't have the bright lights of New York to distract me," he said with a laugh. He lit his hand-rolled cigarette before adding, "And what's the second favor?"

"You'll need to think long and hard about it," she said in an even tone.

Anton put down his coffee, inhaled deeply, and listened carefully as Anna explained in detail how he could help her.

"Have you discussed the idea with your mother?"

"No," Anna admitted. "I think it's best she doesn't find out why I really came to Bucharest."

"How much time have I got?"

"Three, perhaps four days. Depends how successful I am while I'm away," she added without explanation.

"And if I'm caught?" he asked, once again dragging deeply on his cigarette.

"You'd probably go back to jail," admitted Anna.

"And you?"

"The canvas would be shipped to New York and used as evidence against me. If you need any more money for—"

"No, I'm still holding over eight thousand dollars of your mother's money, so—"

"Eight thousand?"

"A dollar goes a long way in Romania."

"Can I bribe you?"

"Bribe me?"

"If you'll take on the assignment, I'll pay for your pupil, Danuta Sekalska, to go to the Slade."

Anton thought for a moment. "And you'll be back in three days," he said, stubbing out his cigarette.

"Four at the most," said Anna.

"Then let's hope I'm as good as you think I am."

"It's Vincent."

"Where are you?"

"Visiting my mother."

"Then don't hang about."

"Why?"

"The stalker knows where you are."

"Then I'm afraid he'll miss me again."

"I'm not even convinced the stalker's a man."

"What makes you say that?"

"I saw Fenston talking to a woman in the back of his car while I was attending your funeral."

"That doesn't prove—"

"I agree, but it worries me that I've never seen her before."

"She could be one of Fenston's girlfriends."

"That woman was nobody's girlfriend."

"Describe her."

"Five foot, slim, dark-haired."

"There will be a lot of people like that where I'm going."

"And are you taking the painting with you?"

"No, I've left it where no one can give it a second look."

The phone went dead.

Leapman pressed the off button. "Where no one can give it a second look," he repeated.

"*Can*, not *will*?" said Fenston. "It must still be in the box."

"Agreed, but where's she off to next?"

"To a country where the people are five foot, slim, and dark-haired."

"Japan," said Leapman.

"How can you be so sure?" asked Fenston.

"It's all in her report. She's going to try and sell your painting to the one person who won't be able to resist it."

"Nakamura," said Fenston.

9/16

29

JACK HAD CHECKED in at what was ambitiously described on a flashing neon sign as the Bucharesti International. He spent most of the night either turning the radiator up because it was so cold or turning it off because it was so noisy. He rose just after 6:00 A.M. and skipped breakfast, fearing it might be as unreliable as the radiator.

He hadn't spotted the woman again since he stepped onto the plane, so either he'd made a mistake or she was a professional. But he was no longer in any doubt that Anna was working independently, which meant Fenston would soon be dispatching someone to retrieve the Van Gogh. But what did Petrescu have in mind, and didn't she realize what danger she was putting herself in? Jack had already decided the most likely place he'd catch up with Anna would be when she visited her mother. This time he'd be waiting for her. He wondered if the woman he'd seen when he stood in line for the plane had the same idea, and, if so, was she Fenston's retriever or did she work for someone else?

The hotel porter offered him a tourist map, which colorfully detailed the finer parts of the city center but not the outskirts, so he walked across to the kiosk and purchased a guidebook entitled *Everything You Need to Know About Bucharest*. There wasn't a single paragraph devoted to the Berceni district where Anna's mother lived, although they were considerate enough to include Piazza Resitei on the larger foldout map at the back. With the aid of a matchstick placed against the scale at the bottom left-hand corner of the page, Jack worked out that Anna's birthplace must be about six miles north of the hotel.

He decided he would walk the first three miles, not least because he needed the exercise, but also it would give him a better chance to discover if he was the target of an SDR.

Jack left the International at 7:30 A.M. and set off at a brisk pace.

Anna also had a restless night, finding it hard to sleep while the red box was under her bed. She was beginning to have doubts about Anton taking on such an unnecessary risk to assist her in her plan, even if it was only for a few days. They'd agreed to meet at the academy at eight o'clock, an hour no self-respecting student would admit existed.

When she stepped out of the hotel, the first thing she saw was Sergei in his old Mercedes parked by the entrance. She wondered how long he'd been waiting for her. Sergei jumped out of the car.

"Good morning, madam," he said, as he loaded the red box back into the trunk.

"Good morning, Sergei," Anna replied. "I would like to go back to the academy, where I'll be leaving the crate." Sergei nodded, and opened the back door for her.

On the journey over to the Piata Universitatii, Anna learnt that Sergei had a wife, that they had been married for over thirty years, and had a son who was serving in the army. Anna was about to ask if he'd ever met her father, when she spotted Anton, standing on the bottom step of the academy, looking anxious and fidgeting.

Sergei brought the car to a halt, jumped out, and unloaded the crate from the trunk.

"Is that it?" asked Anton, viewing the red box suspiciously. Anna nodded. Anton joined Sergei as he carried the crate up the steps. Anton opened the front door for him, and they both disappeared inside the building.

Anna kept checking her watch every few moments and looking back up the steps toward the entrance. They were only away for a few minutes, but she never felt alone. Was Fenston's stalker watching her even now? Had he worked out where the Van Gogh was? The two men finally reappeared carrying another wooden box. Although it was exactly the same size, the plain slats of timber were unmarked in any way. Sergei placed the new crate in the trunk of the Mercedes, slammed the lid down, and climbed back behind the wheel.

"Thank you," said Anna, before kissing Anton on both cheeks.

"I won't be getting much sleep while you're away," Anton mumbled.

"I'll be back, three, four days at the most," Anna promised, "when I'll happily take the painting off your hands and no one will be any the wiser." She climbed into the back of the car.

As Sergei drove away, she stared through the rear window at the forlorn figure of Anton, who was standing on the bottom step of the academy, looking worried. Was he up to the job? she wondered.

Jack didn't look back, but once he'd covered the first mile, he slipped into a large supermarket and disappeared behind a pillar. He waited for her to walk by. She didn't. An amateur would have strolled past and been unable to resist glancing in, and might even have been tempted to enter the building. He didn't hang around for too long, knowing it would make her suspicious. He bought a bacon and egg baguette and walked back onto the road. As he munched his breakfast, he tried to work out why he was being followed. Who did she represent? What was her brief? Was she hoping he would lead her to Anna, was he a selected target for countersurveillance—the unspoken fear of every FBI agent—or was he just paranoid?

Once he was out of the city center, Jack stopped to study the map. He decided to grab a taxi, as he doubted he'd be able to pick one up in the Berceni district, when he might need to make a speedy exit. Jumping into a taxi might also make it easier for him to lose his tail, as a yellow cab would be more conspicuous once they were no longer in the city center. He rechecked his map, turned left at the next corner, and didn't look back or even glance into the shop window with its large plate-glass pane. If she was a pro, it would be a dead giveaway. He hailed a cab.

Anna asked her driver—as she now thought of Sergei—to take her back to the same block of flats they'd visited the previous day. Anna would have liked to call and warn her mother what time to expect her, but it wasn't possible because Elsa Petrescu didn't approve of phones. They were like elevators, she'd once told her daughter: when they break down, no one comes to repair them, and in any case they create unnecessary bills. Anna knew her mother would have risen by six to be sure everything in her already spotless flat had been dusted and polished for a third time.

When Sergei parked at the end of the weed-strewn path of the Piazza Resitei, Anna told him that she expected to be about an hour, and then wanted to go to Otopeni airport. Sergei nodded.

A taxi drew up beside him. Jack strolled round to the driver's side and motioned for him to wind down the window.

"Do you speak English?"

"A little," said the driver hesitantly.

Jack opened his map and pointed to Piazza Resitei, before taking a seat behind the driver. The taxi driver grimaced in disbelief and looked up at Jack to double-check. Jack nodded. The driver shrugged his shoulders and set out on a journey no tourist had ever requested before.

The taxi slipped out into the middle lane and both of them checked the rearview mirror. Another taxi was following them. There was no sign of any passenger, but then she wouldn't have sat in the front. Had he lost her, or was she in one of three taxis he could now see in the rearview mirror? She was a pro; she'd be in one of those taxis, and he had the feeling she knew exactly where he was going.

Jack knew that every major city has its run-down districts, but he had never experienced anything quite like Berceni, with its grim, high-rise concrete blocks that littered every corner of what could only be described as a desolate slum. Even the graffiti would have been frowned on in Harlem.

The taxi was already slowing down when Jack spotted another yellow Mercedes parked by the curb a few yards ahead of them, in a street that hadn't seen two taxis in the same year.

"Drive on," he said sharply, but the taxi continued to slow. Jack tapped the driver firmly on the shoulder and waved frantically forward to suggest he should keep going.

"But this is place you ask for," insisted the driver.

"Keep moving," shouted Jack.

The puzzled driver shrugged his shoulders and accelerated past the stationary taxi.

"Turn at the next corner," said Jack, pointing left. The driver nodded, now looking even more perplexed. He awaited his next instruction. "Turn back around," Jack said slowly, "and stop at the end of the road."

The driver carried out his new instruction, continually glancing back at Jack, the perplexed expression never leaving his face.

Once he'd parked, Jack got out of the car and walked slowly to the corner, cursing his unforced error. He wondered where the woman was, because she clearly hadn't made the same mistake. He should have anticipated that Anna might already be there, and her only form of transport was likely to be a taxi.

Jack stared up at the gray concrete block where Anna was visiting her mother, and swore he'd never complain about his cramped one-bedroom apartment on the West Side ever again. He had to wait another forty minutes before Anna emerged from the building. He remained still as she walked back down the path to her taxi.

Jack jumped back into his own cab and, pointing frantically, said, "Follow them, but keep your distance until the traffic is heavier." He wasn't even sure that the driver understood what he said. The taxi drove out of the side road, and although Jack kept tapping the driver's shoulder and repeating, "Hold back," the two yellow cabs must have looked like camels in a desert as they drove through the empty streets. Jack cursed again, knowing he was burned. Even an amateur would have spotted him by now.

"You do realize that someone is following you?" Sergei said, as he drove off.

"No, but I'm not surprised," Anna replied, but she still felt cold and sick now that Sergei had confirmed her worst fear. "Did you get a look at them?" she asked.

"Only a glimpse," Sergei replied. "A man, around thirty, thirty-five, slim, dark hair; not much else, I'm afraid." So Tina was wrong when she thought the stalker was a woman was Anna's first reaction. "And he's a professional," added Sergei.

"What makes you say that?" asked Anna anxiously.

"When the taxi passed me, he didn't look back," said Sergei. "Mind you, I can't tell you which side of the law he's on."

Anna shivered as Sergei checked his rearview mirror. "And I'm pretty sure he's following us now, but don't look around," said Sergei sharply, "because then he'll know you've spotted him."

"Thank you," said Anna.

"Do you still want me to take you to the airport?"

"I don't have any choice," Anna replied.

"I could lose him," said Sergei, "but then he *would* know that you were on to him."

"Not much point," said Anna. "He already knows where I'm going."

Jack always carried his passport, wallet, and credit card with him in case of just such an emergency. "Damn," he said, when he saw the sign for the airport and remembered his unpacked suitcase sitting in the hotel room.

Three or four other taxis were also heading in the direction of Otopeni airport, and Jack wondered which one the woman was in, or whether she was already at the airport and booked on the same flight as Anna Petrescu.

Anna handed Sergei a twenty-dollar bill long before they'd reached Otopeni and told him which flight she was booked to return on.

"Would you be able to pick me up?" she asked.

"Of course," promised Sergei, as he came to a halt outside the international terminal.

"Is he still following us?" Anna asked.

"Yes," Sergei replied, as he jumped out of the car.

A porter appeared and helped load the crate and her suitcase onto a trolley.

"I'll be here when you return," Sergei assured Anna, before she disappeared into the terminal.

Jack's cab screeched to a halt behind the yellow Mercedes. He leaped out and ran toward the driver's window, waving a ten-dollar bill. Sergei wound the window down slowly and took the proffered money. Jack smiled.

"The lady in your cab, do you know where she's going?"

"Yes," replied Sergei, stroking his thick moustache.

Jack peeled off another ten-dollar bill, which Sergei happily pocketed.

"Well, where?" demanded Jack.

"Abroad," replied Sergei, put the car into first gear, and drove off.

Jack cursed, ran back to his own cab, paid the fare—three dollars—and walked quickly into the airport. He stood still while checking in every direction. Moments later he spotted Anna leaving the check-in counter and heading toward the escalator. He didn't move again until she was out of sight. By the time he had reached the top of the escalator, Anna was already in the café. She'd taken a seat in the far corner from where she could observe everything and, more important, everybody. Not only was *he* being followed, but now the person he was following was also looking out for him. She had already mastered being a tool so she could identify her target. Jack feared that this could end up as a case study at Quantico on how not to trail a suspect.

He retraced his steps back down to the ground floor and checked the departure board. There were only five international flights out of Bucharest that day: Moscow, Hong Kong, New Delhi, London, and Berlin.

Jack dismissed Moscow, as it was due to depart in forty minutes and Anna was still in the café. New Delhi and Berlin weren't scheduled to leave until the early evening, and he also considered Hong Kong unlikely, although it departed in just under two hours, while the London flight was fifteen minutes later. It had to be London, he decided, but he still couldn't take the risk. He would purchase two tickets, one for Hong Kong, and a second for London. If she didn't appear at the departure gate for Hong Kong, he would board the flight to Heathrow. He wondered if her other pursuer was considering the same options, although he had a feeling she already knew which flight Anna was on.

Once Jack had purchased both tickets and explained twice that he had no luggage, he headed straight for Gate 33 to carry out a point surveillance. When he arrived, he took a seat among those passengers who were waiting at Gate 31 for the departure of their flight to Moscow. Jack even gave a moment's thought to going back to the hotel, packing his bags, paying the bill, and then returning to the airport, but only a moment's thought, because if the choice was between losing his bags or losing his quarry, it wasn't much of a choice.

Jack called the hotel manager at the Bucharesti International on his cell phone and, without going into any detail, explained what he needed doing. He could imagine the puzzled expression on the manager's face when he asked for his bags to be packed and left in reception. However, his suggestion that they add twenty dollars to his bill elicited the response, "I'll deal with it personally, sir."

Jack began to wonder if Anna was simply using the airport as a decoy while actually planning to return to Bucharest and pick up the red crate. He certainly couldn't have acted in a more unprofessional manner when he chased after her driver. But if she had worked out that someone was following her, as an amateur her first reaction would have been to try and lose her pursuer as quickly as possible. Only a professional would consider such a devious ploy when trying to shake someone off. Was it possible that Anna was a professional and still working for Fenston? In which case, was he the one being pursued?

Flight 3211 to Moscow was already boarding when Anna strolled by. She looked relaxed as she took her place among those waiting to board Cathay Pacific Flight 017 to Hong Kong. Once she was seated in the lounge, Jack slipped back down to the concourse and kept out of sight while he waited for the final call of Flight 017. Forty minutes later, he ascended the escalator a third time.

All three of them boarded the Boeing 747 bound for Hong Kong at different times. One in first class, one in business, and one in economy.

9/17

30

"I'M SORRY TO interrupt you, m'lady, but a large box of documents has been delivered by Simpson and Simpson, and I wondered where you wished me to put it."

Arabella put down her pen and looked up from the writing desk. "Andrews, do you remember when I was a child and you were second butler?"

"I do, m'lady," said Andrews, sounding somewhat puzzled.

"And every Christmas we used to play a game called Hunt the Parcel?"

"We did indeed, m'lady."

"And one Christmas you hid a box of chocolates. Victoria and I spent an entire afternoon trying to find them—but we never did."

"Yes, m'lady. Lady Victoria accused me of eating them and burst into tears."

"But you still refused to tell her where they were."

"That is correct, m'lady, but I must confess your father promised me sixpence if I didn't reveal where they were hidden."

"Why did he do that?" asked Arabella.

"His lordship hoped to spend a peaceful Christmas afternoon, enjoying a glass of port and a leisurely cigar, happy in the knowledge that you were both fully occupied."

"But we never found them," said Arabella.

"And I was never paid my sixpence," said Andrews.

"Can you still recall where you hid them?"

Andrews considered the question for a few moments, before a smile appeared on his face.

"Yes, m'lady," he said, "and for all I know, they are still there."

"Good, because I should like you to put the box that Simpson and Simpson have just delivered in the same place."

"As you wish, m'lady," said Andrews, trying to look as if he had some idea what his mistress was talking about.

"And next Christmas, Andrews, should I attempt to find them, you must be sure not to let me know where they are hidden."

"And will I receive sixpence on this occasion, m'lady?"

"A shilling," promised Arabella, "but only if no one else finds out where they are."

Anna settled herself into a window seat at the back of economy. If the man Fenston had sent to track her down was on the plane, as she suspected he was, at least Anna now knew what she was up against. She began to think about him and how he'd discovered that she would be in Bucharest. How did he know her mother's address, and was he already aware that her next stop was Tokyo?

The man she had watched from the check-in counter as he ran up to Sergei's taxi and tapped on the window wasn't hoping for a ride, although Sergei had clearly taken him for one. Anna wondered if it had been her phone calls to Tina that had given her away. She felt confident her close friend would never have betrayed her, so she must have become an unwitting accomplice. Leapman was well capable of tapping her phone and far worse.

Anna had purposely dropped clues in her last two conversations to find out if there was an eavesdropper, and they must have been picked up: *going home* and *there will be a lot of people like that where I'm going*. Next time she would plant a clue that would send Fenston's man in completely the wrong direction.

Jack sat in business class sipping a Diet Coke and trying to make some sense of the past two days. *If you're out there on your own, always pre-*

pare for the worst-case scenario, his SSA used to repeat ad nauseam to each new recruit.

He tried to think logically. He was pursuing a woman who had stolen a sixty-million-dollar painting, but had she left the picture in Bucharest, or had it been transferred into the new crate, with the intention of selling the painting to someone in Hong Kong? Then he turned his thoughts to the other person who was pursuing Anna. That was easier to explain. If Petrescu had stolen the painting, the woman was clearly employed by Fenston to follow her until she found out where the picture was. But how did she always know where Anna would be, and did she now realize that he was also following her? And what were her instructions once she'd caught up with the Van Gogh? Jack felt the only way he could redeem himself was to get a step ahead of both of them and somehow stay there.

He found himself falling into a trap that he regularly warned his junior officers to be wary of. Don't be lulled into believing that the suspect is innocent. A jury will make that decision for you. You must always assume they are guilty, and occasionally, very occasionally, be surprised. He didn't remember his instructor saying anything about what to do if you found the suspect attractive. Although there was a directive in the FBI training manual that stated: "Under no circumstances must an agent enter into a personal relationship with any person under investigation." In 1999 the guide had been updated following a congressional directive, when the words "male or female" had been added before "person."

But it still puzzled Jack what Anna intended to do with the Van Gogh. If she was about to try and sell the picture in Hong Kong, where would she deposit such a huge sum of money, and how could she hope to benefit from the spoils of her crime? Jack couldn't believe she was willing to live in Bucharest for the rest of her life.

And then he remembered that she had visited Wentworth Hall.

Krantz sat alone in first class. She always flew first class, because it allowed her to be the last on, and first off, any flight, especially when she knew exactly where her victim was traveling.

But now she was aware someone else was following Petrescu, she would have to be even more cautious. After all, she couldn't afford to kill Petrescu with an audience watching, even if it was an audience of one.

Krantz was puzzled by who the tall, dark-haired man could be and who he was reporting back to. Had Fenston sent someone else to check up on her or was the man working for a foreign government? If so, which one? It had to be Romanian or American. He was certainly a professional because she hadn't spotted him before, or after, his crass mistake with the yellow taxis. She assumed he must be an American. She hoped so, because if she had to kill him, that would be a bonus.

Krantz didn't relax on the long flight to Hong Kong. Her instructor in Moscow was fond of repeating that concentration usually lapsed on the fourth day. Tomorrow.

9/18

31

"THOSE PASSENGERS TRAVELING to onward destinations . . ."

"That's all I need," muttered Jack.

"What do you need, sir?" asked an attentive stewardess.

"Transit."

"Where is your final destination, sir?"

"I have no idea," said Jack. "What's the choice?"

The stewardess laughed. "Are you still hoping to travel east?"

"That makes sense."

"Then it has to be Tokyo, Manila, Sydney, or Auckland."

"Thank you," said Jack, thinking, that doesn't help, but adding out loud, "If I decided to spend the night in Hong Kong, I would have to go through passport control, whereas if I wanted transit . . ."

The stewardess continued to humor him, "When you disembark, sir, there are clear signs directing you to baggage claim or transit. Is your luggage booked through, sir, or will you be picking it up?"

"I don't have any luggage," Jack admitted.

The stewardess nodded, smiled, and left to attend to some of her more sane passengers.

Jack realized that once he disembarked he would have to move quickly if he hoped to locate a concealed vantage point from where he could observe Anna's next move—and not be observed by her other admirer.

Anna stared distractedly out of the cabin window as the plane descended smoothly into Chek Lap Kok airport.

She would never forget her first experience of flying into Hong Kong some years before. To begin with, it felt like a normal approach, and then at the last moment, without warning, the pilot banked steeply and headed straight for the hills. He then descended between the city high-rises, bringing gasps from first-timers, before finally bumping down the short runway into Kow-loon, as if he were auditioning for a part in a 1944 war movie. When the plane came to a halt, several of the passengers applauded. Anna was glad that the new airport meant she would not have to experience a repeat performance.

She checked her watch. Although the flight was running twenty minutes late, her onward connection wasn't scheduled for another couple of hours. She would use any spare time to pick up a guide to Tokyo, a city she had never visited before.

Once they'd come to a halt at the terminal gate, Anna progressed slowly down the aisle, waiting for other passengers to rescue their bags from the overhead lockers. She looked around, wondering if Fenston's man was watching her every move. She tried to remain calm, though in truth her heartbeat must have shot above a hundred every time a man even glanced in her direction. She felt sure he must have already disembarked and would now be lying in wait. Perhaps he even knew her final destination. Anna had already decided on the false piece of information she would drop when she next phoned Tina, one that would send Fenston's man flying in the wrong direction.

Anna stepped off the aircraft and looked around her for the sign. At the end of a long corridor, an arrow directed transit passengers to the left. She joined a handful of travelers heading for other destinations, while the majority of passengers turned right.

When she walked into the transit area, she was greeted by a neon-lit city, half as old as Swatch, lurking in wait for its imprisoned customers to part with their foreign currency. Anna strolled from shop to shop, admiring the latest fashions, electrical equipment, cell phones, and jewelry. Although she saw several items she would have considered in normal circumstances, because of her pecuniary predicament the only shop she thought about entering was a book store displaying foreign newspapers and all the latest best sellers—in several languages. She strolled across to the travel section, to be faced with row upon row of gazetteers of countries as far afield as Azerbaijan and Zanzibar.

Her eyes settled on the section on Japan, which included a shelf devoted to Tokyo. She picked up the Lonely Planet guide to Japan, along with a Berlitz miniguide to the capital. She began to flick through them.

Jack slipped into an electrical shop on the other side of the mall from where he had a clear sight line of his quarry. All he could make out was that she was standing below a large, multicolored TRAVEL sign. Jack would have liked to get close enough to discover which title was causing her to turn the pages so intently, but he knew he couldn't risk it. He began to count down the shelves in an attempt to pinpoint which country had monopolized her attention.

"Can I assist you, sir?" asked the young lady behind the counter.

"Not unless you have a pair of binoculars," said Jack, not taking his eyes off Anna.

"Several," replied the assistant, "and can I recommend this particular model? They are this week's special offer, reduced from ninety dollars to sixty, while stocks last."

Jack looked round as the young girl removed a pair of binoculars from the shelf behind her and placed them on the counter.

"Thank you," said Jack. He picked them up and focused them on Anna. She was still turning the pages of the same book but Jack couldn't make out the title.

"I'd like to see your latest model," he said, placing the special offer back on the counter. "One that could focus on a street sign at a hundred meters."

The assistant bent down, unlocked the display cabinet, and extracted another pair.

"These are Leica, top-of-the-line, 12 by 50," she assured him. "You could identify the label on the coffee they're serving in the café opposite."

Jack focused on the bookshop. Anna was replacing the book she had been reading, only to pick up the one next to it. He had to agree with the assistant, they were state-of-the-art. He could make out the word *Japan* and even the letters *TOKYO* that were displayed above the shelf Anna was taking so much interest in. Anna closed the book, smiled, and headed across to the counter. She also picked up a copy of the *Herald Tribune* as she waited in the line.

"They are good, yes?" said the assistant.

"Very good," said Jack, replacing the binoculars on the counter, "but I'm afraid they're out of my budget. Thank you," he added, before leaving the shop.

"Strange," said the girl to her colleague behind the counter. "I never even told him the price."

Anna had reached the head of the line and was paying for her two purchases when Jack headed off in the opposite direction. He joined another line at the far end of the concourse.

When he reached the front of the line, he asked for a ticket to Tokyo.

"Yes, sir. Which flight—Cathay Pacific or Japan Airlines?"

"When do they leave?" asked Jack.

"Japan Airlines will be boarding shortly, as the flight departs in forty minutes. Cathay's Flight three-zero-one is due to take off in an hour and a half."

"Japan Airlines, please," said Jack, "business class."

"How many bags will you be checking in?"

"Hand luggage only."

The sales assistant printed the ticket, checked his passport, and said, "If you proceed to Gate Seventy-one, Mr. Delaney, boarding is about to commence."

Jack walked back toward the coffee shop. Anna was sitting at the counter, engrossed in the book she had just purchased. He was even more careful to avoid her gaze, as he felt sure she now realized she was being followed. Jack spent the next few minutes purchasing goods from shops he wouldn't normally have visited, all made necessary by the woman perched on the corner stool in the coffee shop. He ended up with an overnight bag, which would be allowed on board as hand luggage, a pair of jeans, four shirts, four pairs of socks, four pairs of underpants, two ties (special offer), a packet of razors, shaving cream, aftershave, soap, toothbrush, and toothpaste. He hung around inside the pharmacy, waiting to see if Anna was about to move.

"Last call for passengers on Japan Airways Flight four-one-six to Tokyo. Please proceed immediately to Gate Seventy-one for final boarding."

Anna turned another page of her book, which convinced Jack that she must be booked onto the Cathay Pacific flight leaving an hour later. This time be would be waiting for her. He tugged at his overnight bag and followed the signs for Gate 71. Jack was among the last to board the aircraft.

Anna checked her watch, ordered another coffee, and turned her attention to the *Herald Tribune*. The pages were full of stories on the aftermath of 9/11, with a report on the memorial service held in Washington, D.C., attended by the president. Did her family and friends still believe that she was dead, or just missing? Had the news that she'd been seen in London already percolated back to New York? Clearly Fenston still wanted everyone to believe she was dead, at least until he got his hands on the Van Gogh. All that would change in Tokyo, if— Something made her look up, and she spotted a young man with thick, dark hair staring at her. He quickly looked away. She jumped off her stool and walked straight across to him.

"Are you following me, by any chance?" she demanded.

The man gave Anna a startled look. *"Non, non, mademoiselle, mais peut-être voulez-vous prendre un verre avec moi?"*

"This is the first call for . . ."

Two more eyes were also watching Anna as she apologized to the Frenchman, settled her bill, and made her way slowly to Gate 71.

Krantz only let her out of her sight after she'd boarded the plane.

Krantz was among the last passengers to board Flight CX 301. On entering the aircraft, she turned left and took her usual window seat in the front row. Krantz knew that Anna was seated at the back of economy, but she had no idea where the American was. Had he missed the flight, or was he roaming around Hong Kong searching for Petrescu?

32

JACK'S FLIGHT TOUCHED down at Narita international airport, Tokyo, thirty minutes late, but he wasn't anxious, because he was an hour ahead of both women, who would still be some thirty thousand feet above the Pacific. Once Jack had cleared customs, his first stop was the inquiry desk, where he asked what time the Cathay flight was due to land. In just over forty minutes.

He turned and faced the arrivals gate, then tried to work out in which direction Petrescu would go once she had cleared customs. What would be her first choice of transport into the city: taxi, rail, or bus? She would have to decide after she'd progressed a mere fifty yards. If she was still in possession of the crate, it would surely have to be a taxi. Having checked out every possible exit, Jack handed over five hundred dollars at a Bank of Tokyo booth in exchange for 53,868 yen. He placed the large-denomination notes in his wallet and returned to the arrivals hall, where he watched people assemble as they waited for the most recent arrivals. He looked up. Above him, to his left, was a mezzanine floor, which overlooked the hall. He walked up the stairs and inspected the space. Although the area was cramped, it was nevertheless ideal. There were two telephone booths fixed to the wall, and if he stood behind the second one, he could look down on any new arrivals without being spotted. Jack checked the board. CX 301 was due to land in twenty minutes. Easily enough time for him to carry out his final task.

He left the airport and stood in the taxi line, which was being organized by a man in a light blue suit and white gloves, who not only controlled the taxis but directed the passengers. When he reached the front, Jack climbed into the back of the distinctive green Toyota and instructed a surprised driver to park on the other side of the road.

"Wait here until I return," he added, leaving his new bag on the backseat. "I should be about thirty minutes, forty at the most." He removed a five-thousand-yen note from his wallet. "And you can keep the meter running. The driver nodded, but looked puzzled.

Jack returned to the airport to find that Flight CX 301 had just landed. He walked back up to the terrace and took his place behind the second phone booth. He waited to see who would be the first through the door with the familiar green and white Cathay Pacific label attached to their luggage. It had been a long time since Jack had waited to pick up *one* girl at an airport, let alone two. And would he even recognize his blind date?

The indicator board flicked over once again. Passengers on Flight CX 301 were now in the baggage hall. Jack began to concentrate. He didn't have long to wait. Krantz was first through the door—she needed to be; she had work to do. She headed for a melee of eagerly waiting locals, who weren't much taller than her. She nestled in behind them before she risked turning around. From time to time, the patient crowd moved like a slow wave, as some people departed, while others took their place. Krantz moved with the tide so that no one would notice her. But a blonde crew cut standing among a black-haired race made Jack's task a lot easier. If she then followed Anna, Jack would know for certain whom he was up against.

While Jack kept one eye on the thin, short, muscular woman with the blonde crew cut, he repeatedly turned back to check on the new arrivals that were now swarming through the exit in little clusters, several with green and white labels attached to their luggage. Jack gingerly took a step forward, praying she wouldn't look up, but her eyes remained doggedly fixed on the new arrivals.

She must have also worked out that there were only three exit routes for Anna to consider, because she was strategically placed to pounce in whichever direction her quarry selected.

Jack slipped a hand into an inside pocket, slowly removed the latest Samsung cell phone, flicked it open, and focused it directly toward the crowd below him. For a moment he couldn't see her, then an elderly man stepped forward to greet his visitor and she was exposed for a split second. *Click,* then once again she disappeared. Jack continually switched his attention back to the new arrivals, who were still pouring out into the hall. As he turned back, a mother bent down to pick up an errant child and she was exposed again, *click,* and just as suddenly disappeared from sight. Jack turned to watch as Anna came striding through the swing doors. He closed his phone, hoping that one of the two images would he enough for the tech guys to identify her.

Jack's wasn't the only head to turn when the slim, blonde American strode into the arrivals hall pushing a luggage cart with a suitcase and a wooden crate on board. He stepped back into the shadows the moment Petrescu paused to look up. She was checking the exit boards. She turned right. Taxi.

Jack knew that Petrescu would also have to join a long line before she could hope to get a cab, so he allowed both women to leave the airport before he came down from the balcony. When he eventually descended, Jack took a circuitous route back to his taxi. He walked to the far end of the hall and then out onto the sidewalk. He ducked behind a waiting bus on his way to the underground parking lot, then continued along the second row of cars and out of the far end of the garage. He was relieved to see the green Toyota still waiting for him, engine running, meter ticking. He climbed into the backseat and said to the driver, "See the blonde with a crew cut, seventh in the taxi line? I want you to follow her, but she mustn't know."

Jack's eyes returned to Petrescu, who was fifth in the line. When she reached the front, she didn't climb into the waiting taxi, but turned round and walked slowly to the back of the line. Clever girl, thought Jack, as he waited to see how Crew Cut would react. Jack tapped his own driver on the shoulder, and said, "Don't move," when Crew Cut stepped into the back of a taxi, which drove off and disappeared around the corner. Jack knew she'd be parked in a side turning only a few yards away waiting for Petrescu to reappear. Eventually, Petrescu reached the front again. Jack tapped his driver on the shoulder and said, "Follow that woman, stay well back, but don't lose her."

"But it isn't the same woman," queried the taxi driver.

"I know," said Jack. "Change of plan."

The driver looked perplexed. Japanese don't understand *change of plan*.

As Petrescu's taxi drove past him and onto the freeway, Jack watched an identical vehicle come out of a side road and slip in behind her. At last it was Jack's turn to be the pursuer and not the pursued.

For the first time, Jack was thankful for the notorious snarl-ups and never-ending traffic jams that are the accepted norm for anyone driving from Narita airport into the city center. He was able to keep his distance while never losing sight of either of them.

It was another hour before Petrescu's taxi came to a halt outside the Hotel Seiyo in the Ginza district. A bellboy stepped forward to help with her luggage, but the moment he saw the wooden crate he motioned for a colleague to assist him. Jack didn't consider entering the hotel until some time after Petrescu and the box had disappeared inside. But not Crew Cut. She was already secreted in the far corner of the lobby with a clear view of the staircase and elevators, out of sight of anyone working behind the reception desk.

The moment he spotted her, Jack retreated through the swing doors and back out into the courtyard. A bellboy rushed forward. "Do you want a taxi, sir?"

"No, thank you," he said, and, pointing to a glass door on the other side of the courtyard, inquired, "What's that?"

"Hotel health club, sir," replied the bellboy.

Jack nodded, walked around the perimeter of the courtyard, and entered the building. He strolled up to reception.

"Room number, sir?" he was asked by a young man sporting a hotel tracksuit.

"I can't remember," said Jack.

"Name?"

"Petrescu."

"Ah, yes, Dr. Petrescu," said the young man looking at his screen. "Room 118. Do you need a locker, sir?"

"Later," said Jack. "When my wife joins me."

He took a seat by the window overlooking the courtyard and waited for Anna to reappear. He noted that there were always two or three taxis waiting in line, so following her should not prove too much of a problem.

But if she reappeared without the crate, he was in no doubt that Crew Cut, who was still sitting in the lounge, would be working on a plan to relieve his "wife" of its contents.

While Jack sat patiently by the window, he flicked open his cell phone and dialed through to Tom in London. He tried not to think what time it was.

"Where are you?" asked Tom, when he saw the name GOOD COP flash up on his screen.

"Tokyo."

"What's Petrescu doing there?"

"I can't be sure, but I wouldn't be surprised if she isn't trying to sell a rare painting to a well-known collector."

"Have you found out who the other interested party is?"

"No," said Jack, "but I did manage to get a couple of images of her at the airport."

"Well done," said Tom.

"I'm sending the pictures through to you now," said Jack. He keyed a code into his phone and the images appeared on Tom's screen moments later.

"They're a bit blurred," was Tom's immediate response, "but I'm sure the tech guys can clean them up enough to try and work out who she is. Any other information?"

"She's around five foot, slim, with a blonde crew cut and the shoulders of a swimmer."

"Anything else?" asked Tom, as he made notes.

"Yes, when you've finished with the American mug shots, move on to Eastern Europe. I've got a feeling she may be Russian or possibly Ukrainian."

"Or even Romanian?" suggested Tom.

"Oh, God, I'm so dumb," said Jack.

"Bright enough to get two photos. No one else has managed that, and they may turn out to be the biggest break we've had in this case."

"I'd be only too happy to bask in a little glory," admitted Jack, "but the truth is that both of them are well aware of my existence."

"Then I'd better find out who she is pretty fast. I'll be back in touch as soon as the boys in the basement come up with anything."

———

Tina turned on the switch under her desk. The little screen on the corner came on. Fenston was on the phone. She flicked up the switch to his private line and listened.

"You were right," said a voice, "she's in Japan."

"Then she probably has an appointment with Nakamura. All his details are in your file. Don't forget that getting the painting is more important than removing Petrescu."

Fenston put the phone down.

Tina was confident that the voice fitted the woman she had seen in the chairman's car. She must warn Anna.

Leapman walked into the room.

33

ANNA STEPPED OUT of the shower, grabbed a towel, and began drying her hair. She glanced across at the digital clock in the corner of the TV screen. It was just after twelve, the hour when most Japanese businessmen go to their club for lunch. Not the time to disturb Mr. Nakamura.

Once she was dry, Anna put on the white toweling bathrobe that hung behind the bathroom door. She sat on the end of the bed and opened her laptop. She tapped in her password, MIDAS, which accessed a file on the richest art collectors around the globe: Gates, Cohen, Lauder, Magnier, Nakamura, Rales, Wynn. She moved the cursor across to his name. *Takashi Nakamura, industrialist. Tokyo University 1966–70, B.Sc. in engineering. UCLA 1971–73, M.A. Economics. Joined Maruha Steel Company 1974, Director 1989, Chief Executive Officer 1997, Chairman 2001.* Anna scrolled down to Maruha Steel. Last year's annual balance sheet showed a turnover of nearly three billion dollars, with profits of over four hundred million. Mr. Nakamura owned 22 percent of the company and, according to *Forbes,* was the ninth richest man in the world. Married with three children, two girls and a boy. Under other interests, only two words appeared: *golf* and *art.* No details of his fabled high handicap or his valuable Impressionist collection, thought to be among the finest in private hands.

Nakamura had made several statements over the years, saying that the pictures belonged to the company. Although Christie's never made such matters public, it was well known by those in the art world that Nakamura had been the underbidder for Van Gogh's *Sunflowers* in 1987, when he was beaten by his old friend and rival Yasuo Goto, chairman of Yasuda Fire and Marine Insurance Company, whose hammer bid was $39,921,750.

Anna hadn't been able to add a great deal to Mr. Nakamura's profile since leaving Sotheby's. The Degas she had purchased on his behalf, *Dancing Class with Mme. Minette,* had proved a wise investment, which Anna hoped he would remember. She wasn't in any doubt that she had chosen the right man to help pull off her coup.

She unpacked her suitcase and selected a smart blue suit with a skirt that fell just below the knees, a cream shirt, and low-heeled navy leather shoes; no makeup, no jewelry. While she pressed her clothes, Anna thought about a man she had met only once, and wondered if she had made any lasting impression on him. When she was dressed, Anna checked herself in the mirror. Exactly what a Japanese businessman would expect a Sotheby's executive to wear.

Anna looked up his private number on her laptop. She sat on the end of the bed, picked up the phone, took a deep breath, and dialled the eight digits.

"*Hai, Shacho-Shitso desu,*" announced a high-pitched voice.

"Good afternoon, my name is Anna Petrescu. Mr. Nakamura may remember me from Sotheby's."

"Are you hoping to be interviewed?"

"Er, no, I simply want to speak to Mr. Nakamura."

"One moment please, I will see if he is free to take your call."

How could she possibly expect him to remember her after only one meeting?

"Dr. Petrescu, how nice to hear from you again. I hope you are well?"

"I am, thank you, Nakamura-san."

"Are you in Tokyo? Because if I am not mistaken it is after midnight in New York."

"Yes, I am, and I wondered if you would be kind enough to see me."

"You weren't on the interview list, but you are now. I have half an hour free at four o'clock this afternoon. Would that suit you?"

"Yes, that would be just fine," said Anna.

"Do you know where my office is?"

"I have the address."

"Where are you staying?"

"The Seiyo."

"Not the usual haunt for Sotheby's, who, if I remember correctly, prefer the Imperial." Anna's mouth went dry. "My office is about twenty minutes from the hotel. I look forward to seeing you at four o'clock. Good-bye, Dr. Petrescu."

Anna replaced the receiver and for some time didn't budge from the end of the bed. She tried to recall his exact words. What had his secretary meant when she asked, "Are you hoping to be interviewed," and why did Mr. Nakamura say, "You weren't on the interview list, but you are now?" Was he expecting her call?

Jack leant forward to take a closer look. Two bellboys were coming out of the hotel carrying the same wooden crate that Anna had exchanged with Anton Teodorescu on the steps of the academy in Bucharest. One of them spoke to the driver of the front taxi, who jumped out and carefully placed the wooden crate in the trunk. Jack rose slowly from his chair and walked across to the window, making sure he remained out of sight. He waited in anticipation, realizing it could well be another false alarm. He checked the taxi rank: four cars waiting in line. He glanced toward the entrance of the health club and calculated he could reach the second taxi in about twenty seconds.

He looked back at the hotel's sliding doors, wondering if Petrescu was about to appear. But the next person who caused the doors to slide open was Crew Cut, who slipped past the doorman and out onto the main road. Jack knew she wouldn't take one of the hotel taxis and risk being remembered—a chance Jack would have to take.

Jack switched his attention back to the hotel entrance, aware that Crew Cut would now be sitting in a taxi well out of sight, waiting for both of them.

Seconds later, Petrescu appeared, dressed as if she was about to attend a board meeting. The doorman escorted her to the front taxi and opened the back door for her. The driver eased out onto the road and joined the afternoon traffic.

Jack was seated in the back of the second taxi before the doorman had a chance to open the door for him.

"Follow that cab," said Jack, pointing ahead of him, "and if you don't lose it, you can double the fare." The driver shot off. "But," continued Jack, "don't make it too obvious," well aware that Crew Cut would be in one of the numerous green vehicles ahead of them.

Petrescu's taxi turned left at Ginza and headed north, away from the fashionable shopping area, toward the city's prestigious business district of Marunouchi. Jack wondered if this could be the appointment with a potential buyer, and found himself sitting on the edge of his seat in anticipation.

Petrescu's green taxi turned left at the next set of lights and Jack repeated firmly, "Don't lose her." The driver switched lanes, moved to within three cars' length of her car and stuck like a limpet. Both cabs came to a halt at the next red light. Petrescu's taxi was indicating right and, when the lights turned green, several other cars followed in her wake. Jack knew Crew Cut would be in one of them. As they swung onto the three-lane highway, Jack could see a string of overhead lights awaiting them, all of them on green. He swore under his breath. He preferred red lights; stopping and starting was always better when you needed to remain in contact with a mark.

They all moved safely through the first green and then the second, but when the third light turned amber Jack's taxi was the last to cross the intersection. As they passed in front of the Imperial Palace gardens, he tapped the driver on the shoulder in appreciation. He leaned forward, willing the next light to remain green. It turned amber just as Petrescu's taxi crossed the intersection. "Go, go," shouted Jack, as two of the taxis in front of them followed Anna across, but instead of the driver pressing hard down on his accelerator and running the lights, he came meekly to a halt. Jack was about to explode, when a police patrol car drew up beside them. Jack stared ahead. The green Toyota had come to a halt at the next light. He was still in with a chance. The lights were running in a sequence and all changed within seconds of each other. Jack willed the patrol car to turn right so they could make up any lost ground, but it remained resolutely by their side. He watched as her green taxi swung left onto Eitaidori Avenue. He held his breath, once again willing the green light not to change, but it turned amber and the car ahead of them came to a halt, having no doubt spotted the patrol car in its wake. When the light eventually returned to green, the longest minute Jack could remember, his driver quickly swung left, only to come face-to-face with a sea of green. It was bad enough that he'd lost Petrescu, but the thought that Crew Cut was probably still on her tail caused Jack to turn and curse the patrol car, just as it turned right and drifted away.

Krantz watched attentively as the green taxi edged across to the inside lane and drew up outside a modern, white marble building in Otemachi. The sign above the entrance, MARUHA STEEL COMPANY, was in Japanese and English, as is common with most international companies in Tokyo.

Krantz allowed her taxi to pass the front of the building before she asked the driver to draw into the curb. She turned and watched through the rearview window as Anna stepped out. Her driver walked to the back of the taxi and opened the trunk. Anna joined him as the doorman came running down the steps to assist. Krantz continued to watch as the two men carried the wooden box up the steps and into the building.

Once they were out of sight, Krantz paid her fare, stepped out of the car, and slipped into the shadows. She never kept a cab waiting unless absolutely necessary. That way, they were unlikely to remember her. She needed to think quickly, in case Petrescu suddenly reappeared. Krantz recalled her brief. Her first priority was to repossess the painting. Once she had done that, she was free to kill Petrescu, but as she had just got off a plane she didn't have a weapon to hand. She was satisfied that the American no longer posed a threat and briefly wondered if he was still roaming around Hong Kong in search of Petrescu, or the picture, or both.

It was beginning to look as if the painting had reached its destination; there had been a full page on Nakamura in the file Fenston had given her. If Petrescu reappeared with the crate, she must have failed, which would make it that much easier for Krantz to carry out both of her assignments. If she walked out only carrying her briefcase, Krantz would need to make an instant decision. She checked to make sure that there was a regular flow of taxis. Several passed her in the next few minutes, half of them empty.

The next person through the door was the taxi driver, who climbed back behind the wheel of his Toyota. She waited for Petrescu to follow, but the empty green cab swung onto the street, in search of its next customer. Krantz had a feeling that this was going to be a long wait.

She stood in the shadows of a department store on the opposite side of the road and waited. She looked up and down a street full of designer label shops, which she despised, until her eyes settled on an establishment that she had only read about in the past and had always wanted to visit: not Gucci, not Burberry, not Calvin Klein, but the Nozaki Cutting Tool Shop, which nestled uneasily among its more recent neighbors.

Krantz was drawn to the entrance as a filing is to a magnet. As she crossed the road, her eyes remained fixed on the front door of the Maruha Steel Company in case Petrescu made an unscheduled reappearance. She suspected that Petrescu's meeting with Mr. Nakamura would last some considerable time. After all, even he didn't spend that amount of money without expecting several questions to be answered.

Once across the road, Krantz stared into the window, like a child for whom Christmas had come three months early. Tweezers, nail clippers, left-handed scissors, Swiss Army knives, long-bladed tailor's shears, a Victorinox machete with a fifteen-inch blade—all played second fiddle to a ceremonial samurai sword (circa 1783). Krantz felt that she had been born in the wrong century.

She stepped inside to be met with row upon row of kitchen knives, for which Mr. Takai, a samurai's descendant, had become so famous. She spotted the proprietor standing in one corner, sharpening knives for his customers. Krantz recognized him immediately, and would have liked to shake hands with the maestro—her equivalent of Brad Pitt—but she knew she would have to forgo that particular pleasure.

While keeping a wary eye on the Maruha Company's front door Krantz began to study the hand-forged Japanese implements—razor-sharp and deceptively light, with the name NOZAKI stamped into the shoulder of each blade, as if, like Cartier, they wished to emphasize that a counterfeit was not acceptable.

Krantz had long ago accepted that she could not risk carrying her preferred weapon of death on a plane, so she was left with no choice but to pick up a local product in whichever country Fenston needed a client account closed indefinitely.

Krantz began the slow process of selection while being serenaded by suzumushi—bell crickets—in tiny bamboo cages suspended from the ceiling. She stared back at the entrance door across the road, but there was still no sign of Petrescu. She returned to her task, first testing the different categories of knife—fruit, vegetable, bread, meat—for weight, balance, and size of blade. No more than eight inches, never less than four.

In a matter of minutes, Krantz was down to three, before she finally settled on the award-winning Global GS5—fourteen centimeters, which, it was claimed, would cut through a rump steak as easily as a ripe melon.

She handed her chosen instrument to an assistant, who smiled—such a thin neck—and wrapped the kitchen knife in rice paper. Krantz paid in yen. Dollars would have drawn attention to her, and she didn't possess a credit card. One last look at Mr. Takai before she reluctantly left the shop to return to the anonymity of the shadows on the other side of the road.

While she waited for Petrescu to reappear, Krantz removed the rice paper from her latest acquisition, desperate to try it out. She slipped the blade into a sheath that had been tailor-made to fit on the inside of her jeans. It fit perfectly, like a gun in a holster.

34

THE RECEPTIONIST COULD not hide her surprise when the doorman appeared carrying a wooden crate. She placed her hands in front of her mouth—an unusually animated response for a Japanese.

Anna offered no explanation, only her name. The receptionist checked the list of applicants to be interviewed by the chairman that afternoon and placed a tick next to "Dr. Petrescu."

"Mr. Nakamura is interviewing another candidate at the moment," she said, "but should be free shortly."

"Interviewing them for what?" asked Anna.

"I have no idea," said the receptionist, seeming equally puzzled that an interviewee needed to ask such a question.

Anna sat in reception and glanced at the crate that was propped up against the wall. She smiled at the thought of how she would go about asking someone to part with sixty million dollars.

Punctuality is an obsession with the Japanese, so Anna was not surprised when a smartly dressed lady appeared at two minutes to four, bowed, and invited Anna to follow her. She too looked at the wooden box, but showed no reaction other than to ask, "Would you like it to be taken to the chairman's office?"

"Yes, please," said Anna, again without explanation.

The secretary led Anna down a long corridor, passing several doors that displayed no name, title, or rank. When they reached the last door, the secretary knocked quietly, opened it, and announced, "Dr. Petrescu."

Mr. Nakamura rose from behind his desk and came forward to greet Anna, whose mouth was wide open. A reaction not caused by the short, slim, dark-haired man who looked as if he had his suits tailored in Paris or Milan. It was Mr. Nakamura's office that caused Anna to gasp. The room was a perfect square and one of the four walls was a single pane of glass. Anna stared out onto a tranquil garden, a stream winding from one corner to the other, crossed by a wooden bridge and bordered by willow trees, whose branches cascaded over the rails.

On the wall behind the chairman's desk was a magnificent painting, duplicating exactly the same scene. Anna closed her mouth and turned to face her host.

Mr. Nakamura smiled, clearly delighted with the effect his Monet had created, but his first question equally shocked her.

"How did you manage to survive 9/11, when, if I recall correctly, your office was in the North Tower?"

"I was very lucky," replied Anna quietly, "although I fear that some of my colleagues . . ."

Mr. Nakamura raised a hand. "I apologize," he said. "How tactless of me. Shall we begin the interview by testing your remarkable photographic memory and first ask you the provenance of all three paintings in the room? Shall we begin with the Monet?"

"*Willows at Vetheuil*," said Anna. "Its previous owner was a Mr. Clark of Sangton, Ohio. It was part of Mrs. Clark's divorce settlement when her husband decided to part with her, his third wife, which meant sadly that he had to part with his third Monet. Christie's sold the oil for twenty-six million dollars, but I had no idea you were the purchaser."

Mr. Nakamura revealed the same smile of pleasure.

Anna turned her attention to the opposite wall and paused. "I have for some time wondered where that particular painting ended up," she said. "It's a Renoir, of course. *Madame Duprez and Her Children,* also known as *The Reading Lesson*. It was sold in Paris by Roger Duprez, whose grandfather purchased it from the artist in 1868. I therefore have no way of knowing how much you paid for the oil." Anna added, as she turned her attention to the final piece. "Easy," she declared, smiling. "It's one of

Manet's late Salon works, probably painted in 1871—" she paused "—entitled *Dinner at the Café Guerbois*. You will have observed that his mistress is seated in the right-hand corner, looking directly out at the artist."

"And the previous owner?"

"Lady Charlotte Churchill, who, following the death of her husband, was forced to sell it to meet death duties."

Nakamura bowed. "The position is yours."

"The position, Nakamura-san?" said Anna, puzzled.

"You are not here to apply for the job as the director of my foundation?"

"No," said Anna, suddenly realizing what the receptionist had meant when she said that the chairman was interviewing another candidate. "Although I am flattered that you would consider me, Nakamura-san, I actually came to see you on a completely different matter."

The chairman nodded, clearly disappointed, and then his eyes settled on the wooden box.

"A small gift," said Anna, smiling.

"If that is the case, and you will forgive the pun, I cannot open your offering until you have left, otherwise I will insult you." Anna nodded, well aware of the custom. "Please have a seat, young lady."

Anna smiled.

"Now, what is your real purpose in visiting me?" he asked as he leaned back in his chair and stared at her intently.

"I believe I have a painting that you will be unable to resist."

"As good as the Degas pastel?" asked Nakamura, showing signs of enjoying himself.

"Oh yes," she said, a little too enthusiastically.

"Artist?"

"Van Gogh."

Nakamura smiled an inscrutable smile that gave no sign if he was or wasn't interested.

"Title?"

"*Self-Portrait with Bandaged Ear.*"

"With a famous Japanese print reproduced on the wall behind the artist, if I remember correctly," said Nakamura.

"*Geishas in a Landscape,*" said Anna, "demonstrating Van Gogh's fascination with Japanese culture."

"You should have been christened Eve," said Nakamura. "But now it's my turn." Anna looked surprised, but didn't speak. "I presume that it has to be the Wentworth *Self-Portrait*, purchased by the fifth marquis?"

"Earl."

"Earl. Ah, will I ever understand English titles? I always think of *Earl* as an American first name."

"Original owner?" inquired Anna.

"Dr. Gachet, Van Gogh's friend and admirer."

"And the date?"

"Eighteen eighty-nine," replied Nakamura, "when Van Gogh resided at Arles, sharing a studio with Paul Gauguin."

"And how much did Dr. Gachet pay for the piece?" asked Anna, aware that few people on earth would have considered teasing this man.

"It is always thought that Van Gogh only sold one painting in his lifetime, *The Red Vineyard*. However, Dr. Gachet was not only a close friend, but unquestionably his benefactor and patron. In the letter he wrote after receiving the picture, he enclosed a check for six hundred francs."

"Eight hundred," said Anna, as she opened her briefcase and handed over a copy of the letter. "My client is in possession of the original," she assured him.

Nakamura read the letter in French, requesting no assistance with a translation. He looked up and smiled. "What figure do you have in mind?" he asked.

"Sixty million dollars," said Anna without hesitation.

For a moment, the inscrutable face appeared puzzled, but he didn't speak for some time. "Why is such an acknowledged masterpiece so underpriced?" he asked eventually. "There must be some conditions attached."

"The sale must not be made public," said Anna in reply.

"That has always been my custom, as you well know," said Nakamura.

"You will not resell the work for at least ten years."

"I buy pictures," said Nakamura. "I sell steel."

"During the same period of time, the painting must not be displayed in a public gallery."

"Who are you protecting, young lady?" asked Nakamura without warning: "Bryce Fenston or Victoria Wentworth?"

Anna didn't reply, and now understood why the chairman of Sotheby's had once remarked that you underestimate this man at your peril.

"It was impertinent of me to ask such a question," said Nakamura. "I apologize," he added, as he rose from his place. "Perhaps you would be kind enough to allow me to consider your offer overnight." He bowed low, clearly indicating that the meeting was over.

"Of course, Nakamura-san," she said, returning the bow.

"Please drop the *san*, Dr. Petrescu. In your chosen field, I am not your equal."

She wanted to say, *Please call me Anna; in your chosen field, I know nothing*—but she lost her nerve.

Nakamura walked across to join her, and glanced at the wooden box. "I will look forward to finding out what is in the box. Perhaps we can meet again tomorrow, Dr. Petrescu, after I've had a little more time to consider your proposition."

"Thank you, Mr. Nakamura."

"Shall we say ten o'clock? I'll send my driver to pick you up at nine forty."

Anna gave a farewell bow and Mr. Nakamura returned the compliment. He walked to the door and as he opened it, added, "I only wish you *had* applied for the job."

Krantz was still standing in the shadows when Petrescu came out of the building. The meeting must have gone well because a limousine was waiting for her with a chauffeur holding open the back door, and, more significant, there was no sign of the wooden box. Krantz was left with two choices. She was confident that Petrescu would be returning to the hotel for the night, while the painting must still be in the building. She made her choice.

Anna sat back in the chairman's car and relaxed for the first time in days, confident that even if Mr. Nakamura didn't agree to sixty million, he would still make a realistic offer. Otherwise why put his car at her disposal and invite her to return the following day?

When Anna was dropped outside the Seiyo, she went straight to the reception desk and picked up her key before heading toward the elevator.

If she had turned right instead of left, she would have walked straight past a frustrated American.

Jack's eyes never left her as she stepped into an empty elevator. She was on her own. No sign of the package and, perhaps more significant, no sign of Crew Cut. She must have made the decision to stay with the painting rather than with its courier. Jack had to quickly decide what he would do if Petrescu reappeared with her bags and left for the airport. At least he hadn't unpacked this time.

Krantz had been standing in different shadows for nearly an hour, only moving with the sun, when the chairman's car returned and parked outside the entrance to Maruha Steel. A few moments later, the front doors slid open and Mr. Nakamura's secretary appeared with a man in a red uniform who was carrying the wooden crate. The driver opened the trunk, while the doorman placed the painting in the back. The driver listened as the secretary passed on the chairman's instructions. The chairman needed to make several calls to America and England overnight, and would therefore be staying in the company flat. He had seen the picture and wanted it to be delivered to his home in the country.

Krantz checked the traffic. She knew she'd get one chance, and then only if the lights were red. She was thankful it was a one-way street. She already knew that the lights at the far end of the road would remain on green for forty-five seconds. During that time, Krantz calculated about thirteen cars crossed the intersection. She stepped out of the shadows and moved stealthily down the sidewalk, like a cat, aware that she was about to risk one of her nine lives.

The chairman's black limousine emerged onto the street and joined the early evening traffic. The light was green, but there were fifteen cars ahead of him. Krantz stood exactly opposite where she thought the vehicle would come to a halt. When the light turned red, she walked slowly toward the limousine; after all, she had another forty-five seconds. When she was only a pace away, Krantz fell on to her right shoulder and rolled under the car. She gripped the two sides of the outer frame firmly and, spread-eagled, pulled herself up. One of the advantages of being four foot eleven and weighing less than a hundred pounds. When the lights turned green and the chairman's car moved off, she was nowhere to be seen.

Once, in the Romanian hills when escaping from the rebels, Krantz had stuck like a limpet to the bottom of a two-ton truck as it traveled for miles across rough terrain. She survived for fifty-one minutes, and when the sun finally set, she fell to the ground, exhausted. She then trekked across country to safety, jogging the last fourteen miles.

The limousine drove at an uneven pace through the city, and it was another twenty minutes before the driver turned off the highway and began to climb into the hills. A few minutes later, another turn, a much smaller road, and far less traffic. Krantz wanted to fall off, but knew that every minute she could cling on would be to her advantage. The car came to a halt at a crossroads, turned sharp left, and continued along what appeared to be a wide, uneven path. When they stopped at the next crossroads, Krantz listened attentively. A passing lorry was holding them up.

She slowly released her right arm, which was almost numb, unsheathed the knife from her jeans, turned to one side and thrust the blade into the right-hand rear tire, again and again, until she heard a loud hissing sound. As the car moved off, she fell to the ground and didn't move an inch until she could no longer hear the engine. She rolled over to the side of the road and watched the limousine as it drove higher into the hills. She didn't attempt to get up until the car was out of sight.

Once the limousine had disappeared over the hill, she pushed herself up and began to carry out a series of stretching exercises. She wasn't in a hurry. After all, it would be waiting for her on the other side of the hill. Once Krantz had recovered, she began jogging slowly toward the brow of the hill. Some miles ahead of her, she could see a magnificent mansion nestling in the hills that dominated the surrounding landscape.

When Krantz came over the rise, she saw the chauffeur in the distance, on one knee, staring at the flat tire. She checked up and down what was clearly a private road that probably led only to the Nakamura residence. As she approached, the driver looked up and smiled. Krantz returned the smile and jogged up to his side. He was about to speak when, with one swift movement of her left leg, Krantz kicked him in the throat, then in the groin. She watched as he collapsed on the ground, like a puppet whose strings had been cut. For a moment, she considered slitting his throat, but now she had the painting, why bother, when she would have the pleasure of cutting someone else's throat tonight. And in any case, she wasn't being paid for this one.

Once again Krantz looked up and down the road. Still clear. She ran to the front of the limousine and removed the keys from the ignition, before returning to unlock the trunk. The lid swung up and her eyes settled on the wooden crate. She would have smiled, but first she needed to make sure that she'd earned the first million dollars.

Krantz grabbed a heavy screwdriver from the tool kit in the trunk and wedged it into a crack in the top right-hand corner of the crate. It took all of her strength to wrench the lid open, only to find her prize was covered in bubble wrap. She tore at it with her bare hands. When the last remnant had been removed, she stared down at the prize-winning painting by Danuta Sekalska, entitled *Freedom*.

Jack waited for another hour, one eye on the door for Crew Cut, the other on the elevator for Petrescu, but neither appeared. Yet another hour passed, by which time Jack was convinced Anna must be staying over-night. He walked wearily up to reception and asked if they had a vacant room.

"Name, sir," asked the booking clerk.

"Fitzgerald," Jack replied.

"Your passport, please?"

"Certainly," said Jack, taking a passport out of an inside pocket and handing the document over.

"How many nights will you be staying with us, Mr. Fitzgerald?"

Jack would have liked to be able to answer that question.

9/19

35

WHEN ANNA WOKE the next morning, the first thing she did was to phone Wentworth Hall.

"It's going to be a close-run thing," warned Arabella, once Anna had imparted her news.

"What do you mean?" asked Anna.

"Fenston has issued a bankruptcy order against the estate, giving me fourteen days to clear the debt or he'll put Wentworth Hall on the market. So let's hope Nakamura doesn't find out, because if he does, it will certainly weaken your bargaining position and might even cause him to have second thoughts."

"I'm seeing him at ten o'clock this morning," said Anna. "I would call you back as soon as I find out his decision, but it will be the middle of the night."

"I don't care what time it is," said Arabella, "I'll be awake."

Once Anna had put the phone down, she began to go over her tactics for the meeting with Nakamura. In truth, she'd thought of little else for the past twelve hours.

She knew that Arabella would be happy with a sum that would clear her debts with Fenston Finance and allow her to make sure that the estate was safe from prying creditors, with enough over to cover any taxes. Anna calculated that sum to be around fifty million. She had already decided she would settle for that amount and the chance to return to New York, no longer with the sobriquet *missing* attached to her name, and be reacquainted with both loops in Central Park. She might even ask Nakamura for more details about the job she wasn't interviewed for.

Anna lingered in a bath that went from boiling to tepid—an indulgence she normally only allowed herself at weekends—as she continued to think through her approach to the meeting with Nakamura. She smiled at the thought of Nakamura opening his present. For all serious collectors, it's as much of a thrill to discover the next master as it is to pay a vast sum for an established one. When Nakamura saw the bold brushwork and the sheer flair, he would surely hang *Freedom* in his private collection. Always the ultimate test.

Anna thought long and hard about what she would wear for their second meeting. She settled on a beige linen dress with a modest hemline, a wide brown leather belt, and a simple gold necklace—an outfit that would be considered demure in New York but almost brash in Tokyo. Yesterday she'd dressed for her opening move, today for closing.

She opened her bag for a third time that morning to check that she had included a copy of Dr. Gachet's letter to Van Gogh, along with a simple one-page contract that was standard among recognized dealers. If she could agree on a price with Nakamura, Anna was going to ask for 10 percent down as an act of good faith, to be returned in full if, after inspecting the masterpiece, he was not satisfied. Anna felt that once he set his eyes on the original . . .

Anna checked her watch. The meeting with the chairman was at ten, and he had promised to send his limousine to pick her up at nine forty. She would be waiting in the lobby. The Japanese quickly lose patience with people who play games.

Anna took the elevator to the lobby and walked across to reception. "I expect to be checking out later today," she said, "and would like my bill prepared."

"Certainly, Dr. Petrescu," said the receptionist. "May I ask if you have had anything from the minibar?"

Anna thought for a moment. "Two Evian waters."

"Thank you," said the clerk, and began tapping the information into his computer as a bellboy came rushing up to her.

"Chauffeur here to collect you," was all he said, before leading Anna out to the waiting car.

Jack was already sitting in a taxi when she appeared at the entrance. He was determined he wasn't going to lose her a second time. After all, Crew Cut would be waiting for her, and she even knew where Anna was going.

Krantz had also spent the night in the center of Tokyo, but unlike Petrescu, not in a hotel bed. She had slept in the cab of a crane, some 150 feet above the city. She was confident that no one would come looking for her there. She stared down on Tokyo as the sun rose over the Imperial Palace. She checked her watch. Five fifty-six A.M. Time to descend if she were to leave unnoticed.

Once Krantz was back on the ground, she joined the office staff and early morning commuters as they disappeared underground and made their way to work.

Seven stops later, Krantz emerged in the Ginza and quickly retraced her steps to the Seiyo. She slipped back into the hotel, a regular guest who never booked in and never stayed overnight.

Krantz positioned herself in the corner of the lounge, where she had a perfect sight line of the two elevators, while she could be seen by only the most observant of waiters. It was a long wait, but then patience was a skill, developed over hours of practice—like any other skill.

The chauffeur closed the back door behind her. Not the same driver as the night before, Anna noted—she never forgot a face. He drove off without a word, and she became more and more confident as each mile passed.

When the chauffeur opened the back door again, Anna could see Mr. Nakamura's secretary waiting for her in the lobby. Sixty million dollars, Anna whispered to herself, as she climbed the steps, and I won't consider a cent less. The glass doors slid open, and the secretary bowed low.

"Good morning, Dr. Petrescu. Nakamura-san is looking forward to seeing you." Anna smiled and followed her down the long corridor of untitled offices. A gentle tap, and the secretary opened the door to the chairman's room and announced Dr. Petrescu.

Once again, Anna was stunned by the effect the room had on her, but this time managed to keep her mouth closed. Nakamura rose from behind his desk and bowed. Anna returned the compliment before he ushered her into a chair on the opposite side of the desk. He sat down. Yesterday's smile had been replaced by a grim visage. Anna assumed this was nothing more than a bargaining ploy.

"Dr. Petrescu," he began as he opened a file on the desk in front of him, "it seems that when we met yesterday, you were less than frank with me."

Anna felt her mouth go dry, as Nakamura glanced down at some papers. He removed his spectacles and looked directly at Anna. She tried not to flinch.

"You did not tell me, for instance, that you no longer work for Fenston Finance, nor did you allude to the fact that you were recently dismissed from the board for conduct unworthy of an officer of the bank." Anna tried to breathe regularly. "You also failed to inform me of the distressing news that Lady Victoria had been murdered, at a time when she had run up debts with your bank"—he put his glasses back on—"of over thirty million dollars. You also forgot to mention the small matter of the New York police being under the illusion that you are currently classified as missing, presumed dead. But perhaps the most damning indictment of all was your failure to let me know that the painting you were attempting to sell is, to use police jargon, stolen goods." Nakamura closed the file, removed his glasses once more, and stared directly at her. "Perhaps there is a simple explanation for such a sudden attack of amnesia?"

Anna wanted to jump up and run out of the room, but she couldn't move. Her father always told her when you've been found out, confess. She confessed everything. In fact, she even let him know where the painting was hidden. Once she finished, Nakamura didn't speak for some time. Anna sat and waited to be escorted unceremoniously from a building for the second time in just over a week.

"I now understand why you didn't wish the painting to be sold for at least ten years and certainly wouldn't want it to be put on public display. But I am bound to ask how you intend to square the circle with your former boss. It is clear to me that Mr. Fenston is more interested in holding on to such a valuable asset than having the debt cleared."

"But that's the point," said Anna. "Once the overdraft has been cleared, the Wentworth estate can sell the painting to whomever they wish."

Mr. Nakamura nodded. "Assuming that I accept your version of events, and if I was still interested in purchasing the *Self-Portrait,* I would want to make some conditions of my own."

Anna nodded.

"First, the painting would have to be purchased directly from Lady Arabella, and only after legal tenure had been properly established."

"I can see no objection to that," said Anna.

"Second, I would expect the work to be authenticated by the Van Gogh Museum in Amsterdam."

"That causes me no problems," said Anna.

"Then perhaps my third condition will cause you a problem," said Nakamura, "and that is the price I am willing to pay, as I do believe that I am, to use that ghastly but appropriate American expression, in the driving seat."

Anna nodded her reluctant agreement.

"If, and I repeat if, you are able to meet my other conditions, I am happy to offer, for the Wentworth Van Gogh *Self-Portrait with Bandaged Ear,* fifty million dollars, which I have worked out will not only clear Lady Arabella's debt but leave enough over to cover any taxes."

"But it could come under the hammer for seventy, even eighty million," Anna protested.

"That assumes *you* are not hammered long before then," Nakamura replied. "I apologize," he added immediately. "You have discovered my weakness for bad puns." He smiled for the first time. "However, I am advised that Mr. Fenston has recently issued a bankruptcy order against your client, and knowing the Americans as I do, it might be years before any legal action can be settled, and my London lawyers confirm that Lady Arabella is in no position to consider the crippling legal costs such a lengthy process would undoubtedly incur."

Anna took a deep breath. "If, and I repeat if"—Nakamura had the grace to smile—"I accept your terms, in return I would expect some gesture of goodwill."

"And what do you have in mind?"

"You will place 10 percent, five million dollars, in escrow with Lady

Arabella's solicitors in London, to be returned if you do not wish to purchase the original."

Nakamura shook his head. "No, Dr. Petrescu, I am unable to accept your gesture of goodwill."

Anna felt deflated.

"However, I am willing to place five million in escrow with *my* London lawyers, the full amount to be paid on exchange of contracts."

"Thank you," said Anna, unable to disguise a sigh of relief.

But Nakamura continued. "Having accepted your terms, I would also expect some gesture of goodwill in return," he said as he rose from behind his desk. Anna rose nervously. "Should the deal go through, you will give serious consideration to taking up the appointment as the CEO of my foundation."

Anna smiled but did not bow. She offered her hand and said, "To use another ghastly but appropriate American expression, Mr. Nakamura, we have a deal." She turned to leave.

"And one more thing before you go," said Nakamura, picking up an envelope from his desk. Anna turned back, hoping she didn't look apprehensive. "Would you be kind enough to pass on this letter to Miss Danuta Sekalska, a huge talent that I can only hope will be allowed to mature." Anna smiled as the chairman accompanied her down the corridor and back to the waiting limousine. They chatted about the tragic events in New York, and the long-term consequences for America. However, Nakamura made no reference to why his regular driver was in hospital recovering from serious injuries, not least to his pride.

But then the Japanese have always considered that some secrets are best kept in the family.

Whenever Jack was in a strange city, he rarely informed the embassy of his presence. They always asked too many questions he didn't want to answer. Tokyo was no exception, but he did need some of his own questions answered, and he knew exactly who to ask.

A con man, whom Jack had put behind bars for several years, once told him that whenever you're abroad and in need of information, book yourself into a good hotel. But don't seek advice from the manager and don't bother with the receptionist; only deal with the head concierge. Information is how he makes his living; his salary is incidental.

For fifty dollars, Jack learnt everything he needed to know about Mr. Nakamura, even his golf handicap—fourteen.

Krantz watched as Petrescu emerged from the building and climbed back into the chairman's limousine. She quickly hailed a taxi and asked to be dropped a hundred yards from the Seiyo hotel. If Petrescu was about to depart, she would still have to retrieve her luggage and settle the bill.

Once the temporary chauffeur had dropped Anna back at the Seiyo, she couldn't wait to check out—she picked up her key from reception and ran up the stairs to her room on the first floor. She sat on the end of the bed and called Arabella first. She sounded wide awake.

"A veritable Portia," was Arabella's final comment after she had learned the news. Which Portia, Anna wondered, Shylock's nemesis, or Brutus's wife? She unclasped her gold chain, unfastened the leather belt, kicked off her shoes, and finally slipped out of her dress. She exchanged her more formal attire for a T-shirt, jeans, and sneakers. Although checkout was at noon, she still had enough time to make one more call. Anna needed to plant the clue.

The ringing tone continued for some time before a sleepy voice answered.

"Who's this?"

"Vincent."

"Christ, what time is it? I must have fallen asleep."

"You can go back to sleep after you've heard my news."

"You've sold the painting?"

"How did you guess?"

"How much?"

"Enough."

"Congratulations. So where are you going next?"

"To pick it up."

"And where's that?"

"Where it's always been. Go back to sleep."

The phone went dead.

Tina smiled as she drifted back to sleep. Fenston was going to be beaten at his own game for once.

"Oh, my God," she said out loud, suddenly wide awake.

"I didn't warn her that the stalker *is* a woman and knows she's in Tokyo."

.

36

FENSTON STRETCHED AN arm across the bed and fumbled for the phone as he tried to keep his eyes shut.

"Who the fuck is this?"

"Vincent's just made a call."

"And where was she calling from this time?" asked Fenston, his eyes suddenly wide open.

"Tokyo."

"So she must have seen Nakamura."

"Sure has," said Leapman, "and claims she's sold the painting."

"You can't sell something that you don't own," said Fenston, as he switched on the bedside light. "Did she say where she was going next?"

"To pick it up."

"Did she give any clue as to where that might be?"

"Where it's always been," replied Leapman.

"Then it has to be in London," said Fenston.

"How can you be so sure?" asked Leapman.

"Because if she had taken the painting to Bucharest, why not take it on to Tokyo? No, she left the picture in London," said Fenston adamantly, "*where it's always been.*"

"I'm not so sure," said Leapman.

"Then where do you think it is?"

219

"In Bucharest, *where it's always been,* in the red box."

"No, the box was just a decoy."

"Then how can we ever hope to find the painting?" asked Leapman.

"That will be simple enough," said Fenston. Now that Petrescu thinks she's sold the painting to Nakamura, her next stop will be to pick it up. And this time Krantz *will* be waiting for her, and then she'll end up having something in common with Van Gogh. But before then, there's another call I have to make.' He slammed the phone down before Leapman had a chance to ask to whom.

Anna checked out of the hotel just after twelve. She took a train to the airport, no longer able to afford the luxury of a cab. She assumed that once she boarded the shuttle, the same man would be following her, and she intended to make his task as easy as possible. After all, he would already have been informed of her next stop.

What she didn't know was that her pursuer was sitting eight rows behind her.

Krantz opened a copy of the *Shinbui Times,* ready to raise it and cover her face should Petrescu look around. She didn't.

Time to make her call. Krantz dialed the number and waited for ten rings. On the tenth, it was picked up. She didn't speak.

"London," was the only word Fenston uttered before the line went dead.

Krantz dropped the cell phone out of the window, and watched as it landed in front of an oncoming train.

When her train came to a halt at the airport terminal, Anna jumped out and went straight to the British Airways desk. She inquired about an economy fare to London, although she had no intention of purchasing the ticket. She had only thirty-five dollars to her name, after all. But Fenston had no way of knowing that. She checked the departure board. There were ninety minutes between the two flights. Anna walked slowly toward Gate 91B, making sure that whoever was following her couldn't lose her. She window-shopped all the way to the departure gate and arrived just before they began boarding. She selected her seat in the lounge carefully, sitting next to a small child. "Would those passengers in rows . . ." The child screamed and ran away, a harassed parent chasing after him.

Jack had only been distracted for a moment, but she was gone. Had she boarded the plane or turned back? Perhaps she had worked out that *two* people were following her. Did she have any idea how much danger she was in? Jack's eyes searched the concourse below him. They were now boarding business class, and she wasn't anywhere to be seen. He checked all the remaining passengers who were seated in the lounge, and he wouldn't have spotted the other woman in his life if she hadn't touched her hair, no longer a blonde crew cut, now a black wig. She also looked puzzled.

Krantz hesitated when they invited all first-class passengers to board. She walked across to the ladies' washroom, which was directly behind where Petrescu had been sitting. She emerged a few moments later and returned to her seat. When they called final boarding, she was among the last to hand over her ticket.

Jack watched as Crew Cut disappeared down the ramp. How could she be so confident that Anna was on the London flight? Had he lost both of them again?

Jack waited until the gate closed, now painfully aware that both women were obviously on the flight to London. But there had been something about Anna's manner since she'd left the hotel—almost as if, this time, she wanted to be followed.

Jack waited until the last airline official had packed up and gone. He was about to return to the ground floor and book himself on the next plane to London, when the door of the men's washroom opened.

Anna stepped out.

"Put me through to Mr. Nakamura."

"Who shall I say is calling?"

"Bryce Fenston, the chairman of Fenston Finance."

"I'll just find out if he's available, Mr. Fenston."

"He'll be available," said Fenston.

The line went silent and it was some time before another voice ventured, "Good morning, Mr. Fenston. This is Takashi Nakamura. How can I help you?"

"I just phoned to warn you—"

"Warn me?" said Nakamura.

"I'm told that Petrescu tried to sell you a Van Gogh."

"Yes, she did," said Nakamura.

"And how much did she ask for?" said Fenston.

"I think, to use an American expression, an arm and a leg."

"If you were foolish enough to agree to buy the picture, Mr. Nakamura, it could end up being your arm and your leg," said Fenston, "because that picture belongs to me."

"I had no idea it belonged to you. I thought that it—"

"Then you thought wrong. Perhaps you were also unaware that Petrescu no longer works for this bank."

"Dr. Petrescu made that all too clear, in fact—"

"And did she tell you she was fired?"

"Yes, she did."

"But did she tell you why?"

"In great detail."

"And you still felt able to do business with her?"

"Yes. In fact I am trying to persuade her to join *my* board, as CEO of the company's foundation."

"Despite the fact that I had to dismiss her for conduct unworthy of an officer of a bank."

"Not *a* bank, Mr. Fenston, *your* bank."

"Don't bandy words with me," said Fenston.

"So be it," said Nakamura, "then let me make it clear that should Dr. Petrescu join this company, she will quickly discover that we do not condone a policy of swindling clients out of their inheritance, especially when they are old ladies."

"Then how would you feel about directors who steal bank assets worth a hundred million dollars?"

"I am delighted to learn you consider the painting is worth that amount, because the owner—"

"I am the owner," bellowed Fenston, "under New York state law."

"Whose jurisdiction does not stretch to Tokyo."

"But doesn't your company also have offices in New York?"

"At last we've found something on which we can agree," said Nakamura.

"Then there's nothing to stop me serving you with a writ in New York, were you foolish enough to attempt to buy my picture."

"And in which name will the writ be issued?" asked Nakamura.

"What are you getting at?" shouted Fenston.

"Only that my New York lawyers will need to know who they're up against. Will it be Bryce Fenston, the chairman of Fenston Finance, or Nicu Munteanu, money launderer to Ceauşescu, the late dictator of Romania?"

"Don't threaten me, Nakamura, or I'll—"

"Break my driver's neck?"

"It won't be your driver next time."

There was a long pause, before Nakamura said, "Then perhaps I ought to reconsider whether it's really worth paying that much for the Van Gogh."

"A sensible decision," said Fenston.

"Thank you, Mr. Fenston. You have convinced me that what I had originally planned might not be the wisest course of action, after all."

"I knew you'd come to your senses in the end," said Fenston, before putting down the phone.

When Anna boarded the flight for Bucharest an hour later, she felt confident that she had shaken off Fenston's man. Following her call to Tina, they would have been convinced that she was on her way back to London to pick up the painting, *where it's always been*. The sort of clue Fenston and Leapman would undoubtedly have argued over.

She had perhaps overdone it a little by spending so much time at the British Airways desk and then heading straight for Gate 91B when she didn't even have a ticket. The little boy turned out to be a bonus, but even Anna was surprised by how much fuss he made when she'd pinched him on his calf.

Anna's only real concern was for Tina. By this time tomorrow, Fenston and Leapman would realize that Anna had fed them false information, having obviously worked out that her conversations were being bugged. Anna feared that losing her job might end up the least of Tina's problems.

As the wheels lifted off Japanese soil, Anna's mind drifted to Anton. She only hoped that three days would have proved long enough.

Fenston's man was chasing her down an alley. At the far end was a high, jagged stone wall covered in barbed wire. Anna knew there was no way out. She turned to face her adversary as he came to a halt only a few feet in front of her. The short, ugly man drew a pistol from his holster, cocked the trigger, grinned, and aimed it directly at her heart. She turned as she felt the bullet graze her shoulder . . . "If you would like to adjust your watches, the time in Bucharest is now three twenty in the afternoon."

Anna woke with a start. "What day is it?" she asked the passing steward.

"Thursday, madam."

9/20

37

ANNA RUBBED HER eyes and set her watch to the correct time.

She had kept her agreement with Anton to be back within four days. Now her biggest problem would be to transport the painting to London, while at the same time . . . "Ladies and gentlemen, the captain has turned on the FASTEN SEAT BELT sign. We will be landing in Bucharest in approximately twenty minutes."

She smiled at the thought that by now Fenston's man would have landed in Hong Kong and would be puzzled why this time he couldn't spot her in duty-free. Would he carry on to London, or risk switching flights for the Romanian capital? Perhaps he would arrive back in Bucharest just as she set off for London.

When Anna stepped out onto the pavement, she was delighted to see a smiling Sergei standing by the door of his yellow Mercedes. He opened the back door for her. Her only problem was she barely had enough cash to cover his fare.

"Where to?" he asked.

"First, I need to go to the academy," she told him.

Anna would have liked to share with Sergei all she had been through, but still didn't feel she knew him well enough to risk it. Not trusting people was another experience she didn't enjoy.

Sergei dropped her at the bottom of the steps, where she'd left Anton before going to the airport. She no longer needed to ask him to wait. The student working at the reception desk told Anna that Professor Teodorescu's lecture on "Attribution" was just about to begin.

Anna made her way to the lecture theater on the first floor. She followed a couple of students in just as the lights were dimmed and slipped into a seat at the end of the second row, looking forward to a few minutes' escape from the real world.

"Attribution and provenance," began Anton, running a hand through his hair in that familiar way the students mimicked behind his back, "are the cause of more discussion and disagreement among art scholars than any other subject. Why? Because it's sexy, open to debate, and rarely conclusive. There is no doubt that several of the world's most popular galleries currently display works that were not painted by the artists whose names are suggested on the frame. It is, of course, possible that the master painted the main figure, the Virgin or Christ for example, while leaving an assistant to fill in the background. We must consider, therefore, whether several paintings, all depicting the same subject, can have been executed by one master, or if it is more likely that one of them, possibly even more, are the works of his star pupils, which several hundred years later are mistaken for the master's," Anna smiled at the words *star pupil* and remembered the letter she had to pass on to Danuta Sekalska.

"Now let us consider some examples," continued Anton, "and see if you can detect the hand of a lesser mortal. The first is of a painting currently on display at the Frick Museum in New York." A slide was beamed up on the screen behind Anton. "Rembrandt, I hear you cry, but the Rembrandt Research Project, set up in 1974, would not agree with you. They believe that *The Polish Rider* is the work of at least two hands, one of which may—I repeat, may—have been that of Rembrandt. The Metropolitan Museum, just a few blocks away from the Frick on the other side of Fifth Avenue, was unable to hide its angst when the same distinguished scholars dismissed the two portraits of the *Beresteyn Family,* acquired by them in 1929, as not executed by the Dutch master.

"Don't lose too much sleep over the problems faced by these two great institutions, because, of the twelve paintings attributed to Rembrandt in London's Wallace Collection, only one, *Titus, the Artist's Son,* has been pronounced genuine." Anna became so engrossed that she began taking notes. "The second artist I would ask you to consider is the great Spanish maestro, Goya. Much to the embarrassment of the Prado in Madrid, Juan Jose Junquera, the world's leading authority on Goya, has suggested that the "black paintings," which include such haunting visions as *Satan Devouring His Children,* cannot have been the hand of Goya, as he points out that the room for which they were painted as murals was not completed until after his death. The distinguished Australian critic Robert Hughes, in his book on Goya, suggests they are the work of the artist's son.

"And now I turn to the Impressionists. Several examples of Manet, Monet, Matisse, and Van Gogh currently on display in leading galleries around the world have not been authenticated by the relevant scholars. *Sunflowers,* for example, which came under the hammer at Christie's in 1987, selling for just under forty million dollars, has yet to be authenticated by Louis van Tilborgh of the Van Gogh Museum."

As Anton turned to display the next slide, his eyes rested on Anna. She smiled, and he put up a Raphael instead of the Van Gogh, which caused a ripple of laughter among the students. "As you can see, I am also capable of attributing the wrong painting to the wrong artist." The laughter turned to applause. But then, to Anna's surprise, he looked back and stared at her. "This great city," he said, no longer referring to his notes, "has produced its own scholar in the field of attribution, who currently works out of New York. Some years ago when we were both students, we used to have long discussions into the night about this particular painting." The Raphael returned to the screen. "After attending a lecture, we would meet up at our favorite rendezvous,"—once again he fixed his gaze on Anna—"*Koskies,* where I'm reliably informed many of you still congregate. We always used to meet at *nine o'clock,* following the evening lecture." He turned his attention back to the picture on the screen. "This is a portrait known as *The Madonna of the Pinks,* recently acquired by the National Gallery in London. Raphael experts are divided, but many are concerned by how many examples there are of the same subject, attributed to the same artist. Some argue that this painting is more likely to be 'school of Raphael,' or 'after Raphael.'"

Anton looked back into the audience to see that the seat on the end of the second row was no longer occupied.

Anna arrived at Koskies a few minutes before the suggested hour. Only an attentive student would have noticed that the lecturer had departed from his prepared script for a few moments to let her know where they should meet. She could not mistake that look of fear in Anton's eyes, a look that is obvious only to those who've had to survive in a police state.

Anna glanced around the room. Her old student haunt hadn't changed that much. The same plastic tables, the same plastic chairs, and probably the same plastic wine that couldn't find an exporter. Not a natural rendezvous for a Professor of Perspective and a New York art dealer. She ordered two glasses of the house red.

Anna could still remember when she had considered a night at Koskies so cool, where she would discuss with her friends the virtues of Constantin Brancusi and U2, Tom Cruise and John Lennon, and have to suck a peppermint on the way home so that her mother wouldn't find out that she'd been smoking and sipping alcohol. Her father always knew—he'd wink and point to whichever room her mother was in.

Anna recalled when she and Anton first made love. It was so cold they both had to keep their coats on, and when it was over, Anna even wondered if she would bother to do it again. No one seemed to have explained to Anton that it might take a woman a little longer to have an orgasm.

Anna looked up to see a tall man coming toward her. For a moment she couldn't be sure that it was Anton. The advancing man was dressed in an army greatcoat too big for him, with a woolen scarf wrapped around his neck, topped off by a fur hat with flaps that covered his ears. An ideal outfit for a New York winter, was her immediate thought.

Anton took the seat opposite her and removed his hat, but nothing else. He knew that the only heater that worked was on the other side of the room.

"Do you have the painting?" asked Anna, unable to wait a moment longer to find out.

"Yes," said Anton. "The canvas never left my studio the whole time you were away, as even the least observant of my students would have noticed it wasn't my usual style," he added, before sipping his red wine. "Though I confess I'll be glad to be rid of the damn man. I went to jail for less, and I haven't slept for the past four days. Even my wife suspects something is wrong."

"I'm so sorry," said Anna, as Anton began to roll a cigarette. "I shouldn't have placed you in such danger, and what makes it worse is I have to ask you for another favor." Anton looked apprehensive but waited to hear what her latest request would be. "You told me you kept eight thousand dollars of my mother's money hidden in the house."

"Yes, most Romanians stash the cash under their mattress, in case there's a change of government in the middle of the night," said Anton, as he lit his cigarette.

"I need to borrow some of it," said Anna. "I'll refund the money just as soon as I get back to New York."

"It's your money, Anna, you can have every last cent."

"No, it's my mother's, but don't let her know, or she'll only assume I'm in some sort of financial trouble and start selling off the furniture."

Anton didn't laugh. "But you *are* in some sort of trouble, aren't you?"

"Not as long as I have the painting."

"Would you rather I held on to it for another day?" he asked, as he took a sip of wine.

"No, that's kind of you," said Anna, "but that would only mean that neither of us was able to get a night's sleep. I think the time has come to take the canvas off your hands."

Anna rose without another word, having not touched her wine.

Anton drained his glass, stubbed out his cigarette, and left a few coins on the table. He pulled his hat back on and followed Anna out of the bar. She couldn't help remembering the last time they'd walked out of Koskies together.

Anna looked up and down the street before she joined Anton, who was whispering intently to Sergei.

"Will you have time to visit your mother?" asked Anton, as Sergei opened the back door for her.

"Not while someone is watching my every move."

"I didn't see anyone," said Anton.

"You don't see him," said Anna. "You feel him." She paused. "And I was under the illusion that I'd got rid of him."

"You haven't," said Sergei, as they drove off.

No one spoke for the rest of the short journey to Anton's home. Once Sergei had brought the car to a halt, Anna jumped out and followed Anton into the house. He led her quickly up the stairs to an attic on the top floor. Although Anna could hear the sound of Sibelius coming from a room below, it was clear that he didn't want her to meet his wife.

Anna walked into a room crowded with canvases. Her eyes were immediately drawn to the painting of Van Gogh, his left ear bandaged. She smiled. The picture was in its familiar frame, safely back inside the open red box.

"Couldn't be better," said Anna. "Now all I have to do is make sure it ends up in the right hands."

Anton didn't comment, and when Anna turned round, she found him on his knees in the far corner of the room, lifting up a floorboard. He reached inside and extracted a thick envelope, which he slipped into an inside pocket. He then returned to the red box, replaced the lid, and began to hammer the nails back in place. It was only too clear that he wanted to be rid of the painting as quickly as possible. Once the final nail was secured, he lifted up the box and, without a word, led Anna out of the room and back down the stairs.

Anna opened the front door to allow Anton to step out onto the street. She was pleased to see Sergei waiting by the back of the car, the trunk already open. Anton placed the red box in the trunk and brushed his hands together, showing how happy he was to be free of the painting. Sergei slammed the lid closed and returned to his seat behind the wheel.

Anton extracted the thick envelope from his inside pocket and handed it over to Anna.

"Thank you," she said, before passing across another envelope in exchange, but it was not addressed to Anton.

He looked at the name, smiled, and said, "I'll see she gets it. Whatever it is you're up to," he added, "I hope it works out."

He kissed her on both cheeks before disappearing back into the house.

"Where will you stay tonight?" asked Sergei, as Anna joined him in the front of the car.

Anna told him.

9/21

38

WHEN ANNA WOKE, Sergei was sitting on the hood of the car, smoking a cigarette. Anna stretched, blinked, and rubbed her eyes. It was the first time she'd slept in the backseat of a car—a definite improvement on the back of a van, somewhere on the way to the Canadian border, with no one to protect her.

She got out of the car and stretched her legs. The red box was still in place.

"Good morning," said Sergei. "I hope you slept well?"

She laughed. "Better than you, it seems."

"After twenty years in the army, sleep becomes a luxury," said Sergei. "But please do join me for breakfast." He returned to the car and retrieved a small tin box from under the driver's seat. He removed the lid and revealed its contents: two bread rolls, a boiled egg, a hunk of cheese, a couple of tomatoes, an orange, and a thermos of coffee.

"Where did all of this come from?" asked Anna, as she peeled the orange.

"Last night's supper," explained Sergei, "prepared by my dear wife."

"How will you explain why you didn't go home?" Anna asked.

"I'll tell her the truth," said Sergei. "I spent the night with a beautiful woman." Anna blushed. "But I fear I am too old for her to believe me," he added. "So what do we do next? Rob a bank?"

"Only if you know one with fifty million dollars in loose change," said Anna, laughing. "Otherwise I have to get that"—she pointed to the crate—"into the cargo hold on the next flight to London, so I'll need to find out when the freight depot opens."

"When the first person turns up," said Sergei, as he removed the shell from the egg. "Usually around seven." He added, before handing the egg across to Anna.

Anna took a bite. "Then I'd like to be there by seven, when they open," she said, "so I can be sure the crate is definitely on board." She looked at her watch. "So we'd better get moving."

"I don't think so."

"What do you mean?" asked Anna, sounding anxious.

"When a woman like you has to spend the night in a car, not a hotel, there has to be a reason. I have a feeling *that* is the reason," said Sergei, pointing to the crate. "So perhaps it would be unwise for you to be seen checking in a red box this morning." Anna continued to stare at him, but didn't speak. "Could there possibly be something inside the box that you don't want the authorities to take an interest in?" He paused, but Anna still didn't comment. "Just as I thought," said Sergei. "You know, when I was a colonel in the army, and I needed something done that I didn't want anyone else to know about, I always chose a corporal to carry out the task. That way, I found, no one took the slightest interest. I think today I will have to be your corporal."

"But what if you're caught?"

"Then I'll have done something worthwhile for a change. Do you think it's fun being a taxi driver when you've commanded a regiment? Do not concern yourself, dear lady. One or two of my boys work in the customs shed, and if the price is right, they won't ask too many questions."

Anna flicked open her briefcase, took out the envelope Anton had given her and passed Sergei five twenty-dollar bills.

"No, no, dear lady," he said, throwing his hands in the air. "We are not trying to bribe the chief of police, just a couple of local boys," he added, taking one of the twenty-dollar notes. "And in any case, I may be in need of their services again at some time in the future, so we don't want expectations to exceed their usefulness."

Anna laughed. "And when you sign the manifest, Sergei, be sure your signature is illegible."

He looked at her closely. "I understand, but then I do not understand," he said, pausing. "You stay here and keep out of sight. All I'll need is your plane ticket."

Anna opened her bag again, placed the eighty dollars back in the envelope, and handed over her ticket to London.

Sergei climbed into the driver's seat, turned on the engine, and waved good-bye.

Anna watched as the car disappeared around the corner with the painting, her luggage, her ticket to London, and twenty dollars. All she had as security was a cheese and tomato roll and a thermos of cold coffee.

Fenston picked up the receiver on the tenth ring.

"I've just landed in Bucharest," she said. "The red crate you've been looking for was loaded onto a flight to London, which will be landing at Heathrow around four this afternoon."

"And the girl?"

"I don't know what her plans are, but when I do—"

"Just be sure to leave the body in Bucharest."

The phone went dead.

Krantz walked out of the airport, placed the recently acquired cell phone under the front wheel of an articulated truck, and waited for it to move off before she slipped back into the terminal.

She checked the departures board, but this time she didn't assume Petrescu would be traveling to London; after all, there was also a flight to New York that morning. If Petrescu was booked on that one, she'd have to kill her at the airport. It wouldn't be the first time—at this particular airport.

Krantz tucked herself in behind a large drinks machine and waited. She made sure she had an unimpeded view of any taxis dropping off their customers. She was only interested in one taxi and one customer. Petrescu wouldn't fool her a second time, because on this occasion, she intended to take out some insurance.

After thirty minutes, Anna began to feel anxious. After forty minutes, worried. After fifty, close to panic. An hour after he'd left, Anna even wondered if Sergei worked for Fenston. A few minutes later, an old yellow Mercedes, driven by an even older man, came trundling around the bend.

Sergei smiled. "You look relieved," he said, as he opened the front door for her and handed back her ticket.

"No, no," said Anna, feeling guilty.

Sergei smiled. "The package is booked for London, and it's on the same flight as you," he said, once he'd climbed back behind the wheel.

"Good," said Anna. "Then perhaps it's time for me to be on my way as well."

"Agreed," said Sergei, turning the key in the ignition. "But you'll have to be careful, because the American is already there waiting for you."

"He's not interested in me," said Anna, "only the package."

"But he saw me take it into the cargo depot, and for another twenty dollars he'll know exactly where it's going."

"I don't care any longer," said Anna without explanation.

Sergei looked puzzled but didn't question her as he eased the Mercedes back onto the highway and continued to follow the signs for the airport.

"I owe you so much," said Anna.

"Four dollars," said Sergei, "plus gourmet meal. I'll settle for five."

Anna opened her bag, took out Anton's envelope, removed all but five hundred dollars, and resealed it. When Sergei came to a halt at the taxi rank outside the main terminal, Anna passed him the envelope.

"Five dollars," she said.

"Thank you, ma'am," he replied.

"Anna," she said, and kissed him on the cheek. She didn't look back, otherwise she would have seen an old soldier crying.

Should he have told her that Colonel Sergei Slatinaru was standing by her father's side when he was executed?

When Tina stepped out of the elevator, she spotted Leapman leaving her office. She slipped into the washroom, her heart beating frantically as she considered the consequences. Did he now know that she could overhear every phone conversation Fenston had, while at the same time being able to watch everything that was going on in the chairman's office? But worse, had he found out that she had been e-mailing confidential documents to herself for the past year? Tina tried to remain calm as she stepped back into the corridor and walked slowly toward her office. One thing she was certain about, there would be no clue that Leapman had even entered the room.

She sat at her desk and flicked on the screen. She felt ill. Leapman was in the chairman's office, talking to Fenston. The chairman was listening intently.

Jack watched as Anna kissed the driver on the cheek and couldn't forget that this was the same man who had extracted twenty dollars from him— a sum that wouldn't be appearing on his expense sheet. He thought about the fact that the two of them had stayed awake all night while she had slept. If he'd dozed off, even for a moment, Jack feared that Crew Cut would have moved in and stolen the crate, although he hadn't spotted her since she boarded the plane for London. He wondered where she was now. Not far away, he suspected. As each hour had passed, Jack became more aware that he wasn't just dealing with a taxi driver, but someone willing to risk his life for the girl, perhaps without even knowing the significance of what was in that crate. There had to be a reason.

Jack knew it would be a waste of time to try and bribe the taxi driver, as he had already discovered to his own cost, but the cargo manager had beckoned him into his private office and even printed out the relevant page of the manifest. The crate was booked on the next flight to London. Already loaded on board, he assured him. Not a bad investment for fifty dollars, even if he couldn't read the signature. But would she be on the same flight? Jack remained puzzled. If the Van Gogh was in the red box on its way back to London, what was in the box that Petrescu had taken to Japan and delivered to Nakamura's office? He had no choice but to wait and see if she boarded the same plane.

Sergei watched as Anna walked toward the airport entrance, pulling her suitcase. He would call Anton later, to let him know he had delivered her safely. Anna turned to wave, so he didn't notice a customer climb into the back of the car, until he heard the door close. He glanced up at his rearview mirror.

"Where to, madam?" he asked.

"The old airport," she said.

"I didn't realize it was still in service," he ventured, but she didn't reply. Some customers don't.

When they reached the second traffic island, Sergei took the next exit. He checked once again in the mirror. There was something familiar about her—had she been in the back of his cab before? At the crossroads, Sergei turned left onto the old airport road. It was deserted. He'd been right, nothing had flown out of there since Ceauşescu had attempted to escape in November 1989. He glanced up at the mirror again, while trying to maintain a steady speed, and suddenly it all came back to him. He now remembered exactly where he'd last seen her. The hair had been longer, and blonde, and although it was over a decade ago, those eyes hadn't changed—eyes that registered nothing when she killed, eyes that bore into you when you died.

His platoon had been surrounded on the border with Bulgaria. They were quickly rounded up and marched to the nearest prisoner-of-war camp. He could still hear the cries of his young volunteers, some of whom had only just left school. And then, once they had told her everything they knew, or nothing at all, she would slit their throats while staring into their eyes. Once she was certain they were dead, with one more sweeping movement of her knife she would hack off the head, then dump it in the middle of an overcrowded cell. Even the most hardened of her henchmen had to avert their eyes.

Before leaving, she would spend a little time looking around at those who had survived. Each night she left with the same parting words, "I still haven't decided which one of you will be next."

Three of his men had survived, and only because a new set of prisoners, with more up-to-date information, had recently been captured. But for thirty-seven sleepless nights, Colonel Sergei Slatinaru could only wonder when it would be his turn. Her last victim had been Anna's father, one of the bravest men he'd ever known, who, if he had to die, deserved to go to his grave fighting the enemy—not at the hands of a butcher.

When they were finally repatriated, one of his first duties as commanding officer was to tell Anna's mother how Captain Petrescu had been killed. He lied, assuring her that her husband died bravely on the battlefield. Why should he pass his nightmare on to her? And then Anton phoned to say he'd had a call from Captain Petrescu's daughter; she was coming to Bucharest, and would he . . . someone else he didn't pass his secret on to.

Once the hostilities had ceased, rumor concerning Krantz was rife. She was in jail, she had escaped to America, she'd been killed. He prayed that she was still alive, as he wanted to be the one to kill her. But he feared that she would never show her face in Romania again, because so many former comrades would recognize her and line up for the privilege of cutting her throat. But why had she returned? What could possibly be in that crate to make her take such a risk?

Sergei slowed down when he reached a barren stretch of land, where the runway had once been but was now covered in weeds and potholes. He kept one hand on the wheel, while the other moved slowly down his left side and reached underneath the seat for a gun he hadn't used since Ceauşescu had been executed.

"Where do you want me to drop you, madam?" he asked, as if they were in the middle of a busy street. He placed his fingers around the handle of the gun. She didn't reply. His eyes glanced up into the rearview mirror, realizing that any sudden movement would alert her. Not only did she have the advantage of being behind him, but she was now watching his every move. He knew one of them would be dead in the next sixty seconds.

Sergei placed his index finger round the trigger, eased the gun from under his seat and began to raise his arm slowly, inch by inch. He was about to hit the brakes when a hand grabbed his hair and jerked back his head in one sharp movement. His foot came off the accelerator and the car slowed to a halt in the middle of the runway. He raised the gun another inch.

"Where is the girl going?" she demanded, pulling his head even farther back so that she could look into his eyes.

"What girl?" he managed to say as he felt the knife touch his skin just below the Adam's apple.

"Don't play games with me, old man. The girl you dropped at the airport."

"She didn't say." Another inch.

"She didn't say, even though you drove her everywhere? Where?" she shouted, the edge of the blade now piercing the skin.

One more inch.

"I'll give you one last chance," she screamed as the blade broke the skin and warm blood began to trickle down his neck. "Where—was—she—going?" Krantz demanded.

"I don't know," Sergei screamed, as he raised the gun, pointed it toward her head, and pulled the trigger.

The bullet ripped into Krantz's shoulder and threw her backward, but she never let go of his hair. Sergei pulled the trigger again, but there was a full second between the two shots. Just long enough for her to slit his throat in a single movement.

Sergei's last memory before he died was staring into those cold, gray eyes.

39

LEAPMAN WASN'T ASLEEP when his phone rang. But then he rarely slept, although he knew there was only one person who would consider calling him at such an ungodly hour.

He picked up the phone, and said, "Good morning, Chairman," as if he was sitting at his desk in the office.

"Krantz has located the painting."

"Where is it?" asked Leapman.

"It was in Bucharest, but it's now on its way back to Heathrow."

Leapman wanted to say, *I told you so,* but confined himself to, "When does the plane land?"

"Just after four, London time."

"I'll have someone standing by to pick it up."

"And they should put it on the first available flight to New York."

"So where's Petrescu?" asked Leapman.

"No idea," said Fenston, "but Krantz is at the airport waiting for her. So don't expect her to be on the same flight."

Leapman heard the click. Fenston never said good-bye. He climbed out of bed, picked up his phone book, and thumbed through until he reached the Ps. He checked his watch and dialed her office number.

"Ruth Parish."

"Good morning, Ms. Parish. It's Karl Leapman."

"Good morning," replied Ruth cautiously.

"We've found our painting."

"You have the Van Gogh?" said Ruth.

"No, not yet, but that's why I'm calling."

"How can I help?"

"It's in the cargo hold of a flight on its way from Bucharest, due to land outside your front door just after four o'clock this afternoon." He paused. "Just make sure you're there to pick it up."

"I'll be there. But whose name is on the manifest?"

"Who gives a fuck? It's our painting and it's in your crate. Just be sure you don't mislay it a second time." Leapman put the phone down before she had a chance to protest.

Ruth Parish and four of her carriers were already on the tarmac when Flight 019 from Bucharest landed at Heathrow. Once the aircraft had been cleared for unloading, the little motorcade of a customs official's car, Ruth's Range Rover, and an Art Locations security van drove up and parked within twenty meters of the cargo hold.

If Ruth had looked up, she would have seen Anna's smiling face in her tiny window at the back of the aircraft. But she didn't.

Ruth stepped out of her car and joined the customs officer. She had earlier informed him that she wished to transfer a painting from an incoming flight to an onward destination. The customs official had looked bored, and wondered why she had chosen such a senior officer to carry out such a routine task, until he was told, in confidence, the value of the painting. His promotion board was due in three weeks' time. If he screwed up this simple exercise, he could forget the extra silver stripe he promised his wife she would be sewing on his sleeve before the end of the month. Not to mention the pay raise.

When the hold eventually opened, they both walked forward together, but only the customs officer addressed the chief loader. "There's a red wooden crate on board"—he checked his file—"three foot by two, and three or four inches deep. It's stamped with an Art Locations logo on both sides, and the number forty-seven stenciled in all four corners. I want it unloaded before anything else is moved."

The chief loader passed on the instructions to his two men in the hold, who disappeared into the darkness. By the time they reappeared, Anna was heading toward passport control.

"That's it," said Ruth, when the two loaders reappeared on the edge of the hold, carrying a red crate. The customs official nodded. A forklift truck moved forward, expertly extracted the crate from the hold and lowered it slowly to the ground. The customs man checked the manifest, followed by the logo and even the stenciled forty-sevens.

"Everything seems to be in order, Ms. Parish. If you'll just sign here."

Ruth signed the form but couldn't make out the signature on the original manifest. The customs officer's eyes never left the forklift truck as the package was driven across to the Art Locations van, where two of Ruth's carriers loaded the crate on board.

"I'll still have to accompany you to the outgoing aircraft, Ms. Parish, so I can confirm that the package has been loaded for its onward destination. Not until then can I sign a clearance certificate."

"Of course," said Ruth, who carried out the same procedure two or three times a day.

Anna had reached the baggage area by the time the security van began its circuitous journey from terminal three to terminal four. When the driver came to a halt, he parked beside a United Airlines plane bound for New York.

The security van waited on the tarmac for over an hour before the cargo hold was opened, by which time Ruth knew the life history of the customs official, even which school he intended to send his third child to if he was promoted. Ruth then watched the process in reverse. The back door of the security van was unlocked, the painting placed on a forklift truck, driven to the side of the hold, raised, and accepted on board by two handlers before it disappeared into the bowels of the aircraft.

The customs official signed all three copies of the dispatch documents and bade farewell to Ruth before returning to his office. In normal circumstances, Ruth would also have gone back to her office, filed the relevant forms, checked her messages, and then left for the day. However, these were not normal circumstances. She remained seated in her car and waited until all the passengers' bags had been loaded on board and the cargo doors had been locked. Still she didn't move, even after the aircraft began to taxi toward the north runway. She waited until the plane's wheels had left the ground before she phoned Leapman in New York. Her message was simple: "The package is on its way."

Jack was puzzled. He had watched Anna stroll into the arrivals hall, exchange some dollars at Travelex, and then join the long line for a taxi. Jack's cab was already waiting on the other side of the road, two sets of luggage on board, engine running, as he waited for Anna's cab to pass him.

"Where to, guv?" asked the driver.

"I'm not sure," admitted Jack, "but my first bet would be cargo."

Jack assumed that Anna would drive straight to the cargo depot and retrieve the package the taxi driver had dispatched from Bucharest.

But Jack was wrong. Instead of turning right, when the large blue sign indicating cargo loomed up in front of them, Anna's taxi swung left and continued to drive west down the M25.

"She's not going to cargo, guv, so what's your next bet—Gatwick?"

"So what's in the crate?" asked Jack.

"I've no idea, sir."

"I'm so stupid," Jack said.

"I wouldn't want to venture an opinion on that, sir, but it would help if I knew where we was goin'."

Jack laughed. "I think you'll find it's Wentworth."

"Right, guv."

Jack tried to relax, but every time he glanced out of the rear window he could have sworn that another black cab was following them. A shadowy figure was seated in the back. Why was she still pursuing Anna, when the painting must have been deposited in cargo?

When his driver turned off the M25 and took the road to Wentworth, the taxi Jack had imagined was following them continued on in the direction of Gatwick.

"You're not stupid, after all, guv, because it looks as if it could be Wentworth."

"No, but I am paranoid," admitted Jack.

"Make up your mind, sir," the driver said, as Anna's taxi swung through the gates of Wentworth Hall and disappeared up the drive.

"Do you want me to keep followin' her, guv?"

"No," said Jack. "But I'll need a local hotel for the night. Do you know one by any chance?"

"When the golf tournament is on, I drop a lot of my customers off at the Wentworth Arms. They ought to be able to fix you up with a room at this time of year."

"Then let's find out," said Jack.

"Right you are, guv."

Jack sat back and dialed a number on his cell phone.

"American Embassy."

"Tom Crasanti, please."

40

WHEN KRANTZ CAME round following the operation, the first thing she felt was a stabbing pain in her right shoulder. She managed to raise her head a couple of inches off the pillow as she tried to focus on the small, white-walled, unadorned room: just the bare necessities—a bed, a table, a chair, one sheet, one blanket, and a bedpan. It could only be a hospital, but not of the private variety, because the room had no windows, no flowers, no fruit, no cards from well-wishers, and an exit that had bars clamped across the door.

Krantz tried to piece together what had happened to her. She could remember spotting the taxi driver's gun pointing at her heart, and that was where the memory faded. She'd had just enough time to turn—an inch, no more—before the bullet ripped into her shoulder. No one had been that close before. The next bullet missed completely, but by then he'd given her another second, easily enough time to cut his throat. He had to be a pro, an ex-policeman, perhaps, possibly a soldier. But then she must have passed out.

Jack checked himself into the Wentworth Arms for the night and booked a table for dinner at eight. After a shower and a change of clothes, he looked forward to devouring a large, juicy steak.

Even though Anna was safely ensconced at Wentworth Hall, he didn't feel he could relax while Crew Cut might well be hovering somewhere nearby. He had already asked Tom to brief the local police, while he continued to carry out his own surveillance.

He sat in the lounge enjoying a Guinness and thinking about Anna. Long before the hall clock struck eight, Tom walked in, looked around, and spotted his old friend by the fire. Jack rose to greet him, and apologized for having to drag him down to Wentworth when he could have been spending the evening with Chloe and Hank.

"As long as this establishment can produce a decent Tom Collins, you'll not hear me complain," Tom assured him.

Tom was explaining to Jack how Hank had scored a half century—whatever that was—when they were joined by the head waiter, who took their orders for dinner. They both chose steaks, but as a Texan, Tom admitted he hadn't got used to the English version that was served up looking like a lamb chop.

"I'll call you through," said the head waiter, "as soon as your table is ready."

"Thank you," said Jack, as Tom bent down to open his briefcase. He extracted a thick file and placed it on the table between them. Small talk had never been his forte.

"Let's begin with the important news," said Tom, opening the file. "We've identified the woman in the photograph you sent through from Tokyo." Jack put his drink down and concentrated on the contents of the file. "Her name is Olga Krantz, and she has something in common with Dr. Petrescu."

"And what's that?" asked Jack.

"The agency was also under the illusion that she was missing, presumed dead. As you can see from Krantz's profile," Tom added, pushing a sheet of paper across the table, "we lost contact with her in nineteen eighty-nine, when she ceased being a member of Ceaușescu's personal bodyguard. But we're now convinced that she works exclusively for Fenston."

"That's one hell of a leap of logic," suggested Jack, as a waiter appeared with a Tom Collins and another half pint of Guinness.

"Not if you consider the facts logically," said Tom, "and then follow them step by step," he added, before sipping his drink. "Um, not bad. After all, she and Fenston worked for Ceaușescu at the same time."

"Coincidence," said Jack. "Wouldn't stand up in court."

"It might, when you learn what her job description was."

"Try me," said Jack.

"She was responsible for removing anyone who posed a threat to Ceauşescu."

"Still circumstantial."

"Until you discover her chosen method of disposal."

"A kitchen knife?" suggested Jack, not looking down at the sheet of paper in front of him.

"You've got it," said Tom.

"Which, I fear, means that there is yet another undeniable link in your chain of logic."

"What's that?" asked Tom.

"Anna is being lined up as her next victim."

"No—there, fortunately, the logic breaks down, because Krantz was arrested in Bucharest this morning."

"What?" said Jack.

"By the local police," added Tom.

"It's hard to believe they got within a mile of her," said Jack. "I kept losing her even when I knew where she was."

"The local police were the first to admit," said Tom, "that she was unconscious at the time."

"Fill me in on the details," said Jack impatiently.

"It seems, and reports were still coming through when I left the embassy, that Krantz was involved in a quarrel with a taxi driver, who was found to have five hundred dollars in his possession. The driver had his throat cut, while she ended up with a bullet in her right shoulder. We don't yet know what caused the fight, but as he was killed only moments before your flight took off, we thought you might be able to throw some light on it."

"Krantz would have been trying to find out which plane Anna was on, after she made such a fool of herself in Tokyo, but that man would never have told her. He protected her more like a father than a taxi driver, and the five hundred dollars is a red herring. Krantz doesn't bother to kill people for that sort of money, and that was one taxi driver who never kept the meter running."

"Well, whatever, Krantz is safely locked up and with a bit of luck will spend the rest of her life in jail, which may not prove to be that long, as we're reliably informed that half the population of Romania would be happy to strangle her." Tom glanced back down at his file. "And it turns out that our taxi driver, one Colonel Sergei Slatinaru, was a hero of the resistance." Tom took another sip of his drink before he added, "So there's no longer any reason for you to worry about Petrescu's safety."

The waiter reappeared to accompany them into the dining room.

"In common with most Romanians, I won't relax until Krantz is dead," said Jack. "Until then, I'll remain anxious for Anna."

"Anna? Are you two on first-name terms?" asked Tom, as he took his seat opposite Jack in the dining room.

"Hardly, though we may as well be. I've spent more nights with her than any of my recent girlfriends."

"Then perhaps we should have invited Dr. Petrescu to join us?"

"Forget it," said Jack. "She'll be having dinner with Lady Arabella at Wentworth Hall, while we have to settle for the Wentworth Arms."

A waiter placed a bowl of leek and potato soup in front of Tom and served Jack a Caesar salad.

"Have you found out anything else about Anna?"

"Not a lot," admitted Tom, "but I can tell you that one of the calls she made from Bucharest airport was to the New York Police Department. She asked them to take her name off the missing list, said she'd been in Romania visiting her mother. She also called her uncle in Danville, Illinois, and Lady Arabella Wentworth."

"Then her meeting in Tokyo must have gone belly-up," said Jack.

"You're going to have to explain that one to me," said Tom.

"She had a meeting in Tokyo with a steel tycoon called Nakamura, who has one of the largest collections of Impressionist paintings in the world, or so the concierge at the Seiyo informed me." Jack paused. "She obviously failed to sell Nakamura the Van Gogh, which would explain why she sent the painting back to London and even allowed it to be forwarded to New York."

"She doesn't strike me as someone who gives up that easily," said Tom, extracting another piece of paper from his file. "By the way, the Happy Hire Company is also looking for her. They claim she abandoned one of their vehicles on the Canadian border, minus its front mudguard, front and rear bumpers, with not one of its lights in working order."

"Hardly a major crime," said Jack.

"Are you falling for this girl?" asked Tom.

Jack didn't reply as a waiter appeared by their side. "Two steaks, one rare, one medium," he announced.

"Mine's the rare," said Tom.

The waiter placed both plates on the table and added, "Enjoy."

"Another Americanism we seem to have exported," grunted Tom.

Jack smiled. "Did you get any further with Leapman?"

"Oh yes," said Tom. "We know a great deal about Mr. Leapman." He placed another file on the table. "He's an American citizen, second generation, and studied law at Columbia. Not unlike you," Tom said with a grin. "After graduating, he worked for several banks, always moving on fairly quickly, until he became involved in a share fraud. His specialty was selling bonds to widows who didn't exist." He paused. "The widows existed, the bonds didn't." Jack laughed. "He served a two-year sentence at Rochester Correctional Facility in upstate New York and was banned for life from working at a bank or any other financial institution."

"But he's Fenston's right hand?"

"Fenston's possibly, but not the bank's. Leapman's name doesn't appear on their books, even as a cleaner. He pays taxes on his only known income, a monthly check from an aunt in Mexico."

"Come on—," said Jack.

"And before you say anything else," added Tom, "my department has neither the financial resources nor the backup to find out if this aunt even exists."

"Any Romanian connection?" Jack asked, as he dug into his steak.

"None that we're aware of," said Tom. "Straight out of the Bronx and into a Brooks Brothers suit."

"Leapman may yet turn out to be our best lead," said Jack. "If we could only get him to testify—"

"Not a hope," said Tom. "Since leaving jail, he hasn't even had a parking ticket, and I suspect he's a lot more frightened of Fenston than he is of us."

"If only Hoover was still alive," said Jack with a grin.

They both raised their glasses, before Tom added, "So when do you fly back to the States? I only ask, as I want to know when I can return to my day job."

"Tomorrow, I suppose," said Jack. "Now Krantz is safely locked up, I ought to get back to New York. Macy will want to know if I'm any nearer to linking Krantz with Fenston."

"And are you?" asked Tom.

Neither of them noticed the two men talking to the maître d'. They couldn't have been booking a table, otherwise they would have left their raincoats in reception. Once the maître d' had answered their question, they walked purposefully across the dining room.

Tom was placing the files back in his briefcase by the time they reached their table.

"Good evening, gentlemen," said the taller of the two men. "My name is Detective Sergeant Frankham, and this is my colleague, Detective Constable Ross. I'm sorry to disturb your meal, but I need to have a word with you, sir," he said, touching Jack on the shoulder.

"Why, what have I done?" asked Jack, putting down his knife and fork. "Parked on a double yellow line?"

"I'm afraid it's a little more serious than that, sir," said the detective sergeant, "and I must therefore ask you to accompany me to the station."

"On what charge?" demanded Jack.

"I think it might be wiser, sir, if we were not to continue this conversation in a crowded restaurant."

"And on whose authority—," began Tom.

"I don't think you need to involve yourself, sir."

"I'll decide about that," said Tom, as he removed his FBI badge from an inside pocket. He was about to flick the leather wallet open, when Jack touched him on the elbow and said, "Let's not create a scene. No need to get the Bureau involved."

"To hell with that, who do these people think—"

"Tom, calm down. This is not our country. I'll go along to the police station and sort this all out."

Tom reluctantly placed his FBI badge back in his pocket, and although he said nothing, the look on his face wouldn't have left either policeman in any doubt how he felt. As Jack stood up, the sergeant grabbed his arm and quickly handcuffed him.

"Hey, is that really necessary?" demanded Tom.

"Tom, don't get involved," said Jack in a measured tone.

Tom reluctantly followed Jack out of the dining room, through a room full of guests, who studiously carried on chatting and eating their meals as if nothing unusual was going on around them.

When they reached the front door, Tom said, "Do you want me to come with you to the station?"

"No," said Jack, "Why don't you stick around. Don't worry, I'm sure I'll be back in time for coffee."

Two women stared intently at Jack from the other side of the corridor.

"Is that him, madam?"

"Yes it is," one of them confirmed.

When Tina heard her door open, she quickly flicked off the screen. She didn't look up, as only one person never bothered to knock before entering her office.

"I presume you know that Petrescu is back in New York?"

"I'd heard," said Tina, as she continued typing.

"But had you also heard," said Leapman, placing both hands on her desk, "that she tried to steal the Van Gogh?"

"The one in the chairman's office?" said Tina innocently.

"Don't play games with me," said Leapman. "You think I don't know that you listen in on every phone conversation the chairman has?" Tina stopped typing and looked up at him. "Perhaps the time has come," Leapman continued, "to let Mr. Fenston know about the switch under your desk that allows you to spy on him whenever he's having a private meeting."

"Are you threatening me, Mr. Leapman?" asked Tina. "Because if you are, I might find it necessary to have a word with the chairman myself."

"And what could you possibly tell him that I would care about?" demanded Leapman.

"About the weekly calls you receive from a Mr. Pickford, and then perhaps we'll discover who's playing games."

Leapman took his hands off the table and stood up straight.

"I feel sure your probation officer will be interested to learn that you've been harassing staff at a bank you don't work for, don't have an office in, and don't receive a salary from."

Leapman took a pace backward.

"When you come to see me next time, Mr. Leapman, make sure you knock, like any other visitor to the bank."

Leapman took another pace backward, hesitated, then left without another word.

When the door closed, Tina was shaking so much she had to grip the armrests of her chair.

41

WHEN THE POLICE car arrived at the station, Jack was bundled out. Once he'd been checked in by the desk sergeant, the two detectives accompanied him downstairs to an interview room. Detective Sergeant Frankham asked him to take a seat on the other side of the table. Something else Jack hadn't experienced before. Detective Constable Ross stood quietly in one corner.

Jack could only wonder which one of them was going to play the good cop.

Detective Sergeant Frankham sat down, placed a file on the table, and extracted a long form.

"Name?" began Frankham.

"Jack Fitzgerald Delaney," Jack replied.

"Date of birth?"

"Twenty-second November, "sixty-three.""

"Occupation?"

"Senior investigating officer with the FBI, attached to the New York field office."

The detective sergeant dropped his pen, looked up, and said, "Do you have some ID?"

Jack produced his FBI badge and identity card.

"Thank you, sir," said Frankham after he'd checked them. "Can you wait here for a moment?" He stood and turned to his colleague. "Would you see that Agent Delaney is offered a coffee? This may take some time." When he reached the door he added, "And make sure he gets his tie, belt, and laces back."

DS Frankham turned out to be right, because it was another hour before the heavy door was opened again and an older man with a weathered, lined face entered the room. He was dressed in a well-tailored uniform, with silver braid on his sleeve, epaulette, and the peak of his cap, which he removed to reveal a head of gray hair. He took the seat opposite Jack.

"Good evening, Mr. Delaney. My name is Renton, Chief Superintendent Renton, and now that we have been able to confirm your identity, perhaps you'd be kind enough to answer a few questions."

"If I can," said Jack.

"I feel sure you can," said Renton. "What interests me is whether you will."

Jack didn't respond.

"We received a complaint from a usually reliable source that you have, for the past week, been following a lady without her prior knowledge. This is an offence in England under the 1997 Protection from Harassment Act, as you are no doubt aware. However, I feel sure you have a simple explanation."

"Dr. Petrescu is part of an ongoing investigation, which my department has been involved in for some time."

"Would that investigation have anything to do with the death of Lady Victoria Wentworth?"

"Yes," replied Jack.

"And is Dr. Petrescu a suspect in that murder?"

"No," replied Jack firmly. "Quite the opposite. In fact, we had thought she might be the next victim."

"Had thought?" repeated the chief superintendent.

"Yes," replied Jack. "Fortunately the murderer has been apprehended in Bucharest."

"And you didn't feel able to share this information with us?" said Renton. "Despite the fact that you must have been aware that we were conducting a murder inquiry."

"I apologize, sir," said Jack. "I only found out myself a few hours ago. But I'm sure our London office planned to keep you informed."

"Mr. Tom Crasanti has briefed me, but I suspect only because his colleague was under lock and key." Jack didn't comment. "But he did go on to assure me," continued Renton, "that you will keep us fully informed of any developments that might arise in the future." Once again, Jack didn't respond. The chief superintendent rose from his place. "Good night, Mr. Delaney. I have authorized your immediate release and can only hope you have a pleasant flight home."

"Thank you, sir," said Jack, as Renton replaced his cap and left the room.

Jack had some sympathy with the chief superintendent. After all, the NYPD, not to mention the CIA, rarely bothered to let the FBI know what they were up to. A few moments later, DS Frankham returned.

"If you'll accompany me, sir," he said, "we have a car waiting to take you back to your hotel."

"Thank you," said Jack, as he followed the detective sergeant out of the room and up the stairs into reception.

The desk sergeant lowered his head as Jack left the building. Jack shook hands with an embarrassed DS Frankham before climbing into a police car that was parked outside the front door. Tom was waiting for him in the back.

"Just another case study for Quantico to add to its curriculum," suggested Tom. "This time on how to cause a major diplomatic incident while visiting one's oldest ally."

"I must have brought a new meaning to the words *special relationship*," commented Jack.

"However, the condemned man is to be given a chance to redeem himself," said Tom.

"What do you have in mind?" asked Jack.

"We've both been invited to join Lady Arabella and Dr. Petrescu for breakfast at Wentworth Hall tomorrow morning—and by the way, Jack, I see what you mean about Anna."

9/22

42

JACK EMERGED FROM the Wentworth Arms just after seven thirty to find a Rolls-Royce parked by the entrance. A chauffeur opened the back door the moment he saw him.

"Good morning, sir," he said. "Lady Arabella asked me to say how much she is looking forward to meeting you."

"Me too," said Jack, as he climbed into the back.

"We'll be there in a few minutes," the chauffeur assured him, as he drove out of the hotel entrance.

Half of the journey seemed to Jack to be from the wrought-iron gates at the entrance to the estate along the long drive that led up to the hall. Once the chauffeur had brought the car to a halt, he jumped out and walked around to open the back door. Jack stepped out onto the gravel drive and looked up to see a butler standing on the top step, obviously expecting him.

"Good morning, sir," he said, "welcome to Wentworth Hall. If you would be good enough to follow me, Lady Arabella is expecting you.'

"'A usually reliable source,'" muttered Jack, but if the butler did overhear him, he made no comment as he led the guest through to the drawing room.

"Mr. Delaney, m'lady," announced the butler, as two dogs, tails wagging, padded forward to greet him.

"Good morning, Mr. Delaney," said Arabella. "I think we owe you an apology. You are so obviously not a stalker."

Jack stared at Anna, who also looked suitably embarrassed, and then turned toward Tom, who couldn't remove the grin from his face.

Andrews reappeared at the door. "Breakfast is ready, m'lady."

When she woke a second time, a young doctor was changing the dressing on her shoulder.

"How long before I'm fully recovered?" was her first question.

The doctor looked startled when he heard her voice for the first time—such a shrill, piping note didn't quite fit her legend. He remained silent until he'd finished cutting a length of bandage with his scissors.

"Three, four days at most," he replied, looking down at her. "But I wouldn't be in a hurry to get myself discharged, if I were you, because the moment I sign your release papers, your next stop is Jilava, which I think you're only too familiar with from your days serving the past regime."

Krantz could never forget the barren, stone-walled, rat-infested building that she had visited every night in order to question the latest prisoners before being driven back to the warmth of her well-furnished dacha on the outskirts of the city.

"I'm told that the inmates are looking forward to seeing you again after such a prolonged absence," added the doctor. He bent over, peeled an edge from the large dressing on her shoulder, and paused. "This is going to hurt," he promised, and then in one movement, ripped it off. Krantz didn't flinch. She wasn't going to allow him that satisfaction.

The doctor dabbed iodine into the wound before placing a new dressing over it. He then expertly bandaged the shoulder and placed her right arm in a sling.

"How many guards are there?" she asked casually.

"Six, and they're all armed," said the doctor, "and just in case you're thinking of trying to escape, they have orders to shoot first and fill in any unnecessary forms later. I've even prepared an unsigned death certificate for them."

Krantz didn't ask any more questions.

When the doctor left, she lay staring up at the ceiling. If there was any chance of escaping, it would have to be while she was still at the hospital. No one had ever managed to escape from Jilava penitentiary, not even Ceauşescu.

It took her another eight hours to confirm that there were always six guards, covering three eight-hour shifts. The first group clocked in at six o'clock, the second at two, and the night shift came on duty at ten.

During a long, sleepless night, Krantz discovered that the half-dozen guards on night duty felt they had drawn the short straw. One of them was just plain lazy and spent half the night asleep. Another was always sneaking off to have a cigarette on the fire escape—no smoking allowed on the hospital premises. The third was a philanderer who imagined that he'd been put on earth to satisfy women. He was never more than a few paces from one of the nurses. The fourth spent most of his time grumbling about how much, or how little, he was paid, and his wife's ability to clean him out before the end of every week. Krantz knew that she could take care of his problem if she was given the chance. The other two guards were older, and remembered her only too well from the past regime. One of them would have been happy to blow a hole right through her if she'd as much as raised her head from the pillow.

But even they were entitled to a meal break.

Jack sat down to a breakfast of eggs, bacon, deviled kidneys, mushrooms, and tomatoes, followed by toast, English marmalade, and coffee.

"You must be hungry after such an ordeal," remarked Arabella.

"If it hadn't been for Tom, I might have had to settle for prison rations."

"And I fear I am to blame," said Anna. "Because I fingered you," she added with a grin.

"Not true," said Tom. "You can thank Arabella for having Jack arrested and Arabella for having him released."

"No, I can't take all the credit," Arabella said, stroking one of the dogs, seated on each side of her. "I admit to having Jack arrested, but it was your ambassador who managed to get him—what's the American expression?—sprung."

"But there is one thing I still don't understand," said Anna, "despite

Tom filling us in with all the finer details. Why did you continue to follow me to Wentworth once you were convinced I was no longer in possession of the painting?"

"Because I thought the woman who murdered your driver would then follow you to London."

"Where she planned to kill me?" said Anna quietly. Jack nodded but didn't speak. "Thank God I never knew," said Anna, pushing her breakfast to one side.

"But by then she'd already been arrested for murdering Sergei?" queried Arabella.

"That's right," said Jack, "but I didn't know that until I met up with Tom last night."

"So the FBI had been keeping an eye on me at the same time?" said Anna, turning to face Jack, who was buttering some toast.

"For some considerable time," admitted Jack. "At one point, we even wondered if you were the hired assassin."

"On what grounds?" demanded Anna.

"An art consultant would be a good front for someone who worked for Fenston, especially if she was also an athlete and just happened to be born in Romania."

"And just how long have I been under investigation?" asked Anna.

"For the past two months," admitted Jack. He took a sip of coffee. "In fact, we were just about to close your file when you stole the Van Gogh."

"I didn't steal it," said Anna sharply.

"She retrieved it, on my behalf," interjected Arabella. "And with my blessing, what's more."

"And are you still hoping that Fenston will agree to sell the painting so that you can clear the debt? Because if he did, it would be a first."

"No," said Arabella, a little too quickly. "That's the last thing I want."
Jack looked puzzled.

"Not until the police solve the mystery of who murdered your sister," interjected Anna.

"We all know who murdered my sister," said Arabella sharply, "and if she ever crosses my path, I'll happily blow her head off." Both dogs pricked up their ears.

"Knowing it is not the same as proving it," said Jack.

"So Fenston has got away with murder," said Anna quietly.

"More than once, I suspect," admitted Jack. "The Bureau has had him under investigation for some time. There are four—" he paused "—now five murders in different parts of the world that have the Krantz trademark, but we've never been able to link her directly to Fenston."

"Krantz murdered Victoria and Sergei," said Anna.

"Without a doubt," said Jack.

"And Colonel Sergei Slatinaru was your father's commanding officer," added Tom, "as well as being a close friend."

"I'll do anything I can to help," said Anna, close to tears, "and I mean anything."

"We've had a tiny break," admitted Tom, "though we can't be sure it will lead us anywhere. When Krantz was taken to the hospital to have the bullet removed from her shoulder, the only thing they found on her, other than the knife and a little cash, was a key."

"But surely it will fit a lock in Romania?" suggested Anna.

"We don't think so," said Jack, after devouring another mushroom. "It has NYRC 13 stamped on it. Not much of a lead, but if we could find out what it opened, it might, just might, connect Krantz to Fenston."

"So do you want me to stay in England while you continue your investigation?" asked Anna.

"No, I need you to return to New York," said Jack. "Let everyone know you're safe and well, act normally, even look for a job. Just don't give Fenston any reason to become suspicious."

"Do I stay in touch with my former colleagues in his office?" asked Anna. "Because Fenston's secretary, Tina, is one of my closest friends."

"Are you sure about that?" asked Jack, putting down his knife and fork.

"What are you getting at?" asked Anna.

"How do you explain the fact that Fenston always knew exactly where you were, if Tina wasn't telling him?"

"I can't," said Anna, "but I know she hates Fenston as much as I do."

"And you can prove it?" asked Jack.

"I don't need proof," snapped Anna.

"I do," said Jack calmly.

"Be careful, Jack, because if you're wrong," said Anna, "then her life must also be in danger."

"If that's the case, all the more reason for you to return to New York and make contact with her as soon as possible," suggested Tom, trying to calm the atmosphere.

Jack nodded his agreement.

"I'm booked on a flight this afternoon," said Anna.

"Me too," said Jack. "Heathrow?"

"No, Stansted," said Anna.

"Well, one of you is going to have to change your flight," suggested Tom.

"Not me," said Jack. "I'm not going to be arrested for stalking a second time."

"Before I make a decision on whether to change flights," said Anna, "I'll need to know if I'm still under investigation. Because if I am, *you* can go on following *me*."

"No," said Jack. "I closed your file a few days ago."

"What convinced you to do that?" asked Anna.

"When Arabella's sister was murdered, you had an unimpeachable witness as your alibi."

"And who was that, may I ask?"

"Me," replied Jack. "As I'd been following you around Central Park, you can't have been in England."

"You run in Central Park?" said Anna.

"Every morning around the loop," said Jack. "Around the Reservoir on Sundays."

"Me too," said Anna. "Never miss."

"I know," said Jack. "I overtook you several times during the last six weeks."

Anna stared at him. "The man in the emerald-green T-shirt. You're not bad."

"You're not so—"

"I'm sorry to break up this meeting of the Central Park joggers' club," said Tom, as he pushed back his chair, "but I ought to be getting back to my office. There's a stack of 9/11 files on my desk I haven't even opened. Thank you for breakfast," he added, turning to Arabella. "I'm only sorry that the ambassador had to disturb you so early this morning."

"Which reminds me," said Arabella, as she rose from her chair. "I must get on with writing some humble-pie letters, my thanks to the ambassador and my apologies to half the Surrey police force."

"What about me?" said Jack. "I'm thinking of suing the Wentworth estate, the Surrey police, and the Home Office, with Tom as my witness."

"Not a hope," said Tom. "I wouldn't care to have Arabella as an enemy."

Jack smiled. "Then I'll have to settle for a lift to the Wentworth Arms."

"You got it," said Tom.

"And now that I feel safe to join you at Heathrow," said Anna, rising from her place, "where shall we meet?"

"Don't worry," said Jack. "I'll find you."

43

LEAPMAN WAS DRIVEN to JFK to pick up the painting an hour before the plane was due to land. That didn't stop Fenston calling him every ten minutes on the way to the airport, which became every five once the limousine was on its way back to Wall Street with the red crate safely stowed in the trunk.

Fenston was pacing up and down his office by the time Leapman was dropped outside the front of the building and waiting in the corridor when Barry Steadman and the driver stepped out of the elevator carrying the red crate.

"Open it," ordered Fenston, long before the box had been propped up against the wall in his office. Barry and the driver undid the special clamps before setting about extracting the long nails that had been hammered firmly into the rim of the wooden crate, while Fenston, Leapman, and Tina looked on. When the lid was finally pried open and the polystyrene corners that were holding the painting in place were removed, Barry lifted the painting carefully out of the wooden crate and leaned it up against the chairman's desk. Fenston rushed forward and began to tear off the bubble wrap with his bare hands, until he could at last see what he'd been willing to kill for.

Fenston stood back and gasped.

No one else in the room dared to speak until he had offered an opinion. Suddenly, the words came tumbling out in a torrent.

"It's even more magnificent than I'd expected," he declared. "The colors are so fresh, and the brushwork so bold. Truly a masterpiece," he added. Leapman decided not to comment.

"I know exactly where I'm going to hang my Van Gogh," said Fenston.

He looked up and stared at the wall behind his desk, where a massive photograph of George W. Bush shaking hands with him on his recent visit to Ground Zero filled the space.

Anna was looking forward to her flight back to the States, and the chance to get to know Jack a little better during the seven-hour journey. She even hoped that he would answer one or two more questions. How did he find out her mother's address, why was he still suspicious of Tina, and was there any proof that Fenston and Krantz even knew each other?

Jack was waiting for her when she checked in. Anna took a little time to relax with a man she couldn't forget had been following her for the last nine days and investigating her for the past eight weeks, but by the time they climbed the steps to the aircraft, together for a change, Jack knew she was a Knicks fan, liked spaghetti and Dustin Hoffman, while Anna had found out that he also supported the Knicks, that his favorite modern artist was Fernando Botero, and nothing could replace his mother's Irish stew.

Anna was wondering if he liked fat women when his head fell onto her shoulder. As she was the cause of his not getting much sleep the previous night, Anna felt she was hardly in a position to complain. She pushed his head gently back up, not wishing to wake him. She began making a list of things she needed to do once she was back in New York, when Jack slumped back down onto her shoulder. Anna gave in and tried to sleep with his head there. She had once read that the head is one-seventh of your body weight. She no longer needed to be convinced.

She woke about an hour before they were due to land to find Jack was still asleep, but his arm was now draped around her shoulder. She sat up sleepily and accepted a cup of tea from the stewardess.

Jack leaned across. "So how was it for you?" he asked, grinning.

"I've had worse," she replied, "and some of them were awake."

"So what's the first thing you're going to do now that you've miraculously risen from the dead?" he asked.

"Call my family and friends and let them know just how alive I am, and then find out if anyone wants to employ me. And you?"

"I'll have to check in with my boss and let him know I'm no nearer to nailing Fenston, which will be greeted with one of his two favorite maxims: 'Raise your game, Jack,' or 'Step it up a notch.'"

"That's hardly fair," said Anna, "now that Krantz is safely behind bars."

"No thanks to me," said Jack. "And then I'll have to face up to an even fiercer wrath than the boss's, when I try to explain to my mother why I didn't call her from London and apologize for not turning up for her Irish stew night. No, my only hope of redemption is to discover what *NYRC* stands for." Jack put a hand in his top pocket. "After I'd checked out of the Wentworth Arms, I traveled on to the embassy with Tom, and thanks to modern technology, he was able to produce an exact copy of the key, even though the original is still in Romania." He pulled the facsimile out of his top pocket and handed it across to Anna.

Anna turned the small brass key over in her hands. "NYRC 13. Got any ideas?" she asked.

"Only the obvious ones," said Jack.

"New York Racing Club, New York Rowing Club, anything else?"

"New York Racquet Club, but if you come up with any others, let me know, because I intend to spend the rest of the weekend trying to find out if it's any of those. I need to come up with something positive before I face the boss on Monday."

"Perhaps you could slow down enough on your morning run to let me know if you've cracked it."

"I was rather hoping to tell you over dinner tonight," said Jack.

"I can't. I'm sorry, Jack, much as I'd love to, I'm having dinner with Tina."

"Are you?" said Jack. "Well, just be careful."

"Six o'clock tomorrow morning suit you?" asked Anna, ignoring the comment.

"That means I'll have to set my alarm for six thirty if we're going to meet up about halfway around."

"I'll be out of my shower by then."

"I'll be sorry to miss that."

"By the way," said Anna, "can you do me a favor?"

Leapman strode into the chairman's office without knocking.

"Have you seen this?" he asked, placing a copy of *The New York Times* on the desk and jabbing a finger at an article from the international section.

Fenston studied the headline: ROMANIAN POLICE ARREST ASSASSIN. He read the short article twice before speaking.

"Find out how much the chief of police wants."

"It may not prove to be that easy," suggested Leapman.

"It's always that easy," said Fenston, looking up. "Only agreeing on a price will prove difficult."

Leapman frowned. "And there's another matter you should consider."

"And what's that?" asked Fenston.

"The Van Gogh. You ought to have the painting insured, after what happened to the Monet."

"I never insure my paintings. I don't need the IRS to find out how much my collection is worth, and in any case it's never going to happen twice."

"It already has," said Leapman.

Fenston scowled and didn't reply for some time.

"All right, but only the Van Gogh," he eventually said. "Make it Lloyd's of London, and be sure you keep the book value below twenty million."

"Why such a low figure?" queried Leapman.

"Because the last thing I need is to have the Van Gogh with an asset value of a hundred million while I'm still hoping to get my hands on the rest of the Wentworth collection."

Leapman nodded and turned to leave.

"By the way," said Fenston, looking back down at the article. "Do you still have the second key?"

"Yes I do," said Leapman. "Why?"

"Because when she escapes, you'll need to make a further deposit."

Leapman smiled. A rarity, which even Fenston noticed.

———

Krantz wet her bed, and then explained to the doctor about her weak bladder. He authorized periodic visits to the bathroom, but only when accompanied by at least two guards.

These regular little outings up and down the corridor gave Krantz an opportunity to study the layout of the floor: a reception desk at the far end of the landing manned by a single nurse; a drug clinic that could only be unlocked if a doctor was present; a linen closet; three other single rooms; one bathroom; and, at the other end of the corridor, a ward containing sixteen beds, opposite a fire escape.

But the outings also served another, more important purpose, and it certainly wasn't anything the young doctor would have come across when reading his medical textbooks or carrying out his ward rounds.

Once they had locked Krantz into her cubicle, also windowless, she sat on the toilet seat, placed two fingers up her rectum, and slowly extracted a condom. She then washed the rubber container in the toilet water, undid the knot at the top, and pulled out a roll of tightly wrapped twenty-dollar bills. She extracted two from the roll, tucked them into her sling, and then carried out the whole process in reverse.

Krantz pulled the chain and was escorted back to her room. She spent the rest of the day sleeping. She needed to be wide awake during the night shift.

Jack sat in the back of the taxi, looking out of the window.

The gray cloak of 9/11 still hadn't lifted from Manhattan, although New Yorkers rushing by no longer stared upward in disbelief. Terrorism was something else the most frenetic city on earth had already learned to take in its stride.

Jack sat back and thought about the favor he'd promised Anna. He dialed the number she'd given him. Sam picked up the phone. Jack told him that Anna was alive and well, and that she had been visiting her mother in Romania, and he could expect her back that evening. Nice to start the day making someone feel good, thought Jack, which wasn't going to be the case with his second call. He phoned his boss to let him know that he was back in New York. Macy told him that Krantz had been taken to a local hospital in Bucharest to undergo an operation on her shoulder. She was being guarded round the clock by half a dozen cops.

"I'll be happier when she's locked up in jail," said Jack.

"I'm told you speak with some experience on that subject," said Macy.

Jack was about to respond when Macy added, "Why don't you take the rest of the week off, Jack? You've earned it."

"It's Saturday," Jack reminded his boss.

"So I'll see you first thing Monday morning," said Macy.

Jack decided to text Anna next: *Told Sam U R on way home. Is he only other man in yr life?* He waited a couple of minutes, but there was no reply. He called his mother.

"Will you be coming home for supper tonight?" she asked sharply. He could almost smell the meat stewing in the background.

"Would I miss it, Ma?"

"You did last week."

"Ah, yes, I meant to call you," said Jack, "but something came up."

"Will you be bringing this something with you tonight?" Jack hesitated, a foolish mistake. "Is she a good Catholic girl?" was his mother's next question.

"No, Mother," Jack replied. "She's a divorcée, three ex-husbands, two of whom died in mysterious circumstances. Oh, and she has five children, not all of them by the three husbands, but you'll be glad to know only four of the kids are on hard drugs—the other one's currently serving a jail sentence."

"Does she have a regular job?"

"Oh yes, Ma, it's a cash business. She services most of her customers on the weekends, but she assures me that she can always take an hour off for a bowl of Irish stew."

"So what does she really do?" asked his mother.

"She's an art thief," said Jack, "specializes in Van Gogh and Picasso. Makes a huge profit on each assignment."

"Then she'll be an improvement on the last one," said his mother, "who specialized in losing your money."

"Good-bye, Mother," said Jack. "I'll see you tonight."

He ended the call, to find there was a text from Anna, using her ID for Jack:

Switch your brain on, Stalker. Got the obvious R. U R 2 slow 4 me.

"Damn the woman," said Jack. His next call was to Tom in London, but all he got was an answering machine saying, "Tom Crasanti, I'm out at the moment, but will be back shortly, please leave a message."

Jack didn't, as the cab was pulling up outside his apartment.

"That'll be thirty-two dollars."

Jack handed the driver four tens and didn't ask for any change and didn't get a *thank you*.

Things were back to normal in New York.

The night shift reported for duty at ten o'clock. The six new guards spent their first two hours marching up and down the corridor, making their presence felt. Every few minutes, one of them would unlock her door, switch on the bare bulb that hung above her bed, and check that she was "present" before he turned off the light and locked the door. This exercise was repeated at regular intervals for the first two hours, but after that it lapsed to every half an hour.

At five minutes past four, when two of the guards went off for their meal break, Krantz pressed the buzzer by her bed. Two more guards appeared, the grumbler with money problems and the chain smoker. They both accompanied her to the bathroom, each holding an elbow. When she entered the lavatory, one remained in the corridor, while the other stood guard outside the cubicle. Krantz extracted two more notes from her rectum, folded them up in her hands and then pulled the lavatory chain. The guard opened the door. She smiled and slipped the notes into his hand. He looked at them and quickly put them in his pocket before rejoining his colleague in the corridor. They both accompanied Krantz back to her room and locked her in.

Twenty minutes later, the other two guards returned from their meal break. One of them unlocked her door, switched on the light, and, because she was so slight, had to go up to the side of the bed to make sure she was actually there. The ritual completed, he walked back into the corridor, locked the door, and joined his colleague for a game of backgammon.

Krantz concluded that her one chance of escaping would be between four and four twenty in the morning, when the two older guards always took their meal break—the philanderer, the smoker, and the dozer would be otherwise occupied, and her unwitting accomplice would be only too happy to accompany her to the bathroom.

Even before Jack had showered and changed, he began to scour the New York telephone directory in search of NYRC. Other than the three Jack had already come up with, he couldn't spot Anna's "obvious one." He switched on his laptop and Googled the words "new york racquet club." He was able to retrieve a potted history of the NYRC, several photographs of an elegant building on Park Avenue, and a picture of the present chairman, Darius T. Mablethorpe III. Jack was in no doubt that the only way he was going to get past the front door was if he looked like a member. Never embarrass the Bureau.

Once Jack had unpacked and showered, he selected a dark suit with a faint stripe, a blue shirt, and a Columbia tie for this particular outing. He left his apartment and took a cab to 370 Park Avenue. He stepped onto the sidewalk and stood staring at the building for some time. He admired the magnificent four-story Renaissance revival architecture that reminded him of a palazzo, so popular with the Italians in New York at the turn of the century. He walked up the steps toward an entrance with the letters NYRC discreetly etched into the glass.

The doorman greeted Jack with, "Good afternoon, sir," holding the door open, as if Jack was a lifelong member. He strolled into an elegant lobby with massive paintings on every available space of suitably attired former chairmen dressed in long white pants and blue blazers, sporting the inevitable racquet. Jack glanced up at the wide, sweeping staircase to see even more past chairmen, even more ancient; only the racquet didn't seem to have changed. He strolled up to the reception desk.

"May I help you, sir?" asked a young man.

"I'm not sure if you can," Jack admitted.

"Try me," he offered.

Jack took the replica key out of his pocket and placed it on the countertop. "Ever seen one of these?" he asked.

The young man picked up the key and turned it over, staring at the lettering for some time, before he replied, "No, sir, can't say I have. It could well be a safety deposit box key, but not one of ours." He turned and removed a heavy bronze key from the board behind him. A member's name was etched on the handle, and NYRC in red along the shaft.

"Any suggestions?" asked Jack, trying to keep any sign of desperation out of his voice.

"No, sir," he replied. "Not unless it was before my time," he added. "I've only been here for eleven years, but perhaps Abe might be able to help. He was here in the days when more people played racquets than tennis."

"And the gentlemen only played racquets," said an older man who appeared from an office at the back to join his colleague. "And what is it that I might be able to help with?"

"A key," said the young man. "This gentleman wants to know if you've ever seen one like it," he added as he passed the key to Abe.

Abe turned the key over in his hands. "It's certainly not one of ours," he confirmed, "and never has been, but I know what the R stands for," he added triumphantly. "Because it must have been, oh, nearly twenty years ago, when Dinkins was mayor." He paused and looked up at Jack. "A young man came in who could hardly speak a word of English and asked if this was the Romanian Club."

"Of course," murmured Jack, "how stupid of me."

"I remember how disappointed he was," continued Abe, ignoring Jack's muttered chastisement, "to find the R stood for *Racquet*. Not that I think he knew what a racquet was. You see, he couldn't read English, so I had to look up the address for him. The only reason I remember anything after all this time is because the club was situated somewhere on *Lincoln*," he said, emphasizing the name of the street. He glanced at Jack, who decided not to interrupt a second time. "Named after him," he explained. Jack smiled at Abe and nodded. "Some place in Queens, I think, but I don't recall exactly where."

Jack put the key back in his pocket, thanked Abe, and turned to leave before he gave him the chance to share any more reminiscences.

Tina sat at her desk, typing out the speech. He hadn't even thanked her for coming in on a Saturday.

Bankers must at all times be willing to set standards that far exceed their legal requirements.

The New York Bankers' Association had invited Fenston to deliver the keynote speech at their annual dinner, to be held at the Sherry Netherland.

Fenston was both surprised and delighted by the invitation, although he had been angling for it for some time.

The committee had been divided.

Fenston was determined to make a good impression on his colleagues in the banking fraternity and had already dictated several drafts of the speech.

Customers must always be able to rely on our independent judgment, confident that we will act in their best interests rather than our own.

Tina began to wonder if she was writing a script for a bankers' sitcom, with Fenston auditioning for the lead. What part would Leapman play in this moral tale, she wondered? For how many episodes would Victoria Wentworth survive?

We must, at all times, look upon ourselves as the guardians of our customers' assets—especially if they own a Van Gogh, Tina wanted to insert—*while never neglecting their commercial aspirations.*

Tina's thoughts drifted to Anna, as she continued to type out Fenston's shameless homily. She had spoken to her on the phone just before leaving for the office that morning. Anna wanted to tell her about the new man in her life, whom she had met in the most unusual circumstances. They had agreed to get together for supper that evening, as Tina also had something she wanted to share.

And let's never forget that it only takes one of us to lower our standards, and then the rest of us will suffer as a consequence.

As Tina turned another page, she wondered just how much longer she could hope to survive as Fenston's personal assistant. Since she'd thrown Leapman out of her office, not one civil word had passed between them. Would he have her fired only days before she had gathered enough proof to make sure Fenston spent the rest of his life in a smaller room in a larger institution?

And may I conclude by saying that my single purpose in life has always been to serve and give back to the community that has allowed me to share the American dream.

This was one document Tina would not bother to retain a copy of.

The light on Tina's phone was flashing and she quickly picked up the receiver.

"Yes, Chairman?"

"Have you finished my speech for the bankers' dinner?"

"Yes, chairman," repeated Tina.

"It's good, isn't it?" said Fenston.

"It's remarkable," responded Tina.

Jack hailed a cab and told him Lincoln Street, Queens. The driver left the meter running while he looked up the address in his much-thumbed directory. Jack was halfway back to the airport before he was dropped off on the corner of Lincoln and Harris. He looked up and down the street, aware that the suit he'd carefully selected for Park Avenue was somewhat incongruous in Queens. He stepped into a liquor store on the corner.

"I'm looking for the Romanian Club," he told the elderly woman behind the counter.

"Closed years ago," she said. "It's now a guest house," she added, looking him up and down, "but I don't think you'll wanna stay there."

"Any idea of the number?" asked Jack.

"No, but it's 'bout halfway down, on the other side of the street."

Jack thanked the woman, walked back out onto Lincoln and crossed the road. He tried to judge where the halfway mark might be, when he spotted a faded ROOMS FOR RENT sign. He stopped and looked down a short flight of steps to see an even more faded sign painted above the entrance. The letters NYRC, FOUNDED 1919 were almost indecipherable.

Jack descended the steps and pushed open the creaking door. He stepped into a dingy, unlit hallway, to be greeted with the pungent smell of stale tobacco. There was a small, dusty reception desk straight ahead of him, and behind it, almost hidden from view, Jack caught a glimpse of an old man reading the *New York Post*, enveloped in a cloud of cigarette smoke.

"I need a room for the night," said Jack, trying to sound as if he meant it.

The old man's eyes narrowed as he gave Jack a disbelieving look. Did he have a girl waiting outside? "That'll be seven dollars," he said, before adding, "in advance."

"And I'll also need somewhere to lock my valuables," said Jack.

"That'll be another dollar—in advance," repeated the man, the cigarette bobbing up and down.

Jack handed over eight dollars in return for a key.

"Second floor, number three, and the safety deposit boxes are at the end of the corridor," he said, passing him a second key. He then returned his attention to the *New York Post,* the cigarette having never left his mouth.

Jack walked slowly down the corridor until he reached a wall lined with safety deposit boxes, which, despite their age, looked solid and not that easy to break into, even if anyone might have considered the exercise worthwhile. He opened his own box and peered inside. It must have been about eight inches wide and a couple of feet deep. Jack glanced back toward the front counter. The desk clerk had managed to turn the page, but the cigarette still hadn't left his mouth.

Jack moved farther down the corridor, removed the replica key from an inside pocket, and, after one more glance toward the front desk, opened box 13. He stared inside and tried to remain calm, although his heart was pounding. He extracted one bill from the box and placed it in his wallet. Jack locked the box and put the key back in his pocket.

The old man turned another page and began to study the racing odds as Jack walked back onto the street.

He had to cover eleven blocks before he found an empty cab, but he didn't attempt to call Dick Macy until he'd been dropped back at his apartment. He unlocked the front door, ran through to the kitchen, and placed the hundred-dollar bill on the table. He then recalled how deep and how wide the empty box had been, before attempting to calculate how many hundred-dollar bills must have been stuffed into box 13. By the time he called Macy, he'd measured a space out on the kitchen table and used several five-hundred-page paperbacks to assist him in his calculation.

"I thought I told you to take the rest of the weekend off," said Macy.

"I've found the box that NYRC 13 opens."

"What was inside?"

"Hard to be certain," replied Jack, "but I'd say around two million dollars."

"Your leave is canceled," said Macy.

9/23

44

"GOOD NEWS," DECLARED the doctor on the morning of the third day. "Your wound is nearly healed, and I shall be recommending to the authorities that you can be moved to Jilava penitentiary tomorrow."

With this, the doctor had determined her timetable. After he had changed her dressing and departed without another word, Krantz lay in bed going over her plan again and again. She only asked to visit the bathroom at two P.M. She slept soundly between three and nine.

"She's been no trouble all day," Krantz heard one of the guards report when he handed over his keys to the night shift at ten o'clock.

Krantz didn't stir for the next two hours, aware that two of the guards would be waiting impatiently to accompany her to the bathroom and collect their nightly stipend. But the timing had to suit her. She would cater for their needs at four minutes past four, not before, when one would receive forty dollars, and he would make sure that the other got a packet of Benson & Hedges. Disproportionate, but then one had a far more important role to play. She spent the next two hours wide awake.

Anna left her apartment to set out on her morning run just before six A.M. Sam rushed from behind his desk to open the door for her—a Cheshire cat grin hadn't left his face from the moment she'd arrived back.

Anna wondered at what point Jack would catch up with her. She had to admit, he'd been in her thoughts a lot since they had parted yesterday, and she already hoped their relationship might stray beyond a professional interest.

"Beware," Tina had warned her over supper. "Once he's got what he wants, he'll move on, and it isn't necessarily sex that he's after."

Pity, she remembered thinking.

"Fenston loves the Van Gogh," Tina assured her. "He's given the painting pride of place on the wall behind his desk."

In fact, Tina had been forthcoming about everything Fenston and Leapman had been up to during the past ten days. However, despite gentle probing, hints, and well-placed questions, by the time they left the restaurant a couple of hours later Anna was no nearer to finding out why Fenston had such a hold over her.

Anna couldn't help remembering that the last time she'd run around Central Park was on the morning of the eleventh. The dark gray cloud may have finally dispersed, but there were several other reminders of that dreadful day, not least the two words on everyone's lips: *Ground Zero*. She put aside the horrors of that day when she spotted Jack jogging on the spot under Artists' Gate.

"Been waiting long, Stalker?" Anna asked, as she strode past him and up around the pond.

"No," he replied, once he'd caught up. "I've already been around twice, so I'm treating this as a cooling-down session."

"Cooling down already, are we?" said Anna, as she accelerated away. She knew she wouldn't be able to maintain that pace for long and it was only a few seconds before he was back striding by her side.

"Not bad," said Jack, "but how long can you keep it up?"

"I thought that was a male problem," Anna said, still trying to set the pace. She decided that her only hope would be to distract him. She waited until the Frick came in sight.

"Name five artists on display in that museum," she demanded, hoping his lack of knowledge would compensate for her lack of speed.

"Bellini, Mary Cassatt, Renoir, Rembrandt, and two Holbeins—More and Cromwell."

"Yes, but which Cromwell?" asked Anna, panting.

"Thomas, not Oliver," said Jack.

"Not bad, Stalker," admitted Anna.

"You can blame it on my father," said Jack. "Whenever he was out on patrol on a Sunday, my mother would take me to a gallery or a museum. I thought it was a waste of time, until I fell in love."

"Who did you fall in love with?" asked Anna, as they jogged up Pilgrim's Hill.

"Rossetti, or, to be more accurate, his mistress, Jane Burden."

"Scholars are divided on whether he even slept with her," said Anna. "And her husband—William Morris—admired Rossetti so much that they don't even think he would have objected."

"Foolish man," said Jack.

"Are you still in love with Jane?" asked Anna.

"No, I've moved on since then. I gave up the pre-Raphaelites for the real thing, and started falling for women whose breasts often end up behind their ears."

"So you must have been spending a lot of your time in MoMA."

"Several blind dates," admitted Jack, "but my mother doesn't approve."

"Who does she think you should be dating?"

"She's old-fashioned, so anyone called Mary who's a virgin, but I'm working on her."

"Are you working on anything else?"

"Like what?" asked Jack.

"Like what R stands for," said Anna, almost out of breath.

"You tell me," said Jack.

"Romania would be my bet," said Anna, the words puffing out intermittently.

"You should have joined the FBI," said Jack, slowing down.

"You'd worked it out already," said Anna.

"No," admitted Jack. "A guy called Abe worked it out for me."

"And?"

"And both of you were right."

"So where is the Romanian Club?"

"In a run-down neighborhood in Queens," replied Jack.

"And what did you find when you opened the box?"

"I can't be absolutely certain," replied Jack.

"Don't play games, Stalker, just tell me what was in the box."

"About two million dollars."

"Two million?" repeated Anna in disbelief.

"Well, it might not be quite that much, but it certainly was enough for my boss to drop everything, stake out the building, and cancel my leave."

"What sort of person keeps two million in cash hidden in a safety deposit box in Queens?" asked Anna.

"A person who can't risk opening a bank account anywhere in the world."

"Krantz," said Anna.

"So now it's your turn. Did anything come out of your dinner with Tina?"

"I thought you'd never ask," replied Anna, and covered another hundred yards before she said, "Fenston thinks the latest addition to his collection is magnificent. But, more important, when Tina took in his morning coffee, there was a copy of *The New York Times* on his desk, and it was open at page seventeen."

"Obviously not the sports section," said Jack.

"No, international," said Anna, as she extracted the article from her pocket and passed it over to Jack.

"Is this a ploy to see if I can keep up with you while I read?"

"No, it's a ploy to find out if you *can* read, Stalker, and I can always slow down, because I know you haven't been able to keep up with me in the past," said Anna.

Jack read the headline and almost came to a halt as they ran past the lake. It was some time before he spoke again. "Sharp girl, your friend Tina."

"And she gets sharper," said Anna. "She interrupted a conversation Fenston was having with Leapman, and overheard him say, 'Do you still have the second key?' She didn't understand the significance of it at the time, but—"

"I take back everything I said about her," said Jack. "She's on our team."

"No, Stalker, she's on *my* team," said Anna, accelerating through Strawberry Fields as she always did for the last half mile, with Jack striding by her side.

"This is where I leave you," said Anna, once they reached Artists' Gate. She checked her watch and smiled: Eleven minutes, forty-eight seconds.

"Brunch?"

"Can't, sadly," said Anna. "Meeting up with an old friend from Christie's, trying to find out if they've got any openings."

"Dinner?"

"I've got tickets for the Rauschenberg at the Whitney. If you want to join me, I'll be there around six, Stalker."

She ran away before he could reply.

45

LEAPMAN HAD SELECTED a Sunday because it was the one day of the week Fenston didn't go into the office, although he'd already called him three times that day.

He sat alone in his apartment eating a TV dinner, and going over his plan, until he was certain nothing could go wrong. Tomorrow, and all the rest of his tomorrows, he would dine in a restaurant, without having to wait for Fenston.

When he'd eaten every last scrap, he returned to his bedroom and stripped down to his underpants. He pulled open a drawer that contained the sports gear he needed for this particular exercise. He put on a T-shirt, shorts, and a baggy, gray tracksuit that teenagers wouldn't even have believed their parents once wore, and finally donned a pair of white socks and white gym shoes. Leapman didn't look at himself in the mirror. He walked back across the room, fell on his knees, and reached under the bed to pull out a large gym bag that had the handle of a squash racket poking out of it. He was now dressed and ready for his irregular exercise. All he needed was the key and a packet of cigarettes.

He strolled through to the kitchen, opened a drawer that contained a large carton of duty-free Marlboros, and extracted a packet of twenty. He never smoked. His final act in this agnostic ritual was to place his hand under the drawer and remove a key that was taped to the base. He was now fully equipped.

He double-locked the front door of his apartment and took the stairs down to the basement. He opened the back door and walked up one flight, emerging onto the street.

To any casual passerby, he looked like a man on the way to his squash club. Leapman had never played a game of squash in his life. He walked one block before hailing a yellow cab. The routine never varied. He gave the driver an address that didn't have a squash club within five miles. He sat in the back of the cab, relieved to find the driver wasn't talkative because he needed to concentrate. Today, he would make one change from his normal routine, a change he'd been planning for the past ten years. This would be the last time he carried out this particular chore for Fenston, a man who had taken advantage of him every day for the last decade. Not today. Never again. He glanced out of the cab window. He made this journey once, sometimes twice a year, when he would deposit large sums of cash at NYRC, always within days of Krantz completing one of her assignments. During that time, Leapman had deposited over five million dollars into box 13 at the guesthouse on Lincoln Street, and he knew it would always be a one-way journey—until she made a mistake.

When he'd read in the *Times* that Krantz had been captured after being shot in the shoulder—he would have preferred that she'd been killed—he knew this must be his one chance. What Fenston would describe as a window of opportunity. After all, Krantz was the only person who knew how much cash was in that box, while he remained the only other person with a key.

"Where is it exactly?" asked the driver.

Leapman looked out of the window. "A couple more blocks," he said, "and then you can drop me on the corner." Leapman took the squash racket out of the bag and placed it on the backseat.

"Twenty-three dollars," the driver mumbled, as he came to a halt outside a liquor store.

Leapman passed three tens through the grille. "I'll be back in five minutes. If you're still around, you'll get another fifty."

"I'll be around," came back the immediate reply.

Leapman grabbed the empty gym bag and stepped out of the cab, leaving the squash racket on the backseat. He crossed the road, pleased to find that the sidewalk was crowded with locals out shopping. One of the reasons he always chose a Sunday afternoon. He would never risk such an outing at night. In Queens, they'd be happy to mug him for an empty bag.

Leapman quickened his pace until he reached number 61. He stopped for a moment to check that no one was taking any interest in him. Why would they? He descended the steps toward the NYRC sign and pushed open a door that was never locked.

The caretaker looked up from his sedentary position and, when he saw who it was, nodded—the most energetic thing he'd done all day—then turned his attention back to the racing page. Leapman placed the packet of Marlboros on the counter, knowing they would disappear before he turned around. Every man has his price.

He peered into the gloom of a corridor lit only by a naked forty-watt bulb. He sometimes wondered if he was the only person who advanced beyond the counter.

Despite the darkness of the corridor, he knew exactly where her box was located. Not that you could read the number on the door—like every-thing else, it had faded over the years. He looked back up the corridor; one of his cigarettes was already glowing in the darkness.

He took the key out of his tracksuit pocket, placed it in the lock, turned it, and pulled open the door. He unzipped the bag before looking back in the direction of the old man. No interest. It took him less than a minute to empty the contents of the box, fill the bag, and zip it back up.

Leapman closed the door and locked it for the last time. He picked up the bag, momentarily surprised by how heavy it was, and walked back down the corridor. He placed the key on the counter. "I won't be needing it again," he told the old man, who didn't allow this sudden break in rou-tine to distract him from his study of the odds for the four o'clock at Bel-mont. He'd been fifty feet from a racing certainty for the past twelve years and hadn't even checked the odds.

Leapman walked out of the door, climbed back up the steps and into the light of Lincoln Street. At the top of the steps, he once again glanced up and down the road. He felt safe. He began to walk quickly down the street, gripping the handle of the bag tightly, relieved to see the cab was still waiting for him on the corner.

He had covered about twenty yards when, out of nowhere, he was surrounded by a dozen men dressed in jeans and blue-nylon windbreakers,
FBI printed in bold yellow letters on their backs. They came running toward him from every direction. A moment later, two cars entered Lincoln, one from each end—despite its being a one-way street—and came
to a screeching halt in a semicircle around the suspect. This time
passersby did stop to stare at the tracksuited man carrying a sports bag.
The taxi sped away, minus fifty dollars, plus one squash racket.

"Read him his rights," said Joe, as another officer clamped Leapman's
arms firmly behind his back and handcuffed him, while a third relieved
him of his gym bag.

"You have the right to remain silent . . . ," which Leapman did.

Once his Miranda rights had been recited to him—not for the first
time—Leapman was led off to one of the cars and unceremoniously
dumped in the back, where Agent Delaney was waiting for him.

Anna was at the Whitney Museum, standing in front of a Rauschenberg
canvas entitled *Satellite,* when her cell phone vibrated in her jacket pocket.
She glanced at the screen to see that *Stalker* was trying to contact her.

"Hey," said Anna.

"I was wrong."

"Wrong about what?" asked Anna.

"It was more than two million."

The clock on a nearby church struck four times.

Krantz heard one of the guards say, "We're off for our supper. We'll be
back in about twenty minutes." The chain smoker coughed but didn't respond. Krantz lay still in her bed until she could no longer hear their departing footsteps. She pressed the buzzer by the side of her bed and a key
turned in the lock immediately. Krantz didn't have to guess which one of
them would be standing in the doorway, eager to accompany her to the
washroom.

"Where's your mate?" Krantz asked.

"He's having a drag," said the guard. "Don't worry, I'll see that he gets
his share."

She rubbed her eyes, climbed slowly out of bed, and joined him in the corridor. Another guard was lolling in a chair, half asleep, at the other end of the corridor. The smoker and the philanderer were nowhere to be seen.

The guard held on to her elbow as he led her quickly down the passage. He accompanied her into the bathroom, but remained outside while she disappeared into the cubicle. Krantz sat on the toilet, extracted the condom, peeled off two more twenty-dollar bills, folded them, and hid them in the palm of her right hand. She then slowly pushed the condom back into a place even the least squeamish guards didn't care to search.

Once she'd pulled the chain, her guard unlocked the door. He smiled in anticipation as she walked back out into the corridor. The guard seated at the far end didn't stir, and her personal minder seemed as pleased as she was to discover that there was no one else around.

Krantz nodded toward the linen closet. He pulled open the door and they both slipped inside. Krantz immediately opened the palm of her hand to reveal the two twenty-dollar bills. She passed them over to the guard. Just as he went to grab them, she dropped one on the floor. He bent down to pick it up—only a matter of a second—but long enough for him to feel the full force of her knee as it came crashing up into his groin. As he fell forward, grasping his crotch, Krantz grabbed him by the hair and in one swift movement sliced open his throat with the doctor's scissors. Not the most efficient of instruments, but the only thing she could lay her hands on. She let go of his hair, grabbed him by the collar, and, with all the strength she could muster, bundled him into the laundry chute. With a heave she helped him on his way, then dived in behind him.

They both bounced down the spacious metal tube, and a few seconds later landed with a thud on a pile of sheets, pillowcases, and towels in the laundry room. Krantz leapt up, grabbed the smallest overall from a peg on the wall, pulled it on, and ran across to the door. She opened it slowly and peered out through the crack into the corridor. The only person in sight was a cleaner, on her knees polishing the floor. Krantz walked quickly past her and pushed open the fire-exit door to be greeted by the word *Subsol* on the wall in front of her. She ran up one flight of steps, pulled up a window on the ground floor, and climbed out onto a flower bed. It was pouring with rain.

She looked around, expecting at any moment to hear the raucous sound of a siren followed by floodlights illuminating every inch of the hospital grounds.

Krantz had covered nearly two miles by the time the philanderer required the privacy of the linen closet for a second time that night. The nurse screamed when she saw the blood all over the white walls. The guard ran back into the corridor and charged toward the prisoner's room. The chair-bound guard at the end of the passage leaped up from his seat as the smoker came rushing in from the fire escape. The philanderer reached her room first. He pulled open the door, switched on the light, and let out a tirade of expletives, while the smoker smashed the glass covering the alarm and pressed the red button.

9/24

46

ONE OF ANNA'S golden rules when she woke in the morning was not to check the messages on her cell phone until she had showered, dressed, had breakfast, and read *The New York Times*. But as she had broken every one of her golden rules over the last two weeks, she checked her messages even before she got out of bed. One from Stalker asking her to call, which made her smile, one from Tina—no message, and one from Mr. Nakamura, which made her frown—only four words: "Urgent, please call. Nakamura."

Anna decided to take a cold shower before she returned his call. As the jets of water cascaded down on her, she thought about Mr. Nakamura's message. The word *urgent* always made her assume the worst—Anna fell into the half-empty-glass category rather than the half-full.

She was wide awake by the time she stepped out of the shower. Her heart was pounding at about the same pace as when she'd just finished her morning run. She sat on the end of the bed and tried to compose herself.

Once Anna felt her heartbeat had returned to as near normal as it was likely to, she dialed Nakamura's number in Tokyo.

"*Hai, Shacho-Shitso desu,*" announced the receptionist.

"Mr. Nakamura, please."

"Who shall I say is calling?"

"Anna Petrescu."

"Ah yes, he is expecting your call." Anna's heartbeat quickened.

"Good morning, Dr. Petrescu."

"Good afternoon, Mr. Nakamura," said Anna, wishing she could see his face and more quickly learn her fate.

"I've recently had a most unpleasant conversation with your former boss, Bryce Fenston," continued Nakamura. "Which I'm afraid"—Anna could hardly breathe—"has made me reassess"—was she about to be sick?—"my opinion of that man. However, that's not the purpose of this call. I just wanted to let you know that you are currently costing me around five hundred dollars a day as I have, as you requested, deposited five million dollars with my lawyers in London. So I would like to view the Van Gogh as soon as possible."

"I could fly to Tokyo in the next few days," Anna assured him, "but I would first have to go to England and pick up the painting."

"That may not prove necessary," said Nakamura. "I have a meeting with Corus Steel in London scheduled for Wednesday, and would be happy to fly over a day earlier, if that was convenient for Lady Arabella."

"I'm sure that will be just fine," said Anna. "I'll need to contact Arabella and then call your secretary to confirm the details. Wentworth Hall is only about thirty minutes from Heathrow."

"Excellent," said Nakamura. "Then I'll look forward to seeing you both tomorrow evening." He paused. "By the way, Anna, have you given any more thought to becoming the director of my foundation? Because Mr. Fenston did convince me of one thing: you are certainly worth five hundred dollars a day."

Although it was the third time Fenston had read the article, a smile never left his face. He couldn't wait to share the news with Leapman, though he suspected he'd already seen the piece. He glanced at the clock on his desk, just before ten. Leapman was never late. Where was he?

Tina had already warned him that Mr. Jackson, an insurance assessor from Lloyd's of London, was in the waiting room, and the front desk had just called to say that Chris Savage of Christie's was on his way up.

"As soon as Savage appears," said Fenston, "send them both in and then tell Leapman to join us."

"I haven't seen Mr. Leapman this morning," said Tina.

"Well, tell him I want him in here the moment he arrives," said Fenston. The smile returned to his face when he reread the headline, KITCHEN KNIFE KILLER ESCAPES.

There was a knock on the door, and Tina ushered both men into the office.

"Mr. Jackson and Mr. Savage," she said. From their dress, it would not have been difficult to fathom which was the insurance broker and which one spent his life in the art world.

Fenston stepped forward and shook hands with a short, balding man in a navy pin-striped suit and crested blue tie, who introduced himself as Bill Jackson. Fenston nodded at Savage, whom he had met at Christie's on several occasions over the years. He was wearing his trademark bow tie.

"I wish to make it clear from the outset," began Fenston, "that I only want to insure this one painting," he said, gesturing toward the Van Gogh, "for twenty million dollars."

"Despite the fact that it might fetch five times that amount were it to come under the hammer?" queried Savage, who turned to study the picture for the first time.

"That would, of course, mean a far lower premium," interjected Jackson. "That's assuming our security boys consider the painting is adequately protected."

"Just stay where you are, Mr. Jackson, and you can decide for yourself if it's adequately protected."

Fenston walked to the door, entered a six-digit code on the keypad next to the light switch, and left the room. The moment the door closed behind him, a metal grille appeared from out of the ceiling and eight seconds later was clamped to the floor, covering the Van Gogh. At the same time, an alarm emitted an ear-piercing sound that would have caused even Quasimodo to seek another vocation.

Jackson quickly pressed the palms of his hands over his ears and turned around to see that a second grille had already barred his exit from the only door in the room. He walked across to the window and looked down at the midgets hurrying along the sidewalk below. A few seconds later, the alarm stopped and the metal grilles slid up into the ceiling. Fenston marched back into the room, looking pleased with himself.

"Impressive," said Jackson, the sound of the alarm still reverberating in his ears. "But there are still a couple of questions I will need answered," he added. "How many people know the code?"

"Only two of us," said Fenston, "my chief of staff and myself, and I change the sequence of numbers once a week."

"And that window," said Jackson, "is there any way of opening it?"

"No, it's double-glazed bulletproof glass, and even if you could break it, you'd still be thirty-two stories above the ground."

"And the alarm . . ."

"Connected directly to Abbott Security," said Fenston. "They have an office in the building and guarantee to be on this floor within two minutes."

"I'm impressed," said Jackson. "What we in the business call triple-A, which usually means the premium can be kept down to one percent or, in real terms, around two hundred thousand dollars a year." He smiled. "I only wish the Norwegians had your foresight, Mr. Fenston, and then perhaps we wouldn't have had to pay out so much on *The Scream.*"

"But can you also guarantee discretion in these matters?" Fenston asked.

"Absolutely," Jackson assured him. "We insure half the world's treasures, and you wouldn't find out who our clients are, were you to break into our headquarters in the City of London. Even their names are coded."

"That's reassuring," said Fenston. "Then all that needs to be done is for you to complete the paperwork."

"I can do that," said Jackson, "just as soon as Mr. Savage confirms a value of twenty million for the painting."

"That shouldn't be too difficult," said Fenston, turning his attention to Chris Savage, who was staring intently at the picture. "After all, he's already assured us that the Wentworth Van Gogh is worth nearer one hundred million."

"The Wentworth Van Gogh most certainly is," said Savage, "but not this particular piece." He paused before turning round to face Fenston. "The only part of this work of art that's original is the frame."

"What do you mean?" said Fenston, staring up at his favorite painting as if he'd been informed that his only child was illegitimate.

"I mean just that," said Savage. "The frame is original, but the painting is a fake."

"A fake?" repeated Fenston, hardly able to get the words out. "But it came from Wentworth Hall."

"The frame may well have come from Wentworth Hall," said Savage, "but I can assure you that the canvas did not."

"How can you be so sure," demanded Fenston, "when you haven't even carried out any tests?"

"I don't need to carry out any tests," said Savage emphatically.

"Why not?" barked Fenston.

"Because the wrong ear is bandaged," came back the immediate reply.

"No it's not," insisted Fenston, as he stared up at the painting. "Every schoolchild knows that Van Gogh cut off his left ear."

"But not every schoolchild knows that he painted the self-portrait while looking in a mirror, which is why the right ear is bandaged."

Fenston slumped down into the chair behind his desk, with his back to the painting. Savage strolled forward and began to study the picture even more closely. "What puzzles me," he added, "is that although the painting is undoubtedly a fake, someone has put it into the original frame." Fenston's face burned with anger. "And I must confess," continued Savage, "that whoever painted this particular version is a fine artist." He paused. "However, I could only place a value of ten thousand on the work, and perhaps—"he hesitated "—a further ten thousand on the frame, which would make the suggested premium of two hundred thousand seem somewhat excessive." Fenston still didn't respond. "I am sorry to be the bearer of such bad news," concluded Savage, as he walked away from the picture and came to a halt in front of Fenston. "I can only hope that you haven't parted with a large sum, and, if you have, you know who is responsible for this elaborate deception."

"Get me Leapman," Fenston screamed at the top of his voice, causing Tina to come running into the room.

"He's just arrived," she said. "I'll tell him you want to see him."

Neither the man from Lloyd's nor the Christie's expert felt this was the moment to hang around, hoping to be offered a cup of coffee. They discreetly left, as Leapman came rushing in.

"It's a fake," shouted Fenston.

Leapman stared up at the picture for some time before offering an opinion. "Then we both know who's responsible," he eventually said.

"Petrescu," said Fenston, spitting out the name.

"Not to mention her partner, who has been feeding Petrescu with information since the day you fired her."

"You're right," said Fenston, and turning toward the open door he hollered "Tina" at the top of his voice. Once again, she came running into the room.

"You see that picture," he said, unable even to turn around and look at the painting. Tina nodded, but didn't speak. "I want you to put it back in its box, and then immediately dispatch it to Wentworth Hall, along with a demand for—"

"Thirty-two million, eight hundred and ninety-two thousand dollars," said Leapman.

"And once you've done that," said Fenston, "you can collect all your personal belongings and make sure you're off the premises within ten minutes, because you're fired, you little bitch."

Tina began shaking as Fenston rose from behind his desk and stared down at her. "But before you leave, I have one last task for you." Tina couldn't move. "Tell your friend Petrescu that I still haven't removed her name from the 'missing, presumed dead' list."

47

ANNA FELT HER lunch with Ken Wheatley could have gone better. The deputy chairman of Christie's had made it clear that the unfortunate incident that had caused her to resign from Sotheby's was not yet considered by her colleagues in the art world to be *a thing of the past*. And it didn't help that Bryce Fenston was telling anyone who cared to listen that she had been fired for conduct unworthy of an officer of the bank. Wheatley admitted that no one much cared for Fenston. However, they felt unable to offend such a valuable customer, which meant that her reentry into the auction house arena wasn't going to prove that easy.

Wheatley's words only made Anna more determined to help Jack secure a conviction against Fenston, who didn't seem to care whose life he ruined.

There wasn't anything suitable at the moment for someone with her qualifications and experience, was how Ken had euphemistically put it, but he promised to keep in touch.

When Anna left the restaurant, she hailed a cab. Perhaps her second meeting would prove more worthwhile. "Twenty-six Federal Plaza," she told the driver.

Jack was standing in the lobby of the New York field office waiting for Anna some time before she was due to arrive. He was not surprised to see her appear a couple of minutes early. Three guards watched Anna carefully as she descended the dozen steps that led to the entrance of 26 Federal Plaza. She gave her name to one of the guards, who requested proof of identity. She passed over her driver's license, which he checked before ticking off her name on his clipboard.

Jack opened the door for her.

"Not my idea of a first date," said Anna, as she stepped inside.

"Nor mine," Jack tried to reassure her, "but my boss wanted you to be in no doubt how important he considers this meeting."

"Why, is it my turn to be arrested?" asked Anna.

"No, but he is hoping that you will be willing to assist us."

"Then let's go and bell the cat."

"One of your father's favorite expressions," said Jack.

"How did you know that?" asked Anna. "Have you got a file on him as well?"

"No," said Jack, laughing, as they stepped into the elevator. "It was just one of the things you told me on the plane during our first night together."

Jack whisked Anna to the nineteenth floor, where Dick Macy was waiting in the corridor to greet her.

"How kind of you to come in, Dr. Petrescu," he said, as if she'd had a choice. Anna didn't comment. Macy led her through to his office and ushered her into a comfortable chair on the other side of his desk.

"Although this is an off-the-record meeting," began Macy, "I cannot stress how important we at the Bureau consider your assistance."

"Why do you need *my* assistance?" asked Anna. "I thought you had arrested Leapman and he was safely under lock and key."

"We released him this morning," said Macy.

"Released him?" said Anna. "Wasn't two million enough?"

"More than enough," admitted Macy, "which is why I became involved. My specialty is plea bargaining, and just after nine o'clock this morning, Leapman signed an agreement with the Southern District federal prosecutor to ensure that if he fully cooperates with our investigation, he'll end up with only a five-year sentence."

"But that still doesn't explain why you've released him," said Anna.

"Because Leapman claims he can show a direct financial link between Fenston and Krantz, but he needs to return to their Wall Street office so he can get his hands on all the relevant documents, including numbered accounts, and several illegal payments into different bank accounts around the world."

"He could be double-crossing you," said Anna. "After all, most of the documents that would implicate Fenston were destroyed when the North Tower collapsed."

"True," said Macy, "but if he is, I've made it clear he can look forward to spending the rest of his life in Sing Sing."

"That's quite an incentive," admitted Anna.

"Leapman's also agreed to appear as a government witness," said Jack, "should the case come to trial."

"Then let's be thankful that Krantz is safely locked up, otherwise your star witness wouldn't even make it to the courthouse."

Macy looked across at Jack, unable to mask his surprise. "You haven't read today's final edition of *The New York Times*?" he asked, turning to face Anna.

"No," said Anna, having no idea what they were talking about.

Macy opened the file, extracted an article, and passed the clipping across to Anna.

Olga Krantz, known as the "kitchen knife killer" because of the role she played as an executioner in Ceauşescu's brutal regime, disappeared from a high-security hospital in Bucharest last night. Krantz is thought to have escaped down a waste-disposal shaft dressed in the clothes of a hospital porter. One of the policemen who had been guarding her was later discovered with his . . .

"I'm going to be looking over my shoulder for the rest of my life," said Anna, long before she'd reached the last paragraph.

"I don't think so," said Jack. "Krantz won't be in a hurry to return to America, now that she's joined nine men on the FBI's most wanted list. She'll also realize that we've circulated a detailed description of her to every port of entry, as well as Interpol. If she were to be stopped and searched, she'd have some trouble explaining the bullet wound in her right shoulder."

"But that won't stop Fenston seeking revenge."

"Why should he bother?" asked Jack. "Now that he's got the Van Gogh, you're history."

"But he hasn't got the Van Gogh," said Anna, bowing her head.

"What do you mean?" asked Jack.

"I had a call from Tina, just before I left to come to this meeting. She warned me that Fenston had called in an expert from Christie's so that he could have the painting valued for insurance. Something he's never done before."

"But why should that cause any problems?" asked Jack.

Anna raised her head. "Because it's a fake."

"A fake?" both men said in unison.

"Yes, that's why I had to fly to Bucharest. I was having a copy made by an old friend who's a brilliant portrait artist."

"Which would explain the drawing in your apartment," said Jack.

"You've been in my apartment?" said Anna.

"Only when I believed that your life was in danger," said Jack quietly.

"But—," began Anna.

"And that also explains," jumped in Macy, "why you sent the red box back to London, even allowing it to be intercepted by Art Locations and delivered on to Fenston in New York."

Anna nodded.

"But you must have realized that you'd be found out in time?" queried Jack.

"In time, yes," repeated Anna. "That's the point. All I needed was enough time to sell the original, before Fenston discovered what I was up to."

"So while your friend Anton was working on the fake, you flew on to Tokyo to try and sell the original to Nakamura."

Anna nodded.

"But did you succeed?" asked Macy.

"Yes," said Anna. "Nakamura agreed to purchase the original *Self-Portrait* for fifty million dollars, which was more than enough for Arabella to clear her sister's debts with Fenston Finance while still holding on to the rest of the estate."

"But now that Fenston knows that he's in possession of a fake, he's bound to get in touch with Nakamura and tell him what you've been up to," said Jack.

"He already has," said Anna.

"So you're back to square one," suggested Macy.

"No," said Anna with a smile. "Nakamura has already deposited five million dollars with his London solicitors and has agreed to pay the balance once he's inspected the original."

"Have you got enough time?" asked Macy.

"I'm flying to London this evening," said Anna, "and Nakamura plans to join us at Wentworth Hall tomorrow night."

"It's going to be a close-run thing," said Jack.

"Not if Leapman delivers the goods," said Macy. "Don't forget what he has planned for tonight."

"Am I allowed to know what you're up to?" asked Anna.

"No, you are not," said Jack firmly. "You catch your plane to England and close the deal, while we get on with our job."

"Does your job include keeping an eye on Tina?" asked Anna quietly.

"Why would we need to do that?" asked Jack.

"She was fired this morning."

"For what reason?" inquired Macy.

"Because Fenston found out that she was keeping me informed of everything he was up to while I was chasing halfway around the world, so I fear that I've ended up putting her life in danger as well."

"I was wrong about Tina," admitted Jack, and looking across at Anna added, "and I apologize. But I still can't make out why she ever agreed to work for Fenston in the first place."

"I have a feeling I'll find out this evening," said Anna. "We're meeting up for a drink just before I leave for the airport."

"If you have any time before takeoff, give me a call. I'd be fascinated to know the answer to that particular mystery."

Anna nodded.

"There's another mystery I'd like to clear up before you leave, Dr. Petrescu," said Macy.

Anna turned to face Jack's boss.

"If Fenston is in possession of a fake, where's the original?" he demanded.

"At Wentworth Hall," Anna replied. "Once I'd retrieved the painting from Sotheby's, I grabbed a cab and took it straight back to Arabella. The only thing I came away with was the red box and the painting's original frame."

"Which you took on to Bucharest so that your friend Anton could put his fake into the original frame, which you hoped would be enough to convince Fenston that he'd got his hands on the real McCoy."

"And it would have stayed that way if he hadn't decided to have the painting insured."

No one spoke for some time, until Macy said, "And you carried out the whole deception right in front of Jack's eyes."

"Sure did," said Anna with a smile.

"So let me finally ask you, Dr. Petrescu," continued Macy, "where was the Van Gogh while two of my most experienced agents were having breakfast with you and Lady Arabella at Wentworth Hall?"

"Plead the Fifth Amendment," begged Jack.

"In the Van Gogh bedroom," replied Anna, "just above them on the first floor."

"That close," said Macy.

Krantz waited until the tenth ring, before she heard a click and a voice inquired, "Where are you?"

"Over the Russian border," she replied.

"Good, because you can't come back to America while you're still regularly appearing in *The New York Times*."

"Not to mention on the FBI's Most Wanted list," added Krantz.

"Fifteen minutes of fame," said Fenston. "But I do have another assignment for you."

"Where?" asked Krantz.

"Wentworth Hall."

"I couldn't risk going back there a second time—"

"Even if I doubled your fee?"

"It's still too much of a risk."

"You may not think so when I tell you whose throat I want you to cut."

"I'm listening," she said, and when Fenston revealed the name of his next victim, all she said was, "You'll pay me two million dollars for that?"

"Three, if you manage to kill Petrescu at the same time—she'll be staying there overnight."

Krantz hesitated.

"And four, if she's a witness to the first throat being cut."

A long silence followed, before Krantz said, "I'll need two million in advance."

"The usual place?"

"No," she replied, and gave him a numbered account in Moscow.

Fenston put the phone down and buzzed through to Leapman.

"I need to see you—now."

While he waited for Leapman to join him, Fenston began jotting down headings for subjects he needed to discuss: *Van Gogh, money, Wentworth estate, Petrescu.* He was still scribbling when there was a knock on the door.

"She's escaped," said Fenston, the moment Leapman closed the door.

"So *The New York Times* report was accurate," said Leapman, hoping he didn't appear anxious.

"Yes, but what they don't know is that she's on her way to Moscow."

"Is she planning to return to New York?"

"Not for the moment," said Fenston. "She can't risk it while security remains on such high alert."

"That makes sense," agreed Leapman, trying not to sound relieved.

"Meanwhile, I've given her another assignment," said Fenston.

"Who is it to be this time?" asked Leapman.

Leapman listened in disbelief as Fenston revealed who he had selected as Krantz's next victim, and why it would be impossible for her to cut off their left ear.

"And has the impostor been dispatched back to Wentworth Hall?" asked Fenston, as Leapman stared up at the blown-up photograph of the chairman shaking hands with George W. Bush following his recent visit to Ground Zero, which had been returned to its place of honor on the wall behind Fenston's desk.

"Yes. Art Locations picked the canvas up this afternoon," replied Leapman, "and will be returning the fake to Wentworth Hall sometime tomorrow. I also had a word with our lawyer in London. The sequestration order is being heard before a judge in chambers on Wednesday, so if she doesn't return the original by then, the Wentworth estate automatically becomes yours, and then we can start selling off the rest of the collection until the debt is cleared. Mind you, it could take years."

"If Krantz does her job properly tomorrow night, the debt will never be cleared," said Fenston, "which is why I called you in. I want you to put the rest of the Wentworth collection up for auction at the earliest possible opportunity. Divide the pictures equally between Christie's, Sotheby's, Phillips, and Bonhams, and make sure you sell them all at the same time."

"But that would flood the market and be certain to bring the prices down."

"That's exactly what I want to do," said Fenston. "If I remember correctly, Petrescu valued the rest of the collection at around thirty-five million, but I'll be happy to raise somewhere between fifteen and twenty."

"But that would still leave you ten million short."

"How sad," said Fenston, smiling. "In which case I will be left with no choice but to put Wentworth Hall on the market and dispose of everything, right down to the last suit of armor." Fenston paused. "So be sure you place the estate in the hands of the three most fashionable agents in London. Tell them they can print expensive color brochures, advertise in all the glossy magazines, and even take out the odd half-page in one or two national newspapers, which will be bound to cause further editorial comment. By the time I finish with Lady Arabella, she'll not only be penniless but, knowing the British press, humiliated."

"And Petrescu?"

"It's just her bad luck that she happens to be in the wrong place at the wrong time," said Fenston, unable to hide a smirk.

"So Krantz will be able to kill two birds with one stone," said Leapman.

"Which is why I want you to concentrate on bankrupting the Wentworth estate, so that Lady Arabella suffers an even slower death."

"I'll get on to it right away," said Leapman, as he turned to leave. "Good luck with your speech, Chairman," he added as he reached the door.

"My speech?" said Fenston.

Leapman turned back to face the chairman. "I thought you were addressing the annual bankers' dinner at the Sherry Netherland tonight."

"Christ, you're right. Where the hell did Tina put my speech?"

Leapman smiled, but not until he had closed the door behind him. He returned to his room, sat down at his desk, and considered what Fenston had just told him. Once the FBI learned the full details of where Krantz would be tomorrow night, and who her next intended victim was, he felt confident that the district attorney's office would agree to reduce his sentence by even more. And if he was able to deliver the vital piece of evidence that linked Fenston to Krantz, they might even recommend a suspended sentence.

Leapman removed a tiny camera, supplied by the FBI, from an inside pocket. He began to calculate how many documents he would be able to photograph while Fenston was delivering his speech at the annual bankers' dinner.

48

AT 7:16 P.M., LEAPMAN switched the light off in his office and stepped into the corridor. He closed his door but didn't lock it. He walked toward the bank of elevators, aware that the only office light still shining was coming from under the chairman's door. He stepped into an empty elevator and was quickly whisked to the ground floor. He walked slowly across to reception and signed out at 7:19 P.M. A woman standing behind him stepped forward to sign herself out as Leapman took a pace backward, his eyes never leaving the two guards behind the desk. One was supervising the steady flow of people exiting the building, while the other was dealing with a delivery that required a signature. Leapman kept retreating until he reached the empty elevator. He backed in and stood to one side so that the guards could no longer see him. He pressed button 31. Less than a minute later, he stepped out into another silent corridor.

He walked to the far end, opened the fire exit door, and climbed the steps to the thirty-second floor. He pushed the door slowly open, not wanting to make the slightest sound. He then tiptoed down the thickly carpeted corridor until he was back outside his own office. He checked to confirm that the only light came from under the chairman's door. He then opened his own door, stepped inside, and locked it. He sat down in the chair behind his desk and placed the camera in his pocket, but did not turn on the light.

chosen this particular time with some thought. Once he had finished one file, he methodically returned it to its place and selected another. His routine didn't alter: search slowly through the contents of the file, select certain items to study more carefully, and then occasionally extract a page to be photographed.

Fenston considered his alternatives before finally settling on something he considered worthy of Leapman.

He first wrote down the sequence of events that would be required to ensure he wasn't caught. Once he was confident that he had mastered the order, he flicked up a switch to stop all outgoing or incoming calls from his office. He sat patiently at his secretary's desk until he saw Leapman open another thick file. He then slipped back into the corridor, coming to a halt in front of his office. Fenston went over the order in his mind and, once he was satisfied, stepped forward. He first entered the correct code, 170690, on the pad by the door, as if he was leaving. He then turned his key in the lock and silently pushed open the door no more than an inch. He then immediately pulled it closed again.

The deafening alarm was automatically set off, but Fenston still waited for eight seconds until the security grilles had clamped firmly into place. He then quickly entered last week's code, 170680, opened the door a second time, and immediately slammed it closed.

He could hear Leapman running across the room, clearly hoping that by entering the correct code he could stop the alarm and cause the grilles to slide back into the ceiling. But it was too late, because the iron grilles remained resolutely in place and the overpowering cacophony continued unabated.

Fenston knew that he had only seconds to spare if he was to complete the sequence without being caught. He ran back to the adjoining office and quickly scanned the notes he'd left on his secretary's desk. He dialed the emergency number for Abbott Security.

A voice announced, "Duty officer, security."

"My name is Bryce Fenston, chairman of Fenston Finance." He spoke slowly, but with authority. "The alarm has been triggered in my office on the thirty-second floor. I must have entered last week's code by mistake, and I just wanted to let you know that it's *not* an emergency."

"Can you repeat your name, sir?"

"Bryce Fenston," he shouted above the noise of the alarm.

"Date of birth?"

"Twelve six fifty-two."

"Mother's maiden name?"

"Madejski."

"Home zip code?"

"One zero zero two one."

"Thank you, Mr. Fenston. We'll get someone up to the thirty-second floor as quickly as possible. The engineers are currently responding to an incident on the seventeenth floor, where we have someone stuck in an elevator, so it might be a few minutes before they get to you."

"No hurry," said Fenston casually, "there's no one else working on this floor at the moment, and the office won't open again until seven tomorrow."

"It's sure not going to take us that long," the guard promised him, "but with your permission, Mr. Fenston, we'll change your category from emergency to priority."

"Okay by me," shouted Fenston above the deafening noise.

"But there will still be an out-of-hours call-out charge of five hundred dollars."

"That sounds a bit steep," said Fenston.

"It's standard in a case like this, sir," came back the duty officer's reply. "However, if you were able to report to the front desk in person, Mr. Fenston, and sign our alarm roster, the charge is automatically cut to two fifty."

"I'm on my way," said Fenston.

"But I have to point out, sir," continued the duty officer, "that should you do that, your status will be lowered to routine, in which case we couldn't come to your assistance until we've dealt with all other priority and emergency calls."

"That won't be a problem," said Fenston.

"But you can be confident that whatever other calls we have outstanding, we still guarantee that yours will be sorted out within four hours."

"Thank you," said Fenston. "I'll come straight down and report to the front desk."

He replaced the receiver and walked back into the corridor. As he passed his office, he could hear Leapman pounding on the door like a trapped animal, but he could only just make out his voice above the shrill scream of the alarm. Fenston continued on toward the elevators. Even at a distance of some fifty feet he still found the piercing drone intolerable.

Once he'd stepped out of the elevator on the ground floor, he went straight to the front desk.

"Ah, Mr. Fenston," said the security guard. "If you'll sign here, it will save you another two hundred and fifty bucks."

Fenston slipped him a ten-dollar note. "Thanks," he said. "No need to rush. I'm the last one out," he assured them as he hurried out of the front door and back down the steps.

As he stepped into his waiting car, Fenston glanced up at his office. He could see a tiny figure banging on the window. The driver closed the door behind him and returned to the front seat, puzzled. His boss still wasn't wearing a dinner jacket.

49

JACK DELANEY PARKED his car on Broad Street just after nine thirty. He switched on the radio and listened to Cousin Brucie on 101.1 FM, as he settled back to wait for Leapman. The venue for their meeting had been Leapman's choice, and he'd told the FBI man to expect him some time between ten and eleven, when he would hand over their camera containing enough damning evidence to ensure a conviction.

Jack was suspended in that unreal world somewhere between half awake and half asleep when he heard the siren. Like all law-enforcement officers, he could identify the different decibel pitch between police, ambulance, and fire department in a split second. This was an ambulance, probably coming from St. Vincent's.

He checked his watch: 11:15 P.M. Leapman was running late, but then he had warned Jack that there could be over a hundred documents to photograph, so not to keep him to the minute. The FBI technical boys had spent some considerable time showing Leapman how to operate the latest high-tech camera so he could be sure to deliver the best results. But that was before the phone call. Leapman had rung Jack's office a few minutes after seven to say that Fenston had told him something that would prove far more damning than any document. But he didn't want to reveal the information over the phone. The line went dead before Jack could press him. He would have been more responsive if it hadn't been his experience that plea bargainers always claim they have new information that will break the case wide open, and therefore the FBI should reconsider the length of their sentence. He knew his boss wouldn't agree to that unless the new evidence clearly showed an unbreakable link in the chain between Fenston and Krantz.

The sound of the siren was getting louder.

Jack decided to get out of the car and stretch his legs. His raincoat felt crumpled. He'd bought it from Brooks Brothers in the days when he wanted everyone to know that he was a G-man, but the higher up the ranks he climbed, the less he wished it to be that obvious. If he was promoted to run his own field office, he might even consider buying a new coat, one that would make him look more like a lawyer or a banker—that would please his father.

His mind switched to Fenston, who by now would have delivered his speech on Moral Responsibility for Modern Bankers, and then to Anna, who was halfway across the Atlantic on her way to meet up with Nakamura. Anna had left a message on his cell phone, saying she now knew why Tina had taken the job as Fenston's P.A., and the evidence had been staring her in the face. The line had been busy when she called, but Anna said she'd phone again in the morning. It must have been when Leapman was on the line. Damn the man. Jack was standing on a New York sidewalk in the middle of the night, tired and hungry, while he waited for a camera. His father was right. He should have been a lawyer.

The siren was now only a couple of blocks away.

Jack strolled down to the end of the road and peered up at the building in which Leapman was working, somewhere on the thirty-second floor. There was a row of blazing lights about halfway up the skyscraper, otherwise the windows were mostly dark. Jack began to count the floors, but by the time he'd reached eighteen he couldn't be sure, and when he counted thirty-two, it just might have been the floor that was blazing with lights. But that didn't make any sense, because on Leapman's floor, there should only have been a single light. The last thing he would have wanted was to draw attention to himself.

Jack looked across the road to watch an ambulance come to a screeching halt in front of the building. The back door burst open and three paramedics, two men and a woman dressed in their familiar dark blue uniforms, jumped out onto the sidewalk. One pushed a stretcher, the second carried an oxygen cylinder, while the third held a bulky medical bag. Jack watched them as they charged up the steps and into the building.

He turned his attention to the reception desk, where one guard—pointing to something on his clipboard—was talking to an older man dressed in a smart suit, probably his supervisor, while the second guard was occupied on the telephone. Several people strolled in and out of the elevators, which wasn't surprising, as they were in the heart of the city where finance is a twenty-four-hour occupation. Most Americans would be asleep while money was changing hands in Sydney, Tokyo, Hong Kong, and now London, but there always had to be a group of New Yorkers who lived their lives on other people's time.

Jack's train of thought was interrupted when an elevator door opened and the three paramedics reappeared, two of them wheeling their patient on the stretcher, while the third was still holding onto the oxygen cylinder. As they walked slowly but purposefully toward the entrance, everyone in their path stood aside. Jack strolled up the steps to take a closer look. Another siren blared in the distance, on this occasion the droning pitch of the NYPD, but it could be going anywhere at that time of night, and in any case Jack was now concentrating on the stretcher. He stood by the door as the paramedics came out of the building and carried their patient slowly down the steps. He stared at the pallid face of a stricken man, whose eyes were glazed over as if they'd been caught in the blaze of a headlight. It wasn't until he'd passed him that Jack realized who it was. He had to make an instant decision. Did he pursue the ambulance back to St Vincent's or head straight for the thirty-second floor? The police siren now sounded as if it could be heading in their direction. One look at that face and Jack didn't need to be told that Leapman wasn't going to be speaking to anyone for a very long time. He ran into the building with the sound of the police siren no more than a block or two away. He knew he had only a few minutes before the NYPD's finest would be on the scene. He paused at the reception desk for a moment to show them his FBI badge.

"You got here quickly," said one of the guards, but Jack didn't comment as he headed for the bank of elevators. The guard wondered how he knew which floor to go to.

Jack squeezed through the elevator doors just as they were about to close and jabbed at the button marked 32. When the doors opened again, he looked quickly up and down the corridor to see where the lights were coming from. He turned and ran toward some offices at the far end to find a security guard and two engineers in red overalls, along with a cleaner, standing by an open door.

"Who are you?" demanded the security guard.

"FBI," said Jack, producing his badge but not revealing his name as he strode into the room. The first thing he saw was a blown-up photograph of Fenston shaking hands with George W. Bush, which dominated the wall behind the desk. His eyes moved quickly around the room until they settled on the one thing he was looking for. It was in the center of the desk, resting on a pile of spread-out papers beside an open file.

"What happened?" demanded Jack authoritatively.

"Some guy got himself trapped in this office for over three hours and must have set the alarm off."

"It wasn't our fault," jumped in one of the engineers, "we were told to downgrade the call, and we've got that in writing, otherwise we would have been here a lot sooner."

Jack didn't need to ask who had set off the alarm and then left Leapman to his fate. He walked over to the desk, his eyes quickly scanning the papers. He glanced up to find all four men staring at him. Jack looked directly at the security guard. "Go to the elevator, wait for the cops, and the minute they turn up bring them straight back to me." The guard disappeared into the corridor without question and headed quickly toward the elevators. "And you three, out," was Jack's next command. "This may be a crime scene, and I don't want you disturbing any evidence." The men turned to leave, and in the split second their backs were turned, Jack grabbed the camera and dropped it into one of the baggy pockets of his trench coat.

He picked up the phone on Fenston's desk. There was no dial tone, only a continuous buzzing noise. Someone had disconnected the line. The same person who triggered the alarm, no doubt. Jack didn't touch anything else in the room. He stepped back into the corridor and slipped into the adjoining office. A screen was fixed to the corner of the desk and was still relaying images from inside Fenston's office. Fenston had clearly not only witnessed Leapman's actions but had enough time to set in motion the most diabolical revenge.

Jack's eyes moved across to the switchboard. One lever was up, illuminating a flickering orange light, indicating that the line was busy. He must have cut Leapman off from any hope of contacting the outside world. Jack looked down at the desk where Fenston would have been sitting when he planned the whole operation. He'd even written out a list to make sure he didn't make a mistake. All the clues were there for the NYPD to gather and evaluate. If this had been a *Columbo* investigation, the switch, the handwritten list left on the desk, and the timing of the alarm going off would have been quite enough for the great detective to secure a conviction, with Fenston breaking down and confessing following the last commercial break. Unfortunately, this wasn't a made-for-TV movie, and one thing was certain: Fenston wasn't going to break down and would never consider confessing. Jack grimaced. The only thing he had in common with Columbo was the crumpled raincoat.

Jack heard the elevator doors open and the words, "Follow me." He knew it had to be the cops. He turned his attention back to the screen on the desk as two uniformed officers marched into Fenston's office and began to question the four witnesses. The plainclothes men wouldn't be far behind. Jack walked out of the adjoining office and headed silently toward the elevator. He'd reached the doors when one of the cops came out of Fenston's office and shouted, "Hey, you." Jack jabbed at the down button and turned sideways, so the officer couldn't see his face. The moment the doors opened, he quickly slipped inside. He kept his finger pressed on the button marked L and the doors immediately closed. When they opened on the ground floor thirty seconds later, he jogged past reception, out of the building, down the steps, and headed in the direction of his car.

Jack jumped in and started the engine, just as a cop came running around the corner. He swung the car in a circle, mounted the sidewalk, drove back onto the road, and headed for St. Vincent's Hospital.

"Good afternoon, Sotheby's."

"Lord Poltimore, please."

"Who shall I say is calling, madam?"

"Lady Wentworth." Arabella didn't have to wait long before Mark came on the line.

"How nice to hear from you, Arabella," said Mark. "Dare I ask," he teased, "are you a buyer or a seller?"

"A seeker after advice," replied Arabella. "But if I were to be a seller . . ."

Mark began to make notes as he listened to a series of questions that Arabella had obviously prepared carefully.

"In the days when I was a dealer," Mark replied, "before I joined Sotheby's, the standard commission was 10 percent up to the first million. If the painting was likely to fetch more than a million, I used to negotiate a fee with the seller."

"And what fee would you have negotiated, had I asked you to sell the Wentworth Van Gogh?"

Mark was glad Arabella couldn't see the expression on his face. Once he'd recovered, he took his time before suggesting a figure, but quickly added, "If you were to allow Sotheby's to put the picture up for auction, we would charge you nothing, Arabella, guaranteeing you the full hammer price."

"So how do you make a profit?" asked Arabella.

"We charge a buyer's premium," explained Mark.

"I already have a buyer," said Arabella, "but thank you for the advice."

9/25

50

KRANTZ TURNED THE corner of the street, relieved to find the pavement so crowded. She walked for about another hundred yards before stopping outside a small hotel. She glanced up and down the road, confident that she was not being followed.

She pulled open the swing doors that led into the hotel and, looking straight ahead, walked past reception, ignoring the concierge, who was talking to a tourist who sounded as if he might come from New York. Her gaze remained focused on a wall of deposit boxes to the left of the reception desk. Krantz waited until all three receptionists were fully occupied before she moved.

She glanced behind her to make sure no one had the same purpose in mind. Satisfied, she moved quickly, extracting a key from her hip pocket as she reached box 19. She turned the key in the lock and opened the door. Everything was exactly as she had left it. Krantz removed all the notes and two passports, and stuffed them in a pocket. She then locked the door, walked out of the hotel and was back on Herzen Street without having spoken to anyone.

She hailed a taxi, something she couldn't have done in the days when the communists were teaching her her trade. She gave the driver the name of a bank in Cheryomushki, sat in the back, and thought about Colonel Sergei Slatinaru—but only for a moment. Her one regret was that she hadn't succeeded in cutting off his left ear. Krantz would like to have sent Petrescu a little memento of her visit to Romania. Still, what she had in mind for Petrescu would more than make up for the disappointment.

But first she had to concentrate on getting out of Russia. It might have been easy to escape from those amateurs in Bucharest, but it was going to be far more difficult finding a safe route into England. Islands always cause a problem; mountains are so much easier to cross than water. She'd arrived in the Russian capital earlier that morning exhausted, having been constantly on the move since discharging herself from the hospital.

Krantz had reached the highway by the time the siren went off. She turned to see the hospital grounds bathed in light. A truck driver who made love to her twice and didn't deserve to die, smuggled her across the border. It took a train, a plane, another three hundred dollars, and seventeen hours before she eventually made it to Moscow. She immediately headed for the Isla Hotel with no intention of staying overnight. Her only interest was in a safety deposit box that contained two passports and a few hundred rubles.

While she was marooned in Moscow, Krantz had planned to earn a little cash, moonlighting while she waited until it was safe to return to America. The cost of living was so much cheaper in the Russian capital than New York, and that included the cost of death: $5,000 for a wife, $10,000 for a husband. The Russians hadn't yet come to terms with equal rights. A KGB colonel could fetch as much as $50,000, while Krantz could charge $100,000 for a mafia boss. But if Fenston had transferred the promised two million dollars, tiresome wives and husbands would have to wait for her return. In fact, now that Russia had embraced free enterprise, she might even attach herself to one of the new oligarchs and offer him a comprehensive service.

She felt sure one of them could make use of the three million dollars stashed away in a safety deposit box in Queens, in which case she would never need to return to the States.

The taxi drew up outside the discreet entrance of a bank that prided itself on having few customers. The letters G and Z were chiseled in the white marble cornice. Krantz stepped out of the cab, paid the fare, and waited until the taxi was out of sight before she entered the building.

The Geneva and Zurich Bank was an establishment that specialized in catering to the needs of a new breed of Russians, who had reinvented themselves following the demise of communism. Politicians, mafia bosses (businessmen), footballers, and pop stars were all small change compared to the latest superstars, the oligarchs. Although everybody knew their names, they were a breed that could afford the anonymity of a number when it came to finding out the details of what they were worth.

Krantz walked up to an old-fashioned wooden counter, no lines, no grilles, where a row of smartly dressed men in gray suits, white shirts, and plain silk ties waited to serve. They wouldn't have looked out of place in either Geneva or Zurich.

"How may I assist you?" asked the clerk Krantz had selected. He wondered which category she fell into—the wife of a mafia boss, or the daughter of an oligarch. She didn't look like a pop star.

"One zero seven two zero nine five nine," she said.

He tapped the code into his computer, and when the figures flashed up on the screen he showed a little more interest.

"May I see your passport?" was his next question.

Krantz handed over one of the passports she had collected from the Isla Hotel.

"How much is there in my account?" she asked.

"How much do you think there should be?" he replied.

"Just over two million dollars," she said.

"And what amount do you wish to withdraw?" he asked.

"Ten thousand in dollars, and ten thousand in rubles."

He pulled out a tray from under the counter and began to count out the notes slowly. "We haven't dealt in this account for some time," he ventured, looking up at his screen.

"No," she agreed, "but you will be seeing a lot more activity now that I'm back in Moscow," she added without explanation.

"Then I look forward to being of service, madam," the clerk said, before passing across two bundles of notes neatly sealed in plastic wallets, with no hint of where they had come from and certainly no paperwork to suggest a transaction had even taken place.

Krantz picked up the two wallets, placed them in an inside pocket, and walked slowly out of the bank. She hailed the third available taxi.

"The Kalstern," she said, and climbed into the back of the cab in preparation for the second part of her plan.

Fenston had kept his part of the bargain. Now she would have to keep hers if she hoped to collect the second two million. She had given a moment's thought to keeping the two million and not bothering to travel to England. But only a moment's thought because she knew that Fenston had kept up his contacts with the KGB, and that they would have been only too happy to dispose of her for a far smaller amount.

When the taxi came to a halt ten minutes later, Krantz handed over four hundred rubles and didn't wait for any change. She stepped out of the cab and joined a group of tourists who were peering in at a window, hoping to find some memento to prove to the folks back home that they had visited the wicked communists. In the center of the window was displayed their most popular item: a four-star general's uniform with all the accessories—cap, belt, holster, and three rows of campaign medals. No price tag attached, but Krantz knew the going rate was $20. Next to the general stood an admiral, $15, and behind him a KGB colonel, $10. Although Krantz had no interest in proving to the folks back home that she had visited Moscow, the kind of person who could lay their hands on the uniforms of generals, admirals, and KGB colonels could undoubtedly acquire the outfit she required.

Krantz entered the shop and was greeted by a young assistant. "Can I help you?" she asked.

"I need to speak to your boss on a private matter," said Krantz.

The young girl looked uncertain, but Krantz just stared at her until she finally said, "Follow me," and led her customer to the back of the shop, where she tentatively knocked before opening the door to a small office.

Sitting behind a large wooden desk, littered with papers, empty cigarette cartons, and a half-eaten salami sandwich, sat an overweight man in a baggy brown suit. He was wearing an open-necked red shirt that looked as if it hadn't been washed for several days. His bald head and thick mustache made it difficult for Krantz to guess his age, although he was clearly the proprietor.

He placed both hands on the desk and looked wearily up at her. He offered a weak smile, but all Krantz noticed was the double-chinned neck. Always tricky to negotiate.

"How can I help?" he asked, not sounding as if he was convinced she was worth the effort.

Krantz told him exactly what she required. The proprietor listened in astonished silence and then burst out laughing.

"That wouldn't come cheap," he eventually said, "and could take some considerable time."

"I need the uniform by this afternoon," said Krantz.

"That's not possible," he said with a shrug of his heavy shoulders.

Krantz removed a wad of cash from her pocket, peeled off a hundred-dollar bill, and placed it on the desk in front of him. "This afternoon," she repeated.

The proprietor raised his eyebrows, although his eyes never left Benjamin Franklin.

"I may just have a possible contact."

Krantz placed another hundred on the desk.

"Yes, I think I know the ideal person."

"And I also need her passport," said Krantz.

"Impossible."

Another two hundred dollars joined the Franklin twins.

"Possible," he said, "but not easy."

Krantz placed a further two hundred on the table, making sextuplets.

"But I feel sure some arrangement could be made," he paused, "at the right price." He looked up at his customer while resting his hands on his stomach.

"A thousand if everything I require is available by this afternoon."

"I'll do my best," said the proprietor.

"I feel sure you will," said Krantz. "Because I'm going to knock off a hundred dollars for every fifteen minutes after"—she looked at her watch—"two o'clock."

The proprietor was about to protest, but thought better of it.

51

WHEN ANNA'S TAXI drove through the gates of Wentworth Hall, she was surprised to see Arabella waiting on the top step, a shotgun under her right arm and Brunswick and Picton by her side. The butler opened the taxi door as his mistress and the two Labradors walked down the steps to greet her.

"How nice to see you," said Arabella, kissing her on both cheeks. "You've arrived just in time for tea."

Anna stroked the dogs as she accompanied Arabella up the steps and into the house, while an underbutler removed her suitcase from the front of the taxi. When Anna stepped into the hall, she paused to allow her eyes to move slowly around the room, from picture to picture.

"Yes, it is nice to still have one's family around one," said Arabella, "even if this might be their last weekend in the country."

"What do you mean?" asked Anna apprehensively.

"Fenston's lawyers delivered a letter by hand this morning, reminding me that should I fail to repay their client's loan in full by midday tomorrow, I must be prepared to pension off all the family retainers."

"He plans to dispose of the entire collection?" said Anna.

"That would appear to be his purpose," said Arabella.

"But that doesn't make sense," said Anna. "If Fenston were to place the entire collection on the market at the same time he wouldn't even clear his original loan.'"

"He would, if he then put the hall up for sale," said Arabella.

"He wouldn't—," began Anna.

"He would," said Arabella. "So we can only hope that Mr. Nakamura remains infatuated with Van Gogh, because frankly he's my last hope."

"Where is the masterpiece?" asked Anna, as Arabella led her through to the drawing room.

"Back in the Van Gogh bedroom, where he's resided for the past hundred years–" Arabella paused– "except for a day's excursion to Heathrow."

While Arabella settled herself in her favorite chair by the fire, a dog on each side of her, Anna strolled around the room, reminding herself of the Italian collection, assembled by the fourth earl.

"Should my dear Italians also be forced to make an unexpected journey to New York," said Arabella, "they shouldn't grumble. After all, that appears to be no more than an American tradition."

Anna laughed as she moved from Titian to Veronese and to Caravaggio. "I'd forgotten just how magnificent the Caravaggio was," she said, standing back to admire *The Marriage at Cana.*

"I do believe that you are more interested in dead Italians than living Irishmen," said Arabella.

"If Caravaggio was alive today," said Anna, "Jack would be following him, not me."

"What do you mean?" asked Arabella.

"He murdered a man in a drunken brawl. Spent his last few years on the run, but whenever he arrived in a new city, the local burghers turned a blind eye as long as he went on producing magnificent portraits of the Virgin Mother and the Christ child."

"Anna, you're an impossible guest, now come and sit down," said Arabella as a maid entered the drawing room carrying a silver tray. She began to set up for tea by the fire.

"Now, my dear, will you have Indian or China?"

"I've always been puzzled," said Anna taking the seat opposite Arabella, "why it isn't 'Indian or Chinese,' or 'India or China'?"

For a moment, Arabella was silenced, saved only by the entry of the butler.

"M'lady," said Andrews, "there's a gentleman at the door with a package for you. I told him to take it around to the tradesman's entrance, but he said he couldn't release it without your signature."

"A sort of modern-day Viola," suggested Arabella. "I shall have to go and see what this peevish messenger brings," she added. "Perhaps I will even throw him a ring for his troubles."

"I feel sure the fair Olivia will know just how to handle him," rejoined Anna.

Arabella gave a little bow and followed Andrews out of the room.

Anna was admiring Tintoretto's *Perseus and Andromeda* when Arabella returned, the cheerful smile of only moments before replaced by a grim expression.

"Is there a problem?" asked Anna, as she turned around to face her host.

"The peevish fellow has sent back my ring," replied Arabella. "Come and see for yourself."

Anna followed her into the hall, where she found Andrews and the underbutler removing the casing of a red crate that Anna had hoped she had seen for the last time.

"It must have been sent from New York," said Arabella, studying a label attached to the box, "probably on the same flight as you."

"Seems to be following me around," said Anna.

"You appear to have that effect on men," said Arabella.

They both watched as Andrews neatly removed the bubble wrap to reveal a canvas that Anna had last seen in Anton's studio.

"The only good thing to come out of this," said Anna, "is that we can transfer the original frame back onto the masterpiece."

"But what shall we do with him?" asked Arabella, gesturing toward the impostor. The butler gave a discreet cough. "You have a suggestion, Andrews?" inquired Arabella. "If so, let's hear it."

"No, m'lady," Andrews replied, "but I thought you would want to know that your other guest is proceeding up the drive."

"The man clearly has a gift for timing," said Arabella, as she quickly checked her hair in the mirror. "Andrews," she said, reverting to her normal role, "has the Wellington Room been prepared for Mr. Nakamura?"

"Yes, m'lady. And Dr. Petrescu will be in the Van Gogh room."

"How appropriate," said Arabella, turning to face Anna, "that he should spend his last night with you."

Anna was relieved to see Arabella so quickly back into her stride and had a feeling that she might prove a genuine foil for Nakamura.

The butler opened the front door and walked down the steps at a pace that would ensure he reached the gravel just as the Toyota Lexus came to a halt. Andrews opened the back door of the limousine to allow Mr. Nakamura to step out. He was clutching a small square package.

"The Japanese always arrive bearing a gift," whispered Anna, "but under no circumstances should you open it in their presence."

"That's all very well," said Arabella, "but I haven't got anything for him."

"He won't expect something in return. You have invited him to be a guest in your house, and that is the greatest compliment you can pay any Japanese."

"That's a relief," said Arabella, as Mr. Nakamura appeared at the front door.

"Lady Arabella," he said, bowing low, "it is a great honor to be invited to your magnificent home."

"You honor my home, Mr. Nakamura," said Arabella, hoping she'd said the correct thing.

The Japanese man bowed even lower, and when he rose came face-to-face with Lawrence's portrait of Wellington.

"How appropriate," he said. "Did the great man not dine at Wentworth Hall the night before he sailed for Waterloo?"

"Indeed he did," said Arabella, "and you will sleep in the same bed that the Iron Duke slept in on that historic occasion."

Nakamura turned to Anna and bowed. "How nice to see you again, Dr. Petrescu."

"And you too, Nakamura-san," said Anna. "I hope you had a pleasant journey."

"Yes, thank you. We even landed on time, for a change," said Nakamura, who didn't move as his eyes roamed around the room. "You will please correct me, Anna, should I make a mistake. It is clear that the room is devoted to the English school. Gains borough?" he queried, as he admired the full-length portrait of Catherine, Lady Wentworth. Anna nodded, before Nakamura moved on "Landseer, Morland, Romney, Stubbs, but then, I am stumped—is that the correct expression?"

"It most certainly is," confirmed Arabella, "although our American cousins wouldn't begin to understand its significance. And you were stumped by Lely."

"Ah, Sir Peter, and what a fine-looking woman—" he paused "—a family trait," he said, turning to face his host.

"And I can see, Mr. Nakamura, that your family trait is flattery," teased Arabella.

Nakamura burst out laughing. "With the risk of being taken to task a second time, Lady Arabella, if every room is the equal of this, it may prove necessary for me to cancel my meeting with those dullards from Corus Steel." Nakamura's eyes continued to sweep the room, "Wheatley, Lawrence, West, and Wilkie," he said, before his gaze ended up on the portrait propped up against the wall.

Nakamura offered no opinion for some time. "Quite magnificent," he finally said. "The work of an inspired hand—" he paused "—but not the hand of Van Gogh."

"How can you be so sure, Nakamura-san?" asked Anna.

"Because the wrong ear is bandaged," replied Nakamura.

"But everyone knows that Van Gogh cut off his left ear," said Anna.

Nakamura turned and smiled at Anna. "And you know only too well," he added, "that Van Gogh painted the original while looking in a mirror, which is why the bandage ended up on the wrong ear."

"I do hope that someone is going to explain all this to me later," said Arabella as she led her guests through to the drawing room.

52

KRANTZ RETURNED TO the shop at 2 P.M., but there was no sign of the proprietor. "He'll be back at any moment," the assistant assured her without conviction.

"Any moment" turned out to be thirty minutes, by which time the assistant was nowhere to be seen. When the owner did eventually show up, Krantz was pleased to see that he was carrying a bulky plastic bag. Without a word being spoken, Krantz followed him to the back of the shop and into his office. Not until he'd closed the door did a large grin appear on his fleshy lips.

The proprietor placed the carrier bag on his desk. He paused for a moment, then pulled out the red outfit Krantz had requested.

"She may be a little taller than you," he said with a half apology, "but I can supply a needle and thread at no extra charge." He began to laugh but ceased when his customer didn't respond.

Krantz held the uniform up against her shoulders. The previous owner was at least three or four inches taller than Krantz but only a few pounds heavier; nothing—as the proprietor had suggested—that a needle and thread wouldn't remedy.

"And the passport?" asked Krantz.

Once again the proprietor's hand dipped into the carrier bag, and, like a conjuror producing a rabbit out of a hat, he offered up a Soviet passport. He handed over the prize to Krantz and said, "She has a three-day layover, so she probably won't discover that it's missing until Friday."

"It will have served its purpose long before then," Krantz said, as she began to turn the pages of the official document.

Sasha Prestakavich, she discovered, was three years younger than her, and eight centimeters taller with no distinguishing marks. A problem that a pair of high-heeled shoes would solve, unless an overzealous official decided to carry out a strip search and came across the recent wound on her right shoulder.

When Krantz reached the page where Sasha Prestakavich's photo had once been, the proprietor was unable to disguise a satisfied smirk. For his next trick, he produced from under the counter a Polaroid camera.

"Smile," he said. She didn't.

A few seconds later an image spewed out. A pair of scissors appeared next, and the proprietor began to cut the photograph down to a size that would comply with the little dotted rectangle on page three of the passport. Next, a dollop of glue to fix the new holder in place. His final act was to drop a needle and thread into the carrier bag. Krantz was beginning to realize that this was not the first occasion he had supplied such a service. She placed the uniform and the passport back in the carrier bag, before handing over eight hundred dollars.

The proprietor checked the wad of notes carefully.

"You said a thousand," he protested.

"You were thirty minutes late," Krantz reminded him, as she picked up the bag and turned to leave.

"Do come and visit us again," suggested the proprietor as she retreated, "whenever you're passing through."

Krantz didn't bother to explain to him why, in her profession, she never saw anyone twice, unless it was to make sure they couldn't see her a third time.

Once she was back on the street, she only had to walk for a couple of blocks before she came across the next shop she required. She purchased a pair of plain, black high-heeled shoes—not her style, but they would serve their purpose. She paid the bill in rubles and left the shop carrying two bags.

Krantz next hailed a taxi, gave the driver an address, and told him the exact entrance where she wished to be dropped off. When the cab drew up by a side door marked STAFF ONLY, Krantz paid the fare, entered the building, and went straight to the ladies' room. She locked herself in a cubicle, where she spent the next forty minutes. With the aid of the needle and thread supplied by the proprietor, she raised the hemline of the skirt by a couple of inches and made a couple of tucks in the waist, which wouldn't be visible under the jacket. She then stripped off all her outer garments before trying on the uniform—not a perfect fit, but fortunately the company she was proposing to work for was not known for its sartorial elegance. Next she replaced her sneakers with the recently acquired high heels, before dropping her own clothes into the carrier bag.

When she finally left the ladies' room, she went in search of her new employers. Her walk was a little unsteady, but then she wasn't used to high heels. Krantz's eyes settled on another woman who was dressed in an identical uniform. She walked across to the counter and asked, "Have you got a spare seat on any of our London flights?"

"That shouldn't be a problem," she replied. "Can I see your passport?" Krantz handed over the recently acquired document. The company's representative looked up Sasha Prestakavich's details on the company database. According to their records, she was on a three-day layover. "That seems to be in order," she eventually said, and handed her a crew pass. "Be sure that you're among the last to check in, just in case we have any latecomers."

Krantz walked across to the international terminal, and once she'd been checked through customs, hung around in duty-free until she heard the final boarding call for Flight 413 to London. By the time she arrived at the gate, the last three passengers were checking in. Once again her passport was checked against the company database before the gate officer studied his screen and said, "We've got seats available in every class, so take your pick."

"Back row of economy," Krantz said unhesitatingly.

The gate official looked surprised, but printed out a boarding card and handed the little slip over to her. Krantz walked through the gate, and boarded Aeroflot's Flight 413 to London.

53

ANNA WALKED SLOWLY down the wide, marble staircase, pausing for a moment at every two or three steps to admire another master. It didn't matter how often she saw them . . . she heard a noise behind her, and looked back toward the guest corridor to see Andrews coming out of her bedroom. He was carrying a picture under his arm. She smiled as he hurried away in the direction of the backstairs.

Anna continued to study the paintings on her slow progress down the staircase. As she stepped into the hall she gave Catherine, Lady Wentworth another admiring look, before she walked slowly across the black-and-white marbled-square floor toward the drawing room.

The first thing Anna saw as she entered was Andrews placing the Van Gogh on an easel in the center of the room.

"What do you think?" said Arabella, as she took a step back to admire the self-portrait.

"Don't you feel that Mr. Nakamura might consider it a little . . . ," ventured Anna, not wishing to offend her host.

"Crude, blatant, obvious? Which word were you searching for, my dear?" asked Arabella, as she turned to face Anna. Anna burst out laughing. "Let's face it," said Arabella, "I'm strapped for cash and running out of time, so I don't have a lot of choice."

"No one would believe it, looking at you," said Anna, as she admired the magnificent long rose silk-taffeta gown and diamond necklace Arabella was wearing, making Anna feel somewhat casual in her short black Armani dress.

"It's kind of you to say so, my dear, but if I had your looks and your figure, I wouldn't need to cover myself from head to toe with other distractions."

Anna smiled, admiring the way Arabella had so quickly put her at ease.

"When do you think he'll make a decision?" asked Arabella, trying not to sound desperate.

"Like all great collectors," said Anna, "he'll make up his mind within moments. A scientific survey has recently shown that men decide whether they want to sleep with a woman in about eight seconds."

"That long?" said Arabella.

"Mr. Nakamura will take about the same time to decide if he wants to own this painting," she said, looking directly at the Van Gogh.

"Let's drink to that," said Arabella.

Andrews stepped forward on cue, proffering a silver tray that held three glasses.

"A glass of champagne, madam?" he inquired.

"Thank you," said Anna, removing a long-stemmed flute. When Andrews stepped back, her gaze fell on a turquoise and black vase that she had never seen before.

"It's quite magnificent," said Anna.

"Mr. Nakamura's gift," said Arabella. "Most embarrassing. By the way," she added, "I do hope I haven't committed a faux pas by putting it on display while Mr. Nakamura is still a guest in my home." She paused. "If I have, Andrews can remove it immediately."

"Certainly not," said Anna. "Mr. Nakamura will be flattered that you have placed his gift among so many other maestros."

"Are you sure?" asked Arabella.

"Oh yes. The piece survives, even shines in this room. There is only one certain rule when it comes to real talent," said Anna. "Any form of art isn't out of place as long as it's displayed among its equals. The Raphael on the wall, the diamond necklace you are wearing, the Chippendale table on which you have placed the vase, the Nash fireplace, and the Van Gogh have all been created by masters. Now I have no idea who the craftsman was who made this piece," continued Anna, still admiring the way the turquoise appeared to be running into the black, like a melting candle, "but I have no doubt that in his own country, he is considered a master."

"Not exactly a master," said a voice coming from behind them.

Arabella and Anna turned at the same time to see that Mr. Nakamura had entered the room. He was dressed in a dinner jacket and bow tie that Andrews would have approved of.

"Not a master?" queried Arabella.

"No," said Nakamura. "In this country, you honor those who 'achieve greatness,' to quote your Bard, by making them knights or barons, whereas we in Japan reward such talent with the title 'national treasure.' It is appropriate that this piece has found a home in Wentworth Hall because, of the twelve great potters in history, the experts acknowledge that eleven have been Japanese, with the sole exception of a Cornishman, Bernard Leach. You failed to make him a lord or even give him a knighthood, so we declared him to be an honorary national treasure."

"How immensely civilized," said Arabella, "as I must confess that recently we have been giving honors to pop stars, footballers, and vulgar millionaires." Nakamura laughed, as Andrews offered him a glass of champagne. "Are you a national treasure, Mr. Nakamura?" inquired Arabella.

"Certainly not," replied Nakamura. "My countrymen do not consider vulgar millionaires worthy of such an honor."

Arabella turned scarlet, while Anna continued to stare at the vase, as if she hadn't heard the remark. "But am I not right in thinking, Mr. Nakamura, that this particular vase is not symmetrical?"

"Quite brilliant," replied Nakamura. "You should have been a member of the diplomatic corps, Anna. Not only did you manage to deftly change the subject, but at the same time you raised a question that demands to be answered."

Nakamura walked straight past the Van Gogh as if he hadn't noticed it and looked at the vase for some time before he added, "If you ever come across a piece of pottery that is perfect, you can be confident that it was produced by a machine. With pottery, you must seek *near* perfection. If you look carefully enough, you will always find some slight blemish that serves to remind us that the piece was crafted by a human hand. The longer you have to search, the greater the craftsman, for it was only Giotto who was able to draw the perfect circle."

"For me, it *is* perfection," said Arabella. "I simply love it, and whatever Mr. Fenston manages to pry away from me during the coming years, I shall never allow him to get his hands on my national treasure."

"Perhaps it won't be necessary for him to prize anything else away," said Mr. Nakamura, turning to face the Van Gogh as if he'd seen it for the first time. Arabella held her breath while Anna studied the expression on Nakamura's face. She couldn't be sure.

Nakamura glanced at the picture for only a few seconds before he turned to Arabella and said, "There are times when it is a distinct advantage to be a vulgar millionaire, because although one may not aspire to being a national treasure oneself, it does allow one to indulge in collecting other people's national treasures."

Anna wanted to cheer but simply raised her glass. Mr. Nakamura returned the compliment, and they both turned to face Arabella. Tears were flooding down her cheeks.

"I don't know how to thank you," she said.

"Not me," said Nakamura, "Anna. Because without her courage and fortitude, this whole episode would not have been brought to such a worthwhile conclusion."

"I agree," said Arabella, "which is why I shall ask Andrews to return the self-portrait to Anna's bedroom, so that she can be the last person to fully appreciate the painting before it begins its long journey to Japan."

"How appropriate," said Nakamura. "But if Anna were to become the CEO of my foundation, she could see it whenever she wished."

Anna was about to respond when Andrews reentered the drawing room and announced, "Dinner is served, m'lady."

"Would you like to go up front, Sasha?" Nina asked, once the captain had instructed the crew to take their seats and prepare for landing. "Then you can disembark immediately after the doors are opened."

Krantz shook her head. "It's my first visit to England," she said nervously, "and I'd prefer to be with you and the rest of the crew."

"Of course," said Nina. "And: If you'd like to, you can also join us on the minibus."

"Thank you," said Krantz.

Krantz remained in her seat until the last passenger had left the aircraft. She then joined the crew as they disembarked and headed in the direction of the terminal. Krantz never left the chief stewardess's side during the long walk down endless corridors, while Nina offered her opinion on everything from Putin to Rasputin.

When the Aeroflot crew finally reached passport control, Nina guided her charge past the long line of passengers and on toward the exit marked CREW ONLY. Krantz tucked in behind Nina, who didn't stop chatting even when she'd handed over her passport to the official. He slowly turned the pages, checked the photograph, and then waved Nina through. "Next."

Krantz handed over her passport. Once again, the official looked carefully at the photograph and then at the person it claimed to represent. He even smiled as he waved her through. Krantz suddenly felt a stab of pain in her right shoulder. For a moment, the excruciating feeling made it difficult for her to move. She tried not to grimace. The official waved again, but she still remained fixed to the spot.

"Come on, Sasha," cried Nina, "you're holding everyone up."

Krantz somehow managed to stumble unsteadily through the barrier. The official continued to stare at her as she walked away. Never look back. She smiled at Nina, and linked her arm in hers as they headed toward the exit. The official finally turned his attention to the second officer, who was next in line.

"Will you be joining us on the bus?" asked Nina, as they strolled out of the airport and onto the pavement.

"No," said Krantz. "I'm being met by my boyfriend."

Nina looked surprised. She said good-bye, before crossing the road in the company of the second officer.

"Who was that?" her colleague asked, before climbing onto the Aeroflot bus.

Krantz had chosen to sit in the back of the aircraft so that few of the passsangers would notice her, only the crew. She needed to be adopted by one of them long before they touched down at Heathrow. Krantz took her time as she tried to work out which of her new colleagues would fulfill that purpose.

"Domestic or international?" asked the senior stewardess, soon after the aircraft had reached its cruising height.

"Domestic," replied Krantz with a smile.

"Ah, that's why I haven't seen you before."

"I've only been with the company for three months," said Krantz.

"That would explain it. My name's Nina."

"Sasha," said Krantz, giving her a warm smile.

"Just let me know if you need anything, Sasha."

"I will," said Krantz.

Trying to relax when she couldn't lean on her right shoulder meant that Krantz remained awake for most of the flight. She used the hours getting to know Nina, so that by the time they landed, the senior stewardess would unwittingly play a role in the most crucial part of her deception. By the time Krantz finally fell asleep, Nina had become her minder.

54

"Wasn't there anything on the film that would assist us?" asked Macy.

"Nothing," replied Jack, as he looked across the desk at his boss. "Leapman had only been in the office long enough to photograph eight documents before Fenston's unscheduled appearance."

"And what do those eight documents tell us?" Macy demanded.

"Nothing we didn't already know," admitted Jack, as he opened a file in front of him. "Mainly contracts confirming that Fenston is still fleecing customers in different parts of the world, who are either naïve or greedy. But should any of them decide it would be in their best interests to sell their assets and clear the debt with Fenston Finance, I suspect that's when we'll end up with another body on our hands. No, my only hope is that the NYPD has gathered enough evidence to press charges in the Leapman case, because I still don't have enough to slap a parking ticket on him."

"It doesn't help," said Macy, "that when I spoke to my opposite number this morning, or to be more accurate he spoke to me, the first thing he wanted to know was did we have an FBI agent called Delaney, and if so, was he on the scene of the crime before his boys arrived."

"What did you tell him?" asked Jack, trying not to smile.

"I'd look into the matter and call him back." Macy paused. "But it might placate them a little if you were willing to trade some information," he suggested.

"But I don't think they have anything we aren't already aware of," responded Jack, "and they can't be that optimistic about pressing charges while Leapman is still out for the count."

"Any news from the hospital about his chances of recovery?" asked Macy.

"Not great," admitted Jack. "While he was in Fenston's office he suffered a stress stroke caused by high blood pressure. The medical term is *aphasia.*"

"Aphasia?"

"The part of Leapman's brain that affects his speech has been irreparably damaged, so he can't speak. Frankly, his doctor is describing him as a vegetable and warned me that the only decision the hospital will have to make is whether to pull the plug and let him die peacefully."

"The NYPD tells me that Fenston is sitting solicitously by the patient's bedside."

"Then they'd better not leave them alone for more than a few moments," said Jack, "because if they do, the doctors won't need to make the decision as to who should pull the plug."

"The police also want to know if you removed a camera from the crime scene."

"It was FBI property."

"Not if it was evidence in a criminal investigation, as you well know, Jack. Why don't you send them a set of the photos Leapman took and try to be more cooperative in the future? Remind them that your father served twenty-six years with the force—that should do the trick."

"But what do they have to offer in exchange?" asked Jack.

"A copy of a photograph with your name on the back. They want to know if it meant anything to you, because it sure didn't to them, or me," admitted Macy.

The supervisor pushed two prints across his desk and allowed Jack a few moments to consider them. The first was a picture of Fenston shaking hands with George W. Bush when he visited Ground Zero. Jack recalled the blown-up version that was hanging on the wall behind Fenston's desk. He held up the picture and asked, "How come the NYPD has a copy of this?"

"They found it on Leapman's desk. He was obviously going to hand it over to you yesterday evening, along with an explanation of what he'd written on the back."

Jack looked at the second print and was considering the words, *Delaney, this is all the evidence you need,* when the phone on Macy's desk buzzed.

He picked it up and listened. "Put him on," said Macy, as he replaced the receiver and flicked a switch that would allow them both to follow the conversation. "It's Tom Crasanti, calling from London," said Macy. "Hi, Tom, it's Dick Macy. Jack's in the office with me. We were just discussing the Fenston case, because we're still not making much headway."

"That's why I'm calling," said Tom. "There's been a development at this end, and the news is not good. We think Krantz has slipped into England."

"That's not possible," said Jack. "How could she hope to get through passport control?"

"By posing as an Aeroflot stewardess, it would seem," said Tom. "My contact at the Russian embassy called to warn me that a woman had entered Britain using a fake passport under the name of Sasha Prestakavich."

"But why should they assume Prestakavich is Krantz?" asked Jack.

"They didn't," said Tom. "They had no idea who she was. All they could tell me was that the suspect befriended Aeroflot's chief stewardess while on their daily flight to London. She then fooled her into accompanying her through passport control. That's how we got to hear of it. It turns out that the copilot asked who the woman was, and when he was told that her name was Sasha Prestakavich, he said that wasn't possible because he traveled with her regularly, and it certainly wasn't Prestakavich."

"That still doesn't prove it's Krantz," pressed Macy.

"I'll get there, sir, just give me time."

Jack was glad his friend couldn't see the look of impatience on the boss's face.

"The copilot," continued Tom, "reported to his captain, who immediately alerted Aeroflot's security. It didn't take them long to discover that Sasha Prestakavich was on a three-day layover, and her passport had been stolen, along with her uniform. That set alarm bells ringing." Macy began tapping his fingers on the desk. "My contact at the Russian embassy called me in the new entente-cordiale spirit of post-9/11," said Tom, "having already briefed Interpol."

"We are going to get there, aren't we, Tom?"

"Any moment, sir." He paused. "Where was I?"

"Taking calls from your contact in the Russian embassy," said Jack.

"Oh, yes," said Tom. "It was after I'd given him a description of Krantz, about five foot, around a hundred pounds, crew cut, that they asked me to fax over a photograph of her, which I did. He then forwarded a copy of the photograph to the copilot at his London hotel, who confirmed that it was Krantz."

"Good work, Tom," said Macy, "thorough as always, but have you come up with any theory as to why Krantz would chance going to England at this particular time?"

"To kill Petrescu would be my bet," said Tom.

"What do you think?" asked Macy, looking across his desk at Jack.

"I agree with Tom" replied Jack. "Anna has to be the obvious target." He hesitated. "But what I can't work out is why Krantz would take such a risk right now."

"I agree," said Macy, but I'm not willing to put Petrescu's life at risk while we try to second-guess Krantz's motives." Macy leant forward. "Now listen carefully, Tom, because I'm only going to tell you this once." He quickly began to turn the pages of his Fenston file. "I need you to get in touch with—just give me a moment," said Macy, as he turned over even more pages. "Ah, yes, here it is, Chief Superintendent Renton of the Surrey CID. After reading Jack's report, I got a clear impression that Renton is a man used to making tough decisions, even taking responsibility when one of his subordinates has screwed up. I know you've already briefed him on Krantz, but warn him that we think she's about to strike again, and the target could well be someone else at Wentworth Hall. He won't want that to happen twice on his watch, and rub in that the last time Krantz was captured, she escaped. That will keep him awake at night. And if he wants to have a word with me at any time, I'm always on the end of a line."

"And do pass on my best wishes," added Jack.

"That should settle it," said Macy. "So, Tom, step it up a notch."

"Yes, sir," came back the reply from London.

Macy flicked off the speaker phone. "And, Jack, I want you to take the next flight to London. If Krantz is even thinking about harming Petrescu, let's make sure we're waiting for her, because if she were to escape a second time, I'll be pensioned off and you can forget any thoughts of promotion."

Jack frowned but didn't respond.

"You look apprehensive," said Macy.

"I can't see why a photo of Fenston shaking hands with the president is *all the evidence you need*—" he paused "—although I think I've worked out why Krantz is willing to risk returning to Wentworth Hall a second time."

"And why's that?" asked Macy.

"She's going to steal the Van Gogh," said Jack, "then somehow get it to Fenston."

"So Petrescu isn't the reason Krantz has returned to England."

"No, she isn't," said Jack, "but once Krantz discovers she's there, you can assume that she'll consider killing Anna a bonus."

55

LIGHTING-UP TIME WAS 7:41 P.M. on September 25th. Krantz didn't appear on the outskirts of Wentworth until just after eight.

Arabella was at the time accompanying her guests through to the dining room.

Krantz, dressed in a black skintight tracksuit, circled the estate twice before she decided where she would enter the grounds. It certainly wasn't going to be through the front gates. Although the high stone walls that surrounded the estate had proved impregnable when originally built to keep invaders out, particularly the French and Germans, by the beginning of the twenty-first century wear and tear, and the minimum wage, meant that there were one or two places where entry would have been simple enough for a local lad planning to steal apples.

Once Krantz had selected her point of entry, she easily climbed the weakened perimeter in a matter of seconds, straddled the wall, fell and rolled over, as she had done a thousand times following a bad dismount from the high bar.

Krantz remained still for a moment as she waited for the moon to disappear behind a cloud. She then ran thirty or forty yards to the safety of a little copse of trees down by the river. She waited for the moon to reappear so that she could study the terrain more carefully, aware that she would have to be patient. In her line of work, impatience led to mistakes, and mistakes could not be rectified quite as easily as in some other profession.

Krantz had a clear view of the front of the house, but it was another forty minutes before the vast oak door was opened by a man in a black tailcoat and white tie, allowing the two dogs out for their nightly frolic. They sniffed the air, immediately picking up Krantz's scent, and began barking loudly as they bounded toward her. But then she had been waiting for them—patiently.

The English, her instructor had once told her, were an animal-loving nation, and you could tell a person's class by the dogs they chose to share their homes with. The working class liked greyhounds, the middle classes Jack Russells and cocker spaniels, while the nouveau riche preferred a Rottweiler or German shepherd to protect their newly made wealth. The upper classes traditionally chose Labradors, dogs quite unsuited for protection, as they were more likely to lick you than take a chunk out of you. When Krantz was told about these dogs, it was the first time she had come across the word *soppy*. Only the Queen had Corgis.

Krantz didn't move as the two dogs bounded toward her, occasionally stopping to sniff the air, now aware of another smell that made their tails wag even faster. Krantz had earlier visited Curnick's in the Fulham Road and selected the most tender pieces of sirloin steak, which would have been appreciated by those guests now dining at Wentworth Hall. Krantz felt no expense should be spared. After all, it was to be their last supper.

Krantz laid the large juicy morsels around her in a circle and remained motionless in the center, like a dumb waiter. Once Brunswick and Picton came across the meat, they quickly tucked into their first course, not showing a great deal of interest in the human statue in the center of the circle. Krantz crouched slowly down on one knee and began to lay out a second helping, wherever she saw a gap appear in the circle. Occasionally the dogs would pause between mouthfuls, look up at her with doleful eyes, tails wagging if anything more enthusiastically, before they returned to the feast.

Once she had laid before them the final delicacy, Krantz leant forward and began to stroke the silky head of Picton, the younger of the two dogs. He didn't even look up when she drew the kitchen knife from its sheath. Sheffield steel, also purchased from the Fulham Road that afternoon.

Once again, she gently stroked the head of the chocolate Labrador, and then suddenly, without warning, grabbed Picton by the ears, jerked his head away from the last succulent morsels and, with one slash of the blade, sliced into the animal's throat. A loud bark was quickly followed by a shrill yelp, and in the darkness Krantz could not see the large black eyes giving her a pained expression. The black Labrador, older but not wiser, looked up and growled, which took him a full second. More than enough time for Krantz to thrust her left forearm under the dog's jaw, causing Brunswick to raise his head just long enough for Krantz to slash out at his throat, though not with her usual skill and precision. The dog sank to the ground, whimpering in pain. Krantz leant forward, pulled up his silken ears and with one final movement finished off the job.

Krantz dragged both dogs into the copse and dumped them behind a fallen oak. She then washed her hands in the stream, annoyed to find her brand-new tracksuit was covered in blood. She finally wiped the knife on the grass before replacing it in its sheath. She checked her watch. She had allocated two hours for the entire operation, so she reckoned she still had over an hour before those in the house, occupied with either serving or being served, would notice the dogs had not returned from their evening constitutional.

The distance between the copse and the north end of the house Krantz estimated to be 100, perhaps 120 yards. With the moon throwing out such a clear light, if only intermittently, she knew that there was only one form of movement that would go unobserved.

She fell to her knees before lying flat on the grass. She first placed one arm in front of her, followed by one leg, the second arm, then the second leg, and finally she eased her body forward. Her record for a hundred yards as a human crab was seven minutes and nineteen seconds. Occasionally, she would stop and raise her head to study the layout of the house so that she could consider her point of entry. The ground floor was ablaze with light, while the first floor was almost in darkness. The second floor, where the servants resided, had only one light on. Krantz wasn't interested in the second floor. The person she was looking for would be on the ground floor, and later the first.

When Krantz was within ten yards of the house, she slowed each movement down until she felt a finger touch the outer wall. She lay still, cocked her head to one side, and used the light of the moon to study the edifice more carefully. Only great estates still boasted drainpipes of that size. When you've performed a somersault on a four-inch-wide beam, a drainpipe that prominent is a ladder.

Krantz next checked the windows of the large room where the most noise was coming from. Although the heavy curtains were drawn, she spotted one affording a slight chink. She moved even more slowly toward the noise and laughter. When she reached the window, she pushed herself up onto her knees until one eye was in line with the tiny gap in the curtain.

The first thing she saw was a man dressed in a dinner jacket. He was on his feet, a glass of champagne in one hand as if proposing a toast. She couldn't hear what he was saying, but then she wasn't interested. Her eyes swept that part of the room she could see. At one end of the table sat a lady in a long silk dress with her back to the window, looking intently at the man delivering the impromptu speech. Krantz's eyes rested on her diamond necklace, but that wasn't her trade. Her specialty was two or three inches above the sparkling gems.

She turned her attention to the other end of the table. She almost smiled when she saw who was eating pheasant and sipping a glass of wine. When Petrescu retired to bed later that night, Krantz would be waiting for her, hidden in a place Petrescu would least expect to find her.

Krantz glanced toward the man in the black tailcoat who had opened the door to let the dogs out. He was now standing behind the lady wearing the silk gown, refilling her glass with wine, while other servants removed plates and one did nothing more than scrape crumbs from the table into a silver tray. Krantz remained absolutely still while her eyes continued to move around the room, searching for the other throat Fenston had sent her to cut.

"Lady Arabella, I rise to thank you for your kindness and hospitality. I have much enjoyed trout from the River Test, and pheasant shot on your estate, while in the company of two remarkable women. But tonight will remain memorable for me for many other reasons. Not least, that I will leave Wentworth Hall tomorrow with two unique additions to my collection—one of the finest examples of Van Gogh's work, as well as one of the most talented young professionals in her field, who has agreed to be the CEO of my foundation. Your great-grandfather," said Nakamura, turning to face his hostess, "was wise enough in eighteen eighty-nine, over a century ago, to purchase from Dr. Gachet the self-portrait of his close friend, Vincent Van Gogh. Tomorrow, that masterpiece will begin a journey to the other side of the world, but I must warn you, Arabella, that after only a few hours in your home, I have my eye on another of your national treasures, and this time I would be willing to pay well over the odds."

"Which one, may I ask?" said Arabella.

Krantz decided that it was time to move on.

She crept slowly toward the north end of the building, unaware that the massive cornerstones had been an architectural delight to Sir John Vanbrugh; to her they formed perfectly proportioned footholds to the first floor.

She climbed up onto the first-floor balcony in less than two minutes and paused for a moment to consider how many bedrooms she might have to enter. She knew that while there were guests in the house there was no reason to think any of the rooms would be alarmed, and because of the age of the building, entry wouldn't have caused much difficulty for a burglar on his first outing. With the aid of her knife, Krantz slipped the bolt on the window of the first room. Once inside, she didn't fumble around for a light but switched on a slimline pen flashlight, which illuminated an area about the size of a small television screen. The square of light moved across the wall, illuminating picture after picture, and although Hals, Hobbema, and Van Goyen would have delighted most connoisseurs' eyes, Krantz passed quickly over them in search of another Dutch master. Once she had given cursory consideration to every painting in the room, she switched off the torch and headed back to the balcony. She entered the second guest bedroom as Arabella rose to thank Mr. Nakamura for his gracious speech.

Once again Krantz studied each canvas, and once again none brought a smile to her lips. She quickly returned to the parapet, as the butler offered Mr. Nakamura a port and opened the cigar box. Mr. Nakamura allowed Andrews to pour him a Taylor's 47. When the butler returned to his mistress at the other end of the table, Arabella declined the port, but rolled several cigars between her thumb and forefinger before she selected a Monte Cristo. As the butler struck a match for his mistress, Arabella smiled. Everything was going to plan.

56

KRANTZ HAD COVERED five bedrooms by the time Arabella invited her guests to join her in the drawing room for coffee. There were still another nine rooms left to consider, and Krantz was aware that not only was she running out of time, but she wouldn't be given a second chance.

She moved swiftly to the next room, where someone who believed in fresh air had left a window wide open. She switched on her flashlight, to be greeted by a steely glare from the Iron Duke. She moved on to the next picture, just as Mr. Nakamura placed his coffee cup back on the side table and rose from his place. "I think it is time for me to retire to bed, Lady Arabella," he said, "in case those dull men of Corus Steel feel I have lost my edge." He turned to Anna. "I look forward to seeing you in the morning, when we might discuss over breakfast any ideas you have for developing my collection, and perhaps even your remuneration."

"But you have already made it clear what you think I am worth," said Anna.

"I don't recall that," said Nakamura, looking puzzled.

"Oh yes," said Anna, with a smile. "I well remember your suggestion that Fenston had convinced you that I was worth five hundred dollars a day."

"You have taken advantage of an old man," said Nakamura with a smile, "but I shall not go back on my word."

Krantz thought she heard a door close, and without giving Wellington a second look returned quickly to the balcony. She needed the use of her knife to secure entry into the next room. She moved stealthily across the floor, coming to a halt at the end of another four-poster bed. She switched on the flashlight, expecting to be greeted by a blank wall. But not this time.

The insane eyes of a genius stared at her. The insane eyes of an assassin stared back.

Krantz smiled for the second time that day. She climbed up onto the bed and crawled slowly toward her next victim. She was within inches of the canvas when she unsheathed her knife, raised it above her head, and was about to plunge the blade into the neck of Van Gogh, when she remembered what Fenston had insisted on if she hoped to collect four million rather than three. She switched off her flashlight, climbed down from the bed onto the thick carpet, and crawled under the four-poster. She lay flat on her back and waited.

As Arabella and her guests strolled out of the drawing room and into the hallway, she asked Andrews if Brunswick and Picton had returned.

"No, m'lady," the butler replied, "but there are a lot of rabbits about tonight."

"Then I shall go and fetch the rascals myself," muttered Arabella and, turning to her guests, added, "Sleep well. I'll see you both at breakfast."

Nakamura bowed before accompanying Anna up the staircase, again stopping occasionally to admire Arabella's ancestors, who gazed back at him.

"You will forgive me, Anna," he said, "for taking my time, but I may not be given the opportunity of meeting these gentlemen again."

Anna smiled as she left him to admire the Romney of Mrs. Siddons.

She continued on down the corridor, coming to a halt outside the Van Gogh room. She opened the bedroom door and switched on the light, stopping for a moment to admire the portrait of Van Gogh. She took off her dress and hung it in the wardrobe, placing the rest of her clothes on the sofa at the end of the four-poster. She then turned on the light by the side of the bed and checked her watch. It was just after eleven. She disappeared into the bathroom.

When Krantz heard the sound of a shower, she slid out from under the canopy and knelt beside the bed. She cocked an ear, like an attentive animal sniffing the wind. The shower was still running. She stood up, walked across to the door, and switched off the bedroom light, while leaving on the reading light by the side of the bed. She pulled back the covers on the other side of the bed away from the lamp and climbed carefully in. She took one last look at the Van Gogh, before neatly replacing the blanket and cover over her head and finally disappearing under the sheet. Krantz lay flat and didn't move a muscle. She was so slight that she barely made an impression in the half light. Although she remained secreted under the sheets, she heard the shower being turned off. This was followed by silence. Anna must have been drying herself, and then she heard a switch being flicked off—the bathroom light, followed by the sound of a door closing.

Krantz extracted the knife from its tailor-made sheath and gripped the handle firmly as Anna walked back into the bedroom. Anna slipped under the covers on her side of the bed and immediately turned on one side, stretching out an arm to switch off the bedside light. She lowered her head onto the soft goose-feather pillow. As she drifted into those first moments of slumber, her last thought was that the evening could hardly have gone better. Mr. Nakamura had not only closed the deal, but offered her a job. What more could she ask for?

Anna was drifting off to sleep when Krantz leaned across and touched her back with the tip of her forefinger. She ran the finger tip down her spine and onto her buttocks, coming to a halt at the top of her thigh. Anna sighed. Krantz paused for a moment, before placing her hand between Anna's legs.

Was she dreaming, or was someone touching her, Anna wondered, as she lay in that semiconscious state before falling asleep. She didn't move a muscle. It wasn't possible that someone else could be in the bed. She must be dreaming. That was when she felt the cold steel of a blade as it slipped in between her thighs. Suddenly Anna was wide awake, a thousand thoughts rushing through her mind. She was about to throw the blanket back and dive onto the floor, when a voice said quietly but firmly, "Don't even think about moving, not even a muscle; you have a six-inch knife between your legs, and the blade is facing upward." Anna didn't move. "If you as much as murmur, I'll slit you up from your crotch to your throat, and you'll live just long enough to wish you were dead."

Anna felt the steel of the blade wedged between her thighs and tried hard not to move, although she couldn't stop trembling.

"If you follow my instructions to the letter," said Krantz, "you might just live, but don't count on it."

Anna didn't, and knew that if she was to have the slightest chance of survival, she would have to play for time. "What do you want?" she asked.

"I told you not to murmur," repeated Krantz, moving the knife up between Anna's thighs until the blade was a centimeter from the clitoris. Anna didn't argue.

"There is a light on your side of the bed," said Krantz. "Lean across, very slowly, and turn it on."

Anna leant over and felt the blade move with her as she switched on the bedside light.

"Good," said Krantz. "Now I'm going to pull back the blanket on your side of the bed, while you remain still. I won't be removing the knife—yet."

Anna stared in front of her, while Krantz slowly pulled the covers back on her side of the bed.

"Now pull your knees up under your chin," said Krantz, "slowly."

Anna obeyed her order, and once again felt the knife move with her.

"Now push yourself up onto your knees and turn to face the wall."

Anna placed her left elbow on the bed, pushed herself up slowly onto her knees, and inched around until she was facing the wall. She stared up at Van Gogh. When she saw his bandaged ear, she couldn't help remembering the last act Krantz had performed on Victoria.

Krantz was now kneeling directly behind her, still gripping firmly onto the handle of the knife.

"Lean slowly forward," said Krantz, "and take hold of the painting on both sides of the frame."

Anna obeyed her every word, while every muscle in her body was trembling.

"Now lift the picture off its hook and lower it slowly down onto the pillow."

Anna managed to find the strength to carry out her command, bringing the portrait to rest on top of the pillows.

"Now I'm going to remove the knife from between your legs very slowly, before placing the tip of the blade on the back of your neck. Don't even give a second's thought to any sudden movement once the blade has been removed, because should you be foolish enough to attempt anything, let me assure you that I can kill you in less than three seconds, and be out of the open window in less than ten. I want you to think about that for a moment before I remove the blade."

Anna thought about it and didn't move. A few seconds later, she felt the knife slide out from between her legs, and a moment later, as promised, the tip of the blade was pressed against the nape of her neck.

"Lift the picture up off the pillow," ordered Krantz, "then turn around and face me. Be assured the blade will never be less than a few inches away from your throat at any time. Any movement, and I mean any movement that I consider unexpected, will be your last."

Anna believed her. She leaned forward, lifted the picture off the pillow, and moved her knees around inch by inch, until she came face-to-face with Krantz. When Anna first saw her, she was momentarily taken by surprise. The woman was so small and slight she even looked vulnerable, a mistake several seasoned men had made in the past—their past. If Krantz had got the better of Sergei, what chance did she have? The strangest thought passed through Anna's mind as she waited for her next order. Why hadn't she said yes when Andrews offered to bring her up a cup of cocoa before she retired to bed?

"Now I want you to turn the picture around so that it's facing me," said Krantz, "and don't take your eye off the knife." She pulled back the blade from her throat and raised it above her head. While Anna turned the picture round, Krantz kept the knife in line with her favorite part of the anatomy.

"Grip the frame firmly," said Krantz, "because your friend Mr. Van Gogh is about to lose more than his left ear."

"But why?" cried Anna, unable to remain silent any longer.

"I'm glad you asked," said Krantz, "because Mr. Fenston's orders could not have been more explicit. He wanted you to be the last person to see the masterpiece before it was finally destroyed."

"But why?" Anna repeated.

"As Mr. Fenston couldn't own the painting himself, he wanted to be sure that Mr. Nakamura couldn't either," said Krantz, the blade of the knife still hovering inches from Anna's neck. "Always a mistake to cross Mr. Fenston. What a pity that you won't have the chance to tell your friend Lady Arabella what Mr. Fenston has in mind for her." Krantz paused. "But I have a feeling he won't mind me sharing the details with you. Once the painting has been destroyed—so unfortunate that she couldn't afford to insure it, such a false economy, because that's when Mr. Fenston will set about selling off the rest of the estate until she has finally cleared the debt. Her death, unlike yours, will be a long and lingering one. One can only admire Mr. Fenston's neat and logical mind." She paused again. "I fear that time is running out, both for you and Mr. Van Gogh."

Krantz suddenly raised the knife high above her head and plunged the blade into the canvas. Anna felt the full force of Krantz's strength as she sliced through Van Gogh's neck, and with all the power she could muster, Krantz continued the movement until she had completed an uneven circle, finally removing the head of Van Gogh and leaving a ragged hole in the center of the canvas. Krantz leaned back to admire her handiwork and allowed herself a moment of satisfaction. She felt she had carried out her contract with Mr. Fenston to the letter, and now that Anna had witnessed the whole spectacle, the time had come for Krantz to earn the fourth million.

Anna watched as Van Gogh's head fell onto the sheet beside her, without a drop of blood being spilt. As Krantz sat back to enjoy her moment of triumph, Anna brought the heavy frame crashing down toward her head. But Krantz was swifter than Anna had anticipated and was able to quickly turn, raise an arm, and deflect the blow onto her left shoulder. Anna jumped off the bed as Krantz cast the frame to one side and pushed herself back up. Anna managed to rise and even take a step toward the door before Krantz leaped off the bed and dived at her, thrusting the tip of the blade into her leg as Anna attempted another step. Anna stumbled and fell, only inches from the door, blood spurting in every direction. Krantz was only a pace behind as Anna's hand touched the handle of the door, but it was too late. Krantz was on her before she could turn the handle. She grabbed Anna by the hair and pulled her back down onto the floor. Krantz raised the knife above her head, and the last words Anna heard her utter were: "This time it's personal."

Krantz was about to perform a ceremonial incision when the bedroom door was flung open. Not by a butler carrying a cup of cocoa, but by a woman with a shotgun under her right arm, her hands and shimmering silk gown covered in blood.

Krantz was momentarily transfixed as she looked up at Lady Victoria

Wentworth. Hadn't she already killed this woman? Was she staring at a ghost? Krantz hesitated, mesmerized, as the apparition advanced toward her. Krantz didn't take her eyes off Arabella, while still holding the knife to Anna's throat, the blade hovering a centimeter from her skin.

Arabella raised the gun as Krantz eased slowly backward, dragging her quarry across the floor toward the open window. Arabella cocked the trigger. "Another drop of blood," she said, "and I'll blow you to smithereens. I'll start with your legs, and then I'll save the second cartridge for your stomach. But I won't quite finish you off. No, I can promise you a slow, painful death, and I will not be calling for an ambulance until I'm convinced there's nothing they can do to help you." Arabella lowered her gun slightly and Krantz hesitated. "Let her go," she said, "and I won't fire." Arabella broke the barrel of her gun and waited. She was surprised to see how terrified Krantz was, while Anna remained remarkably composed.

Without warning, Krantz let go of Anna's hair and threw herself sideways out of the open window, landing on the balcony. Arabella snapped the barrel closed, raised the gun and fired all in one movement, blowing away the Burne-Jones window and leaving a gaping hole. Arabella rushed over to the smouldering gap and shouted, "Now, Andrews," as if she was ordering a beat at a pheasant shoot to commence. A second later, the security lights floodlit the front lawn so that it looked like a football field with a single player advancing toward goal.

Arabella's eyes settled on the diminutive black figure as she zigzagged across the lawn. Arabella raised the gun a second time, pulled the butt firmly into her shoulder, took aim, drew a deep breath, and squeezed the trigger. A moment later Krantz fell to the ground, but still somehow managed to crawl on toward the wall.

"Damn," said Arabella, "I only winged her." She ran out of the room, down the stairs, and shouted long before she reached the bottom step, "Two more cartridges, Andrews."

Andrews opened the front door with his right hand and passed her ladyship two more cartridges with his left. Arabella quickly reloaded before charging down the front steps and onto the lawn. She could just about make out a tiny black figure as it changed direction toward the open gate, but Arabella was beginning to make ground on Krantz with every stride she took. Once she was satisfied that Krantz was within range, she came to a halt in the middle of the lawn. She raised her gun and nestled it into her shoulder. She took aim and was about to squeeze the trigger when, out of nowhere, three police cars and an ambulance came speeding through the gates, their headlights blinding Arabella so that she could no longer see her quarry.

The first car screeched to a halt at her feet, and when Arabella saw who it was that climbed out of the car, she reluctantly lowered her gun.

"Good evening, Chief Superintendent," she said, placing a hand across her forehead as she tried to shield her eyes from the beam that was focused directly on her.

"Good evening, Arabella," replied the chief superintendent, as if he had arrived a few minutes late for one of her drinks parties. "Is everything all right?" he asked.

"It was until you turned up," said Arabella, "poking your nose into other people's business. And how, may I ask, did you manage to get here so quickly?"

"You have your American friend, Jack Delaney, to thank for that," said the chief superintendent. "He warned us that you might require some assistance. So we've had the place under surveillance for the past hour."

"I didn't require any assistance," said Arabella, raising her gun again. "If you'd given me just a couple more minutes, I'd have finished her off and been quite happy to face the consequences."

"I have no idea what you're talking about," said the chief superintendent, as he returned to his car and switched off the headlights. The ambulance and the other two police cars were nowhere to be seen.

"You've let her get clean away, you fool," said Arabella, raising her gun for a third time, just as Mr. Nakamura appeared by her side in his dressing gown.

"I think that Anna—"

"Oh, my God," said Arabella, who turned and, not bothering to wait for the chief superintendent's response, began running back toward the house. She continued on up the steps, through the open door, before dashing up the staircase, not stopping until she reached the guest bedroom. She found Andrews kneeling on the floor, placing a bandage expertly around Anna's leg. Mr. Nakamura came running through the door. He stopped for a moment to catch his breath before he said, "For many years, Arabella, I have wondered what took place at an English country-house party." He paused. "Well, now I know."

Arabella burst out laughing and turned toward Nakamura, to find him staring at the mutilated canvas on the floor by the side of the bed.

"Oh my God," repeated Arabella, when she first set eyes on what was left of her inheritance. "That bastard Fenston has beaten us after all. Now I understand why he was so confident that I'd be forced to sell off the rest of my collection, even finally relinquishing Wentworth Hall."

Anna rose slowly to her feet and sat on the end of the bed. "I don't think so," she said, facing her host. Arabella looked puzzled. "But you have Andrews to thank for that."

"Andrews?" repeated Arabella.

"Yes. He warned me that Mr. Nakamura would be leaving first thing in the morning if he was not to be late for his meeting with Corus Steel and suggested that if I didn't want to be disturbed at some ungodly hour, perhaps it might be wise for him to remove the painting during dinner. This would not only allow his staff to transfer the frame back onto the original, but also give them enough time to have the picture packed and ready before Mr. Nakamura departed." Anna paused. "I put it to Andrews that you might not be too pleased to discover that he had flouted your wishes, while I had clearly abused your hospitality. I think I recall Andrews's exact words," said Anna. "If you were to allow me to replace the masterpiece with the fake, I feel confident that her ladyship would be none the wiser."

It was one of the rare occasions during the past forty-nine years that Andrews had witnessed the Lady Arabella rendered speechless.

"I think you should fire him on the spot for insubordination," said Nakamura, "then I can offer him a job. Were you to accept," he said, turning to Andrews, "I would be happy to double your present salary."

"Not a hope," said Arabella, before the butler was given a chance to respond. "Andrews is one national treasure I will never part with."

9/26

57

MR. NAKAMURA WOKE a few minutes after six, when he thought he heard the bedroom door close. He spent a few moments thinking over what had taken place the previous evening, trying to convince himself it hadn't all been a dream.

He pushed back the sheets and lowered his feet onto the carpet, to find a pair of slippers and a dressing gown had been left by the side of the bed. He placed his feet in the slippers, put on the dressing gown, and walked to the end of the bed, where he'd left his dinner jacket, evening dress shirt, and the rest of his clothes on a chair. He had intended to pack before leaving, but they were no longer there. He tried to recall if he had already put them in his suitcase. He opened the lid to discover that his dress shirt had been washed, ironed, and packed, and his dinner jacket was pressed and hanging up in his suit carrier.

He walked into the bathroom to find the large bath three-quarters full. He placed a hand in the water: the temperature was warm, but not hot. Then he recalled the bedroom door closing. No doubt with just enough force to wake him, without disturbing any other guest. He took off his dressing gown and stepped into the bath.

———

Anna came out of the bathroom and started to get dressed. She was putting on Tina's watch when she first saw the envelope on the bedside table. Had Andrews delivered it while she was in the shower? She felt sure it hadn't been there when she woke. *Anna* was scrawled on it in Arabella's unmistakable, bold hand.

She sat on the end of the bed and tore open the envelope.

WENTWORTH HALL

September 26th, 2001

Dearest Anna,

How do I begin to thank you? Ten days ago you told me that you wished to prove you had nothing to do with Victoria's tragic death. Since then, you have done so much more, and even ended up saving the family's bacon.

Anna burst out laughing at the quaint English expression, causing two slips of paper to fall out of the envelope and onto the floor. Anna bent down to pick them up. The first was a Coutts' check made out to Anna Petrescu for one million pounds. The second . . .

Once Nakamura was dressed, he picked up his cell phone from the bedside table and dialed a number in Tokyo. He instructed his finance director to deposit the sum of forty-five million dollars by electronic transfer with his bank in London. He wouldn't need to brief his lawyers, as he had already given them clear instructions to transfer the full amount to Coutts & Co. in the Strand, where the Wentworth family had maintained an account for over two centuries.

Before leaving the room to go down to breakfast, Mr. Nakamura paused in front of the portrait of Wellington. He gave the Iron Duke a slight bow, feeling sure that he would have enjoyed last night's skirmishes.

As he walked down the marble staircase, he spotted Andrews in the hall. He was supervising the moving of the red box, which contained the Van Gogh with its original frame restored. The underbutler was placing the crate next to the front door so that it could be loaded into Mr. Nakamura's car the moment his chauffeur appeared.

Arabella bustled out of the breakfast room as her guest reached the bottom step.

"Good morning, Takashi," she said. "I do hope that, despite everything, you managed some sleep."

"Yes, thank you, Arabella," he replied, as Anna limped down behind him.

"I don't know how to thank you," said Anna.

"Sotheby's would have charged me a lot more," said Arabella, without explanation.

"And I know that Tina—," began Anna, when there was a firm rap on the front door. Nakamura paused, as Andrews walked sedately across the hall.

"Probably my driver," Nakamura suggested, as the butler pulled open the oak door.

"Good morning, sir," Andrews said.

Arabella swung around and smiled at her unexpected guest.

"Good morning, Jack," she said. "I hadn't realized you were joining us for breakfast. Have you just popped across from the States, or have you spent the night at our local police station?"

"No, Arabella, I did not, but I'm told that *you* should have done," replied Jack with a grin.

"Hello, my hero," said Anna, giving Jack a kiss. "You arrived just in time to save us all."

"Not quite fair," chipped in Arabella, "as it was Jack who tipped off the local constabulary in the first place."

Anna smiled and, turning to Nakamura, said, "This is my friend, Jack Fitzgerald Delaney."

"No doubt christened John," suggested Mr. Nakamura, as he shook hands with Jack.

"Correct, sir."

"Names chosen by an Irish mother, or perhaps you were born on the twenty-second of November, nineteen sixty-three?"

"Guilty on both counts," admitted Jack.

"Very droll," said Arabella, as she led her guests through to the breakfast room, and Anna explained to Jack why she had a bandage around her leg.

Arabella invited Nakamura to take the place on her right. Gesturing to Jack, she said, "Come and sit on my left, young man. There are still one or two questions that I need answered." Jack eyed the deviled kidneys as he picked up his knife and fork. "And you can forget any thought of food," Arabella added, "until you've explained why I'm not on the front page of the *Daily Mail* following my heroic efforts last night."

"I have no idea what you're talking about," said Jack, as Andrews poured him a cup of black coffee.

"Not you, as well," said Arabella. "It's no wonder so many people believe in conspiracy theories and police cover-ups. Now do try a little harder, Jack."

"When I questioned my colleagues at MI5 this morning," said Jack, placing his knife and fork back on the table, "they were able to assure me that no terrorists had entered this country during the past twenty-four hours."

"In other words I got clean away," said Anna.

"Not exactly," said Jack, "but I can tell you that a woman of approximately five foot, weighing around a hundred pounds, with a gunshot wound, spent the night in solitary at Belmarsh prison."

"From which no doubt she will escape," suggested Arabella.

"I can assure you, Arabella, that no one has ever escaped from Belmarsh."

"But they'll still end up having to send her back to Bucharest."

"Unlikely," said Jack, "as there's no record of her ever entering the country in the first place, and no one will be looking for a woman in that particular prison."

"Well, if that's the case, I'll allow you to help yourself to a small portion of mushrooms."

Jack picked up his knife and fork.

"Which I can highly recommend," said Mr. Nakamura, as he rose from his place, "but I fear I must now leave you, Arabella, if I am not to be late for my meeting."

Jack put down his knife and fork for a second time, as everyone left the table to join Mr. Nakamura in the hall.

Andrews was standing by the front door, organizing the packing of the red box into the trunk of a Toyota limousine, when Arabella and her guests walked into the hall.

"I think," said Mr. Nakamura, turning to face Arabella, "that to describe my short visit to Wentworth Hall as memorable would be a classic example of English understatement." He smiled, before taking one last look at Gainsborough's portrait of Catherine, Lady Wentworth. "Correct me if I am wrong, Arabella," he continued, "but isn't that the same necklace you were wearing at dinner last night?"

"It is indeed," replied Arabella with a smile. "Her ladyship was an actress, which would be the equivalent today of being a lap dancer, so heaven knows from which of her many admirers she acquired such a magnificent bauble. But I'm not complaining, because I certainly have *her* to thank for the necklace."

"And the earrings," said Anna.

"Earring, sadly," said Arabella, touching her right ear.

"Earring," repeated Jack as he looked up at the painting. "I'm so dumb," he added. "It's been staring me in the face all the time."

"And what exactly has been staring you in the face all the time?" asked Anna.

"Leapman wrote on the back of a photograph of Fenston shaking hands with George W. Bush: 'This is all the evidence you need.'"

"All the evidence you need for what?" asked Arabella.

"To prove that it was Fenston who murdered your sister," replied Jack.

"I fail to see a connection between Catherine Lady Wentworth and the president of the United States," said Arabella.

"Exactly the same mistake I made," said Jack. "The connection is not between Lady Wentworth and Bush, but between Lady Wentworth and Fenston. And the clue has always been staring us in the face."

Everyone looked up at the Gainsborough portrait.

After a long silence, Anna was the first to speak.

"They're both wearing the same earring," she said quietly. "I also missed it completely. I even saw Fenston wearing the earring on the day he fired me, but I just didn't make the connection."

"Leapman immediately realized its significance," said Jack, almost rubbing his hands together. "He'd worked out that it was the vital piece of evidence we needed to secure a conviction."

Andrews coughed.

"You're quite right, Andrews," said Arabella. "We mustn't keep Mr. Nakamura any longer. The poor man has suffered quite enough family revelations for one day."

"True," said Mr. Nakamura. "However, I would like to congratulate Mr. Delaney on a remarkable piece of detection."

"Slow, but he gets there in the end," said Anna, taking his hand.

Mr. Nakamura smiled as Arabella accompanied him down to his car, while Jack and Anna waited on the top step.

"Well done, Stalker. I agree with Mr. Nakamura, that wasn't a bad piece of detective work."

Jack smiled and turned to face Anna. "But how about your efforts as a rookie agent? Did you ever discover why Tina—"

"I thought you'd never ask," said Anna, "though I must confess I also missed several clues that should have been obvious, even to an amateur."

"Like what?" asked Jack.

"A girl who just happens to support the 49ers as well as the Lakers, has a considerable knowledge and love of American art, whose hobby was sailing a boat called *Christina* that had been named after the owner's two children."

"She's Chris Adams's daughter?" said Jack.

"And Chris Adams Jr.'s sister," said Anna.

"Well that explains everything."

"Almost everything," said Anna, "because not only did Tina Adams lose her home and the boat after her brother had his throat cut by Krantz, but she also had to drop out of law school."

"So Fenston finally crossed the wrong person."

"And it gets better," said Anna. "Tina changed her name from Adams to Forster, moved to New York, took a secretarial course, applied for a temping job at the bank, and waited for Fenston's secretary to resign—a fairly regular occurrence—before she stepped into the breach."

"And held on to her position until she was fired last week," Jack reminded her, as Nakamura bowed low to Arabella before climbing into the back of his limousine.

"And even better news, Stalker," continued Anna, as she returned Mr. Nakamura's wave. "Tina downloaded every document that might implicate Fenston onto her personal computer. She kept everything, from contracts to letters, even personal memos that Fenston thought had been destroyed when the North Tower collapsed. So I have a feeling that it won't be that long before you can finally close the file on Mr. Bryce Fenston."

"Thanks to you and Tina," said Jack. He paused. "But she still lost everything."

"Not everything," said Anna, "because you'll be happy to know that Arabella has given her a million dollars for the part she played in saving the Wentworth estate."

"A million dollars?" said Jack.

"Not to mention the million pounds she's presented to me, 'for the labourer is worthy of his hire' was how Arabella expressed it in her letter."

"St. Luke," said Jack. "'And in the same house remain, eating and drinking such things as they give: for the labourer is worthy of his hire.'"

"Impressive," said Anna.

"And I didn't even get breakfast."

"Well, perhaps I'll take pity on you, Stalker, and let you join me for lunch in first class on the flight home."

Jack turned to Anna and smiled. "I'd much rather you came to dinner with me on Saturday evening."

"Your mother's Irish stew night?" said Anna. "Now that's better than first class. I'd certainly be up for that."

"But before you agree, Anna, that there's something I have to tell you," said Jack, as Mr. Nakamura's car disappeared down the drive and out of the gates.

"And what's that?" asked Anna, turning back to face him.

"My mother is under the illusion that you've already been married three times, you have five children, not necessarily by the three husbands, four of them are on hard drugs, and the other one is currently serving a jail sentence." He paused. "She also thinks that you work in a far older profession than art consultancy."

Anna burst out laughing. "But what will you tell her when she discovers that none of it's true?"

"You're not Irish," said Jack.

AUTHOR'S NOTE

•

Although Van Gogh cut off part of his left ear with a razor following a row with Gauguin, it still remains a mystery why his right ear is covered with a bandage in both self-portraits.

Art historians, including Louis van Tilborgh, Curator of Paintings at the Van Gogh Museum, are convinced that the artist painted the picture while looking in a mirror.

Tilborgh points out that Van Gogh wrote to his brother Theo in September 1888, after buying a mirror to help him with his work (letter number 685 in the 1990 edition of Van Gogh's letters, and number 537 in the 1953 (English) edition of his correspondence).

The mirror was left at Arles when the artist moved on to Saint-Remy. However, Van Gogh wrote another letter to J. Ginoux (May 11, 1890, 634a in the English edition, 872 in the Dutch edition), asking Ginoux to "take good care of the mirror."

Van Gogh is known to have painted two self-portraits with bandaged ear. One can be viewed at the Courtauld Institute at Somerset House in London. The second remains in a private collection.

café allumé sur la terrasse par une grande
lanterne de gaz   dans la nuit bleue
avec un coin de ciel bleu étoilé
Le troisieme tableau de cette semaine
est un portrait de moi même presque
décoloré des tons cendrés
sur un fond véronèse pâle
J'ai acheté exprès un miroir assez bon
pour pouvoir travailler d'après moi même
a défaut de modèle car si j'arrive a pouvoir
peindre la coloration de ma propre tête ce
que n'est pas sans présenter quelque
difficulté je pourrai bien aussi peindre
les têtes des autres bonshommes et
bonnes femmes
La question de peindre les scenes ⟨ou effets⟩ de nuit
Sur place et la nuit même m'intéresse
énormément Cette semaine je n'ai absolument
rien fait que peindre et dormir
et prendre mes repas. Cela veut dire
des séances de douze heures de
6 heures et selon et puis des
sommeils de 12 heures d'un seul
trait aussi.

From Van Gogh's letter to his brother, Theo, September 17, 1888

A Timeline of Bestsellers in the Auction World, 1980–2005

Year	Artist / Title	Price / US$
1980	TURNER *Juliet and Her Nurse*	7,000,000
1981	PICASSO *Yo Picasso*	5,800,000
1982	BOTTICELLI *Giovanni de Pierfrancesco de Medici*	1,400,000
1983	CÉZANNE *Sucrier, poires et tapies*	4,000,000
1984	RAPHAEL *Chalk Study of a Man's Head and Hand*	4,400,000
1985	MANTEGNA *Adoration of the Magi*	10,500,000
1986	MANET *La rue Mosnier aux paveurs*	11,100,000
1987	**VAN GOGH *Irises***	53,900.000
1988	PICASSO *Acrobate et jeune arlequin*	38,500,000
1989	PICASSO *Yo Picasso*	47,900,000
1990	**VAN GOGH *Portrait du Dr Gachet***	**82,500,000**
1991	TITIAN *Venus and Adonis*	13,500,000
1992	CANALETTO *The Old Horse Guards*	17,800,000
1993	CÉZANNE *Nature Morte: les grosses pommes*	28,600,000
1994	DA VINCI *Codex Hammer*	30,800,000
1995	PICASSO *Angel Fernandez de Soto*	29,100,000
1996	John F. Kennedy's rocking chair	453,500
1997	PICASSO *Le Rêve*	48,400,000
1998	**VAN GOGH *Portrait de l'artiste sans barbe***	**71,500,000**
1999	CÉZANNE *Rideau, cruchon et compotier*	60,500,000
2000	MICHELANGELO *The Risen Christ*	12,300,000
2000	REMBRANDT *Portrait of a Lady, Age 62*	28,700,000
2001	KOONS *Michael Jackson and Bubbles*	5,600,000
2002	RUBENS *The Massacre of the Innocents*	76,700,000
2003	ROTHKO *No. 9 (White and Black on Wine)*	16,400,000
2004	RAPHAEL *Madonna of the Pinks*	62,700,000
2004	PICASSO *Garçon á la pipe*	104,000,000
2004	VERMEER *A Young Woman Seated at the Virginals*	30,000,000
2004	WARHOL *Mustard Race Riot*	15,100,000
2005	**GAINSBOROUGH *Portrait of Sir Charles Gould***	**1,100,000**
2005	**Yuan Dynasty vase**	**27,600,000**

Source: *Art & Auction* (September 2005)